ADAMSVILLE-COLLIER HEIGHTS

*Prey To All*

# Prey to All

*Natasha Cooper*

St. Martin's Minotaur ≋ New York

www.minotaurbooks.com

ISBN 0-312-26636-7

First published in Great Britain by Simon & Schuster UK Ltd, A Viacom Company

First U.S. Edition: December 2000

10 9 8 7 6 5 4 3 2 1

*For*
*Richard,*
*not only a beloved cousin but one of my oldest friends*

## ACKNOWLEDGEMENTS

I should like to record my thanks to Mary Carter, Gillian Holmes, Gerald Johnson, Clare Ledingham, Professor Bernard Knight, Monica Myers, Sarah Molloy, Peta Nightingale, James Turner QC, Tom Usher, and Dr Richard Wright.

## AUTHOR'S NOTE

All the prescription drugs referred to in this novel are of the greatest benefit to people for whom they have been correctly prescribed. Nothing I have written is supposed to suggest otherwise.

Natasha Cooper

Created half to rise, and half to fall;
great lord of all things, yet a prey to all;
Sole judge of truth, in endless error hul'd;
The glory, jest, and riddle of the world!
Alexander Pope *An Essay on Man* (epistle ii)

# Prologue

Deb was worried. Mandy's breathing was slower than ever and her face was covered in sweat; but it was warm sweat, not the clamminess that came from doing the rattle. Mandy had already tried that twice since they'd known each other. Both times she'd gone back on smack as soon as she had the chance.

Deb wiped Mandy's face on the corner of her sheet and looked towards the door. Four inches of solid steel, locked now until six thirty. Deb hauled herself up to the top bunk to tug the window further open and let some more air into the cell. Her arms ached and her knees cracked as her weight shifted. She was only forty-seven; she shouldn't be this creaky.

The bunk rocked as she climbed, but Mandy didn't stir. Usually she was such a light sleeper that Deb had only to turn over in bed, or even breathe deeply, to wake her. For once Deb would have welcomed the usual torrent of gross four-letter expletives that greeted any movement.

She pulled at the window. It wouldn't shift. When she stuck her hand through the narrow gap, she realised it didn't matter. There was no wind. Outside the air was hot and damp, licking her hand like a dirty tongue.

Deb let herself drop to the floor, looking for anything that might help. She ran the water in the stainless-steel basin until it was as cold as it ever got, swished Mandy's towel about in it, then squeezed it almost dry. The smell of chlorine from the water roughened her throat as she breathed. She no longer felt it on her hands; these days her skin was as coarse as her mind had become – and her language.

She wiped Mandy's face again, then pulled back the sheet. In the moonlight, her childish body looked as though it had an extra skin of something shiny and transparent, like clingfilm. Deb used the wrung-out towel to wipe her down with firm, sweeping strokes copied from a film she'd seen years ago, all the time thinking of Kate.

Mandy's arms were heavy and flaccid, flopping back on to the mattress as soon as Deb let them go. Even more worried, she pinched the sensitive skin under Mandy's arm. There was no response. Not sure what she was looking for, Deb lifted one of Mandy's eyelids and saw that the pupil was tiny. Her breathing was noisy, but slower than ever.

It must be an overdose, Deb thought, flapping the damp towel to make the air move over Mandy's face. Oh, God, not again; please, please not again.

Mandy had had a visit today, so it was possible that she'd got hold of enough smack to put her out like this. Her friend could have brought it in and got it across the table under the eyes of the screw in charge. There were lots of ways to do that; only some of them involved paying off the screw.

Deb looked at her watch. It was four hours since she'd last summoned Bumface Betty and been bawled out for hysteria and time-wasting. Even after three years, Deb still hated being on the wrong side of any of the screws, and Bumface Betty was the worst. She liked watching inmates battling with rage and did her best to get them going. But she was the only source of help.

Deb left Mandy's side to bang on the door. On this wing there weren't any bells. You just had to bang and shout. Deb did both until her voice was hoarse and her fists hurt. There was no answer. She leaned her aching head against the cold metal of the door, waiting for the flap to whip open so that Bumface Betty could look in.

'What now, Deborah?' she'd said last time. 'Hysterical again? You've been thinking about your kids, haven't you? Turning young inmates into substitutes isn't going to help, you know.'

'I'm not,' Deb had said, because if you didn't challenge Bumface, she'd go on and on until you blew like an overloaded fuse.

'Forget your kids. Face it: your life's here now. Remember that, or you'll make your time a misery for everyone.'

'Isn't it anyway?'

'It doesn't have to be, if you're sensible. Most lifers buckle down and make the best of it. By the time you get parole, if you ever do, your girls won't want to have anything to do with you anyway. You might as well forget them now. It's a waste of time feeling guilty about them.'

I know, I know, I know, thought Deb, banging again. But it's not guilt. I don't feel guilty. It is not my fault I'm in here. And they've got Adam. He's a good man. They'll be all right. So long as they don't trust anyone else. Oh, God! Please, let Kate be all right.

'Help,' she yelled. 'Please, please help.'

Her fists beat at the door, producing no more than a thick thud. She turned her hands round and saw the dirt-marks of bruises beginning to form on the soft pads of flesh between the little fingers and her wrists. The skin burned and the flesh beneath it throbbed.

Glancing over her shoulder to check on Mandy, Deb banged again, ignoring the pain that spread all the way up the little fingers and across the palms.

'For fuck's sake, shut up!' yelled a raucous voice she didn't recognise.

'Who is it?'

'Deb. Gone mad, prob'ly.'

'Well, somebody'd better fucking well make her stop. I need my kip.'

'Help,' Deb shouted. 'Get someone to help. Mandy's ill. Really ill. Could be her brain, heart, kidneys, anything. She needs help. Now.'

There was a small metallic crunch, which Deb could feel vibrating through her bones, as a key was shoved into the lock on the other side of the door. Wearily she pulled herself away, just in time as the door was flung back.

'What's going on?' yelled Bumface Betty, as though she didn't know, as though she hadn't been waiting in silence just outside the door, enjoying Deb's powerlessness. 'You've woken the whole wing, you silly girl.'

Deb didn't answer. She just flattened herself against the wall, gesturing to the bottom bunk.

'Don't touch her. I'll get help.'

Deb let her knees sag and felt her nightie ruck up as her body slid down the wall until she was squatting on her heels. The coldness of the painted brick was a faint comfort until she thought of all the misery the building must have soaked up through the years: misery and hate and anger.

Please don't let her die, she said silently. Whatever happens, please don't let Mandy die, too.

# Chapter 1

The machines swished and thudded like amniotic fluid around Trish as she sat, watching her father. Outside, the sun was dazzling and the air clogged with pollution. In here, blinds covered the windows; the artificial light was dim, and the air cool. The nurses' shoes squeaked against the vinyl floor as they moved from bed to bed, checking, soothing, making sure all was well.

Each bed was like an island protected by its private reefs of machines. The still, silent patient lying in it might be desperately ill, but he wouldn't die if any care could save him. A sensation of absolute competence lapped around Trish.

Paddy Maguire slept on. His jowly face was much paler than usual and the black stubble stood out a good quarter-inch from his skin. Trish should have realised that his old rich colour was as much a sign of the heart-attack to come as his smoking, the gargantuan plates of bacon and eggs he liked, and the floods of cream he poured over every pudding. But she'd never thought about it. There had been too many other things.

He shifted a little under his sheet, his black eyebrows twitching, as though he was dreaming. Trish didn't know how you dreamed when you were on the edge of dying. She hoped it wasn't fear that twisted his face. His head moved sharply to one side and then back to the other. Trish looked for his nurse, who nodded reassuringly and came to check his machines.

Her expression melted into genuine relief. Trish sank back in her chair, letting herself watch again. The dream, if that's what it had been, seemed to be over; Paddy was back to the pale stillness she now recognised as normal for his condition.

He had deserted her, and her mother, before she was half-way through junior school. For years she wouldn't speak to him. When she had eventually allowed herself to meet him, as an adult, she had found a lot to like, against all her instincts. There were his quick jokes, his sly perceptive comments on sacred cows of all sorts, and the hot anger that was so like her own and, like her own, usually triggered by injustice.

She approved of his cussedness, too; his refusal to do and be what everyone else thought he should. Trish pulled herself back from the abyss that opened there.

His Irish voice charmed her, these days, and she liked his flashing eyes and his secret cleverness. Bluff joking Paddy was how people were supposed to see him, and him with a mind like a razor; and a closed mouth when it mattered. She hadn't expected that.

He was like no one else she'd ever known. He was her father. In a weird kind of way she was proud of him these days.

And now here he was, laid out in front of her after a heart-attack, still in danger, and she'd never told him what she felt. Sixty-two. Twenty-five years older than she was. He'd gone before he'd reached the age she was now.

He mustn't die, she thought; not yet. Not before we've clawed back a bit more.

The machines pumped and churned, and Trish waited for a sign that they might get a chance. She felt a hand on her shoulder and looked up, expecting the nurse.

Her mother was smiling down at her. Trish smiled back. She had always admired Meg for her steady courage and her unshakeable kindness, but she hadn't expected this. It was one thing for Paddy's only child to come and watch over him as he lay between life and death, but for the wife he'd dumped in favour of some fly-by-night floozie from the typing pool was something else entirely.

'I'll take over, Trish.' Meg wasn't whispering, but her voice was pitched to suit the soft security of the ward. She was a doctor's receptionist these days and knew all about hospitals and how to behave among the dying.

'It's all right. I . . .'

'No. He's in the best hands here and you've got work to do. They'll be screaming for you in chambers, and it won't do your father any good if you screw up the great career.'

Trish felt her smile broadening.

'That's better,' Meg said. 'Go on now. Hop it, Trish. Bernard's coming to collect me later. He'll drive me home.'

Trish quietly put her papers in her briefcase, eased down the locks so that they wouldn't snap, and stood up. Meg kissed her, then patted her bum to urge her away. Trish went, looking back when she reached the doorway to see Meg leaning down over her erstwhile husband, smoothing the hair away from his forehead. The tenderness in her face made Trish turn back fully to watch.

Meg looked up. Her expression reverted to its more familiar, half-mischievous, wholly confident smile. She nodded, mouthing, 'Hop it.'

Outside the building, Trish paused to breathe normally and fit herself back into her usual role of crisp, efficient member of the Bar, not the yearning, uncertain daughter of a half-known man, who might not survive to talk to her again or answer any of her questions.

It took a moment or two. When she was sure of herself, she felt in her shoulder bag for her mobile and rang for her messages.

There was one from Dave, her clerk, wanting her to get

straight back to chambers to hear about an urgent brief she
must accept if they were to help a child in need of protection
from a potentially abusive parent. Trish felt her jaw clamp
shut like a vice.

The next message was much easier. It asked her to call
Heather Bonwell, who had recently been appointed to the
High Court bench. Trish had often been led by Heather in her
years as a silk and admired her. After her message came one
from Anna Grayling, an old friend who ran an independent
television production company. And after her, Dave again,
nagging for an answer.

Trish rang him as she walked towards her car. His
description of the case made her ears ache. The child's
parents, far too well-educated and endowed to have the
remotest excuse, seemed to be using their four-year-old son as
a means of punishing each other for the failure of their
marriage. His father had been given a residence order at the
divorce because the mother's job took her abroad at very
short notice and she clearly hadn't wanted to be bothered
with maternal responsibility. Now she had lost the job and
seemed to think repossession of her child might do something
for her shaky self-esteem, or so her husband's solicitor
believed.

'And the child?' Trish said into the phone, as she unlocked
the car. 'At four, he could be old enough to express a
preference. What does he say?'

'That he wants to stay with his father. But the mother's
claiming he's been terrorised into saying it. When it's pointed
out to her that he shows no sign of terror, she then says he's
been bribed. Or brainwashed. Anyway, they need counsel
fast. Will you do it? It's for Thursday next week.'

'OK. I'm on my way back now. The traffic looks vile, but
I'll see you when I can.'

'Great. And how's your father?'

What an afterthought! Aloud, she said, 'Holding his own, they say. Thanks, Dave. I'll see you.'

Switching off the phone and letting it drop on to the passenger seat beside her, Trish drove out of the car park and into a seething mass of cars and buses. One day, she thought, it'll be possible to be beamed up, Scotty. And one day the sky will snow diamonds and white chocolate truffles into our upturned faces. One day.

As soon as the traffic stopped moving again, she phoned Heather Bonwell. It turned out that she thought Trish ought to apply for silk.

'Oh, come on,' she said at once. 'I'm not nearly there yet.'

'Thirty-seven, Trish. It's by no means unprecedented and we still need a lot more women. Your income's getting to the point where it should be virtually automatic, and you've a good reputation these days. Think about it.'

'I'm flattered,' Trish said. 'But I think it's a bit soon. I'm not sure I want to be turned down, and I think I would be.'

'Don't leave it too long. Now, will I see you at the next SWAB dinner?'

'Definitely. I'm looking forward to it.' Secretly Trish still preened herself whenever she thought of her invitation to join the exclusive women-only dining club. It had no secretary, no constitution, and no specific objects, but it had become the most powerful source of networking for women in legal London.

The traffic was beginning to shift ahead of her, so she waited to call Anna Grayling until she was stuck again.

'Trish, fantastic!' Anna's voice was extravagantly bright. I wonder what she wants, Trish thought. 'You are such an angel to ring back so quickly. How are you?'

'Fine.' Trish decided to hold the news about her father until she knew how the conversation would progress. 'What's up, Anna?'

'Could we meet? I've got a terrifically interesting proposition to put to you.'

'Can you give me some idea what it is? I've got a lot on just now.'

'It could wait, but I do want to get cracking in the fairly near future. You see . . . It's quite complicated. Have you got a second now for me to give you just the barest smidgeon of an outline?'

'Sure. I'm stuck in traffic.'

'Thank God for mobiles, eh? OK. Here goes. I'm working on a film at the moment, a kind of *Rough Justice* sort of thing, about a woman who's serving life for the murder of her father, and I need a legal adviser.'

'I don't do much crime these days, Anna.'

'But you have done some, and this isn't really about crime. The way I see it, it's about a family on the edge and the dynamic that went awry, horribly awry. Two people are dead, another's incarcerated for life, and one is living in slightly bizarre triumph.' There was a short pause, then Anna's voice again, coming wheedlingly out of the phone: 'Interested yet, Trish?'

'Curious anyway.' Wariness made Trish's voice cool, but it didn't seem to bother Anna.

'You see, families being what you're so good at, and what always get you going, I thought you might enjoy being involved – as well as helping get an innocent woman out of prison.'

Film would be a new experience for Trish. She couldn't stop a tingling of interest.

'Who's the woman?'

'Deborah Gibbert. D'you remember the case? She was convicted partly on the evidence her own sister gave against her.'

'Euthanasia, wasn't it?'

'Not really. If it had been, in the current climate, poor Deb would probably have got off with a suspended sentence for manslaughter.'

'So what was it? How did she do it?'

'She *didn't*. That's the point. She found her father dead one morning when she was staying at their house to help her mother look after him.' Anna paused, as though to allow a question, but Trish didn't have any to ask, yet.

'She did that whenever she could, which wasn't all that often because she's got four kids, a husband, and at that stage she had a part-time job of her own, too.'

'Then I'm amazed she had any spare time for her father.'

'Oh, she's one of those good women. You know the sort, Trish, they try to do everything for everyone, run themselves ragged, short-change everyone, and end up being foul to the very people they most want to help.'

Trish had come across one or two like that and always sympathised with their victims.

'How did the prosecution say she killed him?'

'Used a polythene bag to suffocate him while he was asleep, knowing he wouldn't wake because she'd given him an overdose of antihistamines.'

'That sounds much more like suicide, Anna. Plastic bags almost always mean self-harm.'

A breathy giggle down the phone made Trish's eyebrows lift. It didn't sound as though Anna was quite as desperate to right an injustice as she'd suggested.

'The seriously tricky thing for Deb,' she said, struggling to control the giggle, 'is that the plastic bag wasn't found on the body. The SOCO unearthed it – screwed into a ball – from Deb's wastepaper basket, not even in the same room, you see.'

'Oops.' Now Trish understood the giggle. Black comedy, perhaps, but comedy all the same.

'Exactly. But even worse, anyway from Deb's point of view, is the fact that the lab found her fingerprints on the outside of the bag, but not her father's, and traces of his saliva inside.'

It was the mention of saliva that brought the picture alive. Trish lost all interest in even the blackest comedy. Her head was full of the thought of an old man's panic. Had he woken in time to see through the bag? To know who it was choking him to death?

'What's your friend's explanation?' she asked stiffly.

'Bit too long to go into now, but convincing when you get it from the horse's mouth. At least, it convinced me. If you do decide to help us, you could maybe do a spot of prison visiting and hear it for yourself.'

Something was stirring in Trish's memory: 'You know, I think I do remember the case, and the silk who defended her. Phil Redstone. He's good.'

'Not this time, he wasn't.'

'I'm sure euthanasia came into it,' Trish said, paying no attention to Anna's bitterness. 'Someone wanted the old man rescued from misery and illness. Isn't that right?'

'In a way.' Anna's voice was slower now, as though there was some kind of doubt dragging at it. 'Redstone conducted his case on the basis that Deb's mother confessed as soon as the doctor refused to sign a death certificate. Later on, she told the police she'd smothered her husband because she couldn't bear to see him suffer any more.'

'I *knew* it.'

'The tricky thing was that a couple of other officers were searching the house and finding the bag at the precise moment Deb's ma was dictating a statement about how she'd used a pillow.'

'Ah. Pity.' Trish held the phone a few inches away from her ear, hoping she wasn't boiling her brains, or whatever it was mobiles were supposed to do.

'Yes,' Anna said quickly. 'And to add to Deb's problems, everyone involved agreed that her mother was not physically strong enough to have done it, besides having such iffy balance that she needed a stick even when she was standing still.'

'So the assumption was that the mother confessed only to protect her daughter?' At least the mobile didn't seem to have affected Trish's ability to reason from A to B. That was something.

'Exactly. Reading the trial transcript, I think that's what did for poor Deb more than anything else; you know, that even her mother thought she was guilty. And now she's dead, too, so there's no way of unpicking the mess.'

'Dead? When? How?'

'Oh, even before the case came to trial. She fell, broke her hip and never came out of hospital.'

So, thought Trish, not suicide. Then maybe the daughter did do it after all.

In her experience, most elderly men and women who killed their spouses then went on to commit suicide – or at least tried to. Darby-and-Joan murders, the police called them. They were surprisingly common, almost always the result of desperation as the needs of the weaker half of a devoted couple outgrew the carer's capacity to cope. It was one of the saddest results of old age that she'd come across.

'Which is why,' Anna was saying, 'there weren't any witnesses for Deb. The prosecution had her bitchy sister – giving evidence of how she'd always hated her father – and the doctor, who claimed Deb had ordered him to end her father's life.'

'Hm. If it's true, that sounds a trifle inconvenient for your friend. Did anyone challenge it?'

'I wish you wouldn't keep calling her "your friend" in that sarky way. Yes, it was inconvenient, but it wasn't true.'

'OK. I'm surprised the judge allowed the jury to hear about the mother's confession. But, given that he did, I'm amazed they convicted Deb.'

'She went down because she was a stroppy, outspoken woman, who wouldn't put up with arrogant men ordering her about, or play the game they wanted. And you know how the establishment hates women like that. They were sure she was guilty and wouldn't believe any evidence to the contrary.'

Trish had to smile. Through the sticky windscreen, she could almost see Anna's face, more pug-like than ever in rage. Ever since she'd thrown her unfaithful, financially irresponsible husband out of the house, she'd been battling to empower bullied women. Anna believed it was every woman's right to give full expression to her anger, instead of funnelling it out in psychosomatic illness and tears, ceding her sovereignty to other people in the hope of happiness, and ultimately destroying herself. This case sounded tailor-made for her. For Trish, children took precedence and she liked to reserve most of her efforts for them.

'Look, Anna, the traffic's clearing. I'm going to have to go. I'll phone you later. We might be able to meet tonight. OK?'

'Yes, but, Trish . . .'

'Got to go, Anna, sorry.'

'Deb's innocent, Trish. I'm sure. She didn't do it. She's not the kind of woman who could.'

'We'll talk later,' Trish said, more gently.

In her years at the Bar, she had met far too many people who were utterly convinced that their friend or relation was incapable of the cruelty they'd hidden so successfully. She had often wondered how they recovered enough to trust anyone else again. But then she wasn't very good at trusting people at the best of times, so what did she know?

# Chapter 2

Trish had always hated going to prison, but this was worse than usual. She wasn't here on legal business now, bolstered by a solicitor and her own status. Today she was just a friend of a friend of an inmate, clutching a visiting order, and treated accordingly.

Everyone was bad-tempered with the long wait for security clearance, and the air was heavy with heat and resentment. The officer who had to search Trish had sweated right through her shirt and had hot, damp hands.

Ten minutes later, already longing for the shower she wouldn't be able to have for hours, Trish was ushered into the big visitors' room. Families were gathered down one side of the long row of grey-topped tables with the prisoners opposite them. The noise was indescribable.

Trish sat down as directed, in front of a tired-looking woman about eight or ten years her senior. She had big dark-grey eyes, almost the same colour as the bags underneath them. Her skin was bad, but that could have been the result of prison food and lack of fresh air. Fat blurred the outlines of her face and shoulders. That was normal: most women put on weight in prison.

'So, Anna Grayling sent you,' she said unemotionally, in a voice that could have come from any of Trish's colleagues and sounded out of place with all the others that squealed and echoed around the hard-surfaced room. The air smelt of sweat and cigarettes and about forty-three different sorts of scent.

'Yes. She wants me to advise on the legal background for her film.'

Deborah Gibbert's eyes shifted quickly, as though to check that no one else was listening. She was biting her lip and picking at the skin around her left thumbnail.

'I keep wondering if there's any point in it.'

'Only if you didn't kill your father and want that proved.' Trish tried not to sound unfairly tart.

'No one believed me before. Why should it be different now?' Deborah sounded as though she couldn't care less.

Trish was about to point out that she wasn't here for her own amusement, when Deborah stopped picking and wiped a hand over her eyes, before turning to look towards the officer in charge of the visitors' room.

The officer was a comfortable-looking, middle-aged woman who sat on a raised platform to make sure no visitor was passing drugs or other forbidden items across the tables. As Deborah caught her eye, the officer shook her head.

'What's up?' Trish asked as Deborah looked back at her. 'You seem worried.'

The grey eyes narrowed for a second. It might have been amusement or contempt that made them glitter. Either way they made Trish uncomfortable.

'It's my cell-mate,' Deborah said, after a moment. 'She took an overdose the other day. She's in hospital. It's hard to get news.'

'What did she take?' asked Trish, thinking: Trouble with overdoses does seem to follow you round, doesn't it?

'Smack. They've given her the antidote – you know, naloxone, but I don't know if they got to her in time. Oh, I could kill dr—' Deborah stopped, her face betraying her.

'Drug dealers?' Trish suggested. 'I can sympathise with that.'

'Maybe, but it was a stupid thing to say. The sort of thing people remember and use against you years later.' The words were raw and bitter. Trish could understand that, too.

'Why have you been sharing a cell?' she asked, grabbing the easiest question out of the conflicting ideas that were milling about in her brain. 'Lifers don't usually.'

'No.' The ghost of a good-looking, much younger woman showed for a second in Deborah's face. 'But I was lonely. I decided to trade my privacy for a bit of company. I'm not sure I'd do it again.'

The party at the next table included a whining child, whose mother suddenly cuffed him over the head and told him to fucking well stop squealing and go and play out of her way. He moved a few feet from her chair, his face screwed up and shiny with tears. Trish caught Deborah's expression of hopeless, miserable anger and for the first time thought they might be on the same side.

'Now . . .' Trish caught sight of the clock. 'Look, we haven't much longer. And I need to ask some questions.'

'Go ahead.'

'Can you tell me a bit about your father?' Trish switched on the tiny tape recorder she'd brought with her.

Deborah's eyes stilled and her face tightened. When she spoke again her voice grated like a hacksaw.

'He was a difficult man. You've probably heard that I hated him.' She paused, waiting for a response.

Trish had read the trial transcript and as many of the background documents as Anna had managed to acquire. She'd tried to get more from Deborah's solicitors, she said, but they were waiting to hear whether they were going to get leave to appeal and didn't want to get involved in anything else until they'd got the decision and were sure where they were going next. Trish nodded encouragingly.

'Well, I didn't. But I was afraid of him.'

'Why? What did he do to you?'

Deborah looked up at the grimy, once-cream-coloured ceiling. Her eyes were welling, but her full mouth was twisted, not trembling.

'Nothing physical, so there are no visible scars. It's hard to explain.'

'Try.'

Deborah shrugged, which made her double chin quiver. 'Oh, he'd belittle everything I did, mock, shout, and generally make it clear that I could never be good enough to share the world with him and Perfect Cordelia. That's my brilliant elder sister, you know.' The saw-edged voice was even sharper now, like a flaying knife. Trish could almost feel her skin curling away from it.

'You must have detested her, whatever you felt about your father,' she said lightly.

The shadow of a smile momentarily lifted the corners of Deborah's mouth again. 'Sometimes,' she admitted. 'She egged him on, you see. If he ever showed signs of weakening and began to treat me as . . .' Her voice wobbled out of control and she fell into a battling silence.

Trish waited a moment and then tried a gentle prod: 'Treat you as . . .?'

The other woman took a deep breath, as though to prepare for something impossibly difficult. Her voice was several tones deeper when she eventually managed to bring it out: 'As an acceptable human being.'

'Why did you go back so often to look after him, if he was so awful to you?'

'I couldn't leave my mother to put up with it alone,' Deborah said, her voice braced with indignation. 'She was even more frightened of him than I was.'

Was it that? Trish wondered. Or was there a bit of satisfaction in rubbing his nose in his dependence on a once-despised daughter?

Looking at the other woman's face, Trish thought she might have been unfair. It was equally likely that Deborah had been trying to mend the relationship before it was too late. Either way, it was no wonder that she looked as though she was being eaten from the inside out.

Trish thought of Paddy as he'd been just after the heart attack, lying helpless and mute, fed, hydrated and made to breathe by machine. He was going to need a lot of help when he left hospital. How would she feel then? He'd deserted her when she needed him. Could she trust herself to give him support now?

'If it hadn't been for Mum, I don't think I'd have made it. But every time she defended me, Cordelia hated me even more.' Deborah Gibbert's voice cut the ropes between Trish and her private preoccupation. She remembered how little time there was and looked at her notes.

'Did it ever cross your mind that one way of making your mother's life better would be to give your father a merciful release?' she asked briskly, looking up.

Deborah's eyes were steady as she stared back across the table. 'Never once,' she said, articulating with extra clarity.

'Why? Sorry to sound so sceptical, but I have to be sure.'

Deborah shrugged. 'Maybe it's having been brought up Catholic. Maybe it's cowardice. Or something else. I'm not sure. All I know is that, whatever I might do to myself, I couldn't kill anyone else.' She paused, as though checking her thoughts for accuracy, then she added, 'There is no violence in me.'

Trish didn't believe that. She was certain that, given enough provocation, every single human being could hit out. Still, there was no point saying so now.

'It must make being among the lifers in here pretty difficult.'

'It can be hard,' Deborah said frankly. 'Even though some of the stories I've heard still make me ill with rage. You know there are women here who were regularly beaten up, even had unborn babies kicked out of their wombs, by their husbands?'

Trish nodded. Everyone involved in family law knew all about battered wives and violent men. She suppressed a shudder. Since her own one terrifying encounter with real violence, she'd avoided them whenever she could.

Stop it, she told herself. It's over. He's doing life. He was nothing to do with you personally. Forget him.

'The women put up with it for years.' Deb's quiet voice, more compelling now than when she was talking about her own troubles, pulled at Trish, forcing her to concentrate. 'Then one day, for no apparent reason, they suddenly can't take any more and kill the bastard. I can understand why, but I still can't believe there wasn't another way of getting free.'

Trish thought of the moment when she'd been backed up against the wall, bruised, blood already dripping from her neck, feeling as though her guts were being Hoovered out of her body. 'That's what I've always thought,' she said steadily. 'But there are reasons why they stay. They like the kindness they get afterwards; they try to make it right; they've been told so often that they're bad, hopeless, failures that they've come to think they don't deserve any better.'

'I know.' Deborah's intensity woke all Trish's protective instincts.

She thought of the childhood bullying that Deb had described and reminded herself that sometimes they do hit back.

'Was that what happened to your cell-mate?' She had to stay lawyerly, above the story, and ask sensible questions.

Deborah shook her head. 'No. She was a prostitute, introduced to heroin by her pimp and working the streets to pay him to feed her addiction.' Her bitterness was entirely understandable, and her anger.

'And she killed him? That's surprisingly rare.'

'No. She killed a punter. Beat him over the head with a milk bottle until he was dead. God knows what he'd done to her that was so much worse than the routine stuff she took every day.'

Mandy's past was irrelevant to their meeting, but Deborah's reactions were giving Trish a better idea of her adult character than anything she could have said in her own defence.

'Mandy isn't very bright, you see. She was still trying to revive the punter when the police got there and found her with his blood all over her, and her prints on the bottle.' Deb's eyes welled again. 'Oh, God, I hope she makes it.'

'You're fond of her, aren't you?'

Deb nodded. 'God knows why, because she sometimes drives me mad. But she's never had a chance, you know, no proper mothering or schooling or hope of any kind.' Suddenly she looked almost happy. 'And you've got to be fond of someone in a place like this if you're to stay sane.'

This woman doesn't feel like a killer, Trish thought. 'And now before I'm thrown out,' she said aloud. 'You'd better tell me exactly what happened on the night your father died.'

The drive cross-country to Norfolk had been bad enough, with the dread getting heavier and heavier the closer Deb got to her destination, but arrival at the house was worse. She felt her heart thump and her throat tighten, as it always did.

She parked among the nettles her father no longer had the strength to kill, took her bag from the boot and walked through the puddles in the uneven path up to the house itself, her footsteps lagging like Marcus's whenever she took him and Louis to a party.

She knew how the house would smell. Her throat closed

completely as she pushed open the never-locked front door and met the familiar mixture of dust and rot, misery, and stale urine from the last time her father had missed his aim.

The drawing-room door was pulled open with the usual screech of damp-swollen timber, and her mother stood there, eyes red, lips bitten, hands clutching each other. Things must have been bad today, then.

Deb dropped her bag and hugged her mother, feeling how tiny she'd become, how near the surface all her bones were. Her bent hands clutched and the curved end of the stick pressed against Deb's spine. She'd led the way into the kitchen, turning on the sink taps so that they could have a few moments of private talk without him listening in and yelling at them both.

'It's not his fault,' Deb said at one moment, trying to believe it, 'if the rash is that bad again.'

'I know.' Her mother wiped her eyes on a piece of kitchen paper, which was far too rough for her thin skin. Deb could see where it had raised red patches. 'But it's not just the rash. He's been awful all week, and now . . . I can't . . . Oh, Debbie, I don't know what to do any more. The doctor won't come and I can't manage on my own.'

'I know. That's why I've come. And I'll deal with the doctor. You go and lie down. I'll bring up a hot water bottle and a cup of tea as soon as I've seen him. All right, Mummy?'

'Yes. Sorry.' She sniffed. In a way that brought it home more than anything else. For someone who minded so much about cleanliness and manners, to sniff and rub the back of her hand under her dripping nose was a sign of complete defeat. 'And you ought to sit down after that awful drive. You must be tired.'

'Don't worry about me, Mummy. You go on up and get some rest. You're worn out and it's making things seem even worse than they are. I'll look after things down here.'

Deb watched her mother haul herself towards the stairs, then heard her stick bumping on each tread as she went. The slow, dragging steps and punctuating thumps echoed through the kitchen ceiling. But at last they stopped and the bedsprings creaked. Deb braced herself to face him.

It took no time to make the tea and she laid the tray as he'd demanded last time, with the cup handles to the right and the plate of biscuits between the two cups and the silver milk jug, rather than the one that was part of the tea set.

'Oh, for God's sake,' he said, as though she was torturing him, 'that's a cream jug. Can't you get anything right?'

Deb didn't bother to say anything. There wasn't any point. She poured his tea, carried it to the little table by his chair, found a coaster, and put down the cup and saucer.

His hand shook and some tea slopped into the saucer.

'You've filled it too full,' he said. 'I need a clean saucer.'

Deb went out silently to the kitchen to fetch fresh crockery and started again, telling herself that anyone with half his face and neck covered in painful itching weals couldn't be expected to behave rationally. As she pretended to drink her own tea, she watched him trying not to scratch and failing. His nails, short though they were, cut through the skin.

'I think I'd better ring the doctor,' she said quietly, 'and get you something more for the rash.'

'It won't do any good. Nothing does. It always starts like this when you come.'

Deb couldn't bear to sit and watch and listen to the whole story all over again. She smiled across her gritted teeth, took her tea to the kitchen and tipped it into the sink, before telephoning the doctor.

The receptionist was the usual uncooperative, patronising bitch and said Dr Foscutt was in the middle of evening surgery and couldn't possibly come to the phone. Deb asked for an emergency appointment in half an hour's time.

'What is the emergency?'

Deb explained and the receptionist went away to consult someone, coming back with the words 'Your father's angioneurotic oedema is not life-threatening. He must go on taking the tablets the doctor has already prescribed and you can bring him in next week. I've made an appointment for Thursday.'

There were drums beating in Deb's head, or sledge-hammers. She went back into the drawing room, trying to look and sound calm as she told her father that she had to drive to the surgery to pick up a new prescription. Her mother was blessedly still asleep when she put her head round the bedroom door, so she scribbled a note and put it on the bedside table.

The surgery was full and the receptionist told her crossly that she should've listened to the instructions and stayed at home. 'There's no point waiting. I've told you the doctor can't see you. He's busy. Go home.'

Deb felt something building up in her that had to be let out. She opened her mouth. She couldn't hear any words at first, but she knew she was making a noise. Shocked faces all round the waiting room jerked her into listening to herself. 'You patronising cow. You don't understand a single thing. You shouldn't have any contact with vulnerable patients, and your bloody doctor needs reporting to the health authority. I knew the NHS was in a mess, but I had no idea it was this bad. I'm going to write to every MP in the country and I'll get—'

A door opened and the small angry figure of Dr Foscutt came towards her, his face scarlet and his eyes piercing and cold. He was saying something, but she overrode him, telling him just what she thought of his abandoning two elderly patients with a whole variety of ailments. She told him he should have got the district nurse to call at least once a day, and himself telephoned if he couldn't visit, once a week as an absolute minimum.

'All the patients of this practice know that they must book an appointment if they wish to see me,' he said, his voice shaking with fury that was as bitter as hers. 'And they know that if they wish the district nurse to call, they must telephone by six o'clock the previous evening.'

'Have you no sense of responsibility? These are vulnerable, frightened people in need of help. They are in your care. What the hell do you think you're paid for?'

'Now, come along, Mrs Gibbert. You're hysterical. This is ridiculous behaviour. If you will calm down and wait your turn, I'll see what I can do when I've attended to all the patients who have appointments.'

'I *can't* wait,' she shrieked. 'They're on their own. They're not safe. I won't take any time. I just need you to give me something for my father's rash now. It's unbearable. There must be something you can do. For Christ's sake! If he was a dog and you let him live in that condition you'd be in the dock on a charge of cruelty. And if he was a dog, you'd have had him put down years ago.'

'Mrs Gibbert, control yourself.' Foscutt's whole body was rigid with rage.

Deb gasped. Something brought her back under control with a snap. She looked round the room, half apologetic. The waiting patients looked scared, all but a beady-eyed girl of about twelve, who was loving every minute of it. Deb stuffed her balled fists into the pockets of her Puffa. 'I'm not leaving until you give me something for my father,' she shouted.

'Come into my room at once,' said Foscutt, as though he was her teacher, ready to administer punishment.

Sitting on the opposite side of his desk, with his spectacles perched three-quarters of the way down his nose so that he could look at her over the top, he said, 'Now, tell me calmly what all this is about.'

So she told him, all over again.

'You and your mother are a pair of hysterical women,' he said. 'Your father would do a great deal better with a calmer atmosphere. The rash is stress-related, like the ulcer. Behave better around your father and both would be less severe.'

He was scribbling on his prescription pad. Deb couldn't believe he didn't feel the heat of her fury.

'Now, take this to the dispensing nurse outside and give your father two of these tablets at night.'

'What are they?' Deb demanded.

'I beg your pardon?' He sounded as outraged as if she'd asked him to take off all his clothes.

'I want to know what you're prescribing.'

'I don't have time for this. It's an antihistamine. It should help the skin condition.'

'Has he had this particular one before? They've none of them worked, you know.'

'Make sure he doesn't drive while he's taking the tablets.'

'You really are irresponsible, aren't you? You have no idea of the conditions in which my parents are living. My father hasn't been able to drive for the past two years. I have a good mind to report you to the General Medical Council.' She didn't wait to see how he would take that. She had to get back.

She leaned over his desk and grabbed the prescription pad out of his hands, ripped the top sheet off it, checking that it was signed, and stormed out to give it to the dispensing nurse.

The nurse took the sheet of paper, staring at Deborah in disgust. Echoes of the argument must have reached even this far from Dr Foscutt's room. Deb waited, her hands pushed deep into the jacket pockets so that they couldn't do any damage, while the nurse spent a quite unnecessary amount of time checking the prescription, finding the box of pills, sticking a typed label on it, and making notes in a file.

'There, Mrs Gibbert. And next time please make an appointment. The doctor simply cannot have this kind of interruption. Nor can the patients who have bothered to make appointments.'

Deb didn't trust herself to answer.

As soon as she got home, she gave her father the first two pills and set about cleaning his bedroom and giving the commode a much needed scouring. That done, she allowed herself the rare luxury of sitting at her mother's bedside for half an hour talking quietly about the children. Then she went down to the kitchen, rolled up her sleeves and set about making something soft enough for her father to eat for supper and interesting enough to tempt her mother. Having felt her thinness, Deb thought they must have been missing a lot of meals.

The washing-up took her beyond her father's usual bed-time. Working to his barked instructions, she pulled apart the drawing-room fire and put a guard in front of it, looking apologetically over her shoulder towards her mother, who smiled reassuringly. Deb then turned out the reading light on his table, and folded up the rug he liked to have over his knees in spite of the fire.

By the time she'd helped him up the stairs and gone through the whole ghastly ritual of persuading him to take all his pills with the glass of juice he demanded, even though she was sure it was going to make his ulcer worse, she was too tired to do anything but fall into her own bed. She knew her mother was more than capable of getting herself into bed.

The next two days went better. On Saturday night Deb managed enough sleep to put in the effort necessary to create a proper conversation at breakfast.

She was repaid when they started talking to each other again and occasionally even laughed. Feeling better as soon as she heard the blessed sound, she settled them in the drawing room with the newspaper and set about making a proper Sunday lunch, as they liked.

She really thought she'd be able to go home that evening as she'd originally planned, and phoned Adam to say she'd do her best to get back before he was in bed, but if not she'd sleep in the spare room so as not to wake him.

'How's it going, Deb my darling?' he asked, with all the gentleness she needed.

'Not too bad actually. Not now. They're even being quite nice to each other this morning.'

'I hope it lasts.'

'Me too. How are the children?'

'Terrific. Kate's been playing football with the boys already this morning to give me time to read the paper in peace. She's a sweetie, you know. She does you credit, darling.'

'Oh, Adam.' Deb sighed, but this time in pure pleasure. 'And Millie?'

'Slept right through last night. Dry as a bone. She's the easiest of the lot.'

'Wonderful. I'll see you tonight, if I can. Must go now.'

Even talking to him cheered Deb up and she went about the rest of the lunch preparations singing her favourite childhood songs. Her mother even joined in with 'Sweet Polly Oliver' as they peeled the carrots.

'Will you two stop that caterwauling?' came the inevitable yell from the drawing room.

Deb watched the rare pleasure freezing out of her mother's eyes. She closed her own and prayed that the complaint was a one-off.

But it wasn't. He got more and more unreasonable all through the rest of the day. Deb wasn't sure whether it was natural brutality, extra pain, or an attempt to make sure she didn't leave them alone with each other again. Her mother was in floods of real tears when Deb went to make the tea, so she had to telephone Adam and say she wouldn't be back that night after all.

'Can you manage the school run again?' she asked sadly. 'I hate putting it on you, but . . .'

'You don't have any option, darling. Come back when you can. I'll see if Anne can take Millie again. I expect she will. She said on Friday that it's good for her Paula to have another baby in the house. Don't worry about us, we'll manage.'

But she did worry about them. Millie was only just past her first birthday and the twins were five: noisy and boisterous. Kate did her best to help, but she was only a child, and Adam had his work.

By the time Deb came to put her father to bed, she was ready to hit him and knew she wouldn't have the patience to coax him through the whole pill routine. He could take them or not as he pleased. And if his rash got worse, he'd just have to put up with it. But of course it wasn't that simple, and she knew she'd have to persuade him to take his medicine if she was to have any hope of getting away tomorrow.

'You've already given me the white ones,' he shouted, as she held them out.

'Don't be stupid!' The edge in her voice shocked her, but it seemed to have no effect on him. 'You know I sorted out all the doses when I first got here,' she reminded him more temperately. 'That's what this box is for. I bought it so that we wouldn't have to go through this every single time. This is Sunday evening's compartment. I'm taking the pills from here, one by one, as you like them. I'm not bloody well doing this for my own amusement, you know.'

'You and your mother stuff me with these pills that do me no good at all. You have no idea what it's like. I—'

'Oh, for Christ's sake, get on with it!' she shouted and turned away, so angry that she couldn't bear to look at him for another moment.

Through the open curtains she saw old Major and Mrs Blakemore, goggling up at her. Their shockingly ill-trained golden retriever was leaping around them, but they paid no attention.

Deb forced a smile, waved at them, drew the curtains and turned back. More patiently, she refilled the juice glass and handed over the next pill.

The whole process reminded her of feeding Millie when she wouldn't eat. But at least Millie was only a baby. This was a grown man, who should have known how hellish he made life for everyone around him, and yet who still resented every attempt to make him more comfortable. She couldn't understand why he went out of his way to make people hate him. Especially the people he needed and who tried so hard to look after him.

They got the pills done in the end; then it was time to take out his teeth. Deb picked up the tumbler of water she had ready for him and held it out. He knocked it out of her hand, splashing water all over the carpet, and breaking the glass. She wasn't sure whether it was deliberate.

'You always were the clumsiest child,' he hissed. 'Now you've broken my best glass.'

'It's a garage tumbler, Dad. Not worth anything. Oh, God, don't put your teeth down in all that mess and broken glass. For Christ's sake.'

Gagging at the sight of the teeth, hating the smell of them and of his poor ravaged skin, she felt in her apron pocket for the roll of polythene bags, tore one off, and held it open. Swearing at her, he dropped in the teeth. They snapped together as they fell, as though they had a life of their own. Sickened, she took them at arm's length to the bathroom, filled another glass with water, dropped in a cleaning tablet and added the teeth, looking away.

It shouldn't have taken long to clear up the mess, but there were bits of glass spread all over the carpet between the bed and the wall. She was on her hands and knees, feeling for more in case he put his bare feet out in the night and cut himself, when the telephone rang.

He picked it up and said, 'Hello.' A moment later his whole voice changed. 'Cordelia. Darling, how lovely! It's been a frightful day, and Debbie . . .'

She couldn't bear to listen, so she scrabbled her cloths together and left him to her sister, screwing up the polythene bag and throwing it in her own wastepaper basket.

The officer in charge pressed a buzzer and loudly ordered the inmates back to their cells. Deb stood up, hoping she'd done enough to convince this sharp-eyed laywer. Anna Grayling had said she was one of the best and would do absolutely anything for people she liked. Deb smiled shyly, but Trish was putting away her notes and tape-recorder, so she didn't see. Her face was unreadable. Deb longed for reassurance. As the lawyer stood up, Deb offered her hand.

Trish Maguire took it. Their clammy palms slid against each other.

'Thank you for being so frank,' she said, sounding nearly kind enough. 'I can't promise anything, you know, but I will do my best.'

That sounded so sensible that Deb suddenly said, 'Could you bear to go and see my daughter, Kate? Or at least telephone her?'

'Why?' asked Maguire, curious and wary. Oddly enough that made her seem even more trustworthy.

'Anna Grayling has psyched her up to believe I'll be coming home as soon as the programme's been made.'

'It doesn't work like that.'

'I know. But Kate won't. And I don't want her having to cope with finding out the hard way on top of everything else.

Her life's so hard already . . . Will you see her and explain? Please.'

'I'll do my best,' Maguire said again.

Deb had to trust her. There was no one else.

# Chapter 3

The shabby hospital foyer felt cool and civilised after the prison. Trish paused at the shop on the ground floor to buy grapes to add to the two paperbacks she had with her in case Paddy was well enough to be bored. He had been moved up to an ordinary ward on the eleventh floor. That had none of the professional calm of the intensive care unit, but it was encouraging.

There were eight bays in the ward and six beds in each bay. Most of the patients had two or three visitors. The place was almost as noisy as the prison, and as hot, but it smelt marginally better. Paddy's bed was beside the window, which was a mixed blessing. He had more space and a better view, but the sun blazing through the sealed glass battled with the air-conditioning and made it the warmest corner of the room. He didn't seem to mind, sitting propped up on a mountain of pillows teasing the youngest of the nurses.

She smiled at Trish, flung a cheery little insult at Paddy over her shoulder and flounced off.

'Now what a saucy little colleen, that is.'

'Don't you go all Oirish on me, Paddy,' Trish said, leaning down to kiss him, 'or I'll be seeing little green leprechauns all over the place. Colleen indeed! Really! Now, how are you feeling?'

He looked at her as though checking how far he could push her credulity.

'Come on, tell me honestly.'

'Tired, aching and depressed,' he said, not sounding at all Irish. Then he grinned. 'But it'll go. I've never been depressed for long, after all, and haven't they been telling me I've not much cause to fear another of these things?'

'That's great news. Have they done more tests then?'

'That's right. Today it was an angiogram. The results will be through in the morning.'

'And are they giving you rules about diet and—'

'Don't fuss now, Trish. I've had enough of that from your mother.' The mischief was back in his eyes. 'And from Bella.'

'Right.' Trish had never found the idea of her father's lovers easy to absorb. He'd been apart from Meg for twenty-five years, and there was no reason why he shouldn't have taken up with someone else, but Trish didn't want to hear about it. She didn't mind her mother's relationship with Bernard, but for some reason Bella was difficult to take.

'She's a great girl is Bella.'

'Woman.'

'Woman then.' Trish saw that he was laughing at her. 'She'll be here in about ten minutes. Will you stay now and meet her?'

'I'm not sure.' Trish looked at her watch. These days she hardly ever felt flustered, and she didn't like the sensation. 'I have to get back. George . . . I'll have to cook for George.'

'You ought to meet her, Trish. You'll like her.'

'I'm sure.' She smiled and knew it must look false. 'But maybe not this time. There'll be plenty of chances.'

He shrugged. 'She's busy too, you know. She has a – what do you call it, Trish? A pretty crunchy job of her own. Today would be a good time.'

He was pushing her. And she didn't like that either. She never let anyone tell her what to do. She put the grapes in their bag on his table, and added the two books to the pile at the back. Then she bent down to kiss his forehead. 'I'm sorry. I'll get used to the idea soon. But this time I really do have to run. I'll be back tomorrow, the same sort of time.'

'Sure.' Paddy had turned away to pull some of the fat muscat grapes off their stalks, instead of breaking off a neat bunch. Trish felt her nerves shrieking. She could never bear seeing a bunch massacred like that, with blobs of grape flesh hanging wetly against the whole fruit, ready to rot them.

Outside the ward, waiting for the extraordinarily slow lift with a group of other visitors impatient to get back out into real life, she wondered whether he had done it on purpose to punish her. Or perhaps it had been provocation. Perhaps both the grapes and the demand that she stay to meet Bella had been designed to make himself feel tough again after the massive humiliating terror of the heart-attack.

Impatient with her need to analyse everything, Trish banged the lift button again with her clenched fist. Life would be so much easier if you didn't spend your time wondering about people's subconscious drives and took them as you found them, trusting them to do the same for you.

At last the lift arrived. People were pressing forward behind her even before the doors were open and the new influx of visitors could get out. There was one tall, beautifully dressed woman in her fifties. She had very smooth pale-grey hair and a well-kept face. Catching Trish's eye, she grinned suddenly, revealing a character much quirkier and more interesting than her clothes suggested. Then she was gone, leaving Trish to wonder if she might have been Bella.

Trish rather hoped she had been, but it didn't seem likely that Paddy would attract a woman like that.

George was waiting in the flat when Trish got back, busily cooking for her, or at least arranging the sort of cold food that made eating seem possible on such a stuffy night. He came out of the kitchen at the sound of her key and tried to hug her.

'I'm boiling and sweaty and disgusting,' she said. 'It took ages to get back from the hospital and the car felt like an oven because I was clot enough to have the top down. I'd have been better with the air-conditioning. I need a shower.'

George rubbed her head affectionately and asked if she wanted a drink.

'Later,' she called, as she ran up the spiral stairs, wrenching off her clothes. Their relationship had lasted more than long enough for him to know she wasn't rejecting him, so she took her time in the shower, getting the prison stink out of her hair as well as the grime from her body.

There didn't seem a whole lot of point getting properly dressed again, so she pulled on an old pair of leggings, which felt as soft as pyjamas, and a long T-shirt, slopping downstairs again in her bare feet. George hugged her then and she fitted her long boniness around his ample curves.

'So how was the visit?' he asked later, as she was sitting in front of a plate of tabbouleh and cold spiced chicken. 'And what did you think of Deborah Gibbert?'

'This looks fantastic, George. Thank you.'

'Pleasure. Now, Deborah Gibbert?'

'Well, I can see why Anna likes her,' Trish began, 'but I'm still not sure whether she's innocent. It's a tricky one.'

'I'd be surprised if she was, I must say. Phil Redstone would have got her off if anyone could,' George said. 'He's a good advocate.'

'I know. Usually, anyway. But it sounds to me as though he'd decided to loathe her.'

'Ah.'

That was one of the best things about knowing someone so well, Trish thought, distracted. You didn't have to explain everything.

'And, detesting her, he was sure she'd done it. I don't think he tried half as hard as he would have done if it had been the sainted Cordelia in the dock.'

George looked as if he knew exactly what Trish was talking about, even though she hadn't yet told him about Cordelia. 'Is Deborah untidy?'

Trish nodded. 'And noisy, and bad-tempered.'

'Just the kind of woman to turn Phil off. She must have had a pretty ignorant solicitor if they thought he'd do her justice.'

'Although she could have been tidied up for her first meeting with them,' Trish said.

You often had to act for defendants you disliked, as she always explained when asked by outsiders how any decent barrister could bring herself to speak for someone she thought was guilty. But if you knew your personal feelings were going to affect the work you did for a client, you were supposed to disqualify yourself. That – along with lack of time or expertise – was one of the few acceptable reasons for challenging the cab-rank rule.

Trish used it whenever she could. Dirty doctors had luckily never come her way, or rapists, but she'd been offered several briefs for parents accused of child cruelty or neglect and she had always wanted to turn them down.

Of course, it didn't always work. Sometimes you didn't know what you were doing to your client's chances until it was too late. Maybe that was what had happened to Phil.

'What did you like about her?' George asked, watching her over the top of his glass.

Trish knew he was asking because she needed to talk, rather than from any passionate interest in Deb or her case. She swallowed her mouthful and told him everything. As usual when she was really interested and knew her subject, she didn't think about what she was saying or its effect; she just let the words flow out from some not wholly conscious part of her brain, without any censorship.

At the beginning of her career, she had practised every part of what she'd planned to say in court, over and over again, learning specially important bits by heart. But one day, something else had taken over. When she had fallen silent at last, she had felt as though she'd just come round from some kind of anaesthetic. She'd had absolutely no idea what she'd said. It had terrified her. But her instructing solicitor had later told her he'd never heard her so eloquent or so forceful.

Since then, she had learned to trust herself, and even to welcome the moment when the words took over and she could almost switch off. Of course, with George it was easy. It didn't matter what she said to him. He would neither mock nor betray anything she told him. She became aware that she'd stopped talking.

'Why did she—?' George said, interrupting himself to ask, 'D'you want some more tabbouleh?'

Trish looked down at her plate and discovered she'd eaten everything on it. She'd hardly been conscious of swallowing anything between the torrents of words. 'Yes. Thanks. It's great,' she said, wanting to know how it tasted.

George ladled a lot more on to her plate. The mixed scents of mint, lemon and coriander were all round her. He refilled her glass and sat back to listen. She smiled, cherishing his patience and his interest, determined to repay both the next time he wanted to talk about a difficult case.

'So, to sum up,' he said, as he watched her eat, 'your proto-client was convicted because she was the only able-bodied person in the house when her father died.'

'That's right.' Trish wiped her mouth. 'The doctor didn't believe the death was natural. He refused to sign a death certificate and called the police. They came in force.'

'Not just a country bobby on a bike, you mean?'

'Exactly. They must have trusted the doctor's judgement because they sent two full cars' worth. So, there were two officers searching the house, two interviewing Deb, and two her mother. The mother confessed to suffocating her husband, but said she'd done it with a pillow. Deb said she hadn't touched him, but the SOCOs found the incriminating bag in her wastepaper basket.'

'Which she has just explained to your satisfaction, if not to theirs?'

Trish smiled at George. He was very clear-headed, reducing her rambling explanation to a few crispish propositions.

'That's right,' she said. 'Her account made quite as much sense as the prosecution's, and as far as I can see, there was no scientific evidence to prove their version.'

'OK. Then the autopsy produced the fact that he had had an overdose of an antihistamine called terfenadine, which he had been prescribed only two days earlier, and which had been collected from the surgery by your Deb?'

'Yes.'

'As well as small traces of another, conflicting, antihistamine called astemizole, which he'd never been prescribed?'

'Yes, that's right, too. But Deb herself had been prescribed it the previous year — for hay fever. She admits she didn't finish that packet, but swears she threw the remains away, not liking to have drugs around in a house full of young children.'

'Quite right, too,' said George, picking up his glass and drinking the last of the wine in it. 'But did she just chuck it out with the rest of the household rubbish?'

Trish nodded. 'When I queried that, she pointed out that any council would just laugh if you said you wanted a hazardous-waste pick-up for ten measly tablets.'

'And would ten tablets have been enough to affect him?'

'Presumably, but I'll have to get that checked. Phil should have, but there's nothing in the trial transcript about it.'

George tried to drink again, having forgotten that his glass was empty. Trish pushed forward the bottle. It still seemed extraordinarily full. Perhaps talking so much had stopped her drinking her usual quota.

'Do you suppose,' he said, tipping in about half a glass, 'the reason Phil didn't let her give evidence was because he was afraid she'd betray herself in cross-examination?'

'I think that must have been it, although obviously he didn't tell her that. She says he told her the prosecution had nothing but circumstantial evidence and the best way of dealing with that was to treat it with the contempt it deserved, offer no evidence of their own, and point out to the jury that no one can be convicted without proof.'

'Quite right, too.'

'Maybe. But Deb says she wishes she hadn't gone along with it. She thinks the whole case turned on what her sister and the GP said about her temper and the way she treated her father. She thinks if she'd been allowed to give evidence and been frank about what she felt and why, and how she'd dealt with her fear and anger to enable her to go back and look after him she'd have made a better impression on the jury.'

'It's possible. But it does sound as though she has quite a temper.' George didn't look sympathetic. 'The prosecution's questions would almost certainly have provoked her, and she might well have shown herself in her true colours. She'd have been well and truly dished then.'

Uncontrolled anger had always been one of George's bugbears, Trish reminded herself, as she registered his implicit criticism of Deb. He thought it wrecked your judgement when you let it ride you and had a destructive effect on you and all your targets. Even righteous anger was anathema to him. It was their one major point of conflict. Trish had never seen George lose his temper with anyone or anything. Sometimes that seemed creepy. At others it was reassuring.

'Come on, Trish! Admit it. I can see you liked the woman, but use your professional brain for a moment. It was a judgement call Phil made, and you might have made the same one yourself.'

Trish took a huge swallow of wine to take away the taste of the admission she didn't even have to articulate. George was stacking plates.

'So, what was it that made *you* decide she was innocent?' he asked, scraping the remains into the bin.

Trish organised her thoughts. 'I liked her.'

'Fair enough,' he said, with her favourite smile. 'But you'll need more than that.'

'And I believed her story of the teeth and the bag.'

'Better.'

'Patronising git,' she said cheerfully, and ducked as he threw a tea-towel at her.

'And I can't imagine why – if she had killed him – she wouldn't (a) have worn gloves when dealing with the bag, before pressing his own hands on to it, and (b) left it on his head. She isn't remotely stupid: she'd have known at once that her best defence would have been suicide and that if she were to run that, the bag would have to have been found on his head.'

'OK. I'll buy that.'

'Great,' she said, with enough sarcasm to make him threaten her with the tea-towel again.

'Now, did you see there's going to be that brilliant French film about murder in a chocolate factory tonight?' he said. 'Channel Four. It's on in five minutes. D'you want to see it?'

'Why not? I'll take those out and make us some coffee. You go and warm up the telly.'

# Chapter 4

Trish caught sight of Phil Redstone as she ran upstairs at the Royal Courts of Justice. His face stiffened as he recognised her. 'Trish!' he called.

'Can't stop,' she answered, leaning over the banister, the strap of her bag trailing into space. 'I'm on my way to a hearing. Catch you later?'

'I want . . .'

'Later, Phil. It's OK. Don't worry.'

She went on her way, sure that he must have heard she was looking into the Deborah Gibbert case for Anna's film. Somehow she'd have to reassure him that she wasn't about to rip up his reputation in public. He couldn't be afraid of any kind of legal sanction. Nothing said in court was actionable, and barristers couldn't be sued for negligence in court work.

After all, someone had to lose every case. You couldn't go round complaining about your counsel just because it happened to be you who got the wrong verdict, even if you knew you were innocent. Not all clients understood that, of course, but colleagues should.

But there wasn't time to think about any of it now. For the moment, Trish belonged to Magnus Hirson and his four-year-old son, Alex. She found them waiting with their solicitor outside the court, only about five yards away from Angela Hirson and her team.

The two adults were carefully not looking at each other.

Alex was standing pressed against his father's knee, staring at his mother in terror. Magnus had his right hand loosely draped over Alex's shoulder. The boy was holding his father's index finger in both hands. Trish had been determined to keep him with his father ever since she had read the brief, but the sight of him doubled her need to win. She wished Magnus hadn't brought him, but she knew why he'd done it. The sight of such a child, so small and so vulnerable, occasionally made the aggressive parent think again. Alex's nanny was waiting in the background, ready to take care of him while his parents' lawyers fought over his future.

Trish acknowledged the nanny with a slight smile, then set about talking to Magnus and his son, trying to ease the tension that was wound round them both like binding twine.

The judge, a man Trish had known for a long time, listened patiently and smiled impartially at the two barristers and the court welfare officer as they spoke. Trish tempered her passionate determination with the sort of cool rationality she knew he liked. But in the end he went against her.

She couldn't believe it. She turned to her client. His face was white, stricken, but his eyes were blazing. Trish kept her own eyes still as he glared at her, the anger scorching her.

Outside he put his hand on his son's head, stroking the soft pale-brown hair and murmuring quietly that he would be seeing more of Mummy now and wouldn't that be nice?

'No,' he wailed, with a noise like a seagull. He didn't fling his arms around his father, just pressed himself tightly back against Magnus's legs. 'No.'

Trish knew she should be used to this by now, but it hurt as much as it ever had. She moved slowly backwards, feeling a faint current of air from the flapping of her skirt. Magnus caught the movement and turned away from his desperate son for a second.

'Goodbye, Ms Maguire,' he said casually, not even trying to hide his feelings.

Alex had dug his toes in and was being literally dragged away from his father's side.

'Come on, Trish,' the solicitor whispered in her ear. 'You can't do any more. And this time it's only for tea. He's not being wrenched away for ever. He'll get used to it before the move's made permanent. Children always do.'

They turned away and went downstairs.

'It breaks your heart,' said the solicitor, 'I know. But you did your best, Trish. There's no point tearing yourself apart over it.'

'Hard not to in a case like this.' Trish held out her hand. The solicitor shook it and they parted.

Phil Redstone, she thought, forcing her mind away from Alex and his father. Thank God there was always more work and no time to think about lost cases.

Phil's chambers were quite close to hers, so she called in on her way back and asked the head clerk if she could write Mr Redstone a note. She was invited to use the table in the waiting room and sat down to the task.

Dear Phil,

Sorry I couldn't stop. I had a residence hearing. Lost it. Happens to us all.

I don't know if you've heard about my research into the Deborah Gibbert case, but it's nothing do with any appeal. Just for a telly programme about the law. There's no witch-hunt. In any case, I don't suppose there are any witches to go after, if you see what I mean.

Let's have a drink some time. El Vino's? Give me a ring and let me know, if you'd like to.

Best, Trish

She hoped that would keep him reasonably happy. Her own clerk was waiting when she got back to chambers. When she told him what had happened to the Hirsons, he shrugged, saying: 'Pity. But still, win some, lose some.'

Trish had to grip her hands together to stop herself hitting him. She sought refuge in her own room and an article she was writing about child protection for a new law journal she wanted to support. The fee for the article would hardly pay for e-mailing it to the editor, but it was all in a good cause.

The last paragraph caused her a lot of trouble and she was still fiddling with it when Dave rang through to say that Anna Grayling had arrived.

'Could you ask her to wait for five minutes while I finish this?' Trish said. 'And then I'll be out to collect her.'

But the interruption had destroyed her concentration. She couldn't find the right words to make her conclusion startling enough. With a mental shrug, she eventually filed what she'd done, e-mailed the editor to say he'd get the piece tomorrow, and closed down her system.

'Hi, Anna,' she said, emerging into the waiting room two minutes later. 'Thanks for coming. Shall we go out? I need air.'

'Fine. Whatever.'

They walked out on to the Temple lawn. There were two separate drinks parties already in full swing, but there was still plenty of space near the river side of the gardens, where there were benches and it was cool under the trees. The traffic beat along the Embankment, only just the other side of the railings, but even so it was one of the most civilised spots within reach. The sky over the river was the thin pale blue of a watercolour with just enough wispy white cloud to make it interesting.

'So, what did you think of Deb?' Anna asked, when they were settled.

'I liked her.'

'Oh, fantastic.' Anna shifted on the bench so that she could grab both Trish's hands in a hot, damp clasp.

'Is it that exciting?' Hearing repressive disapproval in her voice, Trish thought she must have caught some of George's dislike of vehemence.

'Yes. You can't think how much I respect your judgement,' Anna said more calmly, letting her go. 'If you hadn't agreed with me about Deb, I'd have dumped the whole idea of the film.'

'I thought you were so keen on her you were determined to do anything you could to get her out of prison.'

'Well, yes. But my confidence has been a bit shot lately, so I needed someone I trust to agree with me. Tell me why you liked her, Trish?'

'Partly because of the way she talked about her cell-mate,' she said, catching the uncharacteristic need for reassurance in Anna's voice and working it out as she spoke. 'And partly because of Deb's determination to protect her daughter, and . . .'

'And?'

'Oh, and because her mother loved her so much that she was prepared to confess to murder to protect her.'

Now it was Anna's turn to look surprised. Trish didn't explain that she couldn't bear the thought of Deb's mother dying in the belief that her so-loved daughter was a killer and might go to prison for the rest of her life. It was for that woman, rather than any of the others, including Anna, that Trish was tempted to work on the film.

'And you,' she asked, knowing that Anna didn't put the same value on mothers as she did, 'what's your particular interest in Deb?'

'Actually,' she said, in a confiding whisper that didn't sound remotely real, 'it's not so much Deb *qua* person as *qua* symbol. If I'm to be truthful, I want to exploit the poor cow.'

'Ah.' A bit of sincerity – even unattractive sincerity – usually made Trish feel more comfortable.

'How?'

'I have to make a popular programme soon. And there's not much that gets people going as quickly as a juicy miscarriage of justice. They love a good let's-kill-all-the-lawyers story. Who wouldn't?'

Trish felt her face hardening. It was unlike Anna to be quite so self-absorbed that she would casually insult a friend she professed to need.

'So, I asked about a bit and came up with Deb. Her story's got everything – ghastly crime, innocent mother of four, faithful wife, dutiful daughter, in prison for a murder she didn't commit because of the shenanigans of the male establishment and the incompetence of her – male – lawyers. What more could a girl want?'

Trish considered the question. She could think of quite a lot, but she didn't know much about television and would have to take Anna's word for it; not something she had ever enjoyed.

'There is just one problem,' she said. 'Or two, rather.'

Anna's face twisted. 'What?'

'I've seen no evidence to prove Deb's innocent, even though her story about the bag sounded credible to me. And you've got no witnesses to speak for her. The only useful one – her mother – is dead.'

'We'll use actors to play out the characters in our version of what happened,' Anna began, 'and—'

'You can't do a film like this entirely with actors. You'll need the real emotion of a suffering family if it's to carry any weight.'

'I know, but we'll have Deb's husband and eldest daughter – and, boy, are they suffering! Then there'll be all the people you'll turn up as you interview the main players.' Anna sounded both more confident and further ahead with the project than she'd suggested. 'You're the best interviewer I know. And, of course, some experts, legal and medical.'

'Who?

Anna put her head on one side, apparently trying to look like a hopeful little wren, but in fact, as Trish was tempted to tell her, impersonating a pug that's eaten its owner's dinner and is about to sick it up.

'Well, you, for a start, Trish, explaining the legal background, Mal—'

'Don't be too sure of that,' she said at once. 'I only agreed to look into the background for you, not expound it on screen. I don't want to be seen in public rubbishing Phil Redstone's work. Particularly not with an appeal in the offing, which is apparently going to be based on his incompetence.'

'Trish, you—'

'No, Anna, listen. This is important. Quite apart from professional loyalty, it could be counter-productive for Deb. Phil persuaded the judge to admit Deb's mother's confession under Section 23 of the Criminal Justice Act 1988. He didn't have to and that was the only thing that might have helped her. You've got to be very careful about this, if you have any real interest in getting Deb out as opposed to making a noteworthy programme.'

'Well, if you won't, you won't. One person who will is Malcolm Chaze, the MP. He's certain Deb's innocent.'

'OK. He would be good. He comes over well. Who else?'

Anna looked blank.

'That's really all?'

'So far. But once you've come up with a realistic alternative killer, we'll—' She broke off artistically.

'Anna,' Trish said, watching her in deep suspicion, 'you are not planning to trick someone on to your programme and then accuse him of this murder on screen, are you?'

'Why not? It would make terrific TV, and I'd be made for life if we got the right man.'

Trish said nothing as she ran through all the things Deb had told her, trying to remember exactly what it was that had sounded convincing in her account of the night her father died. Was it enough to let this probably slanderous project go much further? Trish was so used to being protected against defamation in court that she was bothered about how much the film might expose her.

'Or facing vast damages.'

Anna shrugged. 'You can advise on that when you see the rushes. Come on, Trish. Say you'll help. Concentrate on the thought of getting Deb out. Listen, I need this film to work. And I can't do it without you: I don't know enough about the law. Say you'll do it. Please.'

Trish was still holding out.

'Hear what Malcolm Chaze has to say at least. Shall I fix a meeting for you? Any particular time?'

Anna was pushing much more than Trish liked to be pushed. A lot more. Still, they were old friends. It was an interesting case. And Deb Gibbert did need help.

'Oh, all right.' Trish opened the jacket of her black linen suit and flapped it to get some cooler air through to her skin, forgetting that she wasn't wearing a shirt underneath until she saw Anna's amusement. Luckily there were only trees in front of them.

Deb sat on the edge of the bottom bunk, staring straight ahead. The stainless-steel washbasin was directly in front of her. It made her think of the kitchen at home, with the children trailing in from the garden and Adam getting in the way. He'd driven her mad sometimes, wandering in and leaning against the sink for a chat or washing his hands in it when she was trying to get a meal ready. She used to shout at him for it. Now it seemed the most harmless of habits.

He was a good man. She couldn't remember why she'd been so angry with him. Except that she'd been angry with everyone; everyone except Kate.

'Oh, God, please let Kate be all right,' she said under her breath, so that no one outside the cell could hear. 'Please.'

She'd be able to talk to Kate on the phone again tomorrow morning, so it was silly to get in such a stew now. They always talked on Fridays before Kate left for school. Deb hoarded phonecards to make sure she had enough left by Friday.

Kate tried to be cheerful. Sometimes her stoicism was unbearable. She'd once said, 'Dad's being really kind to me, you know, and patient – even with my hopeless cooking.'

Deb had had to fight hard to keep her tears to herself that day. They were back again now, dripping down the side of her nose and making her choke. Her heart was racing and the hated words were booming around in her brain: you'll never get out; you're stuck here for ever; you'll never get out; you'll die in here. And you deserve it.

# Chapter 5

At six o'clock on Friday evening, the House of Commons terrace was emptier than usual. The country MPs were mostly on the way to their constituencies, but there were enough Londoners glad of the faint breeze off the river to fill most of the tables.

Malcolm Chaze stood out among the rest, as he would have stood out anywhere. Tall and well dressed, he had the kind of smooth, old-fashioned good looks that appeal most to powerful post-menopausal women. They didn't do much for Trish, she was glad to find.

'Debbie was very sweet,' he said, allowing a dreamy note into his voice. 'And thoroughly efficient. I wish my current secretary were as good.'

Trish put down her spritzer, afraid the condensation on the outside of the glass would make it slip out of her hand. 'Deborah was your secretary?'

'No. No. The dean's.' His voice was sharp – irritated – quite different from the one he used in public performances. 'Hasn't anyone told you all this?'

Trish blinked at his impatience and shook her head. 'But then I haven't been on the case very long. Which dean?'

'At Queen's, London. I was a philosophy tutor there and Deb was typing for the dean, which is how we met. I liked her at once.' He laughed, switching easily back into charm mode. The ease made Trish extremely wary.

'Debbie was older than most of the other secretaries there, but she was what at the time we used to call a *bon oeuf.*'

Trish smiled, keeping her teeth together. Childish franglais didn't often make her laugh; and smoothly good-looking, successful men who thought of women in subordinate positions as good eggs made her flesh creep. In her experience it meant the women in question never answered back or thought their own talents or needs as important as those of the men who handed down the tasks and the compliments.

If so, it sounded as though Deb Gibbert had changed since those days. Good for her!

Trish noticed that Chaze was looking closely at her. She relaxed her jaw. 'How nice,' she said, smiling. 'And did you keep up the friendship? I mean, had you seen much of her before her father died?'

'No, we didn't really keep up at all.' Sadness made his voice throb, but Trish wasn't convinced. It wouldn't have been difficult for him to pick up the phone. 'You know how it is, Trish. Or was. She left to get married – most girls of Debbie's type still did in those days – and I went in for politics. Our ways parted and we moved in different worlds. But I'll always be glad she remembered how close we'd been and still trusted me enough to call on me when she found herself in this hellish mess. I went straight down to see her.'

He brushed one finger over his left eyebrow. In anyone else the gesture would have meant that he was removing some sweat, but Chaze wasn't sweating. Too much perfect confidence and self-control. Trish wished she had the trick of it: the air felt like oily flannel against her skin and she could feel the sweat trickling down her spine.

'I wish there was something I could do for her,' Chaze said wistfully.

'Isn't there?' Trish was surprised by her continuing,

instinctive, mistrust of him. It was years since she had had this kind of reaction to a man who was a trifle more pleased with himself than seemed quite justified. No woman at the Bar could survive if she minded a little thing like that. It was almost a qualification in the Temple.

'Only appearing on this film of Anna Grayling's as a kind of character witness for Debbie,' Chaze was saying, with an apparently rueful smile that he must have practised. It was very good. Even Hugh Grant would have been hard pushed to better it.

Stop it, Trish, she ordered herself. You're turning into a bad-tempered old bag. Smoothness and good looks aren't a sign of dishonesty. And self-deprecation can sometimes be real, even in a man like this.

'And writing the article about her case,' Chaze added, keeping the smile going. 'It's all ready, so as soon as Anna gives me the word Debbie will be splashed all over the *Sunday Review*. For my part, I'd have got it in as soon as I'd written it, but Anna wants it out in the same week as the programme. I'm going along with that.'

'It makes sense.'

'And I am, of course, keeping an eye on Debbie's treatment.' He gazed out across the river towards St Thomas's Hospital.

'Really? How?'

'One of the few benefits of being an MP is that people worry about your good opinion.' He grinned again, but this time he looked less smooth and a lot more real in his satisfaction. 'I've made sure the prison governor knows I take an interest. How did she seem when you saw her?'

'Not too bad,' Trish said. 'She had prison skin and a prison figure, and she was worried about her cell-mate, who'd just OD'd on heroin.'

'What?' Chaze's face was in shadow so she couldn't see

much, but bursts of tension came off him like radio waves
pulsating out from a broadcasting mast.

'It does happen, you know, even in prison,' Trish said,
wondering why he was quite so angry. Drugs in prison were
a fact of life.

'It's a fucking disgrace.' The perfectly ordinary expletive
she heard fifty times a day, and often used herself, sounded
shocking from someone whose language had seemed so
artificial until then. He looked at his watch. 'Damn. Too late
to catch the Chief Inspector of Prisons tonight, but I'll put
him on to it on Monday. It's outrageous if that quantity of
drugs is still getting through to inmates. I'll get it stopped if
it's the last thing I do.'

Trish was fascinated by his passion, so much hotter than
anything he'd shown for Deb.

'Sorry,' he said after a while, once more smiling at Trish
with all the deliberate charm of a thirties film star. Any
minute now he was going to tell her he didn't *give* a damn. 'I
detest the thought of her being exposed to that kind of filthy
danger. In her own cell, too!'

Trish wished she could see his eyes more clearly, but the
low sun was right behind him. That might have been chance,
but she decided it was unlikely. With no light falling on the
lines around his mouth and eyes, and his hand elegantly
propping up his head, coincidentally hiding any double-chin,
he could have been her own age. And he *was* a good-looking
man.

'May I ask a very impertinent question?'

As he looked at her, his full mouth thinned. He took away
his hand. Trish saw he didn't actually have a double chin and
felt mean.

'Debbie and I did have a brief affair,' he said, as though
admitting he'd once shaken her hand. 'If that's what you
wanted to know.'

'It was, in fact.'

'I thought so.' He laughed lightly, unconvincingly. 'I'd be glad if you could keep it under your *chapeau*. Not that it's particularly important. I mean, it was donkey's years ago, neither of us was married or even attached at the time, so there's no scandal.'

'It's all right,' Trish said at once. 'I'm not about to leak your past to the tabloids. Why would I? I just want to know where I am.' She smiled a little. 'It helps when assessing evidence.'

'I'll bet. Debbie was lovely then – not beautiful, mind, and a bit, well . . .' He laughed. 'Stocky is the word that comes to mind. But kind and very gentle. I'd been going through a tough time, and she did a lot for me.'

What could the woman he'd described have offered a man like him, Trish wondered, other than the obvious sexual satisfaction?

'I've always known I owed her for that. If I can help her now, it'll do something to settle my debt.' His smile was even better this time, more grown-up and less yearning. 'Hence this meeting with one of the sharpest lawyers of her generation.'

'Tell me what she was like then,' Trish said, discounting the flattery.

She watched him as he talked, liking him better as he forgot to pose, losing himself in a description of a warm, friendly woman, not obviously attractive and clearly rather lonely. Trish wondered if Deb's appeal for him could have had anything to do with the way her uncertainties boosted his own confidence. It seemed pretty unassailable these days, but there was something about him, something about the way he obviously liked to collect admiration, that made her suspicious.

'What do you know about her family?' Trish asked, when he paused.

'Not a lot. I never met the parents. It wasn't that kind of

affair. They were stuck in the depths of wherever it was –
Suffolk?'

'Norfolk.'

'Of course. And they never came to London. Her awful
father didn't approve of the expense or something like that.
But I did meet the sister once or twice.'

'The perfect Cordelia? Good. I want to know about her.
How did she strike you?'

'A hard-faced cow, to be frank. But rather beautiful.'

'Not an Ugly Sister, then?'

'No. But, if you ask me, Goneril or Regan would have
suited her better than Cordelia. I've always thought it was
she, rather than the father, who was the cause of most of
Debbie's problems.'

Trish wasn't sure she agreed. Deb's own account of her
father made him sound unbearable to live with, and she'd
been surprisingly unvitriolic about her sister, considering
what Cordelia had said about her in court.

Even her name had caused Deb problems there, Trish was
sure. Deb herself probably hadn't realised it, but Trish was
well aware of the way the lawyers and the judge would have
reacted to the thought of a father-loving woman called
Cordelia. Everything in their subconscious minds would have
made them long to believe her.

'It sounds to me,' she said, teasing him to see how he
reacted, 'as though Cordelia didn't succumb to your charm.'

'You could say that. She had a lot of offers then, of course.
Even so, it was a blow.' Chaze's laugh was friendly and it
sounded honest. It smoothed away the edges of Trish's earlier
dislike.

She wasn't surprised that Deb had fallen for him. Bruised
by her father's contempt, she must have been wonderfully
reassured by the discovery that she could attract a university
tutor, and a philosopher at that.

'And what about her husband? Did you ever come across him?'

'One or twice. Not an enormously prepossessing bloke, I thought.' Chaze's voice had a seasoning of bitterness now. 'But then I would say that, wouldn't I? He took her off me.'

Good for him! thought Trish.

'He's an engineer of some kind, I believe. She met him when he came to lecture to one of our post-graduate courses. *Malheureusement* for Debbie, I'd have said. I mean, you know how badly engineers are paid.' Chaze laughed again. 'The poor girl has had a very hard time, trying to bring up four children on just about what I pay my current secretary. I've often wondered if that's what soured her.'

Ah, thought Trish, catching a glimpse of nasty pleasure. So perhaps her first reaction to him hadn't been as unfair as she'd thought, and perhaps Deb's preference for her engineer was understandable.

'Soured?' Trish lifted her eyebrows to invite more detail.

'Yes. A lot of witnesses at her trial gave evidence about her verbal violence. When I knew her, she was never even impatient, let alone violent. Now, would you like another drink?' Chaze pulled back the sleeve of his immaculate suit to check his watch: a gold Rolex. 'I'll have to go in a minute or two – I need to get down to the constituency for dinner – but there's time to order you another drink if you'd like one.'

'It's sweet of you, but no thanks. Before you go, are you saying you think she was unhappy in her marriage?'

He shrugged. 'D'you know anyone who isn't?'

Cynic though she was, Trish still believed it was possible for two people to be happy together, if they tried hard enough and were kind to each other. She told him she had several married friends, all of whom were an excellent advertisement for the state.

'I'm not sure I have,' Chaze said bleakly, getting to his feet.

'One last thing,' Trish said. He waited. 'Is there anyone you think might have killed the old man in a way they'd know would implicate Deb?'

As he shook his head, his hair hardly moved. Trish tried not to let the thought of gel and spray add to her prejudice against him. MPs had to take care of their image.

'I take the Phil Redstone line myself,' he said. 'It must have been the mother, at the end of her tether and wanting her husband to be free of pain. After all, that's what she confessed to.'

'But what about the pillow and bag discrepancy?'

'Oh, that's easy. I should think when she told them she'd smothered him, they said something like, "What, with a pillow?" and she would have agreed at once. I expect she was a great agree-er,' Chaze said, looking wisely tolerant. 'Everyone says Debbie's exactly like her, and darling Debbie always did her very best to agree with anything anyone said, however difficult it was for her.'

Trish didn't believe him and knew he saw it in her face. He looked enormously tall as she squinted up at him, the sun making her screw up her eyes. It burst out from behind him, glittering all round his elegant silhouette.

'Now, I'm afraid I really do have to go. It's been *such* a pleasure meeting you.'

Trish didn't get up, but she smiled at him as she thanked him for the drink and the information.

'I feel more optimistic about Debbie's chances than I have for some time,' he said. 'Let me know as soon as there's anything I can do.'

'I will. Thank you.'

As Trish sipped the last of her spritzer, weak and warm now that the ice had melted, she thought about her next move.

The terrace was pleasant with the faint wind off the river,

and Trish never minded sitting alone in a public place, even in the middle of a self-conscious crowd like this one. Several of the other drinkers glanced at her every now and then to make sure she recognised them. A few were clearly wondering whether they should have known who she was. It amused her to meet their half-doubtful smiles with a broad grin and see them rack their brains for her name.

She got bored eventually and walked home along the south side of the river to collect her car for the drive to George's house in Fulham.

By eleven on Saturday morning they were sitting in their matching dark blue towelling dressing-gowns, having breakfast in the garden. There weren't many flowers among the low-maintenance evergreens, but pots of pink and white lilies pumped their richly spicy scent into the air, a few late roses flopped at the end of thin spiky stalks. Daisy-like flowers spread like pools over the hand-made Suffolk bricks, which George had had laid in place of the original scrubby lawn.

A bumble-bee was hovering between flowers, buzzing like mad, and a few sparrows quarrelled at the far end of the garden. Broken snail shells lay in a pile on the bricks, smashed by a hungry thrush, and silvery trails veining several routes to the lace-like hosta leaves showed where slugs had been.

George leaned down to reach for his cup, without looking away from the newspaper. Trish watched him, a slow, contented smile lengthening her mouth. The smell of the coffee reached her, strong and fragrant, and she picked up her own cup to drink again. She did not run to Jamaican Blue Mountain in Southwark, but if that was how George chose to spend his money, that was his business. For herself, the thought of spending thirty-five pounds on a pound of coffee beans that tasted hardly different from any others seemed bizarre, as did the incredible weight of newsprint he had delivered to the house.

He liked to have all four broadsheets and sometimes two or three tabloids as well each weekend. It entailed buying a vast number of recycling bags in which to get rid of them, and hours spent reading them, but why not? It was an innocent pleasure and a tiny extravagance compared to some she'd known.

He sneezed explosively as he opened a magazine, allergic probably to the ink on the coloured pages. Trish got up to refill her cup and collect another croissant from the basket by the pots. The fat bee droned past her, its fur laden now with gold pollen, and settled in one of the regale lilies. She brushed one of the flowers, releasing an extra strong puff of scent, lucky not to have to worry about hay fever or asthma.

A moment later all the happy, self-indulgent peace was driven out of her.

'Did you see this?' she demanded.

'Snoutrage,' George said, looking up to grin at her. 'What is it this time, Trish?'

She knew he didn't like being distracted by snippets from particularly interesting articles, but he'd given up pointing out that he'd be reading the paper himself any time now and didn't need her to tell him what was in it.

'This story here about the parents of some junkie who died in his squalid flat, while he was looking after his two-year-old son.'

'Yes, I saw that. It's in all the papers. Awful for the child, of course. But at least it survived.'

'But now, after all that horror, they're trying to find a reason to repudiate him. It's unspeakable.'

George turned in his chair. His expression was benevolent, but she knew what it hid. It wasn't only uncontrolled anger he disliked; it was vehemence of any kind, especially in her.

She was coming to believe that it frightened him. Once she would have forced him to accept her as she was, but, watching him moderate habits and ways of talking that upset her, she had learned to give a little. And, after all, it wasn't the vehemence of her thoughts he minded, just its expression.

'You mean you're angry that they're having a DNA test done to find out if it's their grandchild before they'll take it into their home?' he suggested casually, much too casually for her current state of mind.

'*Him* not "it",' she said, as sharply as she ever spoke to George. 'Exactly. How could they?'

'Be fair, Trish.'

'Think about the child, for God's sake. He's been brought up by the junkie since birth, and it says here that no one can trace the mother; he was a child of the family. He belonged. And now he may end up in care just because the grandparents . . . Oh, people do make me angry.'

'I know they do.' George put down his paper and cradled the big white cup of coffee in both hands.

His strong, hairy legs were planted square on the stone flags about a foot apart, the dressing gown just covering his knees. He looked what he was: a clever, well-off man in his mid-forties, certain of his place in the world and his opinions, not trying to be young or glamorous. To her he was infinitely more attractive than a smoothie like Malcolm Chaze.

George must have seen the change in her, for his voice was lighter as he said, 'The junkie was in his late forties, wasn't he?'

She nodded.

'Then his parents must be getting on, in their sixties at least, probably seventies. They must have been to hell and back already with a heroin addict for a son.'

Trish scowled, in spite of herself, and drank some more

coffee. The fact that you could be besotted with someone didn't stop you feeling furious with some of their views.

'Trish, be reasonable,' he said again. 'A drug-addicted child is a torment to any parent. I had some clients once who had to take out an injunction to keep their own twenty-six-year-old daughter away from the house.'

'But that's . . .'

'No.' George was firm. He knew where she was coming from, and he wasn't afraid of disagreeing with her. 'It wasn't outrageous.'

Trish shrugged.

'The girl had been an addict for eight years by then. She'd been on the streets; she'd had gonorrhoea. She was sharing a flat with a low-life for whom she went out thieving. She'd had pretty much everything portable from her parents' house. And this was a girl with a good brain, a good education, a supportive family, and no problems with her parents until she got hooked. They did every single thing they could, paid for cure after cure in all the best places. Nothing worked. She was back on drugs within weeks each time.'

'And now?'

George shook his head. A flutter of pink petals from the climbing rose above his head floated down and settled on his hair. Feeling something, he put up his hand to brush them off, looking like a bridegroom embarrassed by confetti. 'I don't know. She's probably dead. They never speak of her. But they're still suffering. They always will. Parents do, you know, Trish. It's not only the children who are made unhappy in families.'

'I know, George.' Trish got up and went to pick the last few pink petals out of his hair. He put his coffee cup on the ground again and put both arms around her waist. She kissed the top of his head. 'Even so, I do think it's an outrage that these particular parents aren't taking the child in. Whatever he's like, whatever he's seen, he'd be reclaimable with proper care.'

George hugged her more tightly. 'You know, I love the way you refuse to back down, but this passion on behalf of stray babies is a bit worrying. Are you about to go broody on me?'

She was surprised he'd noticed and put both hands on his head to tip it up so that she could see his face properly. His eyes were softer than usual.

'I'm not sure,' she said honestly. 'I do keep thinking about it, but it would . . .'

'Change the way we live?'

'Mmm.'

'No more hanging about with the papers at midday on Saturdays? It would mean charging off to football and ballet.'

'And all sorts of other things. Hormone upheavals that might send my brain into outer space and stop me being who I am. I might never get myself back. And we'd have disagreements – quarrels even – about upbringing. You know we would.'

'And school fees,' he said, 'and exam nerves. And worrying that they're out late and might be taking E when they go clubbing. And who they want to marry, and whether they're paying enough into their pension schemes, and—'

'Oh, stop it,' she said, laughing. 'I know I'd worry too much. But it's a thought that does keep cropping up.'

'I know.'

Something in his voice made her say carefully, 'You too?'

He nodded.

'Then we will have to think about it,' she said, breathing carefully. It was all rather alarming.

'But we've plenty of time,' he said, picking up her doubts.

'A bit, anyway.' She took her hands away from his head and moved back out of his grasp. 'I must dress. May I have first bath?'

'Naturally.'

She took *The Times* Metro section with her, so she could read the book reviews in the bath. She wished George had two bathrooms and that one of them had a proper shower. She'd lost the habit of baths years earlier. Still, they spent all the week at her place; it was his turn from Friday to Sunday. Wallowing like a mudfish was a small price to pay.

# Chapter 6

'Ms Maguire?' said the stringy-looking man, who bent down to the open window.

'Yes. And you must be Adam Gibbert. Do, please, call me Trish.'

'Thank you, and thank you for coming all this way. It means a lot to us all that you've taken Deb on like this. D'you want to park over there, behind the Volvo? There's just about space, and you'll be safer off the road with a car like that.'

'Great.'

Trish waited until he'd moved out of her way, then manoeuvred her big soft-top Audi behind his battered estate car. The gravel crunched under her wheels and slipped as she turned the tyres.

Adam Gibbert shut the gate at the bottom of his garden and she watched in the mirror as he came back to the car. He was tall and walked painfully, which made him look much older than Deb. Trish knew the age difference was only four years, which made him younger than Malcolm Chaze, his one-time rival. He didn't look it.

He was wearing clean cream-coloured cord trousers, but they were split at the hem and beginning to fray. His shirt was made from dark green and blue checked cotton, like a primitive tartan. It seemed too vigorous a colour combination for his wattled neck and worried face. She thought he'd come over quite well on screen.

'Come on in. Kate's been determined to cook you a traditional Sunday lunch with all the trimmings, so it may be a bit late. But we can have a drink straight away.'

'Lovely. I brought some wine.' Trish leaned back into the car to find the bottle that had been rolling about under the passenger seat. She hoped it would be drinkable, and that he wouldn't be insulted by it. Knowing that he was strapped for cash and trying to bring up four children while their mother served out her sentence, Trish hadn't wanted to take lunch off him without giving something in return. Gibbert looked at the label with real interest and then glanced up, smiling shyly. 'It'll be a treat to drink something like this again. How very kind of you! Now, come on in and meet Kate and the rest of the family.'

He stroked his elder daughter's back as he introduced her to Trish and she saw the girl smile at him. But the smile seemed forced. She didn't look happy. Her oval face was still plump, but the shape of the appley cheeks suggested there might be striking bones under the puppy fat, and her long-tailed eyes were a deep, shining brown with glossy mink-like lashes.

'Would you like some help?' Trish asked, when they'd shaken hands. 'Or would the greatest help be our getting out of the way?'

A flashing smile transformed the weary patience in Kate's eyes. Her face was shiny with sweat and there was flour all down the front of her sagging black T-shirt, and in her long brown hair. She was in the process of putting a pastry lid on a pie dish full of browning lumpy chunks of cooking apple.

'Do you know how to make gravy?'

'In fact I do,' Trish said. 'The man I live with has managed to teach me after about three years together.'

'Oh, brilliant. Could you do that, then? And, Dad, will you get the little ones washed? They're mucking about in the garden and it always takes ages to clean the mud off.' She brushed the lank fringe out of her eyes with a floury wrist, sighing. A small piece of rolled dough fell off one of her fingers and lodged in her hair. She didn't notice.

When her father had gone, Kate sighed again and rubbed her forehead, as though it was aching. 'The potatoes have been in for ages.'

Trish knew the state of complete absorption in a tricky task that made you assume everyone nearby had taken each step with you and knew exactly what you were talking about.

'But I don't think they're going to be properly crisp. I can't work out how to get them like that. And the lamb will be done . . .' Kate looked at the clock. 'Oh, no! It was ready five minutes ago. But the pie . . .' She bit her lips. Trish saw her battling for control.

'Shall I get the lamb out?' Trish said, careful not to sound as though she was taking over. 'It won't have spoiled, I'm sure. And it'll do it good to rest while we get everything else done. In this weather, it won't get cold. I think you're amazing to cook a proper lunch for everyone like this.'

'Thanks.' The girl's taut shoulders relaxed a little and a sloppy grin made her look much younger. 'D'you think you could put a pan of water on? We're going to have peas. They take five minutes, I think. I'll just finish the pie.'

Trish did her best not to get in the way. When Adam Gibbert came in with the rest of his family and proceeded to stand over them while they washed their hands at the kitchen sink, forcing Kate to walk right round the kitchen table to put the pie in the oven, Trish wanted to shake him. Couldn't he see what he was doing? There must be other places in the house where they could wash.

She looked at Kate and saw a remarkable tolerance in her face. Her smile was almost maternal as she watched his back.

Then she looked up and apparently read Trish's expression without difficulty.

As Gibbert took the younger three children into the dining room with a tray of cutlery, Trish remembered that Kate was just seventeen and in the first year of her A level course. What could Adam Gibbert have been thinking of to make her do the family's cooking at such a stage? Trish stirred the gravy with such vigour that some splashed up over the side of the old-fashioned ridged cream enamel roasting pan.

'Sorry,' she said at once. 'I'll mop that up when it's cool.'

'You know, you're really kind.'

'Oh, Kate,' Trish said, laughing over her shoulder. 'You shouldn't sound so surprised.'

The girl blushed. 'No. I mean I'm sorry. It's just that a barrister, you know . . . I was expecting you to be frightening. D'you think you will be able to get my mother out?' Suddenly she looked terrified and started to brush the flour off her front. 'That was a stupid thing to say. Sorry. I'm in a real mess. Sorry.'

Trish put down the big spoon and abandoned the gravy for the moment. 'Listen, Kate. Obviously I'm going to do my best for your mother. But you must face the fact that there isn't a lot—'

'Oh, I know. Please don't think I'm expecting you to get her out next week. I know things don't . . .' She was crying, the tears puddling with the flour on her face to make flat greyish cakes on her skin. 'I know I mustn't build too much on the TV programme.' Kate wiped her face with a tea-towel. 'Sorry. I'll be all right in a minute. It's just that I know she didn't do it. I know it. If the law wasn't such a lottery, she wouldn't be in prison now. And Anna's told me that you're the best, that if anyone can prove the legal system got it wrong, you will. But, honestly, I promise I'm not going to blame you if you don't. I know it's like moving the Taj Mahal with a knitting needle. I know it is.'

Her tears were falling faster than she could mop them up. It looked as though her attempt to reassure Trish was one more burden than she could bear. She started howling like a much younger child. Trish found a clean tea-towel and offered it silently, waiting until the storm was passing. When Kate was fairly quiet again, Trish took the towel back.

'Kate, your mother is lucky to have a daughter like you.'

'Thank you,' she whispered, then turned aside to pour a shower of frozen peas into the boiling water. Some of them bounced into Trish's gravy pan.

'And so are the rest of your family. Now, shall we put the case to one side while we get lunch on the table? Then perhaps you and I can have a private talk afterwards. How would that be?'

'That would be great. You are kind. I do try not to cry in front of the little ones, but when I talk about her, I can't always help it. She's so . . .'

'As I say, she's lucky to have you. Now, I think this gravy's done. What shall I put it in?'

After lunch, while Adam took the boys and Millie out to play football, Trish and Kate did the washing-up and talked. Kate cried occasionally, but for most of the time she achieved impressive self-control. Trish didn't discover any new facts, but she did get a better picture of the dead man.

'He used to make such a fuss about all the pills he had to take,' Kate said at one moment, as she carried the clean meat plates to their appointed cupboard.

Trish, who was doing the washing because she didn't know where anything went, asked if there had been many pills.

'Oh, millions. There were so many things wrong with him, you see. And he hated swallowing them. And he hated being told what to do, specially by Granny and Mum. When it was Cordelia looking after him, he took everything without fuss. But she didn't do it any differently from Mum and Granny. He just behaved better with her.'

'D'you know why?'

Kate pushed away her fringe again. Her eyes were shrewd. Now that she had recovered and was letting her mind run ahead of her emotions, she looked quite different from the beleaguered cook who'd first greeted Trish: older and more sophisticated, but also slightly out of place in this old-fashioned kitchen with its metal cupboards, battered saucepans and blue-and-white marbled lino floor.

'I think he felt she did him credit, so he liked her better, and he didn't get anything out of making her miserable. My English teacher would say that there wasn't any psychological advantage in turning her into the enemy.'

'Whereas there was with your mother and grandmother?' Trish suggested, impressed.

'Yes, I think so. I've thought about it a lot, you see. He despised them, so he had to put himself above them. Making them scared and miserable was a way of doing that. He could feel bigger and better.' Kate frowned, looking unhappy but a lot tougher. 'But he wasn't. He might have been cleverer, although I don't think he was as clever as he thought. And Mum isn't nearly as stupid as he made her think she was.'

'I think you're right.' Trish meant it. 'What do you think happened to your grandfather?'

'I don't know.' Kate picked up the roasting tin that Trish had laboriously scoured and thrust it into the oven to dry in the residual heat. 'I really don't. If it wasn't for the fact that they didn't find the plastic bag on his head, I'd have said he must have committed suicide. But the bag was in Mum's room.'

'And there was really no one else in the house?' Trish

watched closely for the betraying blush. She couldn't help it. Here was a bright girl, who clearly adored her mother; a girl who could easily have retrieved the spare antihistamines from the rubbish bin, and known enough to check out the pills' potential for damage. But no blush came.

'No one any of us knew about,' Kate said. 'I suppose there could have been a burglar, but there was no sign of a break-in and nothing was taken.'

As she saw Kate frown, Trish hurried to ask another question before the girl could guess what she was thinking. 'Can you remember when your mother had bad hay fever that last summer before your grandparents died?'

'Of course. She was sneezing and wheezing and her eyes watered all the time. It was awful. I made her go to the doctor to get some pills, and she did in the end. They were called ast-something. I can't remember exactly what.'

'Astemizole.'

'Yes. That's right, I think. But she wouldn't have taken them to my grandparents' house. The hay-fever season was long over and she'd have no need to take them. I know she wouldn't. She said she didn't and she doesn't lie. Ever.'

'Do you know what she did with the spare pills?'

Kate shook her head. Her eyes welled with tears. But she didn't look away. 'She didn't tell me and I didn't ask. Why would I?'

'No, of course you wouldn't. Now, where should I put this saucepan?' Trish asked. Kate took it from her, wiped it, and bent down to put it in its place at the back of a cupboard. Then she started knotting the black plastic rubbish bag before hauling the whole thing out and carrying it outside.

When she came back, Trish said, 'You're very good at all this domesticity, Kate. You must have had a lot of practice. Have you always done such a lot in the kitchen?'

'No, of course not. Only since the trial. Mum always did it.

I'm only trying to copy her. But there's so much I don't know how to do: cooking and things. The rubbish is easy.'

'Did she do that, too?'

'Of course. Except sometimes at weekends when Dad helped.'

'I see.'

'You want to know if I can swear she'd thrown away the pills, don't you?'

Trish nodded.

'Well, like I said. I don't know. I wish I could tell you something that would be useful, but I don't know anything. I've racked and racked my brains, and I can't think of anything.' Kate's voice had been rising with every word, but now she was breathing slowly, obviously trying to get herself back together. 'You see, you've come all this way for nothing.'

'It hasn't been for nothing, Kate. For one thing, I had a delicious lunch. And for another, I've got yet more support for my own certainty that your mother didn't do it.'

Kate put down the bundle of knives she was drying and hugged Trish. Over Kate's shoulder, Trish saw Adam Gibbert coming back into the house with the other children. He looked surprised to see them, and worried, too. Trish tried to signal reassurance. It didn't seem to work.

Later, he left the rest of the brood with Kate while he escorted Trish back to her car. On the way he told her, while tears welled in his eyes, that he knew what all the extra work was doing to Kate and that she oughtn't to have to do it when she was working so hard for her A levels, but that he didn't see what else was to be done. He helped her with the subjects he knew, and he took on as much of the childcare as he could, all the shopping and a lot of the cooking. But it was still far too much of a burden for a girl of her age.

'Maybe you need some paid help.' Trish tried not to sound critical.

He bit his lip, still looking unhappy rather than ashamed. After a moment he said he couldn't afford it, adding, 'For a time I thought Deb's sister might help out, but she won't. And I can't borrow – I've nothing except the house to borrow against and I can't risk that. It's the kids' only security.'

'I must say I'd have thought Cordelia might have helped out in the circumstances. She is the children's aunt, after all.'

'I know. I'd have hated to accept anything from her after the way she treated Deb in court – and when they were teenagers – but we need help so badly I'd have forced myself to take anything she offered for the children's sake. But she never offered anything. And when I abased myself and actually asked for help, she turned us down flat.'

'Even though she's rich?'

He nodded. 'All she would offer was to take Millie and bring her up as her own – you know, with a nanny and private schools and all that.'

Trish felt her eyes stretch at the thought of Deb's reaction to such a proposition.

'I know,' Adam said, once more displaying more sensitivity than his behaviour in the kitchen had suggested, 'it was a pretty aggressive move, wasn't it? I didn't tell Deb. I knew how much she'd hate it. It could have been generously meant, but it . . .' His voice, which had hoarsened as he wrestled with his indignation, dwindled into a dry cough and then nothing.

'Have you any theories about what really happened to your father-in-law?'

Adam rubbed both hands over his lined, greying face as though he was washing. 'None.' He sounded so hopeless, so tired, that Trish believed him. 'All I can assume is that there was some kind of accident. But then that doesn't fit with the evidence of the bag.'

He leaned against Trish's car, propping his arm on the roof and rubbing his head with his free hand.

'What is your wife's greatest fault?' she said abruptly.

Gibbert stood up, moving away from the car as though it was coated with anthrax. 'What do you mean?' Clearly angry, he wouldn't meet her eyes, looking from side to side as though he was searching for something easy to fix on.

'Everyone has faults,' Trish said gently, 'and no one knows them better than a spouse. If I'm to understand Deb, I need to know what hers are. What came into your mind the instant I asked my question?'

'Outrage.' For a moment he did look directly at her. Then he twitched his gaze away and stared at some straggling petunias that had been planted in a shell-edged plot beside the edge of the drive. The wobbliness of the lines and an arrangement of random sticks suggested it could be Millie's private garden. Adam bent down to straighten one of the sticks.

'Apart from outrage,' Trish said, not letting him distract her, 'it may feel disloyal to talk about her faults, but honesty, real, complete honesty, is the only thing that's going to help me help her now.'

'Temper.' Adam stood up again with a scarlet petunia between his hands. Shredding the petals and dropping the bits like gouts of blood around his feet, he looked over Trish's head to the far distance, where a pinkish haze hovered over an ugly conifer forest. 'Deb doesn't get angry like everyone else. She's miles more patient than anybody I know. But when something does eventually get to her, she blows up more quickly and vio— and fiercely than other people. And she . . .' He covered his face again. There was still some of the mangled petunia sticking to his fingers. His voice came out muffled and worrying: 'I can't do this.'

'Has Deborah ever, to your knowledge, taken impulsive action in a temper that she's later come to regret?' Trish was implacable.

'Once or twice.' The words were wrenched out of him. He turned away and stumbled back towards the house, tripping and sliding through the gravel as he went.

Trish watched as the front door opened. Kate stood there with the other children. Millie was clinging to Kate's leg, crying into the stiff black denim of her jeans. Kate took her hand from Millie's blonde head and held out her arms to her father. He lurched forwards as though he was another child she had to comfort. Trish was too short-sighted to see the expression on Kate's face, but she recognised the helpless guilty misery of his hunched shoulders and the protectiveness of Kate's stroking hands.

No wonder he doesn't want any paid help, Trish thought, as she soberly unlocked her car and slid into the driving seat. She sat, without putting the key into the ignition, trying to imagine what it must be like to believe your wife guilty of murdering her father and yet have to keep up a pretence of believing in her innocence.

# Chapter 7

Adam pulled himself together and hustled Kate upstairs to her room to work or rest. 'I don't mind which,' he said, pushing her towards the stairs. 'But you need time to yourself.'

'But tea,' she protested. 'And then baths. You need—'

'No, Kate, I'll be fine. You go on. I can manage.' He smiled at her and saw relief chasing doubt to and fro in her eyes. 'Honestly.'

'Call me if you need anything?'

'Of course. Now, go on. I'll see you later if you feel like some supper. We can have sandwiches with some of the cold lamb. But don't bother to come down if you're not hungry. I'll be fine.'

'OK. Thanks, Dad.'

He watched her climbing easily on her long, long legs until she disappeared round the turn of the stairs. He worried about her so much. She had far too big a load to carry, but he was already beaten to his knees with his own and he couldn't help any more with hers.

He hoped she'd find a way to deal with her genetic inheritance somehow. She was a credit to her upbringing, honest and kind and serious, but you never knew when inherent characteristics were going to emerge out of the manufactured self. Like with Deb: so kind on the surface and so volcanically angry beneath it. Just like her terrifying father, in spite of everyone saying she was her mother all over again. If only . . .

Stiffening himself, Adam turned to face his responsibilities, smiling as brightly as he could. 'Now, kids, how about cooking something for tea?'

'Yeah, great,' said Louis, while Marcus scowled. 'Flapjacks?'

'And chocolate cornflakes,' shrieked Millie.

'Must we?' sighed Marcus, sounding as though he were in his sixties.

'Not if you don't want to, and if you can amuse yourself quietly. But I don't want you disturbing Kate. She's done enough for today.' Adam knew Marcus would sneer and pretend to loathe the idea of cooking, only to sidle into the kitchen eventually and join in.

Adam tied tea-towels round the waists of the other two and set them to measuring and mixing, while he tried to make himself believe he could carry on for as long as it took. Provided it was just the family, he thought he probably could manage, but if he were faced with any more penetratingly perceptive women like Anna Grayling's pet barrister, he might crack.

It had been shaming to see Trish Maguire pick up his certainty of Deb's guilt. He should have hidden it better. But he didn't know how. He could manage to keep it from the little ones and, he thought, from Kate. He wasn't so sure about Deb herself, but at least now they had only the odd hour alone together and there was plenty else to talk about. It had been hell for the year she'd been on bail waiting for the trial.

They'd gone on sleeping – or more often not sleeping – in the same bed, just as they'd always done, and Adam had tried not to think about her father's death, or what she might do if he himself triggered one of her rages. Setting them off had been all too easy throughout the long, anguished months of her bail.

He'd tried so hard to go on thinking about her as the gentle, uncertain, hurt woman he'd fallen in love with, and the mother of his children, but more and more as she retreated into her angry silences, or burst out with diatribes about his and everyone else's failings, he'd seen her as the killer of her father. And he'd hated himself for it.

He knew the barrister had understood. He just hoped she hadn't picked up the rest. Even to himself it was hard to admit that he was afraid of his own wife.

'Where's the treacle, Dad? Dad!' Louis's voice broke in. From the irritation in his round blue eyes, which were so like Deb's, it was clear he'd been asking the question for some time.

Adam found the heavy green-and-gold tin and reminded Louis how to weigh out the necessary 150 grams. Marcus was back already, loitering on the edge of the busy little group, flinging sarcastic comments around, but not yet joining in. He would, given time. Adam had no trouble understanding him or knowing how he'd react. He felt safe with Marcus. Louis was more difficult, as emotional and incalculable as Deb, as well as looking out of her eyes. Funny that twins, even fraternal twins, could have turned out quite so different.

He wished he believed in God – or any god. Then he could have prayed: Don't let any of them see how terrified I am that their mother may get out of prison.

While she was locked up, the children were safe. They could believe in her innocence and love her, write their pathetically brave letters and draw their pictures of what they'd been doing and what they thought she'd like to see. If she came out and they were faced with her little spurts of temper and the few but appalling bigger ones, they too might come to question her innocence.

Adam knew he was a coward. He'd discovered it a long time ago. If he'd been braver, he'd have told Anna Grayling what he believed and she'd have dropped her plans for the TV programme. But perhaps the barrister would tell Anna for him and that might be enough. Trish Maguire certainly knew. She'd sussed him for the weak man he was, terrified of his own wife and appalled at the idea of ever having to live with her again.

'What's the matter, Daddy?'

Millie was looking so frightened he realised he must have groaned aloud. He made himself grin again.

'Lumbago,' he said.

'What's that?'

'It's a kind of backache old men get,' he said, tweaking one of her blonde curls. 'They used to say that the only cure for it was to make a roll of old flannel filled with hot salt, like a kind of swiss roll, and lay it on the afflicted part.'

'There's some salt here,' she said, scrambling off the chair on which she'd been perching to stir her sticky mixture. There was chocolate goo all over her hands and face and a goodly lot down her front too. 'We can put it in the cooker and make it hot and I'll get my flannel . . .'

'Oh, Millie, my darling,' he said, swinging her up into his arms in spite of the chocolate, 'you are a sweetie, but it's not that bad. We can keep the hot salt for another day. Now, we need to get you some paper cases, don't we?'

'Millie's feet are in my way, Dad,' said Marcus, elbowing them both aside. 'Move her, for goodness sake. Then I can stir. You are useless. Lumbago's no excuse.'

Out of the mouths of babes and sucklings, Adam thought.

The letter was already limp from overhandling, even though Deb was trying to ration herself. She knew if she read it as often as she wanted, it would lose its power, but it was hard not to take it out of her pocket for a quick look every time she felt low.

Her door was open and the others were milling about outside, making the usual racket. It amazed her that the women who were penned up with her could produce such a volume of noise for so many hours at a time. Ghetto-blasters, raucous laughter, tuneless singing, and, of course, the screams of the self-harmers and the attention-seekers.

Anna Grayling's letter opened itself between her fingers and her eyes caught the magic sentences again:

Trish really liked you, Deb, and she's told me she's sure you're innocent. She fights like a tiger for people she takes on, so I know you're going to be all right. It may take time, but it will come right in the end, and you will be going home. I'm sure of it. You'll be with Kate again, probably before she takes those A levels of hers.

# Chapter 8

Trish let herself into George's house as quietly as she could. He'd had a briefcase full of work, and she didn't want to disturb him before he'd finished.

'Trish? That you?'

She could feel the smile stretching her cheek muscles as the sound of his voice reached her from the garden. He never worked out there, so he must have finished the briefcase. He'd be prepared to talk.

'I was beginning to get worried. Traffic hell?'

'Yes. And a lot of tough questions to ask.' Trish plumped down on the chair beside his and pushed off her shoes. Her bare feet were grubby from exhaust fumes, but as the soles met the cooling bricks and her toes flexed she sighed in pleasure. She knew George wouldn't mind the grime.

'You look as though you need a drink,' he said. 'Then you can tell me all about it. Pimm's? I've made a jug.'

'I'd rather have wine, actually,' she said, wrinkling up her nose. 'Pimm's isn't really my—'

'Nor it is. I can't think why I keep forgetting.'

He disappeared into the kitchen, leaving Trish to wonder why she should mind that he'd forgotten something as trivial as her dislike of the sickly drink. There were so few days hot enough to persuade George to mix himself some Pimm's that the subject had hardly ever cropped up. There was no reason for him to remember.

'Here.' He handed her a tall, dewy glass of white wine, which tasted like her favourite New Zealand sauvignon. She felt his hand on her head. 'Someone's been horrible to a child, haven't they, Trish? One of Deborah Gibbert's? Do you want to talk about it, or would you rather . . .?'

She looked up quickly. Her taste in drinks might occasionally escape his memory, but not the important things.

'Not this time. This time it's an adult who's suffering.' She told him about her discovery that Adam Gibbert, like Deb's mother, believed her guilty. 'So no wonder the police and the CPS and the jury thought so too.'

'But you're still convinced she's innocent?'

'Not convinced. I never have been. But I still think she could be. Don't ask me why.'

'Why?'

She laughed. He could always make her feel better, less stressed, more rational.

'Because you liked her?' he suggested.

'That, yes. And . . .' Trish tried to fix on the conviction that sat like a stone at the bottom of the muddy river of ideas and suspicions in her mind. She thought of Deborah's face as she explained why Kate mustn't be given false hope. Trish had taken that as devoted mothering; was it in fact the sign of a woman aware that no one would ever find any evidence that she wasn't guilty?

'Because she's a good mother?'

Trish reached up to take his hand from her head and kiss it. 'You know me too well, George. Though lots of them say she has a terrible temper.'

He moved away to sit in his own chair and lifted his heavy tumbler of tea-coloured liquid, picking a fly out of it with a small bunch of borage flowers.

'But you knew that. A terrible temper, clearly, and a sharp tongue, and an inability to hide outrage.' George's face softened into a smile that made her flex her toes again in pleasure. 'She sounds just like you, my love.'

'Bastard.' Trish stuck out her tongue. 'Maybe that's why I liked her.'

'So what are you going to do next?'

'Interview the doctor who treated her parents, if I can, and find out whether there was any reason for him to want Deb to be guilty. Interview the old couple's neighbours in case they've got anything useful; then see Deb's sister to find out what she really thinks, now she's had a chance to cool off.'

'And maybe find out a bit more about the real Deb who may be hiding behind the mask you saw?'

'That, too. There can't be anyone who knows her better,' said Trish, who had no sisters.

'I wouldn't be too sure of that,' said George, who had two.

He laughed and, when Trish had asked what was so funny, told her horror stories from their adolescence. It sounded as though it had been a hell of unwittingly shared boyfriends and terrible rivalries, of clothes borrowed and spoiled, an enmity that sometimes threatened to swamp the whole family, and an absolute defence of each other in the face of outside threat, which made a nonsense of all the rest.

Trish liked it when George talked about his past. He didn't often do it, but it always made her wish she'd known the dogged, fat child who'd battled with the school bullies. They'd tormented him about his shape and his specs and his swotty tendency to come top in all exams.

'Are you going to see your father this evening?' he said, as the last of the sun sank behind the houses opposite and the light turned from yellow to pale grey.

'Yes, I must. I haven't been in for a couple of days.' Trish stretched and checked the time. 'I suppose I'd better go now or visiting hours will be over. Thank you, George, you've sorted me all over again.'

She finished her wine and got out of the low deck-chair in one easy movement. 'I'll let myself out,' she said, when she'd kissed him. 'Will I see you tomorrow?'

'Sure, if you're not busy. Shall I come to Southwark?'

'Lovely. I'll cook something.'

George raised an eyebrow. Trish aimed a punch at him and said with great dignity that she was beginning to enjoy cookery these days and would have something on the table by the time he got to the flat.

'I shall look forward to it all day,' he said, with an expression of fainting ecstasy on his face, which meant that she left him laughing.

It didn't take long to get to the hospital and there were plenty of parking spaces between the concrete pillars. Trish had hoped to buy more grapes at the hospital shop, but it was shut, so she was empty-handed when she got up to the ward.

There were a few visitors still hovering around the beds and she squeezed past their chairs on her way to the corner, only to see screens around her father's bed. Slowly, with feet that felt as though they'd been dipped in lead, she walked towards a gap in the screens. Then she stopped. Her breath stuck in her throat and her hands were sweating.

The bed was empty, stripped, and smelling of disinfectant.

But he was getting better, she told herself, wondering how she could possibly have left him for forty-eight hours without visiting or even phoning to find out if he needed anything.

She looked round at the patient opposite, whom she thought she recognised, and then at the others nearby. One of them must know when it had happened. None of them said anything. One after another, as she met their gaze, they turned away.

Trish waited another moment, staring at the bare mattress and picturing her father's fleshy, unshaven face with the bright black eyes. Then she walked briskly away, the heels of her flat sandals clicking on the polished vinyl floor.

There was no one at the nurses' station near the lifts. Trish waited, not knowing what else to do. There seemed to be no medical staff of any kind. She was teetering on the brink of fury; all that was holding her back was the knowledge that she'd left him alone for forty-eight hours and it had happened then. She was partly responsible for this appalling hole that had been torn in her life. She'd been out of reach when he died. She'd never told him any of the things she'd come to understand about him and about herself. Her teeth clenched against the pain and guilt.

A nurse appeared and Trish burst out, 'Why didn't anyone tell me about my father?'

'Who is your father?'

'Paddy Maguire,' said Trish, and heard a note of pride wobbling somewhere in her voice.

The nurse leaned over the paper-strewn counter for a clipboard. She had stumpy legs, so she had to strain to reach it, perching on one foot.

'Ah, Maguire, Patrick.' She looked up and seemed surprised at the sight of Trish with her eyes heating up and her mouth trembling.

'When did it happen?'

'Ten thirty yesterday morning,' said the nurse, consulting her notes again. She was utterly matter-of-fact. 'He called for a minicab and left half an hour later.'

'What?' Trish felt the heat transferring itself from her eyelids to her brain as the misery and guilt metamorphosed into a lava-flow of fury. 'You mean you allowed a man who's just had a massive heart-attack to go home alone? In a minicab?'

'It wasn't that massive,' said the nurse pettishly. 'He's made a good, quick recovery.'

'But why wasn't I told?'

'And you are?'

'His daughter, I told you. My name's Trish Maguire. I've given your colleagues all my numbers and asked to be told as soon as there's any change. Why didn't anyone ring me?'

'Well, I don't know, do I? I've only just come on duty. But he was fine. They wouldn't have discharged him if he hadn't been.'

Trish felt as though the pent-up feelings were about to split her skull and emerge as a red-hot river that would devour everyone and everything in its path. The nurse seemed to understand. She backed away, reaching for the phone. 'I'll call the doctor, shall I?'

'I think you'd better.' Trish retreated to a row of orange chairs, hugging her midriff so tightly she could feel the edge of her watch pressing through her T-shirt. She sat down and tried to control her temper.

Twenty minutes later a harassed young man in a flapping white coat appeared and looked at the fat little nurse, who gestured towards Trish.

'Ms Maguire? You wanted to know about your father?'

'Yes. You let him go, alone, without telling me anything about it.'

'Yes.' The young man rubbed his eyes like a small boy. His blue plastic label said he was the senior house officer. He had probably been on duty all weekend. Trish tried to feel kinder. 'The results of the angiogram came through. He was fine. There was nothing more we could do for him here, and we like to send patients home at the weekend, if we possibly can.'

'I'll bet you do,' said Trish, surprising herself as much as him with the force of her scorn. 'And what did you send him home with? An aspirin?'

'No. He said he had plenty of aspirin at home.'

'I was joking,' she said grimly.

'Were you?' The doctor looked puzzled. 'Aspirin is used to

thin the blood in patients who don't need Warfarin.'

'Rat poison?' Nothing would surprise Trish about this place – or the medical profession.

'It's an anti-coagulant,' the doctor said impatiently, as though she should have known exactly what treatment heart patients might be offered. But she'd never had close dealings with one before. 'It's used for patients at risk of thromboses – clots.'

'But when I was first in here, they told me that if he recovered this time he'd have to take the greatest care because it was likely he'd have another heart-attack.'

'It's always possible, of course, though in his case we don't think so – at the moment anyway.'

'What action have you taken to make sure it doesn't?'

'Nothing, beyond the aspirin,' said the doctor, not looking at all sheepish. He glanced at his watch, clearly anxious to be gone. 'It was decided he'd do fine without either an anti-coagulant or digoxin.'

'What about his diet?' Trish thought of the mountains of egg, bacon and fried bread, and the Niagaras of cream, the ziggurats of cheese.

The young doctor shrugged and muttered something about Paddy's GP. Trish told him that it sounded as though the hospital had been irresponsible in the extreme and quite possibly negligent. She stormed out without waiting for an answer, and drove far too fast to her father's flat.

He'd offered her a set of keys months earlier and she'd declined them. Now she wished she hadn't been so standoffish. What if he were lying on the floor in the throes of another attack? She rang the bell. When she heard his heavy footsteps coming to the door, she felt her knees sagging.

'Trish, m'dear! How nice of you. Come on in. I was never expecting you on a Sunday night.'

She looked at him, hardly able to believe that he was

standing grinning at her, looking entirely at ease, wholly healthy and fully dressed. She leaned against the architrave, licking her lips and trying to get control of her own heart's beating.

'Now what's the matter wit' you?' He held out his arms.

To her astonishment she leaned into his embrace. 'I thought you were dead,' she said, into his shoulder.

'Well, I'm not. So come and have some whiskey on it. And cheer up, now. It's not as bad as all that, is it, to find me still alive?'

Sniffing, she laughed and told him he knew what she meant. She wasn't all that keen on Irish whiskey and she'd already drunk a glass of George's wine, but she couldn't refuse a small one. She felt more foolish than she could remember since childhood, and thoroughly embarrassed at the scene she'd made in the hospital. She supposed she ought to write an apology to the exhausted young doctor she'd bawled out.

George was always telling her she had to learn to trust people. He'd given up telling her not to lose her temper. But he was right. It hadn't done her any good. Her head was still ringing and she felt sick.

Paddy bustled about, providing a cushion for her back and crisps to soak up the alcohol, and every time she tried to make him sit down, he told her he wasn't an invalid and that so long as he kept drinking the whiskey to keep his arteries open and didn't indulge too much in the bacon and the butter, he'd be fine. She drank some whiskey to keep him company and began to let herself believe that she hadn't lost him.

# Chapter 9

'The doctor won't be able to see you until next week,' said the receptionist, her voice oozing satisfaction.

'I'm not a patient,' Trish said crisply into the phone, glad that the woman couldn't see her face. 'I'm researching the background to a film about Deborah Gibbert's case. Do you know what I mean?'

'Of course. But . . . Could you hold on a moment?' Trish waited, hearing several other phones ringing and a blurry mixture of voices, punctuated by a child's frightened wailing. When the receptionist picked up the phone again, she sounded breathless. 'The doctor cannot possibly spare the time to talk to you.'

Thinking about a country GP in late middle age, Trish took a gamble on his likely political affiliations. 'Could you tell him that I'm calling on behalf of Malcolm Chaze, the MP, who is particularly interested in the case and planning to discuss all its implications on screen in due course?'

'The doctor's busy with a patient. He's already said he can't help you. I can't interrupt him again.'

'Please try once more, and tell him about Malcolm Chaze. He's already written the first of a series of articles on the subject, you know. It should be coming out any day now.'

Another, longer, pause ended with the receptionist panting and irritable. 'Dr Foscutt is most fearfully busy, but he has authorised me to say that if you come here later on this morning, he'll try to squeeze you some time at the end of surgery. Be here by twelve.'

That didn't leave much time to drive into the wilds of Norfolk, but there weren't many days when Trish had neither court nor chambers commitments, so she agreed. She might have to sit up half the night working on her trial papers to make up for the trip, but she had to find out what the doctor knew and whether he was as ghastly as Deb had claimed.

Picking her way with difficulty through the East End towards the M11 twenty minutes later, she wished she had never set out. But once she had reached the motorway and could put her foot down, it wasn't so bad. She'd always loathed Norfolk, cold, flat, featureless and associated in her mind with painful memories of an old boyfriend, but she did like fast driving.

Accustomed in childhood to the cosiness of Buckinghamshire, with its beech woods and beautiful seventeenth-century red brick, Trish had to work to appreciate the huge skies and bleached emptiness of East Anglia.

The doctor's village turned out to have a kind of bleak charm, with neat white cottages and a few bigger houses built of grey flint and stone. Parking was easy, but it amused Trish to find that the surgery shared a car park with the local pub.

The waiting room was still full. It was clear she wasn't going to get in to see Dr Foscutt for some time. As she sat down and opened her newspaper, the mainly elderly patients in the waiting room resumed the conversations they had broken off to stare at her. One woman, who had a great bruise spreading up over one side of her face, confided to her neighbour that she just didn't know what she'd do if she fell again when the Meals-on-Wheels lady wasn't due for more than twenty-four hours. She just couldn't get up on her own any more and there wasn't anyone else to help. The neighbour was sympathetic but wanted to talk about the time she'd had to wait six hours for the hospital transport service to get her home after the last X-ray. But that wasn't nearly as long as the first woman had had to wait when she'd gone in for her biopsy and some machine or other wasn't working so they'd wanted to send her straight home without doing the operation at all.

Their patience was astonishing, and their stoicism. Trish had heard doctors in London complaining of the hordes of 'worried well' who clogged their surgeries, along with people surprised by an excess of earwax or uncomfortable with a heavy cold. Such people clearly didn't bother Dr Foscutt.

One woman, who looked about seventy and was describing *sotto voce* how embarrassing she had found her last barium meal, suddenly blushed. Trish realised she had been staring and raised her newspaper to give the woman some privacy.

The voices became little more than a distant buzz as Trish read the law reports. She was vaguely aware of phones ringing and patients moving around as she read. Leafing back through the paper, she came to the opinion page, opposite the letters, and saw Malcolm Chaze's face, looking out at her.

Darkly glamorous, but serious too, the portrait headed a diatribe about drugs in prison. He wrote with passionate anger, usually balanced by clear argument. His last three paragraphs went over the top, but by then he had found a way to introduce Deb:

It is a shocking system that locks up for life an innocent woman like Deborah Gibbert but cannot control the evil of illegal drugs. For the past six months, Mrs Gibbert, a devoted wife and mother, has been sharing a cell with a heroin addict. Somehow the young addict got hold of enough of the drug for a dangerous overdose. Taken to hospital for treatment, she may not recover.

How could this happen in a place where she was meant to be guarded twenty-four hours a day? Someone in that prison must know who supplied the heroin. But no one will talk. Without witnesses, there is no hope of identifying, let alone convicting, the dealer.

Something has gone fatally wrong in society and it is up to all of us to put it right. If the law has to be changed and some cherished freedoms curtailed to rid our land of this evil, then so be it. I for one will work for the rest of my days to . . .

'Ms Maguire?' The receptionist was standing in front of Trish, her face tight with impatience.

'Sorry,' Trish said, dropping the paper in her lap.

'Dr Foscutt can see you now. Please don't keep him too long. He's got a heavy list this afternoon, and then there's evening surgery.'

'I'll do my best to be quick.' Trish got up as she was folding up her paper and stuffed it into the briefcase she was holding open against her bent knee.

Dr Foscutt did not impress her. Slight, but very erect in his green tweed suit, he was a couple of inches shorter than she, and he clearly resented it. In fact, Trish thought, he looked as though he might resent quite a lot. He waved her to a chair on the far side of his desk.

She sat down, looking straight into his chilly grey-green eyes, and repeated her introductory spiel.

'I know Ian Whatlam's death took place four years ago,' she finished, 'but I'm sure you haven't forgotten it.'

The doctor fiddled with his spectacles, tapping them on his blotter, opening them and squinting at the lenses. He looked away from Trish, feeling in all his pockets, apparently searching for a special cloth to polish and repolish the glass.

'It was a dreadful time,' he said, as he put on the spectacles, settling his shoulders in a series of flurrying movements. 'I do not know when I have been more disturbed by anything. Of course I have not forgotten.'

Trish opened her mouth to ask a helpful question, but he didn't need help.

'I agreed to see you this morning because it is of crucial importance to show the public that assisted deaths are wholly unforgivable.' His declamatory style must have come from long practice. 'If your television programme is designed to do the opposite, I shall—'

'It isn't.'

He looked surprised. 'Have you not come here to persuade me that Deborah Gibbert was justified in what she did because it released her father from intolerable pain?'

Intrigued, Trish shook her head and watched the muscles under the thin skin of his face twitch and tighten. 'What on earth would be the point?' she said. 'Deb's been convicted of murder and is in prison. There's no question of getting her off on some kind of mercy-killing excuse at this stage.'

'Then what *are* you trying to do, Ms Maguire?' The question was so straightforward that Trish was almost prepared to forgive him for his speechifying.

'Show that she didn't kill him,' she said, letting herself frown, as though puzzled by his mistake. 'And that all the facts which were given in evidence in court could be construed in at least two quite different ways.'

Dr Foscutt raised his eyes to the ceiling and sighed with all the gustiness of a pantechnicon letting out its air brakes. Trish hoped he'd be prepared to reproduce it on camera.

'And I am here now to establish exactly what was wrong with her father and how you treated him,' she went on, hoping she looked unthreatening. 'And his wife, of course.'

'Good gracious me! You cannot possibly expect me to disclose patient records to you, a complete stranger.'

'You disclosed them to the court.'

'That was entirely different.'

'I see. Why did you suppose I wanted to talk about assisted deaths?' Trish asked, watching as the spectacles hit the blotter again, bounced up and down in his hand like a miniature pogo stick.

'My receptionist told me that's what you wanted.'

'I don't—'

'And, in any case, it was Deborah Gibbert's only possible defence, even though it is no defence either in law or in morality. I wanted to make that plain to you. Do you understand, Ms Maguire?'

'I understand what you're telling me, but it's not quite accurate.' Trish was well used to explaining the same point over and over to lay clients, so she was able to keep her voice free of both irritability and excessive patience. 'Deb's defence was that she had neither suffocated her father nor given him an overdose of antihistamines.'

'That's as ludicrous now as it was then,' he said, fast and angrily. 'The autopsy proved that someone had done just that, and there was no one else in the house who was physically, let alone emotionally, capable of it.'

'Except her mother.'

Dr Foscutt's face reddened and his narrow upper lip began to quiver. Trish quite expected his spectacles to snap between his tightening fingers.

'Helen Whatlam required a stick to walk – and balance – with. Think about that, Ms Maguire, if you can think about anything beyond your extraordinary enthusiasm for a callous killer like Deborah Gibbert.'

Trish thought of her face as a plaster mask and her feelings as nasty little rodents threatening to gnaw holes in it and give him a glimpse of her real loathing.

'I don't suppose you have ever tried to put an unconscious

man's head in a polythene bag, have you, Ms Maguire?'
Foscutt was sneering, so the mask must have been thick
enough to contain her feelings.

'No.'

'Well, neither have I, but I can assure you it would take two
hands.'

'Perhaps she leaned against the wall for balance.'

'And perhaps the fairies did it,' he said surprisingly. He
hadn't appeared to have a sense of humour. 'Ms Maguire, this
is a shocking waste of my time and no doubt of yours too.
You must know perfectly well that if Helen Whatlam had
committed the crime, her fingerprints would have been on the
polythene bag.'

'Yes, but she said she used a—'

'Please do not waste my time with this kind of nonsense.'
Dr Foscutt put both hands on the edge of his desk, as though
to push himself to his feet.

'Have you never been tempted to help a suffering patient on
his – or her – way, Dr Foscutt?' Trish asked quickly. There
was something in the man that worried her – and, judging by
his body language, it worried him too. He was so tense she felt
he would twang if she plucked him.

She watched as he coughed and put on his spectacles again.
His hands lay on the pristine blotter in front of her. They were
not shaking any more, but the joints were white. Trish could
see him working to make himself relax. His fingers stretched,
and his chest expanded as his lungs pumped in and out. His
lips moved as he sucked them. At last he was ready to
pronounce.

'Ms Maguire, I do not know what gossip you may think
you have picked up.'

Aha! thought Trish, but she waited without prodding.

'But I can assure you that I have never taken – nor would I
ever take – part in any kind of euthanasia. You must be as

well aware of the law as I: no doctor may assist his patient to die, but every doctor may give pain relief to a dying patient, even though he knows that the analgesia will also work to shorten the period of dying.'

'Yes,' Trish said, even more interested. Gossip, she thought, what gossip? 'Naturally I know that. Was Mr Whatlam being given pain relief?'

'My goodness me!' The doctor's lips spread tightly against his teeth, as though he was trying to smile without ever having known how that should feel. 'How many times must I reiterate that I will not reveal details of a patient's treatment?'

'Very well. Then what can you tell me about Deborah Gibbert's last visit to the surgery?'

'She was a difficult woman,' he said, leaning back in his chair and taking off his glasses again. He folded them and tapped one end on the blotter. This time the tapping was relatively slow, no more than one gentle knock every five seconds.

How odd that he should be relaxing, Trish thought. Why was Deb's last visit so much less worrying than his views on euthanasia? From her account in the prison, it had been dreadful. Trish smiled sweetly and waited.

'Unlike her mother, who was a delightful woman and very patient with her husband, Mrs Gibbert had no understanding whatsoever of the limitations imposed on the medical profession.'

So perhaps that was why you wanted Deb to be the killer and not her mother, Trish thought. Aloud she said, 'And so what did she do – Deb, I mean – on that last visit here?'

'She harangued me, in front of a waiting room full of patients, if you can believe it.' Dr Foscutt's voice had begun to shake again. He pursed his lips, which made him look like an elderly geisha before she'd put on her makeup. 'She told me that if a dog were in the pain her father was forced to endure, its carers would be hauled into court by the RSPCA.'

'And you took that, did you, as a plea to shorten his life?'

'Most certainly I did. There was no other construction to be put upon the words, whatever her counsel alleged at the trial. Lawyers can twist almost anything anyone says to their client's advantage. The concepts of truth and the sanctity of actual fact appear to be quite foreign to them.'

He paused, as though giving Trish an opportunity to protest, but she saw no point in even trying to explain the limits and demands of *her* profession.

'And, by the way, I do not believe for one instant that that woman was concerned to end her father's suffering.'

'Dr Foscutt—'

But he was well away and nothing Trish could say was going to stop him now.

'If Deborah Gibbert had had an ounce of decency or kindness, she would have been able to do her duty by her father. But she hadn't and so she couldn't. She killed him to save herself inconvenience.'

'So you, yourself, never had one moment's doubt about her guilt?' Trish asked slowly, using her voice to lower the emotional temperature in the room, which was becoming unbearable.

'I would remind you once again, Ms Maguire, that the autopsy confirmed my original suspicions that his heart had stopped during suffocation, and a court of law convicted her. *Ergo*, she is guilty. These researches of yours are a waste of time, as I hope you will explain to Mr Chaze when you report back to him.'

'As I understand it, Dr Foscutt—' Trish broke off. His habit of punctuating every comment with her name must be catching. She started again: 'As I understand it, there are no definitive indications of suffocation to be found at autopsy.'

He glared at her, as though trying to intimidate her with the force of his unshareable expertise.

'Fluff and feathers in the larynx appear only in novels, petechial haemorrhages are much rarer than most people think, and if cardiac inhibition occurs because of suffocation, they are highly unlikely to be present at all.'

'You are well informed, Ms Maguire.' A mouthful of vinegar couldn't have made him any sourer.

'Thank you. Now, are you sure your patient's heart couldn't simply have stopped of its own accord?'

'Quite positive. He was not a well man, but he had no history of cardiac symptoms whatsoever. His death could not have occurred as a result of natural causes. These fairy-tales you are inventing are ludicrous, a function, I am afraid, of your inexperience. And now I must ask you to leave. I have important work to do.'

So have I, thought Trish. She felt like throttling him, and listing all the cases she had successfully prosecuted and defended. No wonder Deb had lost her temper in this room. Sleepless probably, desperately worried about both her parents, and faced with a man who could listen to what she was saying yet not hear a word of it, she must have felt murderous, too.

Could she have decided to treat her father herself? What if she had remembered how much the antihistamine she'd taken the previous year had helped her, and been determined to get some more to ease her father's terrible skin condition?

It would have been relatively simple to get a prescription for herself from a doctor who knew nothing about her or her circumstances. Trish thought of the monstrous carbuncle that had once driven her to a practice in Northumberland. She'd been staying with friends who had recommended the surgery. The doctor who saw her had taken one look at her back and prescribed penicillin. She hadn't had to provide any identification, only a name, address, and the name of her doctor. Any of them could have been false.

'You know,' said Dr Foscutt, speaking in a very clear voice as though Trish were deaf – or very stupid, 'I don't wish to be rude, but there is a type and class of woman who, at a certain age, becomes extraordinarily difficult to deal with. Deborah Gibbert was an almost perfect example. You, yourself, are a little young yet for that kind of behaviour.'

You may not wish to be rude, Trish thought, but you're managing pretty well. Then she remembered the poor young houseman she had savaged, and felt guilty all over again.

'Mrs Gibbert would not listen to anything anyone said to her. She had several bees in her bonnet and made herself thoroughly unpleasant to everyone here, including the district nurse. When her mother tried to take the blame for her crime, I was ripe for murder myself.'

Trish felt her eyebrows pushing up towards her hairline. From a man who claimed to have such reverence for human life, that remark was pretty rich.

'Now,' said Dr Foscutt, almost shouting, 'I must ask you – once again – to leave my surgery. I have several domiciliary calls to make.'

'I thought you didn't do that? Go to people's homes?'

'Of course I do. This is a country practice. When patients request a home visit, I make one. And now, if you'll excuse me, Ms Maguire?'

'But I understood from Deb Gibbert that—'

'What I would not do,' he said, standing up and reaching for his open bag, 'was drop everything every time poor Helen Whatlam thought up a new anxiety. She used to telephone in a panic of some kind every week. My partners and I have two thousand patients on our books, Ms Maguire. Have you any idea of the responsibility that represents? Or the time it takes to look after them all?'

This seemed to be a speech he had made several times before. Trish didn't try to respond or to stop it. She just listened.

'My goodness me, if I took to making house calls to reassure all the hypochondriacs and the chronically ill who are already receiving all the available treatment, I should have no time to see other patients with genuinely treatable complaints. I suggest that you learn a little more about the life of a busy general practitioner before you start criticising us in the way that woman tried to do. Good day to you.'

'Before I go, there is just one thing on which I'd very much like some instruction from an expert,' she said, with what she hoped was a shy smile.

He didn't respond any more than he had to her earlier eagerness, but he didn't order her out of the room again. She let the smile die since it wasn't doing her any good.

'It's this business of the astemizole that was found in the victim at autopsy.'

Dr Foscutt didn't move. His face seemed stuck in its tight, affronted pout.

'I don't understand how it could have got there. Had you ever prescribed it for him, or for his wife?'

'I thought you said you had read the trial transcripts, Ms Maguire.'

'I have.'

'In that case, you will know that I provided all my case notes for both the Whatlams and thus proved to the court that I had written no prescriptions for astemizole to either of them, or to their daughter. Is that quite clear, Ms Maguire?'

'Yes, but I've been wondering why you didn't. It's a very effective antihistamine, isn't it?'

Dr Foscutt's face grew redder as she watched and his hands were shaking again.

'Very. But, Ms Maguire, in a practice like this we have to

watch our budgets. Non-proprietary terfenadine happened to cost less, therefore non-proprietary terfenadine was the drug of choice. Do you understand what I am saying to you?'

'Yes, I think I can just about manage to grasp it, thank you.' Trish stood up, stuffing her notebook in her shoulderbag. She detested him as much as he clearly loathed her, but she wasn't giving in to him. She held out her hand.

'It was good of you to spare the time to see me, Dr Foscutt, and I hope that when plans for the film are further advanced, you might consider repeating some of this on the screen. I know Malcolm would be pleased.'

Dr Foscutt stood stiffly on his side of the desk. He was not going to take her hand. Trish let it drop to her side.

'The receptionist will unlock the door for you.' He did not look at her again, packing his bag with prescription forms and drug bottles. When it was ready, he had to glance up again. He seemed surprised that Trish was still there, although he must have known she hadn't moved.

'What I cannot understand,' he said, hustling her to precede him out of the surgery, 'is what a respected Member of Parliament like Mr Chaze is doing involved in a sordid affair like this one.'

Trish smiled. 'Oh, he's sure Deborah Gibbert is innocent. He's known her for years, you see.'

The doctor's expression was a reward in itself. Trish waited by her car until he had roared off in an old Rover, which spluttered and farted up the road in a cloud of dirty exhaust.

# Chapter 10

Dr Foscutt drove home to an outrageously late lunch. It was true he had domiciliary visits to make, but not until half past three. Lunch was sacred. A man couldn't give of his best to his patients unless he looked after himself. Luckily Molly was an excellent cook.

He kissed her cheek as he always did when he came home, and counted his blessings. She had aged, like him, but she had never lost the sweetness with which she had started out on married life thirty years ago. She was his calm centre, his certainty, and the one and only reason why he could still cope with the unending, usually unreasonable, demands of his patients and their friends and relations.

Moving in step with her towards the dining room, he thought of the grace with which she had conducted herself throughout a life that couldn't have been easy. She had taken on his parents' house, which was much too big for a modern servantless life, and apparently loved it as much as he did; she had given birth to three healthy sons, brought them up with wisdom and kindness, grieved when they left home and always welcomed them back with a smile.

She allowed the morning's messages to trickle out in bearable quantities as she shook out her napkin and he carved the cold joint. It was pork, his favourite. He had forgotten through the morning's frustration that they'd had roast pork yesterday. He particularly liked cold crackling with cold apple sauce. And Molly had made a dish of potatoes and onions in cream to go with it. She was a remarkable woman. He smiled fully for the first time that day as he handed her a plate full of neatly carved slices.

'Are you having a bad day, dear?'

'No worse than usual,' he said briskly, as he poured small glasses of cider for them both. Molly helped herself to salad.

'You've got the red shaky look you have when you've been angry. Was it the awful mother of that poor girl with Crohn's disease again?'

He occasionally forgot how perceptive she could be and nodded to show his gratitude as he told her that for once Mrs Frankel had left him alone. She'd been convinced by some journalist that her daughter's Crohn's was the result of the MMR vaccine he'd administered six years ago. He detested the media for what they did to patients with these ludicrously exaggerated scare stories. If everyone who'd written about the autism and the Crohn's and God knew what else they thought had been caused by MMR looked back at the records to see the much bigger number of children whose infertility, blindness, encephalitis, and brain damage had been caused by complications of measles, mumps and rubella, they'd—

'Then if not her, who was it, Archie?' Molly said, luckily breaking in before the fury overtook him completely.

He smiled at her and saw her look reassured. Then he told her a little about the proposed television programme and the impertinent young lawyer who had come along to interrogate him. Her pretences must have been false, he'd decided, when she used the MP's name.

Molly listened in silence, her forehead disfigured by deep furrows. She sighed as he finished. He saw that she hadn't eaten anything. He had a piece of meat on the prongs of his fork and was carefully covering it with apple sauce, on to which he dropped a knife-point's worth of salt. Too much for his blood pressure probably, but he liked it, and he didn't have many pleasures.

'I've often wondered why Debbie did it,' Molly said, staring out of the window towards the black-and-white pattern made by the neighbouring farmer's Friesians. 'It seemed so unlike her. She must have done it for Helen's sake. Debbie always did everything she could to help her mother.'

'Did you see much of her?' he asked, in surprise. He couldn't remember Molly's ever having volunteered a comment about Deborah Gibbert.

'When she was here? A little. I used to sit with Ian Whatlam on Saturdays sometimes so that Helen could go to evening mass. And occasionally Debbie would arrive while I was there, and we'd talk. I liked her so much.'

'You never said.' He was no longer eating either. He could not remember when he had felt so disturbed.

'I didn't want to worry you.' Molly smiled at him. There seemed to be a kind of courage in her eyes. He wasn't sure why she needed courage to talk to him, even about something like this. 'You needed a lot of support over Ian's death and all through the trial. I tried to give it to you undiluted by any of my own feelings.'

He was not a demonstrative man, but he reached out to pat her hand. She smiled again. He found himself facing the first ever doubt about Deborah Gibbert.

'Do you mean you don't think she did it?'

'Oh, no. I'm sure you're right that she did it.' Molly sounded utterly convinced and he began to breathe more easily again. He would trust her judgement anywhere. 'Besides, there was no one else who could have done it, was there? We both know Helen would never have been strong enough, even if she could have overcome her faith and what it required of her and Ian. No, no, my dear. You mustn't worry about that. I just wish I could understand why Debbie didn't ask for help. We could have intervened if we'd known how bad things were.'

The cold pork was suddenly hard to chew. He did his best, swallowing more cider than usual to get it down. Molly changed the subject by asking about one of his younger patients who had a terrible head injury after a motorcycling accident.

'I don't know what we're going to do,' he admitted. He put down his knife and fork, wondering how he was ever going to last until his sixty-fifth birthday. Could he manage five more years of this perpetual juggling with his patients' needs, finding locums so that he and the other partners could occasionally have a holiday, filling in all the endless forms, battling his patients up the hospital waiting lists, having to read yet more insults to the profession from the government and ill-informed pundits in the press.

While his patients behaved properly, and accepted that he was doing his best for them, he might last out, but if they went on ranting at him, cross-questioning him about his treatments, criticising, demanding things that were out of his power to give them, reading up their illnesses on the Internet, he might break. He might—

'Try to eat something, my dear.' Molly's voice called him back from the edge. 'You'll wear yourself out if you don't.'

He forced himself to focus on her, sitting on his right at his father's mahogany table, loyal, kind, on his side. His throat opened and the food began to taste good again.

'There's nowhere in the area that can take him,' he said. 'I'm told that there's a nursing home near Portsmouth that specialises in cases like his, but I can't see how to make the budgets stretch to it.'

'So, what will happen?'

'His family will have to do their best, with outpatient

treatment where necessary, and the district nurse when she can be spared.'

He caught sight of Molly's face and added more impatiently, 'I know what their life will be like, but what's the alternative? No more hip operations for anyone for a year? Putting off all biopsies in the practice? Something's got to give.'

'"It is expedient that one man should die for the people",' she quoted, not exactly appositely. 'I know. I know, Archie. And it can't be you and your health. Try not to worry too much. Here, you don't want any more of that, do you? I've a nice rice pudding keeping warm. Wouldn't you rather go straight on to that?'

He felt like kissing her hand as she took his half-eaten food away.

Trish saw the Whatlams' house from miles away: a square red-brick building with white stone coigns, which should have been pretty but wasn't. There was a windswept for-sale sign nailed to one of the gateposts and the small front garden was neglected. What must once have been a lawn was now a tattered mess, and a few collapsing roses blew about in the mangled borders.

Presumably few people were prepared to buy a house where a murder had been committed, but Trish was surprised that the efficient Cordelia Whatlam hadn't taken steps to have this one properly maintained. If the place were ever to find a buyer it would need to look a lot more kempt.

She parked the car in a layby opposite the gates and got out for a closer look. Not far away, she could see a large grey church with a cluster of houses round its skirts. Two of the long ground-floor windows of the house were broken, and all of them were thick with dust. The white paint on the panelled front door was splitting and the brass knocker was greenish-black.

A dog barked. Trish looked round quickly to see a beautifully kept golden retriever dancing along beside an elderly couple. They were dressed in the kind of saggy khaki quilted jackets and toning tweeds that looked as though they'd been deliberately designed to blend in with an English hedge. The man raised his hat and they both murmured, 'Good afternoon.'

'Good afternoon.' Trish produced her frankest smile. Remembering everything she had read about the day before Mr Whatlam died and the neighbours who always walked their golden retriever down the lane, she added, 'You couldn't by any chance be Major and Mrs Blakemore, could you?'

'Have we met somewhere?' asked the man, a little embarrassed. 'My memory's not what it was, I'm afraid. Or my eyesight.'

'No, we've never met.' Trish held out her hand. 'Trish Maguire. I'm a . . . a friend of Deborah Gibbert.'

He shook her hand firmly, then introduced her to his wife, as though she hadn't been there when Trish gave her name. They, too, shook hands.

'I'm so glad Debbie still has friends,' he said, while his wife nodded vigorously.

'Are you? I understand you overheard her last argument with her father?'

'That's right.' The major turned aside to order the dog to sit. It paid no attention, snuffling at an interesting hole in the bank by the edge of the road. 'We told the truth in court.'

'I'm sure you did. It never occurred to me that you wouldn't have,' Trish said hurriedly.

'But we were appalled at the way what we said was used,' Mrs Blakemore said. 'Appalled. Poor old Ian Whatlam was one of the most difficult men in the world, always, and of course he got even worse once he was ill. Both Helen and

Debbie had such trouble with him. I wish . . .' She turned away. Trish waited, then looked enquiringly at the major.

'I think my wife wishes we'd known quite how bad things were. We could have helped, d'you see, if we'd understood how desperate Helen was, and Debbie. But they were good women, loyal – wouldn't want to betray him to his friends. We didn't know the full story until the trial.'

'So you don't think Debbie was guilty of murder?'

'Good Lord, no. A woman like that? It's absurd. Whatever she did, she can't have known it would kill him. I wrote, d'you see, to the Crown Prosecution people to tell them what I thought of the way they'd used our evidence and not allowed us to explain.'

Trish tried to visualise the transcripts. How had Phil Redstone cross-examined these two? She couldn't remember, so she asked.

Mrs Blakemore had herself under control again. 'He asked whether we could have been mistaken about the day when we'd heard the argument, and we hadn't been. We were late bringing Ponto out for his walk because we'd had to wait in for the Aga man, and he hadn't come until after six, which put back dinner by an hour and a half. There couldn't be any doubt at all. I said so, and then I was excused. I tried to say what I felt about Debbie, but the lawyers cut me off.'

Such was the woman's sincerity – and age – that Trish didn't really mind the way the last word had come out as 'orf'.

'Have you seen Debbie in that place?'

'Yes.' Trish smiled at them both. 'It's not pleasant, but she is holding on. And she has found friends there.'

All over Mrs Blakemore's face tiny muscles relaxed. She smiled, her lips trembling a little. 'Helen would be so relieved. It was terrible for her, when she was dying, to know that Debbie might go to prison.'

'Helen confessed to it herself, d'you see,' said the major,

looking at his dog. 'To save Debbie.'

'I know,' Trish said.

He nodded and raised his hat again, rocking a little on his feet as though to get them moving once more. His wife took his arm and smiled at Trish. 'He can't stand for long. The arthritis isn't so bad when he's walking. It's in his knees, you see.'

'I quite understand. I'm sorry. It was very good to meet you both. Thank you for being so frank. If you can bear to help me a little more, I'll walk along beside you. Is there anyone you know of in the village who could have wanted Mr Whatlam dead?'

'I don't think so,' said the major, after a pause for thought. 'He was a very difficult old man but, d'you see? He hadn't got out much for years. What with the gout and everything. There wasn't anyone with any kind of personal grudge against him round here.'

'Yes, I do see. Thank you. The only other thing I wanted to ask . . .'

'Yes?'

'Was about the doctor. I've heard gossip that he once helped one of his patients to die. Could that be right?'

The major looked at his wife. There was new colour under her cheekbones. To Trish's surprise it turned out to be a sign of anger.

'That's malicious nonsense,' she said, sounding much more forthright. Her husband nodded approvingly. 'There was an elderly woman with liver cancer who used to live in the village. She needed very large doses of painkillers and the morphine pump she had failed one day. The district nurse called Dr Foscutt, who administered morphine by mouth while a new pump was found. The woman died the next day and one of her relations accused the doctor of killing her.'

'That seems pretty unfair,' Trish said. 'Was there any

reason – a will or anything like that – to make the relation suspicious?'

'She hadn't much to leave,' said the major gruffly. 'Her pension died with her, and the cottage was rented. But she did leave him a tea-service she'd cherished and he'd once admired. It wasn't worth much, but it was all she had. And the doctor was all she had, too, because the great-nephew or whoever he was never did anything for her.'

'I see. One of the hazards of the medical profession, I imagine,' Trish said, feeling more sympathy for the doctor. No wonder he'd reacted so strongly to talk of euthanasia. 'Thank you for telling me. It clears up a lot.'

'Good. Give our love to Debbie, will you, when you next see her?' said Mrs Blakemore, taking her husband's arm. 'We don't write. She wouldn't want letters from us. But I'd like her to know we think of her. If you think it would help.'

They moved slowly away, the retriever charging ahead of them and having to be called back to heel. Trish tried not to think too much about old age, concentrating on the benefits of staying in London instead of being lost in this endless flat space, miles from anyone and anything that might help.

# Chapter 11

The car was full of the disciplined passion of Bach's cello suite, played by Sue Sheppard. Trish had thought it would be suitable music for the drive back to London, with the solo cellist having to provide both the melody and the accompaniment. Anna's expectations and Deb's need were weighing on her.

The half-dancing, half-austere throbbing sound put some welcome distance between her and her memories of the doctor. But it couldn't stop her thinking of Deb going to the surgery in desperation and meeting hostility and rejection. Imagining Deb's feelings on the drive back to her parents' house made Trish feel as though she might have let her liking for the woman make her dangerously credulous.

No music on earth could have stopped her mind working to rearrange the few facts she had, first one way and then another, trying to see how they could be made to fit the story she so much wanted to believe.

At first it had comforted her to find that Foscutt was quite as awful as Deb's account had made him sound. But the more she thought about him the less happy she became. Deb had turned to him because there was no one else. When he failed her she must have felt like an animal in a trap.

And she wasn't stupid, whatever her father had told her all her life. She'd have known his death would spring the trap at once, and for ever.

Back in the cool sanctuary of her Southwark flat, Trish made her coffee strong and reread the whole of the trial transcript, searching it for hints of evidence that could have been misused or mislaid. She couldn't find anything to confirm any of the stories.

Impatient with herself, and with Anna for involving her in so much work on such a hopeless project, Trish decided to abandon the case for the moment. She knew she'd have to check her answering machine for urgent messages before she got back to her own work, but she dreaded hearing Anna's voice.

It burst into the room as soon as the machine's clicks had stopped, and that was only the first of four messages, all harping on the same theme. Have you found the real killer? What *have* you found out? Why aren't you working harder? What are you going to do next? Trish had spoken to her twice the night before and once before she set off for Norfolk.

Her father, her work, her friends, her own needs: none of these seemed to have impinged on Anna's consciousness. Trish finished her coffee as she listened to the rest of the messages, even though she knew the caffeine wouldn't improve her temper. Then, deliberately calm, she rang back.

'What have you found out?' Anna demanded, as soon as they were connected.

'Not a lot,' Trish said, with impressive calm. At least, she thought it impressive; Anna didn't notice. 'I've just got back from the doctor.'

As she described their meeting, she drew stick figures of all the characters in the story. A female emerged on the paper, clumsily drawn, carrying the screwed-up polythene bag in her hand. Trish drew a doorway, then a passage and another door. She redrew the figure with the bag entering the second door.

Helen Whatlam was said to have been shorter than her daughter. Trish drew another basic stick figure, then added a balloon for her stomach and a slight hump to her back and a walking stick dangling from one hand. Deciding that the sketch looked more like an emu than anything human, she put down the pencil. Her imagination was much more effective.

In her mind she could see Helen Whatlam gingerly opening the door into her husband's bedroom. She used her stick carefully and quietly to help her across the long expanse of carpet between the door and the bed. There was a pillow under her arm. Reaching her husband's bed, without waking him, she put the pillow over his face and leaned on it, the pillow and the body taking the place of the stick that usually kept her from falling.

It could play, Trish told herself, as she said into the phone: 'After all, it is what Helen Whatlam said she'd done. I'm not surprised Phil Redstone tried to make the jury believe it.'

'Yeah, but he failed.' Anna's voice was packed with impatience, like an unexploded bomb. 'We have to do something different, for Christ's sake.'

'Maybe. But you're luckier than Phil was. You can dramatise the story, have actors playing the parts and a seductive voiceover putting Deb's version of what she did with the plastic bag, making it much more convincing than a hammy playlet of the prosecution's invention. You're not constrained by the rules of evidence. You might swing it.'

'It's not enough,' Anna snapped. 'We need evidence that someone else killed him, even if not the name of the person. Can't you see that, Trish? You of all people! I thought that's what you were going to do, not just waste time regurgitating all the old arguments that we all know aren't going to do anything for anyone.'

Trish took a moment to bite her tongue. 'And what have

you been doing to further *your* project, while I've been flogging up the M11 for you?'

'Now, just hang on a moment.' Anna sounded nearly as angry as Trish felt. 'I've been working my socks off. You've no idea how much is involved in getting together the proposal for a film like this before the commissioning editors will even look at it.'

'Anna . . .'

'I've got to put together a whole team from best boys and gaffers to cameramen and props buyers, but I can't hire them until I've got a commission. I've got to use people I can trust, people I've worked with before, and the good ones are booked up months and months ahead, so I spend hours keeping them on side, promising that I'm nearly there. I'm researching locations, finding a studio we can afford, working out budgets, finding a good scriptwriter, editors, sound mixers . . . Besides cutting every possible cost to the bone. It's a nightmare.' She moderated her machine-gun voice a little. 'But I suppose I can't expect you to understand. It's not your field.'

'Anna—' Trish broke off as she heard her mobile ring. It was probably just as well. 'Look, I've got to go. I'll ring later. 'Bye.'

'Trish?' said a vigorous, masculine voice over the mobile. 'Malcolm Chaze here. I rang your chambers, but they said you were working at home. I wondered if you were still on Deb's case, and if there was anything I could do to help.'

That was so much more tactfully put than Anna's demands that Trish was able to say she hadn't yet managed to find anything very useful, but was still hoping to get somewhere in the end. She didn't add that she was beginning to wonder about Deb's innocence. Trish could hear the doubts in her voice. She wondered if he would.

'You sound nearly as frustrated as I feel,' Chaze said

sympathetically. 'Would you like to come round and have a drink? We could cheer each other up, brainstorm our way through what little there is and see if we can't come up with a useful plan of campaign. Or at least some more helpful lines of inquiry. How would that be?'

Trish thought it might be good. George wasn't due to come to the flat that evening and she'd had enough of her own company and Anna's nagging. If the phone rang once more, she thought she might lose it and scream at the unfortunate caller. She said she could be at Westminster at whatever time would suit.

'Why don't you come here, to Pimlico? It's much more civilised and we can talk without worrying about being overheard. Would you mind?'

'Not at all. Give me the address.'

When she emerged at Pimlico tube station, she was furious with London Transport, herself, Anna, the passengers who wouldn't get a move on, and the poor tourists who hadn't yet learned that they couldn't stand on both sides of the escalator without driving regular commuters into a state of murderous fury.

Upstairs, at street level, the air seemed a little cooler, even marginally fresher. Trish checked her directions and turned right. Chaze's house turned out to be in the middle of one of the better Pimlico streets. It was a tall white building with two windows on each storey and neat little black-iron balconies on the first floor.

Trish rang the bell and was admitted by a scared-looking young woman who said she was Malcolm's secretary, Sally Hatfield, doing a bit of overtime to clear things up after the end of the Parliamentary session.

The fear in her face interested Trish, who had not put Chaze down as a frightening man.

'I'm fantastically sorry, Ms Maguire,' Sally went on in the kind of gaspy, exaggeratedly grand accent that always set Trish's teeth on edge, 'but Malc's a bit tied up just at the mo. Could you bear to come back in a bit? You know, in about half an hour?'

'About' came out as 'abite'. Trish's teeth felt like millwheels mashing the last few husks of the day. 'He told me to come now,' she said, checking her watch. 'Look, I'm sorry if it's inconvenient, but I don't particularly want to hang about in a pub, or go home and have to flog out again. It's too hot for that. Can't I wait for him here?'

Sally looked ready to burst into tears or be sick, but she shrugged, then tried a smile. 'Well, OK, yah. I s'pose. I mean, do come in. Fine. Right. Come into the drawing room and have a drink. I'll try to get him to hurry up.'

'Thank you.' A little puzzled by what sounded like incipient hysteria, Trish followed her guide into a long yellow-painted double drawing room, where a well-stocked drinks tray stood on top of a low mahogany bookshelf, heavily decorated with gilded swags. The books were an eclectic collection, obviously there because someone had read and valued them, not because they were beautifully bound or fashionable. Trish liked what she saw.

'Would you like a drink?' Sally asked, in a quite unnecessarily loud voice.

Trish accepted a glass of wine and couldn't imagine why the other woman was making such a noise crashing bottles around and kicking things that got in her way. Then, as a bitterly angry female voice echoed down through the ceiling, Trish understood: Malcolm Chaze was having a stonking great row upstairs, presumably with his wife, and his young secretary was embarrassed at the thought of a stranger's overhearing it.

'You're making a fool of me, Malcolm. And I won't have it.'

The secretary shuddered as she handed Trish her wine in a heavy cut-crystal goblet and asked her, almost shouting, whether she enjoyed working at the Bar.

'Yes. Thank you. Don't worry about it.' Trish gestured towards the ceiling. 'This sort of thing happens to everyone. I'm not going to gossip about it.'

The young woman gave her a huge, wavering smile. 'You are a brick. Thanks. That's really good of you. They'll stop soon,' she said, in a much less offensively posh voice.

But the insults that fell through the ceiling became more and more violent. It was impossible not to listen to them. Trish sat on one of a pair of matching tangerine-and-yellow-striped sofas, while Sally perched on a kilim-covered ottoman in front of her, crossing her slender legs so that the patent-leather pump dangled from her left foot.

Glass crashed on glass upstairs, as though a heavy scent bottle was being banged down on the glass covering of a dressing table. 'I'm prepared to put up with your hours, the fact that you're never available when *I* need a walker for a work dinner even though you always force me to trot out with you when you need someone.'

There was a low, buzzing murmur. Chaze, probably aware that Trish had arrived, must be trying to damp down the row.

'I don't give a shit. I'm even prepared to watch these idiot girls rolling over for you. What I'm not prepared to do is take any steps—'

There was another crash of glass, followed by splashing sounds as Sally Hatfield dropped her drink. She slid off the ottoman, down on her knees, dabbing at the puddle with a tissue she'd been keeping up her sleeve. She was whispering vicious self-criticisms. Trish saw her cut her hand on a sharp stalagmite of lead crystal and offered to help.

Sally stood up suddenly, dripping blood, muttering that she

really had to get it strapped up and find a cloth and would Trish mind being left on her own for a sec?

'No. You carry on. Don't worry about me. I'll wait here till he's free.' It would be much easier to listen to the row if she didn't have to keep pretending not to for Sally's sake.

Mrs Chaze was still batting away upstairs: 'I can see it makes them work themselves into the ground for you, and I don't much mind falling over their lapdog bodies whenever I come home. I'm even prepared to go your revolting constituency once in a while. But I am not, absolutely not, prepared to watch you making a fool of yourself over an old girlfriend who everyone knows killed her own father. You're making me ridiculous and you're risking your one asset: your reputation for brains and common sense.'

'No, I'm not.' This time Chaze's voice was clearer. 'Deb Gibbert is part of my campaign for better access to real justice. I've told you over and over again. Everyone knows that. It has nothing to do with you or my past with her, which was over donkey's years ago. There's going to be a high-profile campaign, which will do nothing but good for us both. It'll be a winner for us both in the publicity stakes. You'll see.'

Trish could feel her eyebrows crawling up towards her hair. What an unpleasant bloke he was making himself sound! But if his wife had been Lady-Macbething him to greater heights, perhaps it was the only way he could think of to get her off his back.

'Don't be childish,' she snapped. 'One, it'll only help if you do get her out, and from all I've heard that's shooting at the moon. Two, everyone knows she's one of your innumerable exes. And worse. The story going round is that you've been carrying a torch for her for years and you're still besotted. If you do make this idiotic television programme, I'll—'

'You'll what?' At last Chaze sounded as though he was as angry and contemptuous as his wife. 'Leave me?'

'I might.'

'Don't be ridiculous. It helps your business to be married to an MP. Don't think I don't know that's why you stay, or that you'd been planning to leave when you thought I wouldn't get the seat back at the last election.'

'So we're nothing but a mutual self-help society. Is this what you're telling me?'

'Can you think of another single reason for us to exist as a couple? I'm not sure I could if I racked my brains for a month.'

There was no audible answer from his wife.

Sally came back with cloths, newspapers and a bucket of Flash. While she mopped up the mess of gin, broken glass and blood, Trish shuddered at the hostility that seeped down through the floorboards. She was tempted to shudder even more violently ten minutes later when Chaze himself appeared in the doorway of the long room, impeccably dressed and apparently quite untroubled.

'Trish,' he called. He was holding out his hand as he came towards her, looking as though she was his dearest friend. 'How lovely to see you! How've you been getting on?'

Sally muttered something and slid out of the room with her bucket. He didn't look at her. All his attention was on Trish.

'Not too badly,' she said, getting to her feet to shake hands. There was the sound of feet in high heels running down the stairs, followed almost immediately by the slamming of the front door. A cabinet of antique glasses shook and the walls vibrated in the aftershock.

'My wife,' he said easily. 'She does so much that she's usually late, and always in a rush. Now, to Debbie's business.'

As he walked into the light from the double windows overlooking the street, Trish saw that the argument had left its mark after all. There was hurt in his eyes, which she hadn't seen there before, and his smile seemed more vulnerable. For the first time she saw the damaged child in him, and that had its usual effect on her.

When he touched her hand and urged her to sit down again, she felt that she knew him much better than their one meeting justified. She liked him. She wanted to comfort him. Warmth filled her, and confidence. She knew her eyes were shining with affection, and she could see his immediate response. She moved closer to him, the warmth increasing, until she realised what she was doing and cut it off at its source.

She knew that her response to other people's unhappiness was part of her own subconscious need. It had got her into a lot of trouble in the past, and in the end done little good for the people she had tried to help. Slowly she was learning how to use her instinct and channel it into her work so that she didn't wake expectations in friends and acquaintances that she was never going to meet.

Malcolm Chaze was a source of information, she told herself, and quite possibly PR for Anna's programme. He was not a hurt child. His unhappiness was no reason to like or trust him.

She controlled her smile and sat at the far end of one of the sofas. He joined her, sitting much closer to her than necessary. She described everything she'd been doing for Anna, censoring only her own anger at Anna's unreasonable demands. Her professional detachment was clear in her voice and she was glad to see him move back towards the far end of the sofa.

'It sounds excellent,' he said, when she finished her account. He was gazing at her as though he had adored her for years and she was the most brilliant, beautiful woman on the planet. Recognising the operation of his own instinctive need to make people respond to him, she felt better about herself. 'You've got much further than you suggested on the phone.'

'Not nearly far enough. And there's something that's really worrying me.'

'Oh? What's that?'

'I detested the doctor.'

'That seems quite fair,' Chaze said, laughing. 'He sounds utterly detestable.'

'I know. But don't you see? When Deb encountered him that last time, she was already raw. She needed help and he didn't give it to her. There was no one else.'

Chaze was still watching her admiringly.

'If it had been me in her place, his patronising dismissal could have tipped me over the edge, made me do something I'd never—'

'You mustn't think like that, Trish. Not ever.' The words came out very fast. They sounded sincere. But he was a politician: he would be able to turn on sincerity like a tap. 'I've told you already, Trish. I *know* Deb couldn't have committed murder.'

'Even though her father was driven to constant verbal cruelty by the pain he was in, and her mother was being broken a little more with every turn of the wheel as she struggled to care for him?'

Chaze shook his elegant head. His hair didn't move. He got up to pour himself a goblet of wine to match Trish's.

'If you can't accept that she did it deliberately, then how about an accident? Say she was so desperate to relieve his skin condition that she gave him some of the antihistamines that had helped her in the past, unaware of the danger of mixing them with his own?'

'No, Trish.' A hint of impatience scratched at his voice. He gulped some wine in a way that made her stare. 'Not even an accident makes sense to anyone who knows Debbie.' Chaze drank again, as though to give himself courage. Catching her eye, he deliberately put the glass on a silver coaster on the table beside the sofa arm. 'It's not sentimentality,' he said, wiping his hands on a large white cotton handkerchief. 'Or even the vanity of a man who thinks he has only to sleep with a woman to know everything about her.'

She acknowledged that one with a smile, thinking, So he does know something about himself.

'You see, I know Debbie. Even though it's years since we were close, I know how she thinks and what moves her; what makes her angry and how she behaves when she loses her temper.'

'How?' Trish asked urgently, remembering Adam's fear.

'She runs away, and cuts the person who made her angry right out of her life. She doesn't stay for a confrontation.'

'She could have changed. You said her marriage had done things to her.'

'True. But however much she's changed, I know she couldn't kill.'

'But . . .'

He stretched out a hand and laid it palm upwards on the striped cushion between them. The skin was faintly shiny, but did not look damp. Liars usually sweated buckets. But then he'd have had plenty of practice: politicians were always having to lie – or at least shade the truth, which came to much the same thing.

'Trish, I believe in Debbie. And I have to see her free. That would—' He broke off, apparently unable to say any more.

Trish noted the wobble in his voice and the slow moistening under his eyelids. It was years since he'd had anything to do with Debbie. What was going on in his mind? He coughed.

'It would make up for some of the things I've got wrong in the past,' he said more firmly, hiding behind the big wine-glass again. It was empty when he put it down.

'We all make mistakes when we're young,' he told her

seriously, even though she hadn't asked for any explanation. She wondered how much of his determination to help Deb came from his need to prove his wife wrong about his motives and character. 'We misjudge people, make the lives of the ones we care about more difficult than they need to be. I've done my share of that, God knows. More than my share. If I can help Debbie now, I can . . . I suppose it would allow me to believe in myself again.'

Trish had to exert considerable will not to look up at the thin ceiling.

'It must sound very selfish: to want to help Debbie because it would make me feel better.'

She could hear the subtext shrieking at her: reassure me; reassure me; tell me I'm an OK person. She resisted her urge to do exactly that and produced the most austere piece of comfort she could find: 'Selfishness wouldn't matter if it got her out.'

'Thank you,' he said quietly, still looking vulnerable.

It was time to wind this up and get home. 'So, as far as I can see,' she said briskly, 'our only real hope of getting her out is to come up with another source for the astemizole and a doctor who'll say that it was enough – in combination with the prescription drugs – to kill him without any suffocation at all.'

'That's a terrific idea,' said Chaze, losing most of his sadness and looking almost energetic again. 'But *are* there any doctors who'll do things like that?'

'Only if it's true,' Trish said drily. 'Anna's got researchers checking out all the medical details, but nothing's come through yet.'

She wondered why she hadn't counter-attacked when Anna complained of her lack of progress. Something must be softening parts of her brain, and Anna's.

'And then, of course, there will still be the terfenadine overdose to be explained.'

'You'll do it, Trish, if anyone can.' Chaze settled back into the sofa's softness, recrossing his long legs. His face was languorously peaceful again and he looked at her out of eyes that seemed full of confidence.

She couldn't help noticing that his suit was made of superfine wool and that the cut was so good it didn't ride up anywhere or crumple. She had a feeling she was meant to have noticed.

'But I'm not surprised you sounded depressed on the phone,' he said, comfortably re-established now in the master's role. 'It's a tall order. I'm so glad that Debbie's got you on her side. The one piece of luck the poor girl has ever had.'

'Thank you.'

'I hope when it's all over and we've got her home, you and I will be able to work together again.' He patted the sofa cushion beside him, as though inviting her to cosy up to him. 'I think we make an excellent team, you and I. You'd be an immense help to me in my war on drugs.'

'You know, I've been thinking that what really needs changing in this country isn't so much the obvious wickedness of drug-dealers as the everyday mistreatment of the elderly. You could do a lot worse than taking that on.'

'Trish, Trish! I've got more than enough on my plate. I've set my hand to the plough; I can't abandon it now.'

Were clichés and mixed metaphors worse than franglais? she asked herself. Aloud she said, 'But lots of people are campaigning for that. There's even a Drugs Tsar. But there isn't any Elderly Tsar that I've ever heard of. No one's in charge. Look what happened to Deb's parents: middle-class, articulate and reasonably well-off, but desperate. Think what must happen to people of that age who don't have resources like theirs.'

'The state can never take the place of the family,' he said, parroting his party's latest back-to-the-hearth campaign.

'You mean, Deb should have abandoned husband, children and job to be her parents' nurse-housekeeper?' Trish said. 'Is that what you're saying? Or do you think Cordelia should have given up her business and become a drain on the benefits budget?'

His face took on the withdrawn but faintly smiling expression every politician learned to use when put on the spot and made to face the real human cost of some piece of spin-doctor's rhetoric.

'The welfare state was built on the assumption that women's domestic labour was free and would be freely available for ever,' Trish said, recognising the soap box only as she got on to it. 'Sorry. This isn't a political meeting. But something needs to be done.'

'I'm sure you're right. And if you start a campaign, I'll lend you my support. But I'm already committed. Now, how are you getting on with Phil Redstone, by the way?'

'He's not being co-operative at the moment, which is understandable. Deb's appeal is mostly based on his incompetence. The idea of being pilloried in a television programme as well must be vile. I keep telling Anna that I won't be party to a witch hunt, but I know she'd like to see him publicly humiliated.'

'Professional solidarity,' Chaze said, with a bitterness that sat oddly with his smooth professional persona. 'The curse of all miscarriage-of-justice cases. Doctors, lawyers, car dealers, police officers . . . you're all the same.'

Trish withheld her defence and got to her feet, holding out her hand. Chaze took it, gripping lightly and pulling her towards him so that he could kiss her cheek. His own was smooth as cream.

'I'm just worried about Debbie,' he murmured, his lips moving against her skin. 'It makes me bad-tempered. Will you forgive me? As I said, you're doing a fantastic job and we couldn't do without you.'

Smooth bugger, Trish thought uncharitably, as she left the house.

# Chapter 12

Letting her head turn sideways on the pillow, Trish saw that George was still asleep, flat on his back, mouth a little open. He looked comfortable. Safe. He had arrived at the flat a couple of hours after she'd left Malcolm Chaze last night, saying that the legal dinner had been excruciatingly dull and could he stay?

They had made love, avoiding the subject of each other's broodiness, and Trish had slept better than she had for weeks. She stretched now under the sheets, feeling sleek and serene as her long legs slid luxuriously under the light summer duvet. The flakes of the digital clock flicked over for half past six and the radio burst into sound.

George's faintly blue eyelids twitched but did not open. His hand reached for her and brushed her thigh. She moved her leg a little closer to him.

'MP Malcolm Chaze was found shot in the front hall of his house in Pimlico at half past eleven last night,' said the newsreader.

Trish shot up, the thin coverings falling away from her body. George coughed and muttered a protest, dragging the duvet back. His eyes opened and began to focus.

'Laura Chaze, the MP's wife, found him when she returned from the theatre. He was lying, shot in the head, just inside the front door. The couple had no children.'

Trish felt George's arm round her shoulders, pulling her

back against the pillows. She remembered Chaze's farewell gesture last night and gripped the edge of the duvet between both hands.

George buried his face in her neck. She felt his lips moving and heard his voice buzzing against her skin.

'What? I can't hear.'

'I was just weak-minded enough to be thanking God that you'd left his house in time,' George said, moving back and blinking. He reached for his glasses, then his dressing gown. 'I need coffee. Shall I make you some?'

Trish glanced at the clock, no longer hearing the news-reader's voice. 'Why not? There's just time. But then I'll have to run.'

Alone, hearing the sound of George's bare feet slapping against the wrought-iron treads of the spiral staircase, Trish thought about Malcolm Chaze and how he'd died – and why.

'Did you like him so much?' George asked, when he brought up her big, white cup almost overflowing with strong coffee.

'What?' She stared up at him. 'What d'you mean? I hardly knew him.'

'You look horrified,' he said. 'Your eyes are huge, and I bet your pulse is racing. I've never seen you so stary, except the time they rang to tell you about Paddy's heart-attack.'

She shook her head, taking the cup from him. When she'd drunk some coffee, she licked her upper lip to get the foamed milk off it. 'I quite liked Chaze, I suppose, even though I still wasn't sure I could trust him, but it's not that.'

In spite of the heat and the coffee, she was shivering and felt very sick. Being pregnant must be like this. She wasn't sure why she'd ever thought she might like to bring a child into such a world.

'A lot of it's probably shock,' George said, perching on her side of the bed. He didn't try to touch her, which was lucky. She felt her face clench.

'I'm not trying to belittle your feelings, Trish,' he said, reading her without difficulty, 'but it is a shock – and to hear it like that, as you burst out of sleep. Not surprising it's affected you.'

She put down the cup and leaned against him, taking some solace from his warm solidity. 'I think,' she said slowly, 'it's the thought that this might have something to do with his campaign to free Deb Gibbert.'

George pushed her away from him so that he could look at her face. 'Are you telling me you think someone out there could be so afraid of what Malcolm Chaze might turn up about the killing of an old man in Norfolk that he had Chaze shot?'

'Put like that it sounds a bit melodramatic,' Trish said, reaching for her coffee cup. She was proud of the steadiness of her hand.

'Come on, Trish. Chaze was a politician. He must have had a million enemies.'

'Maybe. But it is a bit pat, isn't it? His death coming just twenty-four hours after he first publicly announced that he was going to prove her innocent. Didn't he say something about "If it's the last thing I do"?'

'I need some of your coffee,' George said, grabbing the cup. 'Trish, will—'

'I will be careful,' she said, taking the cup back.

'And will you talk to the police?'

She appreciated his use of a question, knowing how much he wanted to issue instructions. 'Shit! Look at the time, George! Are you bathing this morning?'

'If that won't get in your way.'

'Great. I can have the shower then. Budge up out of the way.'

Their morning routine was so slick that they moved off in their separate directions, meeting at intervals as they fetched ironed shirts from the hangers in Trish's long wardrobe and more coffee from the kitchen, but never getting in each other's way. George's shaving took about as long as Trish's makeup, so they met again at the front door, impeccably tidy, briefcases in hand, ready to face their clients.

Dave was hovering in the doorway of the clerks' room when Trish ran into chambers. He wasn't holding a stopwatch, but he might have been. She felt like reminding him that she employed him and not vice versa.

'What, Dave?' she said, not stopping but merely slowing down as she passed him.

'I need to talk to you about the Greer case. We—'

'Not now, Dave. I'm in court this morning.'

'I know,' he called bitterly down the passage after her. She closed her ears to the words and their implication and shut the door of her room so that she could gather herself and her papers together in peace.

Trish spent a bruising day in front of a judge who had always been hostile to her and today kept interrupting as she examined her witnesses. Trying to think of her fury as a spoiled lapdog that had to be kept quiet, she smiled at the bench, answered all the irrelevant unnecessary questions, waited patiently while the judge made notes of what she said, then returned to her proper job.

The lapdog had a good run once she was back in the robing room, but even there she tried to keep it on the lead. If she were ever to take up Heather Bonwell's suggestion of applying for silk, she'd need judges and senior members of the Bar on her side. Slagging off one of them where she could be overheard would be idiotic.

Her opponent rolled up his gown and stuffed it in his red-brocade bag.

'What about a drink in El Vino?' he said, slinging the bag over his shoulder with a jauntiness that seemed unlike him. But he didn't win nearly as often as she. Trish explained that she had to get back to chambers to collect an urgent message and hoped he wasn't going to tell the assembled barristers in the wine bar that she was a bad loser.

It wasn't long before she was back at her desk, phoning the Pimlico police. When she asked for the number of the incident room dealing with the Chaze murder, she was put through to a constable, who said he was collecting all information offered by the public. Trish said politely that she wanted to talk to someone actually involved in the investigation.

The young-sounding officer told her patiently that there were three separate incident rooms and that his job was to sift the information that came in and funnel it through to the right people.

'Who are the officers in charge?' she asked, hoping that she would know at least one. She'd met quite a few senior members of the Met and it wouldn't be too much of a coincidence if one of these was known to her.

The constable was determined not to give her any names, but she was persistent and experienced. Eventually he surrendered and told her who they were. Two were super-intendents, whose names meant nothing to her, but one was a DCI she knew. He was in command of the smallest of the three incident rooms, and his name was William Femur.

Trish almost cheered when she heard that. He was the man who'd put her attacker behind bars for life. She owed him rather than the other way round, but she had enough faith in him to believe he would listen to her. The constable didn't agree but reluctantly took her name and asked her to hold on.

'Trish Maguire? Is it really you?' asked Femur's familiar gravelly voice, two minutes later.

'You remember me, then?'

'How could I forget?' There was a sharp edge as well as a smile in his voice, which pretty much summed up their relationship.

'Good. I want to come and talk to you about Malcolm Chaze.'

'Don't tell me, he was a client of yours and you've some secret information no one else could possibly know, which will prove he's been—'

'No,' Trish said quickly, picking up Femur's real annoyance, in spite of the coating of humour. 'Nothing like that. But I saw him last night. Well, yesterday evening.'

'So I shouldn't have been frivolous. OK. I can accept that. I'll get the relevant incident room to send someone round to chambers to take your statement.'

'Couldn't I maybe drop in on my way home and talk to *you*? Presumably you're working fairly near his house.'

There was a sigh. Then came Femur's voice, harsh now without the amusement. 'Is this really necessary?'

'If I didn't think so, I wouldn't have bothered to ring you. We're both busy.'

'All right.' He gave her the address. 'I should be able to give you a few minutes in about half an hour's time, but I can't take long.'

'I'll be there.'

Femur was much as Trish remembered him: an ordinary-looking bloke in his fifties, untidy in his plain dark-grey suit, with a chewed-up tie knotted askew under his collar. Only when he saw her and his hard-grey eyes turned diamond-shaped as his cheeks pressed upwards in a smile of recognition did he show any individuality.

'Trish Maguire. You haven't changed.'

'Good. I won't take much of your time,' she said, very fast, 'but you need to know—'

'It's OK, provided you're not going to fly any stupid kites. I could do with a short break. Cup of tea?'

'No, thank you. Look, I went to see Chaze yesterday because we've been working together on the background to a campaigning TV programme of Anna Grayling's about Deborah Gibbert. D'you remember the case?'

The diamond-shaped eyes were shut now. 'Don't. This is a standard-issue contract-killing, almost certainly drug-related. Don't try to complicate it for me.'

'I'm not here to cause trouble,' she said at once. 'Last time you were angry because I withheld information. Now I want to give you all I've got, but you don't want it. Surely you must need to know what had been preoccupying Chaze in the weeks before his death, and who he might have pissed off. Mayn't I tell you about it?'

'If you must.' Weariness showing in every gesture, Femur pulled forward a thick pad of lined paper and pulled off the top of a felt-tip pen. 'Fire away.'

Trish described the way Anna had embroiled her in the case, the little she had found out, and everything she could remember that Chaze had said about Deb and his campaign for justice. Femur's expression lightened a little as she talked. 'You do make a good witness, I'll give you that,' he said, when she stopped. 'But even if your Deborah Gibbert is innocent you can't expect me to believe that the real killer of her father would put out a contract like this one.'

'Put like that, it does sound a little unlikely.' She thought of George and how well the two men would get on. 'Are you *sure* it was a contract killing?'

'There's no reason why you shouldn't know. We gave a press conference this morning and it'll be all over the news tonight. The neighbours saw a motorbike messenger call at Chaze's house last night at around nine thirty. We have several independent sightings as well as CCTV footage. No one paid any attention. All MPs have deliveries at all times of the day and night. Chaze clearly let the man in and was then shot, in the privacy of the hall, with a silenced gun. The messenger shut the door behind him, retreated to his bike, clipboard in hand – again we have several witnesses – and rode off.'

'Did anyone get the number?'

Femur frowned. 'Only the CCTV. But the plates were false. He was wearing a helmet and leathers. There's nothing to pick him out from a thousand others of his type.'

'So you haven't a hope of catching him.' To Trish's surprise, the words came out quite steadily.

'Probably not.' Femur pushed his hands over his creased face. 'Christ knows why I'm telling you all this. Except that there's nothing secret about it.'

'I'm hardly likely to take advantage of it anyway,' Trish said, fighting to keep the professional mask in place. It was stupid to be afraid, she told herself. She'd been unlucky enough to be assaulted once. That didn't mean it would ever happen again. 'But there is one other thing I came to tell you. Chaze and his wife were having the most terrific row when I arrived at the house last night.'

Femur's eyelids sank again. His mouth looked different, tight. Trish wished she could see his eyes. She didn't know whether he was bored, irritated or concerned. He picked up his felt-tip and nodded. At dictation speed, Trish repeated everything she could remember of Mrs Chaze's diatribe and the fury she'd been showing at the thought of her husband's campaign to free Deb Gibbert.

'So, this time you're suggesting Laura Chaze was so angry with her husband that on her way to a performance by

Fascinating Aida she stopped to phone a handy contract killer to get rid of the husband who'd been bugging her. Have I got that right?'

'Doesn't it help you build up a picture of his last hours?' said Trish, despising herself for her need to hear again that the gunman roaring around London disguised as a motorbike messenger couldn't be interested in anything she might be doing.

'Oh, sure,' Femur was saying.

Trish stopped thinking about the past and the possibly dangerous future and concentrated on the moment.

'But that's not what I need right now. If you'd heard the contract being put out, or even threats to Chaze's life, I'd be interested. But this kind of speculation is wasting my time.'

Trish hadn't taken up more than fifteen minutes, and she'd done no more than any good citizen should. 'Is Constable Lyalt still on your team?'

'Sergeant Lyalt now. Yes, she is. But I don't want you bothering her either. She's busy.'

'Fine.'

'But I do want you to give your statement to the constable, who's waiting outside. His name's Owler.'

'Fine,' Trish said again, surprised by Femur's hostility.

He looked up from his notes. There was a bleak smile around his mouth. 'And I'm grateful you took the trouble to come in.'

'Good.' Trish left him to whatever was bugging him.

# Chapter 13

Femur was having another bad night. He couldn't stop thinking about Trish Maguire's thin face and brilliant eyes, or her link with Malcolm Chaze. The coincidence made him edgy. And he didn't know how to take it. He didn't really believe she was part of a set-up to tempt him to make a public fool of himself, but could it really be coincidence that had brought her of all people back into his working life?

He had exposed a corrupt officer last year, and even though everyone wanted the bad apples chucked out of the barrel, no one loved the chucker. It had been during that particular case when he'd met Trish Maguire for the first time. Could it just be coincidence?

That time she had had access to information that she'd withheld for so long that a man who should have lived had died. He still hadn't forgiven her for that. But she had paid for it in the assault she'd suffered.

Thinking about that, Femur realised it was enough to explain her anxiety over her tenuous link to Malcolm Chaze. Femur had seen enough beaten women to know what the experience of being attacked in their own home did to them. It took some of them years to get over it, and a lot looked over their shoulders for the rest of their lives. Maguire's sufferings at the hands of the psychopathic thug Femur had eventually managed to get put away for life must still be affecting her judgement.

He had no such excuse, and he had to decide what to do with the information she'd brought him. He didn't have an unlimited budget and he couldn't go chasing wild geese. It was tempting to file and forget the Deborah Gibbert connection. But officers who'd done that sort of thing in the past had come a cropper when the loony suggestion they'd dismissed out of hand turned out to be true. He couldn't afford that sort of mistake at this stage in his career.

Shit, he hadn't worried like this since his early years in CID. He must be losing it. Or maybe it was the drink. There'd been too much of that recently. He hadn't been counting the whiskies last night, but his head and his gut, as well as his mouth, told him there'd been too many. Maybe that was all these worries were, fallout from the drink. His liver had probably woken him as it tried to mash up the alcohol and now it was sending mad thoughts through his brain. When the hangover had gone in the morning, he'd be able to think sensibly again and decide what to do about Maguire.

He tried to wrestle his bedclothes into shapes that didn't dig into him the moment he tried to relax. One thing he didn't have to worry about, thank God, was waking Sue with his restlessness. She'd gone to stay with some friend in Spain a week ago.

He wasn't sure she was coming back, and he wasn't altogether sure he minded as much as he ought. Life at home might be messier without her, but it was a damn sight easier. More peaceful. It did piss him off, though, that she'd lied about the friend. Yes, it was the lies, not her absence, he minded.

Stephanie Watson, Sue had called the friend. Femur wasn't sure why he'd bothered to check up, but a quick call to the airline had told him there were no Stephanies on Sue's flight at all, although there was a Stephen Watson. A few covert enquiries among the neighbours and Sue's sister produced the further information that the art teacher at the adult education classes Sue had been taking was called Stephen.

The two of them had run out of affection and things to talk about long ago, so what did it matter? Thank God for work. He lay on his back and stared up at the dark ceiling.

But it was work that had brought sodding Trish Maguire back into his life, threatening to disturb the calm, orderly investigation he'd planned. He and his team had to probe Chaze's personal life for any clues to the motive for his death and the identity of his killer, and the person who'd taken out the contract.

Femur had decided that the widow would be interviewed first, then Chaze's immediate staff and close friends, including any current girlfriends they might turn up and any cuckolded husbands. The team would then go on to more distant relations and less intimate friends. If nothing came out of those interviews they'd go back and back through all his contacts, all his lovers, and all the ramifications of an apparently colourful past. They'd spread their inquiries in ever-widening ripples from the centre of the victim's life until they'd found their answers or exhausted every possible lead.

It was the latter possibility that he expected. Most murders in Britain might be domestic, but not the ones where the victim was shot in the head by a man on a motorbike. That sounded like a contract, and a contract nearly always meant drugs, or maybe terrorism.

Unfortunately Femur and his team would not be looking into either. While the team in Incident Room I were tackling the physical evidence found at the scene and the house-to-house inquiries, Incident Room II would be digging into the victim's political background. Lucky buggers.

Chaze had been in the House of Commons for years and, even though he'd never been a minister, he'd served on various 'sensitive' select committees. Everything he'd said then, everything he'd heard, and every secret document he'd seen would have to be checked for possible links to the killing. He'd had some input in the Balkans, apparently, some with the new MI5 organised-crime department, and some with counter-terrorism. Any of them could have led to his death.

But that investigation was the plum assignment and Femur didn't get those any more. He couldn't blame Maguire for that. She was OK, really. It wasn't her fault he'd been sidelined, even if she had been involved in the case that had caused all the problems.

He looked at the clock. It was already five. There didn't seem any point lying in bed any more. In his present state of mind, tossing and turning wasn't going to do him much good. Specially not tossing, he told himself, with an attempt at gallows humour. So he got up and cooked himself some eggy bread and a large mug of tea.

It was so hot, even though it was still early, that he took his breakfast out into the garden and stared glumly at the unmown grass and the roses that needed dead-heading. If Sue were here, she'd have had him out with the mower and the secateurs long ago.

Uncomfortable, irritable, more depressed than he should've been, he locked up the house and headed back to the incident room determined to talk to the officers who'd investigated Deborah Gibbert's case. With luck they'd be able to knock this wild goose on the head, then he'd be free to grill Chaze's widow, who, according to the officers who'd seen her yesterday, wasn't grieving half as much as she should. Bloody women.

'If you ask me,' DCI Ben Hatchett from Norfolk said, almost spitting down the phone a couple of hours later, 'this TV programme about the Gibbert case is so much horse-shit. We've already heard about it and we're not worried. Not at all.'

Femur sat more comfortably in his chair.

'Your MP's death can't have anything to do with it.'

'Right. Though, as I see it,' Femur said, determined to banish the ghost of Trish Maguire's suspicion completely, 'you didn't have any incontrovertible evidence against Gibbert, did you? Means? Maybe. Opportunity? Certainly. But no evidence.'

'Except the bag she'd used – in other words, a lot more than other forces have had in cases they've won. For Christ's sake, Femur! There were Gibbert's prints on the outside and no one else's, her father's saliva inside. It's as near incontrovertible as you're likely to get in this kind of killing.'

'But what about this story of the daughter picking up his teeth with the bag?'

'Bollocks to that. She's been watching too many cop shows on telly.'

'Although, if she'd been thinking like that, wouldn't she have got rid of the bag altogether? It wouldn't have been that difficult in the middle of the country. There were probably goats or pigs in the farm next door. They eat anything, don't they?'

'Whose side are you on, Femur?' asked the Norfolk officer indignantly.

'Yours,' Femur answered at once. 'Ours, I mean. But I have to get it clear. You're sure, are you, that he couldn't have done it himself?'

'And taken the bag off once he was dead, you mean?' Sarcasm dripped from his voice.

'Right. Of course. Then why didn't she leave it there?'

'Because, according to all reports, she's not over-bright. You should have heard her sister on the subject! I'll send you copies of the SOCO reports and the pathologist's if that'll stop this nonsense,' Hatchett offered.

'That would be good. Thanks.'

Femur put down the phone, rubbing his chin. Odd how satisfying that could be, feeling the odd bristle where his shaving hadn't been up to scratch against the softness of the inside of his hand. Up and down; up and down; soft then rasping. Satisfying.

'You OK, Guv?'

He stopped feeling his bristles and focused on Caroline Lyalt's bright face. His scowl softened. 'At least I wasn't looking for hairs on the palms of my hands,' he said, making her blink. 'You look bright and breezy this morning.'

'I am. Even though I'm not hopeful that we'll crack this one.'

'Me neither.'

'But I have been reading Trish Maguire's statement. Guv, you don't think . . .'

He shook his head. 'No. But I think we will have to follow it up; both the Gibbert connection and the row Maguire overheard Chaze having with his wife. I could have done without her intervention, you know, Cally.'

'There's a secretary, Sally Hatfield,' she said casually. 'DC Pepper saw her yesterday. I've been reading the statement she gave him, and she lists Maguire as the last visitor she admitted to the house before she went home on the night Chaze died. We'd have had to talk to Trish Maguire anyway, Guv.'

His head was still thumping and, despite the breakfast, and the toothpaste, his mouth felt like shit. He knew Caroline was right about Maguire, but he wasn't going to say so.

'Was Chaze bonking the secretary? If you believe the tabloids, all MPs are at it all the time.'

Caroline grinned. 'Not this one. At least not yet. I doubt if it would have taken long, if he was up for it: she definitely was. But, as far as I can tell, things hadn't gone much further than silent adoration.' She hesitated, seemed to be assessing how much he could take, then added, 'Unlike with Deborah

Gibbert in the days when they were both working at London University.'

Femur's hands were cradling his aching head before he'd realised he'd moved. 'Don't do this to me, Cally. I thought the only connection between them was that he'd taken up her case – presumably to grab publicity for himself before the next election.'

'No. There's more. They're old friends. Didn't you get to that bit in Maguire's statement?'

'I told her to give it to Steve Owler. I was going to read it when there was time this morning. I thought I'd got all the salient bits in my head.'

'According to Maguire, it was Chaze's old affair with Gibbert that made him sure she's innocent. That's why he got involved in the first place.' Now there was compassion in her face; compassion of a kind he'd only ever seen directed at victims and their families. He must sort himself out. He couldn't go round being pitied, even by a woman as sensible as Sergeant Caroline Lyalt.

'Could you ever kill one of your parents?' he asked abruptly.

'Like Deborah Gibbert? No, Guv.'

'Not even if they were in agony the doctor couldn't do anything about?'

'No. I'm too much of a wimp probably.'

'And too law-abiding,' he said, with a faint smile.

'I'm not sure about that. I hope so.'

'So do I.'

'But, Guv, begging to be put out of his misery can't have applied to Gibbert's father.'

So, he thought, you've been reading it up, have you? Then there must have been something in Trish Maguire's statement that made you suspicious, too. Bugger it.

'Why not?'

'Because he'd have asked the other sister. Everyone's clear that he didn't like Deborah. You'd really have to trust and love someone you asked to bump you off.'

'You could be right,' Femur said. 'Now, what have you got for me about the private life of Malcolm Chaze, MP? Which, after all, is our only investigation. He must have pissed off someone.'

'Loads of people,' Caroline said, giving him a typed list of all the most likely names her officers had turned up so far.

Femur read it, muttering as he thought of all the big drug-importers he should've been allowed to check out. At the end, he looked up, feeling marginally more intelligent and in control. 'Get regular briefing reports from the other two incident rooms, will you? Check them for any names that match ours. That way none of us will waste manpower on crossed wires or dead ends, and we won't do a Yorkshire Ripper and miss the obvious.'

'It's under control, Guv.' Caroline checked the notes in her hand. 'First reports from ballistics suggest there's nothing special about the bullet, which is a pain. Hairs and fibres haven't produced anything yet, but it's early days and they've got lots to work on. IR One's pursuing the bike's origins, but haven't come up with anything yet. It's a bog-standard model, sold in the thousands, plenty on the second-hand market, plenty nicked every week.'

'That's helpful.'

'The house-to-house hasn't produced anything either, and they're collecting the CCTV footage in wider and wider circles as they follow the bike through London. So far they've lost it somewhere over Vauxhall Bridge. Fewer cameras on that side of the river, you see.'

'So, nothing hard yet?'

'Nothing. Don't fret, Guv, the other teams haven't got any further than us.'

Her eyes were full of pity again. He'd have to break her of the habit soon or he might give in to it. 'So you've got it all under control, have you? I might as well sit on my arse for the whole investigation, Sergeant, while you run it,' he said, ashamed of the sarcasm even as it emerged from his mouth, but not quite ashamed enough to put a cork in it.

'You know, Guv, this could be one of those impossible ones,' she said easily, more than tough enough to take his bad temper. 'Frankly I don't see how anyone's going to come up with any realistic suspects without a tip-off or a lucky break.'

'You could be right. The one almost untraceable kind of murder. Christ! I wish I could get that woman out of my head.'

'Trish Maguire?'

'Right. I think I'll have to see Gibbert. You're right, we can't ignore a lead like this, even if it does look like a dead end. Set it up with the prison, will you, Cally? And you'd better come with me. You usually get more out of miserable women than I do.'

She nodded and went off to sort it without another word. Thank God for women like her. He didn't know what he'd do if she left or transferred to another force. Retire probably. It was time, clearly, but life without the Job would be pretty damn bleak. Freelance security advising? No thanks. Still, if Sue really had buggered off for good, he'd have to sort out his life. Moving on out of the Job might just get rolled up into that.

When Chaze's killer's been charged, then you can think of going on to something else. But not yet. Stick with it till there's a result.

Deb Gibbert was sitting in a heap, slumped against the edge of the sticky interview table. She'd had enough. First the news that there was something more wrong with Mandy, even though she was well out of the coma now. Then, on top of that, Malcolm's death.

It was beginning to look as though there was some awful fate in store for everyone Deb had ever loved. She couldn't bear to imagine what might be waiting for Kate and the other children. If she thought about it too much she'd go mad. There wasn't anything she could do to protect them.

She'd wept for Malcolm, but she was dry-eyed now, and blank-eyed, too. Everything she'd learned of the police since she'd been arrested had taught her not to cry in front of them. She wasn't even going to try to help this time. She'd follow the lead of all the other fat, miserable, stupid women in this hellish place and offer no more than hopeless apathy.

Once she'd tried to help the police, answering all their questions as fully as possible, offering suggestions, making gallons of tea. All that had got her was arrest, charge, and a life sentence.

She didn't look at either of the officers, instead concentrating on picking at a break in the plastic laminate of the table in a way that would have driven her to fury if anyone had done it to her.

'We're very sorry about the death of your friend Malcolm Chaze,' said the male officer. Deb didn't look up. She couldn't remember his name and didn't care anyway. 'We'd like you to tell us everything you know about him and his life.'

'Me?' She was so surprised – and so angry – that she had to look up. The policeman's face was tired but friendly. He even looked trustworthy, but it had to be a trick. She wondered what they really wanted. It couldn't be her memories of Malcolm. Everyone must know she'd had nothing to do with him for years, except for that one visit two months ago, when he'd come to talk to her about Anna Grayling and the possibility of a campaign to get her out.

'Even a policeman should have the wit to realise I couldn't

shoot him from in here.'

'We're not here because we think you could have had anything to do with it, Mrs Gibbert, obviously,' said the woman officer, talking as though Deb might be an intelligent being, worthy of consideration. 'But we're talking to everyone who's seen him in the last six months. One of them is you. He is on record as having visited you here eight weeks ago.'

'Yes, he did.'

Deb had dreaded the visit. It would be the first time they'd met since the awful day when she'd decided she couldn't go on with him. She'd been so angry then that for nearly the first time in her life she'd screamed and yelled. Malcolm had looked stunned. If he'd been within reach, she might even have hit him, but he'd kept sensibly out of the way. When she flung herself out of his room, he'd shouted after her, something about talking it through, but she'd ignored him and gone.

In the prison, he'd sat with all the other visitors, looking, in his wonderful suit, so out of place and so disdainful that she'd felt more humiliated than she'd been since the day they convicted her. She'd become even more aware of her fatness than usual. Her clothes seemed especially horrible, and smelly, and her hair stringy and very grey. But as they'd talked and he'd smiled the old, secret smile, she'd realised they could be friends again.

By the time he had to go, they'd got back to something important she'd thought she'd thrown away a long time ago.

'What did he talk about when he came here?' asked the woman sergeant.

'The past mostly.'

She smiled like a friend and Deb felt herself responding. She quickly pulled the apathy back over herself like a blanket. Until she knew what they were really after, she wasn't going to fall for friendliness, any more than she had fallen for threats in the old days. Her few remaining stomach muscles sagged under their muffling flesh.

'There can't be many people who've known him as long as you. Tell us what he was like – as a man, not a Member of Parliament.'

Deb shrugged, still keeping up her show of resistance. But it was hard. She was digging the nails of one hand so sharply into the palm of the other that she expected to see blood. But there was only sweat.

'Apart from that visit it's years since I had anything to do with him, let alone cared . . .'

'Men – people – don't change much in eighteen years in my experience,' said the woman. 'How would you describe Malcolm when you were going out with him?'

Deb had opened her mouth to answer before she thought. She realised she wasn't going to be very good at this apathy business. A lifetime of trying not to be angry, to be kind, to be liked, to do what was expected of her, was hard to shed, even now that she'd had to admit how often she'd failed.

'On the surface he was brilliant, charismatic,' she started, in her own voice. Sergeant Lyalt's face lit up straight away. Deb was smiling back before she could stop herself, and adding, 'But behind the mask, I realised he was incredibly insecure. I think that's why I . . . liked him so much, being a bit that way myself.'

'You and me both,' said the sergeant. 'But it was clever of you to spot it in Chaze. No one else we've talked to so far saw it. What made you guess?'

Deb's back was straightening, and her fingers uncurling. She felt better already. 'I don't know that there was anything specific, but I cared about him, so I wanted to protect him. I suppose it was that. Of course, he did hate being laughed at or teased.'

'Who laughed at him?'

'Oh, you know, other tutors at the university, who thought his extra-curricular seminars on the evils of drugs were naïve and silly. And . . . Well, I suppose some of my friends, who were a bit snobbish.' Deb considered her past with detached interest, thinking how odd it was after three years in prison and fifteen years of hard labour before that in the horrid little house outside Birmingham to remember the life she'd once lived.

She'd never really been part of the smart East Anglian set, who spent the week in London and then went back to huge cold houses for the weekend, but she knew some of them and they'd invited her to their bigger parties. It had been a blissful relief to be able to take someone like Malcolm with her, both as protection and as an excuse to leave early.

'He minded snobs, did he?'

'Yes,' Deb said. 'He despised them and their pre-occupations, but he wanted to be liked, even, I think, to be one of them. As you probably know, Malcolm didn't come from a very well-off family. Well, I didn't either. I mean, we never had any money, but we sort of knew people. That sort of people. Malcolm didn't, and he wanted to.'

Deb remembered the battles she'd fought to try to make him go home with her for weekends with her parents. Only when she'd understood why he couldn't bear the idea had she given up hope of seeing her bloody father realise that a good-looking, clever man like Malcolm Chaze could find Despised Deb attractive.

'He used to make mistakes . . . what to wear when, how to pronounce things. I mean, there he was, incredibly clever and teaching philosophy and absolutely looked up to by all his students. But sometimes there were things – trivial social things – I knew better than he did.'

'Like what?'

'Oh, you know, silly social rules. Names like Featherstonehaugh and Marjoribanks and things like that.' Deb closed her eyes for a second. She could still remember her own mortification and Malcolm's when she'd taken him to Siggy and Pog Featherstonehaugh's party and he'd mispronounced their name when he thanked them for inviting him. He'd only seen it on the invitation and she'd only ever referred to them as Siggy and Pog, so why should he have known? They'd been sweet about it, of course, but some of the other guests had giggled.

'But he must have been, what . . .? Thirty-five or so?'

'Yes, but he'd worked so hard all his life that he hadn't mixed much outside the trendy lefty academic world. He didn't like the trendy lefties much, and he wanted to get into Parliament and kind of join in a more conventional kind of world, and so . . .'

Was that what he saw in me? she asked herself suddenly, much too late. Was it my few connections to a kind of motheaten sub-aristocracy that made him think I was worth having? That could explain a lot.

'You said the other tutors mocked his anti-drugs work. He must have felt very strongly about it if he hated being laughed at as much as you say,' said the sergeant.

'He did. At the time I used to think he must be incredibly brave to go on with it. I admired that.'

'Right,' said the male officer, leaning forward. 'Do you think he could have been doing something similar before he was killed? You know, standing up to someone with a strong enough vested interest to have him shot?'

Deb stared at him. He seemed to be serious. But why was he asking her? How could she possibly know? She said as much.

'I wondered if he'd talked to you about his work. Said something maybe about a secret campaign, or an enemy he was stalking. Anything like that. Anything he was trying to do that might have frightened someone.'

'Only the person who really killed my father,' she said drily. Then, catching the officer's expression, she felt little bubbles of hope fizzing through her blood. 'Is that why you're here? Has someone finally realised that I didn't do it?'

Femur looked serious. 'It has been suggested as a possible motive for the murder, yes.'

Deb felt her whole body lightening, as though the bubbles might make her levitate right off her chair. 'Who by?'

'You must've heard about this film that's being made,' Sergeant Lyalt began, as the bubbles burst and Deb slumped back against the edge of the table.

'I thought you meant someone official was taking an interest.' Tears – stupid and humiliating – welled up in her eyes. She bit her lip to try to stop them. It didn't work. They spilled over on to her face and dripped down towards her chin. She wiped them off with both hands, but she couldn't stop them. More and more chased themselves down her cheeks. She pulled up her T-shirt to wipe her face, then let it drop as she felt a draught on her gut.

She was making a noise now, too, and she couldn't do anything about that either. A thin, strangulated, hoarse shriek came out of her mouth, broken by syncopated gasps.

The man turned away, but Sergeant Lyalt pulled a packet of Kleenex out of her bag and opened it for her. Deb grabbed a handful and tried to blot the tears, but the paper was soon soaked. Her nose was running with disgusting thin snot. It was all over her mouth and chin. Still she couldn't stop, howling for Malcolm and Mandy and herself and Kate and everyone. Her head hit the table as she gave in to it. She felt as though she was sicking up all her grief. And anger. A gentle hand stroked her back, but that only made it worse.

Only when they started to ask questions about Mandy did she begin to recover. Talking about Mandy and the drugs and who could've brought them into the prison helped. Half an hour later, Deb was almost in control of herself again.

It was only when she was talking about Mandy's last visitor, Spike Hamper, that she realised how they'd tricked her, suckered her in by making her believe they might help her. God, she'd been a fool. She told them she was going back to her cell and there wasn't anything they could do about it. That was her only satisfaction, that and the look on their smug faces.

'Phew.' Femur looked up at the sky. 'Thank God we're out of there. You did well, Cally. I couldn't have coped with all that without you. And I'd have run as soon as she cracked up and we'd never have got the name of the pusher-pimp. I suppose you'd better get on to IR Two and pass it on,' Femur said, sounding too tired to give any more real orders.

'Must I hand it over? It's a much better line of inquiry than following up all the players in an obscure domestic murder. Even if the wrong woman *is* inside for that.'

'Cally, don't do it to me.'

'Guv?'

'Don't tell me you think Gibbert really is innocent.'

'How could I not?' she said, with surprisingly archaic formality. She must have been listening to her Jess again. 'You do.'

'You know me too well,' he said, sighing. 'Still, that's not our problem. That belongs to Norfolk and maybe the Criminal Cases Review Commission. Chaze and whoever put the contract out on him are the only people we've got to worry about.'

'Maybe, Guv. But you know what struck me most in there, apart from Gibbert's almost certain innocence?'

'No. What?'

'That there had to be something personal in Chaze's anti-drugs campaign, and that would make it our business.'

'Why personal?' He wasn't that interested, and Caroline's energy made him feel tired, but he sympathised with her resentment at the thought of handing over good information to another incident room.

'No one would make himself ridiculous, like Gibbert said Chaze did, unless he had a real urgent, personal reason to care so much about drugs.'

Femur began to breathe more easily. That was the thing – one of the things – about Caroline Lyalt that made her such a rarity. She knew when to stop and when to push, and he'd trust her judgement anywhere.

'It's possible.'

'If Chaze had had a lover, or a sister maybe, even a friend who'd been damaged by drugs, that could have set him off. Don't you think, Guv?' She seemed to be driving him to some kind of enthusiastic response.

'Could be,' he said, doing his best for her.

'So, what if the dealer's become respectable now, and doesn't want his past revealed? Say he'd just put two and two together and realised that the MP who's always banging on about drugs is a bloke who could blow his cover.'

'So he had him shot? Come on, Cally. Be reasonable.'

'Someone had him shot, Guv. You've said all along that it must've been drug money that paid for the hit.'

'Right. It's a thought,' Femur said, managing to grin at her. He sympathised with her need to be involved in the discovery of the killer. 'How's Jess? You haven't mentioned her for weeks.'

Caroline's face softened. All the muscles around her mouth flowed into a smile that blazed through his own greyness to the part of him that was still capable of pleasure. Or at least optimism. 'She's great, thanks, Guv. Working. Successful. Happy.'

'And you?' he asked, with a gentleness only she could wake in him these days. And then only sometimes.

'I'm happy, too.'

He leaned towards her, then stopped as he realised he'd been about to kiss her in gratitude that someone in this whole miserable bloody world should have got so much that she deserved. Since he couldn't do that, he patted her shoulder instead.

'It's a telly she's doing,' Caroline said, looking as though she knew pretty well what was in his mind, 'so she's around in the evenings. Why not come back and have some food with us tonight? She's cooking. And she's a damn good cook, too. You need a break, Guv. And the flat's not that far from the incident room. Anyone wants either of us, they can phone. How about it?'

'Won't I put you out?' he asked, wondering how much she knew or guessed about Sue bunking off.

'Never. Jess always cooks for the five thousand. And she'd like to see you.' Caroline grinned. 'She's always banging on about how much she likes you. Come on. Get the prison out of your nostrils and off your tongue.'

'Put like that, how could I resist?' he said, then remembered that 'put like that' was a phrase Trish Maguire used.

He must get her out of his head. The Malcolm Chaze killing had nothing to do with an alternative suspect for the murder of Deborah Gibbert's father. Caroline was right: Spike Hamper, who could have supplied Gibbert's cell-mate with enough smack to put her in hospital for weeks, was a much likelier bet. And Caroline's second scenario had possibilities, too; a few anyway. And more than Gibbert's family. He grinned at her.

'Let's go.' And sod Trish Maguire, he added to himself.

# Chapter 14

Trish was sitting in her favourite chair in El Vino's, absorbing the full blast of Phil Redstone's resentment. She wasn't surprised, and she didn't blame him for it, which was one reason why it was so excruciating. The other was that she was still feeling as though she'd had at least three layers of skin peeled away. She had to forget Malcolm Chaze's murder and her own fear and make Phil relax; otherwise she'd never last long enough to get anything out of him.

She had bought an expensive bottle of burgundy and watched him down two glasses before she'd even begun on her first. She refilled his glass and took advantage of a short pause in his diatribe to say, 'Phil, I'm not doing this in some kind of attempt to prove you incompetent.'

'No? Then why? I know you were furious two years ago over that child-killing case. Isn't this some kind of revenge?'

'God, no!' But I was angry, she thought. For about an hour after we left court, I felt as though it would be your fault if that paedophile maniac killed anyone else after you'd rubbished our case and set him loose again. 'I'm a professional. I know how it works. What you did then wasn't personal. And this isn't personal either.'

'That was a case,' he said, swallowing the wonderful raspberry-like wine as though it were any old plonk. Trish sipped and let the taste – sunny, fruity, amazingly elegant – burst open in her mouth. 'This is different. This is holding me up to ridicule on television for your own greater media glory.'

'No, it's not.' Trish felt as old as his great aunt. 'Come on, Phil. Give me a break. The producer wants to change the climate of opinion surrounding your erstwhile client, who seems to be known to everyone who noticed the original case as the all-time witch who took revenge on her fragile elderly father for trivial – and imaginary – childhood difficulties. The loss of Malcolm Chaze is going to—'

'You mean *he* was involved in this pantomime of yours?'

Trish swallowed the insult with difficulty. 'It's hardly that, and yes, he was. His death is going to hurt Deb in more ways than one.' Seeing how surprised – even shocked – Phil looked, Trish explained a little of the background, adding, 'Did you ever meet him?'

He shook his head, but he looked worried. 'Have you talked to the police about this?'

'Of course I have.'

'And do they think there's a connection?'

'No. They treated me like a melodramatic girlie, wasting their time.'

Phil leaned back against the chair and stretched out his legs with a satisfied sigh.

'But I still think there could be a link,' said Trish, watching his knee tighten under the smooth black cloth of his trousers.

'I can see it would be bloody convenient for you.' Phil laughed almost convincingly. 'But I have enough faith in you to be sure you'd never swallow anything as ludicrous as that.'

'You're very flattering. And I may be wrong. Either way, we still need a lot of answers before we can start shooting the film.'

'D'you really think any TV company is going to buy a project about an obscure domestic killing without a high-profile personality like Chaze to front it? I know you're doing well these days, Trish, but not that well.'

'The story's as powerful as it ever was,' she said coolly, not giving him the satisfaction of even showing she'd noticed the insult. 'An innocent woman's serving life for a murder she didn't commit.'

'OK. Ask your questions.' He shrugged. 'But I doubt if anything I can tell you will do you much good.'

Trish drank again, trying to concentrate on the wine for a second.

'You didn't have to prove Deb Gibbert innocent in court, so you didn't try,' she began. Phil nodded kindly, as though she'd proved to be brighter than he'd expected. Patronising prick, she thought. 'All you had to do was show that the prosecution hadn't proved her guilty. I understand that.'

'That's something, I suppose.' He was looking down into his glass, so she couldn't see his eyes.

'But this film is different. It's designed to show that Deb shouldn't be in prison, so it will try to establish her innocence. It's a different kind of animal altogether.'

'I can accept that. But I don't like the idea that a fellow member of the Bar is out to criticise my work. Would you?'

'Frankly I'd hate it,' she said. 'Especially if I'd always thought my client guilty and getting no more than she deserved.'

Phil had begun to smile, but as the sense of what Trish had said reached him his face hardened. Something began to flicker in his eyes, like the first few tiny flames that might, unchecked, grow into a fireball.

'You did, didn't you?' Trish said, pressing now because she thought his petulance was unprofessional. And because he was being greedy with her splendid wine.

'I honestly can't remember,' he said, clearly lying through his teeth. Trish began to think more kindly of Deb's loathing of him, and Anna's determination to expose his failings.

'I took the view,' he went on, with quite unnecessary

pomposity, 'that the police had a confession from someone else, and my client had given a statement that included a wholly credible explanation for their only bit of scientific evidence against her.'

'Did you believe it yourself? That story of the poly bag, I mean.'

'That's irrelevant.' The flicker in his eyes had been doused. So, she thought, it's not the question of Deb's guilt that worries him.

'True. And what about the conflicting antihistamines?'

'There was no evidence to prove that my client had administered them. And her mother confessed to that, too. There was no reason for my client to have been charged, tried or convicted. No reason at all. The prosecution had not established anything whatsoever beyond a reasonable doubt.'

The little speech had been delivered with conviction and clarity. Trish wondered whether Phil had practised it in those awful moments of wakefulness at three in the morning, when memories of lost cases can return like a torturer's favourite instruments to keep you conscious while he extracts all the horrible facts you've hidden even from yourself.

'That seems eminently reasonable, Phil,' she said, smiling to placate him. He didn't respond. 'I assume you had a second autopsy done before you decided to call no evidence?'

The flicker started again. He must have had an autopsy done, Trish told herself, wishing Anna had managed to get hold of a full set of case papers. Had somebody lost part of them? Or shredded them?

Phil began to laugh and ruffled his hair. It would have been a picture of an untroubled man, but for his eyes. They betrayed him.

'You did have one done, didn't you, Phil?'

'Trish, for heaven's sake. I know this is for telly, but come on. Give me a break. No one ever disputed the fact that the poor bugger was suffocated after being given an overdose But of course I had the autopsy results checked.'

'Good.' Then why are you so worried?

'Unfortunately, as is so often the case with defence autopsies, our man merely confirmed the prosecution's findings. What's so odd about that?'

'Nothing. What did he say about the extra antihistamines in the body? Was there any explanation apart from malice aforethought?'

Phil smiled luxuriously, reaching out to pick up the bottle to refill their glasses. But he didn't look at her. She was sure he knew that he couldn't control his eyes in the way he managed his mouth, his breathing, and even his hands. He was an excellent performer. But everyone has one betraying habit.

'The antihistamines never seemed to me to be the crux of the thing,' he said, sounding casual again. 'OK, the old man should never have been given both sorts, but no one – not even the prosecution's pathologist – ever suggested there was enough astemizole to kill him.'

'I've been missing a subtlety then,' Trish said, realising that Phil must have been rereading his notes of the case. Without checking, he couldn't have remembered the name of the drug that hadn't been prescribed. He really must be worried. 'I thought it was the very presence of astemizole that persuaded everyone they had a case of murder on their hands.'

'Not in itself, Trish. This was where the line between fact and interpretation became almost impossibly narrow. As I said, there was only a very small quantity of astemizole, not enough to do him harm, even with the terfenadine overdose, but quite enough to suggest that someone had been giving him things they shouldn't.'

'Oh?'

'Yes. The prosecution's theory was that my client had tried

to make her father dopey enough not to fight back – or make enough noise to wake her mother – when she put the bag on him. They alleged that she could have noticed that his terfenadine hadn't made him sleep deeply enough on previous nights, so when she was intending to bump him off, she added a bit of her own astemizole to help things along.'

Trish, who had read all this in the trial transcript but wanted to see how Phil presented it, swigged some more wine.

'Phil,' she said, a little later, 'don't take this wrong, but why didn't you call any evidence?'

'You know very well that it's the prosecution's job to prove—'

'That would do very well for the media,' Trish said quickly, 'and it might do for the TV film, but this is me. Were you afraid Deb would crack under cross-examination?'

Phil produced a sound that was half-way between a sigh and a laugh as he sagged against the leather chairback. 'Trish, put yourself in my place. You're faced with a client so angry she feels as though she's permanently wired. She leaps down your throat at every question, however innocuous. You know she savaged the doctor before her father died, apparently begging for him to be killed – or put out of his misery, if you prefer. You know the police detest her – and suspect her – because of the things she's said to them. You know her own sister's given statements about her verbal cruelty to their father. Would you dare expose a woman like that to cross-examination by Mark Savory, of all people?'

'Maybe not.' Trish liked Phil better now that he was being frank. And he had a point. 'But weren't there any witnesses you could have produced to speak for her?'

'Such as who? The teeth-and-bag episode, if it ever happened, took place in her father's bedroom. The only other person in the house that night was her mother, now dead. I could have called character witnesses, but if I'd done that and not called my client, it would have been even more obvious why. The only safe way of conducting the case was to major on the hopelessness of the prosecution's evidence and the barminess of the police refusal to believe in the mother's confession.'

'Right.'

'And their case *was* hopeless. You must admit.'

'Yes, I do, even though the jury didn't. But didn't your pathologist come up with anything you could have used?'

He sighed. 'No. What I wanted was something to prove that the suffocation had been by means of a pillow, not a bag. That would have clinched it, despite what they all said about the mother's physical weakness. Unfortunately our pathologist couldn't give me anything.'

'In that case, why did you put the question, in exactly those terms, to the prosecution's man in court?' Trish asked, trying not to let any of her astonishment show.

Phil was lifting the glass to his lips again, but at the end of her question he banged it down on the table again. 'So you *are* trying to rubbish my work. I thought so.'

Trish felt his anger, cold now but very sharp, and tried not to recoil.

'All I'm saying, Phil, is that with hindsight it might have been better for your client if you'd asked merely whether or not there was anything in the autopsy to prove that suffocation had been effected by means of a plastic bag. If you'd asked it like that, he'd have had to admit there wasn't.'

His eyes were flickering again. So, he knew he'd cocked up. Good. That also explained, of course, why he was quite so angry at the thought of Anna's film and Deb's solicitors' attempt to get leave for the new appeal.

'I don't need you to tell me my job, Trish.' His tone was ostensibly polite, but the subtext was that she was a child of no account, daring to question a great man, who would one day sit on the bench and eat little girls like her for breakfast. She just looked at him.

'I managed to make the police officers who had taken my client's statement admit that there was nothing to prove her story false,' he said huffily. 'Unfortunately I couldn't get the jury to accept what I'd shown to be true. That was my client's bad luck. But you know how it goes as well as I do.'

'Win some, lose some?' Trish said, remembering Dave's casual comment. The thought of all the work that was piling up for her in chambers, and Dave's likely punishment for the last few days' unscheduled absences, made her stomach lurch.

'Exactly.'

Trish tried a brief smile. There was a slight relaxation in his facial muscles, but not enough to make him look at ease. 'Will you come on the programme?' she asked.

'To be made a fool of? Certainly not.'

'No,' she said patiently. 'To explain the limits of what counsel can do with the evidence that exists, how a defence case is conducted, and why you chose to offer no evidence.'

'Who'll be the presenter, Trish? You?'

'God, no. A professional. I'd be hopeless. And anyway I wouldn't want to do it. I'm just a backroom gofer.' And I'm not sure I'm ever going to forgive Anna for involving me – or myself for taking it on.

'I couldn't possibly agree without knowing who would conduct the interview, and until I'd seen the script.'

Trish hardly heard him, because George had appeared in the doorway. She was on her feet, wishing that there was still some burgundy left for him. He kissed her, then shook hands with Redstone.

'I hadn't expected to find you involved in this particular party, George,' he said, looking thoroughly put out.

So, thought Trish, Phil must get quite a lot of briefs

from George and not want to piss him off. Why didn't he tell me?

'I'm not,' George said cheerfully. 'I've come to collect the little woman and take her off to cook my dinner.'

Trish had to suppress a smile at the sight of Phil's face. He'd never seen them together and had no idea of their private jokes. She was glad that George seemed to have got over the morning's *Angst*. As she coughed, choking on the amusement, Phil looked at her in astonishment.

'Sorry,' she said. 'It's just George, Phil. He likes a bit of misogynist make-believe.'

'She can get a bit up herself,' George said confidingly. 'Needs reminding of her proper place in the hierarchy.'

Redstone's eyes were slowly returning to normal. 'I can see you two play a lot of very weird games. I must go.'

'Thank you for talking to me, Phil. Oh, just before you go?'

'What?'

'Did you get the doctor's notes checked for forgery or tampering?'

He looked at her as though she was a woodlouse crawling out from under damp floorboards. 'Of course I did, ESDA test and all. They were genuine all right.'

'Pity. But thanks.'

'OK. That wine's too good for George,' he said, pointing at the empty bottle. 'He's never had much of a palate.'

'Wanker,' Trish muttered, when he'd gone. 'He drank most of it as though it was Ribena.'

'What a waste! Would you like me to get another bottle or shall we go home?'

'Let's go.'

As they walked together over the bridge towards Southwark, he said, 'By the way, I had a meeting today with someone from social services at Westminster.'

Trish looked at him in surprise.

'And I asked about your protégé. Apparently he's being fostered by one of their most experienced couples. He isn't—'

'My protégé?' She was all over the place and couldn't think what he meant.

'The dead junkie's child. Remember Saturday's papers? Wake up, Trish. The two-year-old. You haven't forgotten, have you? You were beating up such a rage about him you'd practically covered yourself in foam. I thought you'd like to know.'

She shook her head. 'I hadn't forgotten. I suppose this means the grandparents' DNA test proved he wasn't theirs?'

'Yup. But he'll be all right with Westminster social services. They're good people there.'

'Thank you for bothering to ask. George, you are . . .'

He bent to kiss her lightly. She knew she didn't have to tell him how much she cared these days, but sometimes she liked doing it, for herself as much as for him.

'Did they tell you how the child is?' she asked, as they set off again.

'Not himself addicted, but malnourished and with various problems caused by deficiencies of one sort or another.'

'Brain?'

'Thought to be OK, but development may be slow. They won't know for a year or two yet.'

'Poor child. I wish I could help.'

'I know. But you can't do anything. Tearing yourself apart won't help. Now, how's your father?'

'Not bad. He says he's going back to work next Monday. I'm sure it's too soon, but he insists his GP says it's OK, and he's so bored at home he says he'll top himself if he doesn't get out soon. Oh, God, I forgot.'

'What?'

'I meant to apologise to the house officer I bawled out for

letting him go home without telling me, but what with Malcolm Chaze and everything . . . it's no excuse, though. Damn. I really screamed at the poor bloke.'

'I shouldn't worry about it, Trish. He's probably used to relatives panicking themselves into a frenzy. And anyway, you were justified.'

Trish looked at him in amazement.

'You were justified,' he said again, seeing her surprise. 'You'd asked the hospital to tell you if there was any change and left all your phone numbers. The fact that the change was for the better doesn't let them off the hook. They should have rung you.'

In spite of the heat, she flung her arms round George's comfortable bulk.

Later, he poured himself a glass of wine to take into the kitchen and insisted that she go upstairs to shower. Clean and changed, she was downstairs in time to answer the phone when it rang.

'Trish? It's Anna. I've been trying to get you ever since I heard about Malcolm.'

'Yes, I know. I'm sorry, I've been too busy to ring you back.' Trish sat down, swinging her legs up on the sofa. The smells of George's cooking were teasing her nostrils. There was lemon in the air, she decided as she sniffed, and maybe garlic as well as fish, and hot butter.

'I don't know what we're going to do about the film now.' There was a high, vibrating note in Anna's voice that suggested hysteria. 'We needed Malcolm to sell it. How could he . . .'

'Anna, for God's sake! He's been murdered.'

'Oh, I know. And it's ghastly for him and his wife. But we . . . Oh, shit, Trish.'

'Trish?' George was calling from the kitchen. 'Two more minutes.'

'Anna, I'm going to have to go soon.'

'I heard.'

'Anna? Are you crying.'

'No, of course not.' There was a distinct sniff down the phone.

'Come on, tell me. What's up? Were you and Malcolm . . .?'

'No. Don't be ridiculous.' She sniffed again. 'It's just that I *have* to get this programme commissioned.'

'Why? Come on. Out with it.'

'Trish, I hadn't meant to tell you this, but it's my last chance. The bank are going to pull the rug if I don't sell a big one in the next month. It's that urgent. I'm facing bankruptcy. And if that happens, I'll lose the house. I'm forty-two, I'll never get another one, I don't know what'll happen to me. I'll . . .'

'Anna, you—'

'Trish, when I found Deb and realised she had to be innocent, I was sure I was on to a winner. Then I couldn't find an alternative killer. The commissioning editors said they'd had so many miscarriage-of-justice cases that they wouldn't go for it unless I could at least suggest that someone else was responsible and show why.'

'But weren't they worried about defamation?'

'We didn't get as far as that. They kept saying they needed drama, not just a kind of legal home-study lesson. So I tried. I really tried. But I don't know enough, and I'm not a good interviewer like you, and I didn't get anywhere. I read that bloody typescript over and over again, and I couldn't see any gaps. In the end I thought I'd gone mad, and invested all this time – and a fair bit of money – and got the bank all excited at the idea of the project for nothing. And Malcolm, who was on my side, but didn't seem able to do very much. So I came to you.'

'I wish you'd told me.'

'I thought if anyone could find the killer and save me, you could. I've been . . . desperate, Trish.'

Oh, shit, she thought. So now, as well as my own safety, my father's health, my clients, Deborah Gibbert and her daughter, I've got to worry about Anna and her future. A sense of persecution battled with Trish's instinct to take control and tell everyone how to sort out their problems.

'Try not to get in too much of a state,' she said at last. 'I'll phone Cordelia Whatlam in the morning and see her as soon as I can. She may produce something useful. Anna, hang on in there. Malcolm's championship was important for Deb, but he wasn't the be-all and end-all of the film. If we get some really crunchy information, the channel will go for it even without a celebrity. I promise you I'll do my best.'

'I know. And I know you'll fight like a tiger for Deb and for me. I'm sorry. I should've told you before about the bank, but it gets frightening to be so desperate. You think if people knew how bad things were, they'd put you on a lower rung, and pay no attention, just because—'

'Anna, stop it. You're hysterical. I've said I'll do my best. I'll ring you tomorrow evening, either way. In the meantime, hurry your researchers up with the medical stuff. We need that. Now. I've got to go. 'Bye.'

The fish was halibut, in fat juicy steaks, slicked with melted butter just turning brown, and studded with the murky green of capers. A bright emerald flicker of chopped parsley fell on to the fish as Trish watched, and neat yellow lemon quarters were laid at either end. She looked up at George's serious face. He could have been a surgeon carrying out a life-or-death operation. The scents of the dish were fresh and pungent. He poured wine and cold fizzy water, then pushed forward a big dark blue bowl of salad.

Trish put away all thought of Malcolm Chaze and the army of people who were depending on her. This was

George's time, and hers. They deserved it undiluted. She slid her silver knife into the halibut and parted one slightly veined chunk from the rest. It gave way with a satisfactory little squelch.

# Chapter 15

'I don't have to listen to this.' In spite of the outrage in her voice, Laura Chaze looked the picture of ease, sitting on her striped silk sofa with her legs crossed. 'All right, so I've told friends I wanted Malcolm out of my life. But not like this, for Christ's sake!'

Femur coughed, the clashing scents of her skin and the room catching in his throat. He didn't like the house, the pot pourri, or the lacquered finish of the widow herself. And he definitely didn't like what his officers had learned about the woman's behaviour to her husband in the last few months, or the things she'd said about him to friends.

Some of her reported threats had been so violent that he'd had to come this morning himself to face her with the suggestion that she could have put out the contract on her husband's life. So far her reaction hadn't told him anything except that she was a hard-faced bitch.

The memory of Deborah Gibbert's howling anguish made this woman's composure even more suspicious. An empty filing cabinet would have shown more emotion. He held on to his loathing with difficulty.

'Why did you want to be rid of him?'

Mrs Chaze raised her plucked eyebrows.

'Come on,' Femur said irritably. He wasn't going to use kid gloves with a bitch like this. 'We need to know everything about his personality and his activities in the last few months if we're to get anywhere. You must have known him better than most, even if you couldn't feel any kindness for him.'

Young Steve Owler, his AMIP constable, twitched. Femur paid no attention. Owler was a good lad, but too squeamish. If this woman wanted to play hard-ball, she'd find the police could give as good as they got.

'Very well, Chief Inspector Femur. The man I married was idealistic, on the left of his party, wanted to make a difference to the lives of the disadvantaged. Or so I thought.'

He glanced round at the richly decorated room and disliked her even more. Why should a woman who was at home in this kind of silky smartness take to a man because he planned to make a difference? Or want a room like this if she cared about 'the disadvantaged'? Compared to her, he was one of the disadvantaged himself.

'But once I'd got to know him, I found he was quite different: utterly vain and, under the superficial arrogance, needing the constant reassurance that only fresh batches of adorers can supply. Pathetic. And boring. I'm afraid I ran out of reassurance to offer him some time ago.'

She recrossed her legs. She had great legs and made the most of them. The rest of her was beginning to show her age: her neck had enough lines to date a tree stump, and her face was beginning to pouch around the eyes and under the chin.

Stop it, Femur, he told himself. You've no reason to hate her. Yet. So concentrate. What did she just say? Under the arrogance, her husband had needed reassurance.

Deborah Gibbert had talked like that, too. Interesting, Femur thought. None of the men he'd talked to so far had noticed it. Maybe it was the impression of underlying vulnerability that made Chaze so successful with women – anyway, at the beginning of his affairs. Or maybe it was the combination of that and his so-called charisma. He must ask Cally. She'd know, even though men didn't turn her on.

Maybe a bit of weakness is what women think they're going to want in a man. Only they don't really. It bugs them in the end. Even Sue had been gentle with his fears when they first married; later, once she'd had the kids, he had only to express the mildest anxiety for her to round on him for being pathetic. Oh, stop it, he told himself again, weary to his soul. This woman is not Sue. And you're here to do a job. So get on with it.

'Did he give you any hint that he'd been worried by a stalker or any kind of verbal threat?' She might relax enough to give them something useful if she thought they were flailing about, suspecting everyone. 'Did you have any dodgy phone calls here, for instance?'

Owler relaxed against the sofa back.

'No.' Laura Chaze turned her thin wrist so she could look at her watch. Femur knew he was supposed to be impressed by how much it must have cost. He didn't know and couldn't give a toss anyway. 'I have a meeting in twenty minutes,' she said, 'so I can't stay much longer. I have instructed Malcolm's secretary, Sally Hatfield, to make you free of my study upstairs, and to answer any questions you may have. She's waiting for you there. You can look through my diary, my financial records, whatever else you want. And Malcolm's, as far as I'm concerned. That will give you far more information than this kind of laborious question-and-answer session, which must be as boring for you as it is for me.'

'Thank you,' Femur said. There wasn't much else he could say, given that he had no grounds to arrest her. Yet. And there might be something useful in her records. He'd leave Owler to comb those, send him more bodies if anything looked hopeful, and get back to the incident room himself and clear his head of his problems so that he could think straight about this. He'd like her to be the villain, but he had to be a lot more sure before he did anything stupid like dragging her out of the house in handcuffs for all the papers to record. He could see the headlines now, 'Another Police Blunder. Grieving Widow Bullied By Police While the Real Killer Goes Free'.

She was on her feet now, small but as charged with energy as a laser gun. 'I can assure you that you won't find any items in my diary about "find contract killer", but you'll want to check my financial records for unexplained payments.'

'How much d'you suppose that would cost?' Steve Owler said suddenly.

Femur hid a smile, thinking: So, not so squeamish after all. Good lad. But this lady's probably too well insulated to shock with such a small charge.

Laura Chaze stopped half-way to the door and looked at them both with amusement, which made her face twice as lively as before. 'I have no idea. Five hundred? Five thousand? I wouldn't know. It doesn't come within my area of expertise, constable. But then I would say that, wouldn't I? Goodbye.'

'Wait, Mrs Chaze.' Femur was pleased to see her hesitate. He owed it to Caroline Lyalt to ask one more question: 'Have you any idea why your husband was so ferociously anti-drugs? It's the first thing everyone mentions about him.'

Her face cleared like a white sink given a good dose of bleach. Her voice was a bit like bleach, too: smooth in itself, but scouring in its effect. 'Like all the other issues he's engaged with, it's an ideal platform for an ambitious MP. Nearly everyone you need to vote for you agrees that drugs should be controlled. Even the respectable constituents who take the stuff themselves want the criminal element well policed. And the underclass are never going to vote for anyone anyway.'

'So, it wasn't anything personal?'

'I don't think so.' She took two steps back into the room, which Femur took as a compliment. 'His only close encounter with drugs was in his last year at school, I think. But he didn't like it, unlike most people who tried the stuff at the end of the sixties. So he never tried it again.'

'Right. And you didn't know him then?'

'No. We met about ten years ago at a fund-raising dinner.' She looked from Femur to his constable and back again, a cynical smile changing the shape of her lips. 'I suppose you could say we fell in love. It seems hard to believe now.'

'It didn't last?'

'No, Chief Inspector, it did not.' There wasn't much emotion in her voice beyond the kind of contempt for the class dummy who took twice as long as everyone else to pick up the simplest point.

'Was he unfaithful?'

'Surely you know that much. Of course he was.'

'But you stayed with him?'

'Just.' He watched her as she realised that wasn't enough of an answer. She took a step back towards the door. 'He kept promising me it would be the last time, and I kept accepting it. You think I'm hard, Chief Inspector, but I was naïve enough to go on trying to believe him, trying to make our marriage work. I gave up when I realised he'd never put in the same kind of effort.'

He was too old to blush, but it did sound as though she had just cause to be angry.

'And I can tell you that living with Malcolm would have made even Patient Griselda a trifle snappy. Now I really must go. If you need to ask more questions, phone my secretary and give me enough warning to clear my diary for you.'

'Right.'

'And, Chief Inspector Femur, I do hope you catch whoever sent the killer. I can't see how you're going to do it, but I wouldn't want Malcolm's death to go unavenged. Do you understand me?'

He waited for long enough to see how she dealt with the

pause. All he was offered was a picture of controlled impatience and several glances at the expensive wristwatch. 'I think so,' he said at last. 'Before you go, what drug did he experiment with at school? LSD? That could have given him a bad trip.'

'I have a feeling it was heroin, but I couldn't swear to it.' She was opening the door as she spoke. 'Luckily, weak-willed though he could be, he had enough presence of mind to resist addiction to whatever it was.'

'Heroin would have been an unusual school drug in the sixties.'

'You'll have a better idea of that than me. But I think that's what he said the only time we ever talked about it.' She stepped across the threshold, but she was still looking back over her shoulder. 'I wasn't interested enough to check up, I'm afraid.'

'Right. We'll look into it. Which school was it?'

'St John's, Henley. He got a scholarship.' Now she was sounding impatient. 'You shouldn't have to ask me that; it's a matter of public record. Surely your people aren't too incompetent to have looked up *Who's Who*?'

She had gone.

'Right. That was a pretty good waste of time. Steve, you'd better make a start upstairs. I'll get back and put someone on to his schooldays in case there's anything in this heroin business.'

'Is there any point going through her papers, Guv? If she'd wanted to make a big payment, she'd have flogged a piece of jewellery, or that watch, and paid cash. A woman like that isn't going to leave a paper trail for us to follow.'

Christ! thought Femur. Bollocked by a suspect, then by my own constable. I must be losing it. 'I know, Steve,' he said, more patiently than he felt. 'We won't find anything, but we have to go through the motions. More to the point, it'll give you a chance to cross-question the secretary, who'll know a lot more about Chaze than his wife, and about their dealings with each other.'

'Sergeant Lyalt's already had DC Pepper . . .'

'I know she has. But you're a good-looking lad, you may get more out of her than Pepper or Lyalt could. Get on with it, will you?'

'Sure, Guv.' Owler still hesitated, looking sympathetic and anxious, which was unlike him. Femur shook his head. He knew what was coming and he didn't want to hear it. 'And, Guv, you look like shit. You ought to have some food, or sleep or something.'

'Sod off and get on with it,' Femur said. Odd that Owler still had to learn that sympathising with your senior officer was worse than telling him how to do his job. It would do the lad good to plough through files of domestic accounts.

For himself, Femur would get back to the incident room and tell Caroline that her intuition about the drugs could have been half right, even though she'd been giving Chaze credit for too much unselfishness. It sounded like it had been his own trauma that had driven him, not a girlfriend's.

Trish was in the corridor of the Royal Courts of Justice, waiting for her case to be called and reading Malcolm Chaze's powerful plea for justice for Deborah Gibbert. At the foot of the last column was a tiny, italic statement: 'Anna Grayling's film about Deborah Gibbert, *Torn from the Family*, is to be shown on television later in the year.'

There was no suggestion from the loitering ushers that the case was about to begin, so Trish signalled to her instructing solicitor that she was going to make a phone call. He nodded, quite unworried. She took her mobile round the corner into the main hall and rang Anna.

'Oh, yes,' she said cheerfully, a moment later. She sounded

not only unlike the woman who'd wept down the phone but almost from a different species. 'It would have been mad to let this fantastic opportunity drop. I mean, Trish, don't misunderstand me. I—'

'If you're in a hole, Anna, stop digging.'

'OK. But face it, from the point of view of our campaign for Deb, it would have been seriously stupid not to take advantage of the publicity. And the weight of this message from a dead man is going to help her. That's all I was trying to do.'

'Maybe. But what's this about "the film is to be shown?" Have they made a commitment this morning?'

'Well, not exactly. But I've just been speaking to them and it's virtually certain now that—'

'Anna! Stop it. Let me get this right. You are using Malcolm's murder to bounce one of the television companies into buying your film. Yes?'

'Well, yes. And it looks as though it's working. But, Trish, I'm fighting for my future here. And Deb's freedom.'

'Just so I know. Now, how are your medical researchers doing?'

There was a pause. 'Well, Trish, the thing is, you see . . . actually . . .'

Trish felt the old lava-flow of anger beginning to stir. 'You mean you haven't got anyone talking to a geriatrician yet?'

'It's more than that actually. I can't . . . I haven't the funds yet to . . . Until I get a commitment, I can't get the bank to let me have any . . . I'm sorry, Trish.'

'There are no researchers. Is this what you're telling me?'

'Yes.'

'Oh, shit, Anna. Why didn't you tell me?' Trish thought of the hours she'd expended on the project, the lists of questions she'd typed and e-mailed to Anna. All to no purpose. What a waste of time! No wonder she hadn't got all the case papers she'd wanted. 'Who's been producing the few scraps you have sent me?'

'Me, actually; in between finding studios, trying to persuade camera crews, grips—'

'I don't need the full list again,' Trish said, holding on to her irritation. 'I know you've got difficulties, too. Fine. But I don't have time to do everything. I've got a demanding job and a convalescent father. Get me the medical information now or I'm off the case. Understood?'

'You sound very cross.'

'And you sound like a child. Anna, why couldn't you have been honest with me? I've put in hours on this thing. If it had been a case, you'd be paying me tens of thousands of pounds.' The lava tide was surging so powerfully that Trish knew she had to break off the conversation. Anna was desperate; it wouldn't help to swear at her now.

'I don't know why you're sounding so holy. You haven't even talked to Cordelia yet, and she has to be the key.'

Trish counted three. 'You're right, Anna. But I've go to go now. 'Bye.'

She snapped her phone shut and stuffed it in the pocket of her black suit under the flapping gown. Her jaw felt as though it would never relax, and she suspected her face was white. All the blood seemed to drain away from her head when she was as angry as this. She hoped she'd get at least ten minutes before she had to go into court. Starting out in this state would not augur well for her client.

Luckily the ushers were still loitering happily where she'd last seen them, and everyone else was reading their papers. Trish sat down again on the hard bench and went back to Malcolm's article.

He had set out the little real evidence the prosecution had had, then followed it with everything he knew of Deb, along with testimonials from all sorts of people who'd known her.

The article ended with a passionate denunciation of the injustice that had locked her up for life and risked the ruination of her children's lives. It was a powerful piece.

A hand tapped her on the shoulder. She looked up quickly.

'We're on, Trish. You OK?'

'Sure. Why d'you ask?'

'You look shaky.'

She smiled and saw the solicitor breathe more easily. 'I'm just in a rage about something else. Don't worry.' She stood up, shook out her gown, and slotted into her professional persona. This was something she could do. She knew the brief backwards. She'd see her client right.

Five hours later, she was back in the flat, lying on her sofa with a long glass of mineral water, wondering if she'd ever be cool again. The case had gone reasonably well, but something had been wrong with the air-conditioning and the court had been unbearably stuffy. Even though her suit was made of thin linen, the gown had meant she was wearing two layers of black cloth. In this weather, that alone, even without the constricting Lycra tights, would have been an ordeal.

She tried to believe it was the heat that made it impossible to suppress some very uncharitable thoughts about her old friend Anna. Cashing in on murder was a thoroughly nasty business. So was lying to your friends, and exploiting them.

'Oh, forget it,' Trish said aloud, weary and dissatisfied with herself. She picked up the newspaper again.

There was a huge glamorous photograph of Malcolm Chaze in the middle of the page beside a much smaller one of Deb, looking dowdy and a most unlikely girlfriend for a man like him. There was something about his face that made Trish curious.

As she looked at it more carefully, she kept seeing another face superimposed on it: younger and infinitely less assured, but very similar. She shook her head. The idea was absurd. And yet, if you took thirty-odd years off Malcolm Chaze's face, made it female, added a lot of long hair and removed the fringe, wasn't it a dead ringer for Kate Gibbert's?

They had the same shaped forehead and fine dark hair; the same pointed chin; and the same appealing smile.

The dates fitted, too. Trish wondered whether it had ever occurred to Adam Gibbert that Deb might already have been pregnant by someone else when they got engaged. He could hardly have missed the likeness between Kate and Deb's old lover, even if it had taken Trish far too long to notice it, and he was neither vain nor stupid enough to ignore the obvious reason.

Malcolm's campaign to get himself on the front pages and the television news hadn't taken effect until fairly recently. Had Adam belatedly woken up to the fact that 'his' beautiful, helpful daughter, the one person who made his impossible life bearable, belonged to someone else?

Trish had seen at once that Adam was a man on the edge, hanging on by his fingernails. It wouldn't have taken much more to kick him over.

She sat down again with the paper between her damp hands, looking at the dead man's face. She didn't know how to get a hitman herself, but it couldn't be hard to find out. And Adam might not have needed one. Much the easiest way for him to get rid of Malcolm Chaze would have been to dress up in leathers and a helmet and do the job himself. He'd have had to get a gun, of course, but from what Trish had read in the papers that wasn't particularly difficult.

Tempted to phone Femur and ask if he'd thought to question Adam, Trish knew she couldn't. She'd already infuriated the police by pointing out one connection with Deb Gibbert; Femur hadn't listened then. Why should he pay any more attention now?

She thought of writing to Deb to ask for confirmation, but there didn't seem any point. Now that she'd seen the likeness, she couldn't think why she hadn't noticed before, and she had no doubt at all about Kate's true parentage. She wished she'd known before she had talked to Deb in the first place, but the things she wanted to ask couldn't be put in a letter. If she went to the prison again, she'd ask them then.

George was due at a Law Society dinner that evening, so she wouldn't see him. She picked up the phone to find out how Paddy was and whether he needed anything.

He didn't, but he said he'd like to see her. Trish thought wistfully about a cool shower and a peaceful early night, but got straight into her car to drive along the south side of the river to his Battersea flat.

# Chapter 16

Cordelia Whatlam's double-fronted mews house dripped pink geranium petals from terracotta planters on every window-sill. Trish picked her way towards it across painfully knobbly cobbles, avoiding the glossy, expensive cars that took up every possible parking space.

She should have been in chambers still. As it was, she'd been up at five to go through all the papers that were piled on her desk. She'd dealt with a lot and left a huge long note for Dave before she'd left to fulfil her promise to Anna. It stuck in her craw, but she was going to do what she'd agreed, even if Anna had messed her about.

Even so, she'd hoped she wasn't turning into a woman like Deb herself. What was it Anna had said in the beginning? Something like: 'Deb tries to do everything for everyone, runs herself ragged, short-changes the lot of them and is foul to the very people she most wants to help.'

Well, if this visit didn't produce any useful information and Anna didn't turn up anything on the medical evidence, it would be time to cut loose. If Anna's business folded and she lost her home, that would be tough, but Trish hadn't caused the problem and she would have given the solution her best shot. If she failed, she failed. She couldn't be responsible for everyone. And, she told herself, surprised at the metaphors her brain was spouting, this might be the Last Chance Saloon, but she wasn't in a Western. But it meant she was smiling when the glossy black door in front of her opened.

A slender, dark-haired woman stood there, with her eyebrows raised and a polite smile on her neat, pink lips. Trish had been expecting someone menacing, or at least predatory, but this woman looked almost fragile and very much as Deb would if she shed four stone and dressed at Armani.

'Ms Whatlam?'

'Yes.' Cordelia Whatlam's voice was less than welcoming. Her sleek hair was cut short and tucked behind her ears. Neat globular gold earrings hung from them, looking like little melons. She was wearing beige linen trousers under a loose black shirt-like jacket. She looked cool, in every sense of the word. 'You must be Trish Maguire. You'd better come in.'

Polite but hostile, Trish thought. Very hostile. Oh, well, it wasn't that surprising, was it? 'Thank you,' she said, stepping across the threshold.

Cordelia led the way through the shady house to a small, flower-splashed courtyard. A highly decorated pottery fountain was playing in the middle, catching the light in each droplet and making what was only a tiny backyard look positively exotic.

'This is gorgeous, and so unexpected.' You creep, Trish added to herself. Careful you don't overdo it.

But it seemed that Cordelia Whatlam wasn't going to be distracted. Standing beside her fountain, with the same small, polite smile on her face, she said quietly, 'May I ask why you of all people are involved in this farce?

Me of all people? thought Trish. She doesn't know anything about me. The hostility was shocking. Trish took a moment to compose her response.

'How would you feel if someone came to tell you they were trying to get Charles Chompton out of prison and asked your help to do it?'

Trish stiffened. She might have got most of her fears under control, but that didn't mean they weren't there.

'You must have known I'd check you out before I let you into my house.'

'Yes,' Trish said carefully. 'That would be only sensible.'

'So, how would you feel if I were digging around for legal tricks that would free the man who raped and killed your friend and nearly did the same to you? Hm?'

'Frankly, I'd hate it.' Trish remembered she'd used exactly the same phrase to Phil Redstone and wondered whether he and Cordelia were in touch. He'd have been a good source for this information about her past. The thought of the pair of them cooking up a nasty plot like this to stop her fighting for Deb was unpleasant in the extreme.

'This is a little different.' She was determined not to show any weakness. 'Deb is your sister. Don't you have any feelings for her at all?'

'Not many that would help you. I suppose you'd better sit down. I'm prepared to listen to what you have to say, but I can't give you long.' Cordelia looked at her watch, a gold Panther that glittered in the sun and showed off her faintly tanned skin. It was so smooth it looked like the shell of a big, old-fashioned brown boiled egg.

'I hope someone has told you that Debbie was always a fantasist,' she said casually. 'As a child she'd tell herself stories so vivid that she'd get muddled between what was real and what was not.'

'A lot of children do that.'

'Most of them grow out of it. Debbie hasn't. Think of that ridiculous story about my father's false teeth.'

'I must say I did find that one convincing. And it's certainly a lot more convincing than some stories that other juries have believed.'

Cordelia raised her eyebrows, but she did not otherwise

question Trish's capabilities or experience.

'So you yourself never doubted that she'd deliberately murdered him?'

Cordelia didn't bother to answer. The scorn in her face was enough, and she knew it.

'Not even at three in the morning when you can't sleep? Have you never, ever, wondered whether perhaps your mother's confession was real?'

'Never. Not even in my darkest moments.' Cordelia shivered artistically, even though there was no wind to move the hot air over their skin. 'And there have been plenty of them.'

'I'm sure.'

'My mother was incapable of killing my father. Physically incapable, emotionally incapable, and in any case barred by her faith. She took her religion with total seriousness, however much it cost her. Is that something you can understand, Ms Maguire?'

There was so much aggression in the last question that Trish decided to answer. 'I was brought up a Protestant myself, and in any case lapsed a long time ago, but I have enough respect for people who haven't to take their beliefs seriously.'

'Lucky you.' Cordelia leaned back against the squidgy cushions in her chair. 'You must accept that the confession was made to protect Debbie. You see, even my mother, who adored her, knew she'd done it.'

'How can you be sure?'

'Because she told me, just before she died.'

'Does anyone else know that?'

'No. She begged me never to tell anyone. She lay in that hospital bed, looking like death, and all she could think about was protecting Debbie.'

'And telling you the truth about her own confession,' Trish

said, thinking, The poor woman, trying to do right by her two warring daughters, dying in the knowledge that they hated each other.

'Did she ask you to look after Deb?' she asked gently, and watched Cordelia's face pale under the makeup. She didn't speak.

'Is that why you were prepared to talk to me today?' Trish tried but failed to ignore the difference between Cordelia, sitting so elegantly in her glorious miniature garden, and Deb, miserable and stubbornly fighting her fear in the smelly, noisy prison visiting room.

'We were close once. When we were children. I always fought her battles, defended her against anyone who was . . . oh, impatient with her slowness, or bullied her. That was my role.'

Trish thought there ought to have been a speech bubble coming out between Cordelia's smooth lips, saying, 'Wasn't I generous?'

'And then she kicked me in the teeth. Don't get me wrong, I don't hate her now. I can't forgive her, but I don't hate her any more.'

Trish nodded and waited for more. Cordelia recovered her cool and sat in passive elegance, giving nothing more away.

'What went wrong between you?' Trish asked, as the silence became too oppressive for her. 'It wasn't just your father's death, was it? It sounds as though it started before that.'

'Of course it did. It started when she set out to wreck my relationship with him.' Cordelia's voice had a hiss in it. 'She never took the trouble to understand him and she hated the fact that I could.'

'That doesn't seem fair, but it does sound as though he made life hard for her.'

'It didn't have to be like that,' Cordelia burst out, sounding and looking a lot less smooth. 'That's what she wouldn't face. She could have had just as good a relationship with him if she'd tried a bit harder. But she just couldn't be bothered. She preferred to put her energies into trying to poison my relationship with him – and with my mother. And when she saw she couldn't do that, she killed him.'

'She must have been very unhappy,' Trish said, feeling as though she'd been dumped in the middle of a minefield without a map.

'I can't bear it when people use that as an excuse.' Cordelia's voice was rock steady and her eyes had hardened to match. 'So dog-in-the-manger: "I can't be happy, so I'm going to make damn sure no one else is."'

'Perhaps . . .' Trish was thinking as she spoke '. . . it has more to do with having to struggle so hard to deal with their own misery that they just can't take on anyone else's. Or maybe even see it.'

'No. It's lack of empathy. Debbie had absolutely none. She couldn't believe anyone else might suffer. It never occurred to her that my father and I might not be trying to do her down, might be unhappy because of what she was doing to *us*.'

'She knew about your father's pain.' Trish couldn't help the quick protest. 'That was what sent her to the doctor and caused all the trouble with him.'

Cordelia's eyes flashed. 'She wasn't sympathetic. She was angry because it made him difficult to deal with.' The scorn in her voice ripped into Trish. 'I'd seen her yelling at him when he was in so much pain that he could hardly breathe, let alone eat or sleep. She had a temper like you've never seen.'

'D'you think—?'

Cordelia had too much to say to wait for the question. The words were bursting out of her now: 'For Christ's sake! Half his medical problems were caused by the agitation Deb aroused in him. They were always worse when she was there.'

'I don't understand.'

'A lot of his ailments – the ulcer, the angioneurotic oedema, the anxiety – were stress-related,' Cordelia said more quietly, 'and, by God, Deb knew how to generate stress.' Once again she shivered, huddling her body into her arms as though she was cold. She couldn't have been. In spite of the shade and the fountain, the little courtyard was like an oven. 'Have you seen her?' she demanded abruptly.

'Yes.'

'How is she?'

Trish tried to decode the intention behind the question. 'How do you expect?'

Something attracted Cordelia's attention in the flower-bed beside her chair. She was looking down at it, her face turned almost completely away from her visitor. She picked a small spider off one of the plants, winding its fragile silk thread around her finger and tugging. Then she squashed the minute creature between her finger and thumb and scraped the resulting mess from her skin with a lemon-balm leaf. The sweetly spicy citrus smell was so strong that it reached Trish, who was sitting at least four feet away.

'You know, my only consolation is that I managed to phone just before she did it. He didn't die entirely un-comforted, but . . .'

Trish saw that there was a line of liquid hovering on the edge of Cordelia's lower lids. It dried in a moment.

'I have to go out now,' she said, getting to her feet. 'If you've got any more questions, the best thing would be to write to me. OK?' She led the way towards her front door. Trish had to follow. 'You know,' Cordelia said, pausing with her hand on the latch, 'I can't forgive her, but we are sisters. One day I might be able to see her again. But not yet.'

Trish didn't answer. She couldn't imagine Deb's reacting well to a request for a visiting order from Cordelia.

'So she still hates me?'

'I can't imagine it's easy to forgive people whose evidence puts you in prison for life, can you?'

'It's a lot harder to forgive someone who's killed your father.' Barbed wire couldn't have been sharper than Cordelia's voice. 'Deb will get out one day, even though she hasn't got Malcolm to fight for her any more. I'll never have my father back.'

Back in Southwark, Trish wandered about the enormous space of her warehouse flat, trying to shed the feelings Cordelia had aroused in her and fit herself back into her own serenely happy life. Her family hadn't been perfect by any means, but compared with Deb's, it wasn't a bad substitute.

The phone rang. It was Anna, of course, unrepentant and nagging for yet another update. Trish gave her a quick résumé of the last meeting, adding, 'So, even if Cordelia agreed, I don't think it would be a good idea to get her on the screen. She's utterly convinced Deb did it. And I think she might have the same effect on the audience as she did on the jury.' I wonder, Trish thought, if an ability to tell yourself stories so vivid you have to believe in them is a family trait?

'D'you think she could have killed her father, planted evidence to incriminate Deb, and then had Malcolm Chaze shot because she was afraid he'd turn up the truth?'

'Does it seem likely to you, Anna?' Trish didn't have the patience to take idiotic suggestions seriously.

'She could have driven down there that night after her visitor left,' Anna said, with dignity. 'I've been checking her out ever since she refused to see me. I thought if I could get her to agree to be interviewed on camera, I could get the presenter to point that out and see how she behaved. At the very least it would make her angry and that would have to help Deb.'

'You could shoot yourself in the foot,' Trish said, recognising the biting anxiety behind Anna's determined strength. 'I think you'd do better to see if Adam has any photographs of Deb and Cordelia in childhood. You know, the sort of thing most families have – the two girls fighting over a toy, or hugging each other, something like that. You could get a montage going for the beginning of the film, showing the little darlings as happy sisters, then as angry ones, then – if any – as violent ones. You could have a voiceover quoting some of Cordelia's evidence, then another with what the Blakemores have said about Deb's kindness.'

'It could make a good intro. Yes. You might have a second career here, Trish.'

I'd rather keep my own, thanks, she thought. At least I don't have a bank telling me what I can and can't do. 'And I need those medical details, Anna. Like yesterday.'

'They're coming. They're coming. They won't be long now,' Anna said, in a rush. 'I'm calling in almost the last of my favours. There's the bell. Got to go. Sorry. Goodbye.'

Half an hour later, Trish was standing in her kitchen, stirring a complicated sauce for the steak she was planning to grill for George, and rereading everything that had been said at the trial itself about old Mr Whatlam's medical condition. The two activities did not sit well together and she was beginning to feel sick. She wished she knew more about old age and its ills and the best way of dealing with them.

Deb's diatribe about the hopelessness of Dr Foscutt's treatment of her parents had definitely been sincere, but Trish couldn't work out from the details of the examination and cross-examination propped up against the Magimix whether it had been justified or not.

There did seem to have been an inordinate number of things wrong with the old man: gout, migraine, prostate, depression, the ulcer and the angioneurotic oedema that had been so bad during Deb's visit, as well as an infinity of scrapes and bruises. He didn't heal well, it seemed, and he'd been forever banging himself or breaking his wrist or his fingers.

There was the sound of heavy feet clumping up the iron staircase outside the flat. George, she thought in satisfaction. She could have let him in, but she liked hearing him unlock the door with the keys she'd given him as soon as she'd realised he cared as much as she did. Such a little thing, but it added up with a whole raft of others into a safety of familiar pleasures.

But the bell rang. So, not George, she thought, as she turned off the heat altogether and went to the door.

There was a spyhole, which she hardly ever bothered with, but tonight she did look through it. Standing in front of her was an enormously tall man in motorcycle leathers with a helmet on his head. He had a thin brown package in his hands on top of a clipboard. He was wearing black leather gloves.

Trish was sweating and her heart was walloping at her ribs, much faster than usual, but her mind was still working. Thank God. She told herself grimly to be proud of it. She looked as carefully as she could with her restricted field of vision, but she could see no gun. The messenger's leathers looked far too tight to be concealing anything. And his bike with its capacious panniers was way down in the street. So perhaps the package was going to be a bomb. Or perhaps, she told herself, he's a bike messenger. He rang again, then thumped his gloved fist on the heavy door.

As her vision cleared, she saw that the package was only an A4 brown envelope, not particularly thick. She put the door on the chain and opened it.

'Yes.'

'Maguire? Package.'

She looked at it through the narrow gap, staring at the flap.

There didn't seem to be any wires. The envelope was addressed in neat handwriting she didn't know. 'Who's it from?' she asked, and was irritated to hear her voice high and trembling.

His voice boomed out from his all-embracing helmet, 'Pick-up address was 14 Fratchet Mews, Holland Park.'

Cordelia Whatlam's house. He thrust his clipboard through the gap, asking for a signature and her name in caps at the side. She scrawled her name, took the envelope and quickly banged the door shut.

She could hear his feet hitting each step of the iron staircase and checked through the kitchen window. He kicked the struts holding up his bike and roared off out of her sight. She felt all over the envelope, running her fingers up and down each part. There were no wires. A paperclip or two, and paper, but that was all.

Oh, stop being paranoid, she told herself, and ripped open the flap. Nothing blew up. All she found was a sheaf of handwritten letters with a typed note paperclipped to the top one:

Ms Maguire, you seemed so sure of my sister's innocence that I thought you might be interested in these letters. Deb wrote most of them during her time on bail; but there are a couple from the prison. I could see she's charmed you. She can be very charming. These will show you the kind of woman she is.

I'm sorry I was unhelpful, but, as I told first Anna Grayling and then Malcolm, I know the jury reached the right verdict and I am not prepared to have anything to do with the film. I saw you today because I've been told you're sensible and informed. I thought you might be able to knock this nonsense on the head once and for all.

I hope I was right. We're not likely to meet again, but, as

I say, if there is anything you have to ask me, please do it in writing. You may have to wait for an answer because I'm off to the Far East on a buying trip next week and I won't be around for some time.

Yours, Cordelia Whatlam

Trish thought she'd had enough of them all for the day. George would soon be home and she'd promised him a good dinner. She put Cordelia's envelope on her desk with the trial transcript, unchained the door, and went back to her pots and pans.

She was still at the hob, dealing with the last stages of the sauce, when she heard George letting himself in. His arms came round her as she stirred her pan and she leaned back, turning up her face. He did his best to kiss her.

'If I were a contortionist or a giraffe, I'd do this better,' he said.

Trish laughed and turned within the circle of his arms so that she could kiss him properly. She wasn't wearing much, having already had her shower, and the thought of food suddenly seemed comparatively uninteresting.

'Are you very hungry?' she murmured. He stroked her left eyebrow, then her nose, and at last her lips, with one large finger. He tasted salty.

'No,' he said slowly, pulling out the sound. He kissed her again and slid his hands up under her T-shirt. 'I don't know that I am.'

Trish only just remembered to turn off the heat under the sauce.

# Chapter 17

'I think the boss is losing it, Sarge.'

Caroline Lyalt looked up from her list of Malcolm Chaze's past girlfriends – a lot longer than it should have been in her opinion – and considered DC Owler. He was wearing tight black jeans and a round-necked black T-shirt under a loose grey linen jacket. His pretty face under the short hair looked worried rather than gleeful, so she decided not to ignore the comment.

'Why?'

'He savaged Chaze's widow yesterday on no evidence except that she wasn't as distraught as he thought she should be, and he's had me and three others ransacking her papers and cross-examining her husband's secretary about her ever since. He has no reason to suspect her. It's a waste of time and money.'

'You know as well as I do, Steve, that most murders are domestic.' God, you can sound sententious, she told herself.

'Not when they're contract killings, like this one. We should be looking in his past for—'

'She's a sophisticated woman with a lot of money and she's in a ruthless business. It's a legitimate line of inquiry, Steve.'

'Maybe, but not to this extent. I think the boss is—'

'Losing it. You said.' Caroline thought of the way Femur had changed as Jess fed and petted him in their big kitchen. 'But he's not. And if you're looking for the moment to jump ship and hitch a better ride, don't. You owe that man.'

'Christ, Sarge, I know that. But he's crashing the budgets for nothing. Just because he hates women, I mean, women who . . .'

Caroline looked at him and knew what he was thinking and why he was scowling. If he'd been less sure of himself, he'd have been blushing. Well, she wasn't going to help him. If he wanted to go on working at AMIP he had to get used to the fact that she was gay.

'He rescued you from a minor, thoroughly dirty local nick,' she said coldly, 'where you'd have eked out your days on burglary and mugging, and he got you into AMIP. You ought to remember where your loyalties lie.'

'Why d'you dislike me so much?' he asked suddenly, hooking a chair towards him with one foot and sitting down with his arms crossed along the back.

'I don't.' She smiled at him, carefully keeping her gaze fixed on his hairline so she didn't have to meet his eyes. 'But I don't trust you.'

In the days when she was still a constable and had to pretend not to notice that the boss's favourite sergeant didn't like her – or the way the boss would sometimes consult her and not the sergeant – she used to tell herself that when it was her turn to feel someone treading on her tail she'd behave better. She hoped she was, but there was no way she was shutting her eyes to disloyalty like this.

'Sarge . . .'

'I can see you watching him these days, waiting for the moment when he's not useful to you any more.'

Owler didn't comment. He moved, though, as if he was uncomfortable.

'I know you don't want to be tied to a has-been,' Caroline went on. 'No one does, and you're an ambitious little thing. I've always known that.'

His alluring face twisted again. He'd registered the insult all right. Good. She'd meant him to.

She thought of what she'd recognised in the kitchen last night: that Femur was lonely and deeply troubled about something in a way she'd never seen before. But she wasn't going to ask questions. When he was ready to talk, he'd talk. Until then she'd support him as well as she could. One or two of her fans in the Job had taken her out for a drink recently and warned her to move on, not to let herself get tainted by that case and her association with Femur. But she owed him. He'd given her a leg up in the Force and he'd given her a kind of stability, too. In the days when life with Jess had been hard, he'd always been there, unobtrusively, noticing when she was pissed off or miserable and sorting her out.

If he really was cracking up, she'd shield him until the case was done, then take him back for another of Jess's suppers and show him that it was time to go before he buggered up what was left of his reputation. Jess would help. He'd come to like her, too, and he was easier with the pair of them than any other straight man of his generation she'd come across so far.

Caroline saw Owler looking at her in gratification and realised she must be smiling. Dream on, sunshine, she said in her head. Aloud, she asked him what he'd found among Laura Chaze's papers.

'Fuck all, Sarge. Like I knew we would.'

'Did you get anything from the secretary?'

'Only confirmation of the marital rows. She was hacked off by his affairs. He thought she ought to put up with them, like his mates' wives did. And she was well pissed off by his campaign to get Deborah Gibbert out of prison.'

Caroline felt like sighing. Trish Maguire's dark intense face floated into her mind, saying, 'I told you so.'

'Tell me more,' she said.

Owler repeated everything Malcolm Chaze's secretary had said about the last row her boss had had with his wife. Caroline didn't think there was much there.

'Anything else?'

'Only that Mrs C got even more vicious after the girl she'd never seen before came to the house a few weeks back.'

'Girl? What girl? And why didn't you tell me that before?'

'I was coming to it. Give me time.' He was all injured innocence, the little rat.

It crossed Caroline's mind that he might be stacking up some private stores of information to feed to one of the other incident rooms, hoping to show up her and the boss. Well, if that was his nasty little plan, he'd find himself neck deep in shit before she'd let it happen.

'What's her name?'

'The secretary said she thought Kate, but she couldn't hear much. She didn't open the door, see; she was working in the little study by the front door – they call it the boot room – inputting some document into his laptop because the scanner was on the blink. She heard the bell ring. Laura Chaze yelled out, "I'm busy, Malcolm, answer that." "Must I?" he yelled back.'

'All this verbatim reporting, Constable, I'm impressed. But are you sure it's accurate?'

He pulled out his notebook and flipped it open with one hand, like a Georgette Heyer hero with his snuff-box. Yeah, yeah, she thought, clever clogs.

Jess had introduced her to the books and she liked them because they made her laugh; touched her sometimes, too. But now she kept her face stern. She wasn't going to give Owler any more encouragement.

'It's an accurate record of what I was told, Sarge. I can't be sure it's what my informant heard, but it's what she told me.'

'Good point.' He wasn't stupid. He might even turn into a

useful officer one day, when he'd been a bit bruised by life and learned what hurts and why and what it's worth taking on the chin.

'Then she heard his steps, the door opening, his voice all cold saying, "Yes?", then a breathless quite young girl's voice, saying, "I'm Kate." Then there was a long pause till he said, "You'd better come in." They went into the drawing room, past the office, and Sally – the secretary – said she caught a glimpse of a tall, thin, dark-haired girl. Lots of hair, drawn back in a slide at the back of her head: old-fashioned, she said. About five minutes later, Chaze breezed in and told her she'd done enough and ought to go home, since it was a Saturday. She never saw the girl again.'

Caroline was glad he'd seen fit to give her the full story, but she was angry all the same that he'd kept it so long. 'And what construction did you put on all that?' He just shrugged. 'You didn't have a shot at working out who she could be?' Caroline did give him a smile this time, wanting to soften him up. 'That's unlike you, Steve.'

'A constituent? A relation? I didn't think it was that important. She's hardly going to have been a major drug-dealer – or even a runner for one. They don't come girl-shaped with well-spoken voices and old-fashioned hair. At least, not in my experience they don't.'

'Probably not.' Caroline went on smiling blandly at him, pushing the irritation down well below anything Owler would be able to see. 'Well done. I'm not sure how much further it'll take us, but you've done good. Thanks. Now, more important, how are Incident Room One doing with the gun dealers?'

'I don't know yet. I've—'

'They've been sending through reports every day. Haven't you bothered to read them?'

'Not yet. The boss made me—'

'Well, get on with it, then. That's hard information we need out there. Right up your street.'

'But the shooters and the snouts don't come under our brief,' he said, betraying his resentment. So maybe it wasn't just Femur's dwindling reputation that was whittling away at his loyalty, but envy of the other team's more interesting work. If so, he wasn't alone in that.

'No, but the more we know, the more we can use as a lever when we do find a suspect. Which we might well do. Get on with it. Check the facts, find the gaps, make a few lists. Man's work, Steve. Like trainspotting.'

The look in his narrow dark eyes was poisonous, but at the door he turned back and gave her a bit of smile back. 'You're right, Sarge. Sorry.'

She nodded. So maybe the boss was on to something after all when he claimed that Steve Owler was a good, honest, intelligent copper in the making. And maybe she was a jealous cow, too, not wanting to lose her status as Femur's most cherished body on the team.

When Owler had gone, Caroline checked the time and put in a call to Trish Maguire's chambers. Her clerk said she was in a con but that he'd get her to call the incident room as soon as she was free.

Caroline spent the intervening twenty minutes toothcombing the lists of all known girlfriends and mistresses of Malcolm Chaze, from his schooldays until his death, for criminal records. She grinned privately. Jess always got cross when she used the expression, banging on about how it was a fine-toothed comb you were supposed to use to pick nits, and that no one combs their teeth, but Caroline used it like most of her colleagues. You had to talk in the language of your world, even if it wasn't right. Otherwise you were just being a snotty cow and getting up people's noses.

Several of Chaze's old squeezes had motoring offences

recorded against them; a few, minor convictions for possession of soft drugs; one, with possession with intent to supply. But there was no one with any real drug habit that Caroline could find, at least not one who had come to the attention of the police. Her next set of checks would be against suicides and accidental deaths. That was going to take a lot longer.

She was still on the B suicides when Trish Maguire phoned back.

'What a surprise, Sergeant Lyalt,' she said, in her deep, classy voice, which always made Caroline think of Jess. That was probably why she'd liked Maguire from the start, and why she trusted her. She'd better watch that: an officer like her couldn't go round trusting a brief. And just because Maguire sounded like Jess, that didn't make her the same kind of person at all.

'What can I do for you?'

'You knew Malcolm Chaze quite well,' Caroline said. 'Can you put a surname to a young, probably teenage, girl with long dark hair, who was visiting him a short while before the killing? He called her Kate.'

'Why have you come to me? You must be talking to his wife and staff. They could tell you straight away.'

Such suspicion, Caroline thought, as she said aloud, 'The widow's had enough to take right now, and the last time I talked to the secretary she howled so much I couldn't get anything out of her. Do you know who this Kate is?'

'May I ask how you've come across her?'

'So you do know. Great.'

'I have an idea, but that's all it is. How does she fit in to your inquiries?'

'She probably doesn't, but we've heard that relations between the Chazes deteriorated after her visit. We have to find out why. If you won't help, you won't. We'll go crashing about in our size tens and hope we don't hurt too many innocent people.'

There was silence down the phone. Caroline waited to be told that Maguire wasn't susceptible to that sort of black-mail. But eventually she said, 'The person who springs to mind is Deborah Gibbert's eldest child, Kate. She fits the description.'

Facts and inferences clicked into place in Caroline's brain. She could almost hear the satisfying clunk.

'And Chaze and Deborah Gibbert were once lovers. And you overheard Mrs Chaze saying she could put up with girlfriends but drew the line at "steps", didn't you?'

'Yes.'

'Could she have been talking about stepchildren?'

'It's possible.' Trish didn't sound too happy about it. 'Is that all, Sergeant Lyalt? I'm pretty busy here.'

There was a sound of shuffling papers, as though Maguire was determined to prove her desk was covered with work.

'That's all for the moment. Thanks. I'll be in touch.'

Caroline put down the phone and looked up to see Femur standing in front of her desk.

'I need a drink, Cally.'

'OK.' Without a protest, she locked away her lists in the drawer of the borrowed desk. 'There's a nice little pub just round the corner. Shall we go?'

'How do you know Pimlico so well, Sergeant?'

He was smiling again in almost the old way; his eyes were still hurt, but the rest of him was looking better.

'Jess has friends who live here. We sometimes go with them to this pub and drink The Macallan.'

'Sounds good to me. I want . . . I need . . . Can I talk to you about Sue?'

Caroline got up from the desk and put her hand on his shoulder. Odd how you could feel like the mother of a man old enough to be your dad. 'Let's wait till we've a Scotch in our hands, Guv. That'll make it easier for us both.'

She put out the lights, sent him off ahead and had a quick word with the officers who were still at work. She delivered the orders as though transmitting them from Femur, then said she'd be back in an hour. They showed no signs of resenting – or suspecting – the orders.

Her only other pause on the way to the conversation she didn't much want to have was at the most private of the available phones.

'Jess?' she said, as soon as they were connected. 'Sorry about dinner, but I've got to work.'

'OK,' said Jess. 'Nothing'll spoil. It's all cold. I'll have mine when I get hungry and bung yours in the fridge for when you're free. Don't kill yourself, will you, Angel? Remember, I have a stake in you.'

Caroline sometimes wished Jess wasn't an actor. It was hard to tell whether she was hurt. Or angry.

'Me, too. See you later,' she said, and followed her guv'nor out into the sweaty dusk. The chosen pub had a garden, but it would probably be full to overflowing at this time of day.

Trish put down the phone with added respect for the young sergeant. Almost at once it rang again.

'Dave here. I've had Sprindler's on the line. They're in a state because one of their clients, Deborah Gibbert, needs help and is begging to see you. It's legal aid, and not your area, but apparently you've already been down to see her in an informal way. Can that be true?'

It was a loaded question. Trish knew how jealously Dave guarded his right to allocate his employers' time. 'It's part of the TV work I'm doing for Anna Grayling,' she said, quickly adding, 'nothing to do with chambers. Why should she need a brief in prison?'

'Apparently,' Dave said, his voice leaking acid suspicion and disapproval like a corroded car battery, 'her cell-mate has died of a drugs overdose.'

'Oh, shit. Mandy. But she was getting better. What happened?

'The girl took a huge dose of heroin, which caused her to fall into a coma. She came out of that, but mysteriously did not recover. Now she's died of liver failure. The PM established that it had been caused by an overdose of paracetamol . . .'

'Why didn't they test for that at the beginning?'

'I don't know, do I?' Dave sounded martyred as well as irritable.

'They could have saved her if they had. But presumably one overdosed prostitute-junkie serving a life sentence doesn't merit full toxicological testing. Bastards.'

There was a heavy sigh from Dave.

'Sorry,' Trish said, sounding anything but apologetic. 'You were saying?'

'While it's possible that the heroin could have been cut with paracetamol, they think Deborah Gibbert could have given paracetamol to the young woman when she was high and not noticing what anyone was doing to her.'

'How would Deb have got that much?'

'She's been given a lot recently for headaches. They think she could have been hoarding instead of taking it. You know how they do that, those women in prison: hold the tablets in their mouths as long as someone's looking, then spit them out into a container.'

'Yes,' said Trish sadly. 'But where would she hoard them? Hadn't they had any cell searches?'

'Naturally. But nothing too rigorous until after the heroin-coma. She was something of a trusty, I gather. They've torn the place apart now, of course, but they've found nothing.'

Trish's heart sank. She knew what prison officers could do to a cell when they were frustrated in a search for drugs. She could understand their anger, but it tipped some of them over into the kind of vindictiveness that sickened her. There was no point in asking Dave what they'd done and how much Deb had lost in the way of torn photographs or broken possessions, so she concentrated on the facts of the cell-mate's death.

'But there's no evidence of Deb's involvement?'

'No. But she has a record for doping and killing people after all.'

Trish thought for a few moments. 'Look, Dave, I can't get involved now, if I'm to go on with this TV lark, and it's not my field. She needs a solicitor after all, not counsel at this stage. Tell Sprindler's to send someone down with a holding brief to make sure Deb doesn't incriminate herself now and we'll try to work out something better in the morning.'

'You won't, Ms Maguire. You're due in court at ten.'

'Yes, Dave,' she said meekly. As soon as she'd got him off the line, she phoned Anna to warn her of the latest twist in Deb's story, phoned George to say she'd be back late in Southwark, and phoned her father to make sure he was all right and didn't need her that evening. Sure of them all, she got back to work for tomorrow's case. Not since her first year at the Bar had she ever gone into court underprepared. The memory of one humiliating fiasco would live with her always.

It wasn't till she left chambers a couple of hours later that she realised how hot it still was. The dank, dark old buildings of the Temple didn't overheat until much later in the summer. No direct sunlight reached her room, only a little grey light from a dingy brick-lined well. Outside, the sun had sunk behind the buildings, but there was still plenty of heat left to rise from the pavements and hover against her face. She contemplated walking home, then saw a taxi with its light on.

It was weakness that tempted her to hail it, but she was tired enough to give in.

George greeted her with a long, tall spritzer, almost pushed her into a recumbent position on her favourite sofa. She kicked off her shoes and wondered if she had the energy to wriggle out of her tights, too. But she didn't. He said something about finishing off the dinner as Trish let her head slide back against the purple cushion and felt its softness cradling the ache at the back of her skull. His voice burbled on, telling her the news of his day and who he'd spoken to, and how his current cases were going.

She was listening, probably she could even have reproduced some of his news if she'd been challenged, but it was wonderfully peaceful to let it flow over her without having to concentrate. Her eyes closed. George's voice had much the same effect as the pumping machines in the intensive care unit: rhythmic, safe, strong, comforting. He was in charge; she could let go.

She came to not much more than an hour later to see him grinning at her over the top of the *Evening Standard*.

'Hi, there.'

'Hi, yourself,' she said, blinking but not moving anything else. Then she ran her tongue over her dry lips. 'Ugh.'

'I took your drink away when it looked as though you might soak your front. Are you hungry?'

She thought about it, blinked, then nodded. 'Um. Maybe.'

'Good. Because there's a nice pair of artichokes ready with a new sauce. And it's quarter past ten. If you don't eat now, you'll never do it. And you haven't any weight to spare.'

Trish was on her feet by then, bending over him to kiss him in gratitude for the tolerance and the cookery and the fact that he was there.

Caroline was so weary she was almost crawling by the time

she reached her own sanctuary. Jess was in bed and asleep, but she'd left a pretty plate of cheese-and-asparagus quiche and salad in the fridge with a note on it, saying, 'Eat me.'

Caroline ripped off the clingfilm and ate with her fingers, stuffing in the food to get it down fast enough to deal with her hunger. Then she had a quick shower and slid into bed, her gut already aching with indigestion.

Jess half woke and stretched out a hand. When it met Caroline's shoulder, Jess smiled in her sleep and moved a little closer. Caroline lay in the warm dark, with her legs stuck out at the side of the duvet and tried to calm down enough to sleep.

All the figures in the case danced on the inside of her eyelids like a nursery frieze. But each one carried the weight of her need to help Bill Femur. He'd been mashed up by the powers-that-be over the last case; he'd been pulverised by Sue's departure; and Caroline thought he could be on the edge of a major breakdown.

Somehow she had to keep Steve Owler corralled; or at least out of the way so that he couldn't see how near the edge the boss had got. And, of course, she had to find a lead to Malcolm Chaze's killer – or at least the person who'd paid the killer. She didn't like the idea of people supplying death by mail order, but it was the orderer who deserved the biggest punishment, not the supplier. Like it was the drug-dealers they ought to go after, not the consumers. And the punters, not the prostitutes. At least that's what she thought.

Forms filled her vision. She was trying to work out the answer to one of the questions, peering at the box that needed a tick. Or was it a cross? She couldn't see properly.

She flopped over, sticking her legs further out of the duvet. Catching sight of the clock, she realised she must have been asleep for hours.

Deborah Gibbert woke again and wondered how many

officers had flicked open the spyhole to watch her as she slept. She felt their gloating like a layer of grease all over her, and she hated them. The resentful dread she'd felt for her father was like a drift of chiffon compared to this all-covering goo. If she'd understood what it was like to hate when she'd been interrogated after his death, she'd have been able to convince the whole bloody world she wasn't guilty.

Her back was agony from the disgusting, pavement-like mattress underneath her. The cell stank in the unmoving air. Stress always went for her tummy and she'd been up and down with the runs as though she'd eaten a dodgy Egyptian meatball like the one that had ruined a long-awaited trip up the Nile with Adam the year before Millie was born.

She thought of bloody Cordelia the last time she'd seen her outside court. Cordelia would probably be sitting in her shady courtyard sipping some pink champagne and eating caviare.

She had to get out of here. With Mandy dead and the screws all convinced she'd been murdered, life wasn't going to be endurable. If the film didn't work, she could always . . .

But Kate needed her. She couldn't put her head in a plastic bag while Kate was still so vulnerable.

Deb had tried to phone her back after their row, but something had been wrong with the line and she hadn't got through. There were only a couple of units left on her phonecard after the call to Sprindler's.

She tried to turn over, but the mattress was even worse agony on her front. It squashed her breasts flat and pushed her back out of line. Her breasts were nearly as sore as when she'd first tried to feed Kate. Oh, Kate.

Her hard little head, covered in silky black hair, had pressed against Deb's chest and her urgent gums had bitten hard into the already sore nipples. It had been agony, but worth it. There was no one in Deb's whole life she'd ever loved as much as Kate.

No wonder bloody Cordelia was jealous. She'd always been jealous of everything. Jealous of their mother's preference, jealous of Malcolm, jealous of the babies, jealous even of Adam, whom she'd professed to despise.

That had always been her favourite tactic. If Deb had something Cordelia couldn't have, she'd affect contempt, to make it seem worthless. And for years Deb had been a sucker for that and believed she and everything she liked and everyone she cared about was crap. God, she was a fool. And Cordelia was a bitch!

Standing in the dock, listening to Cordelia's hate, had been like standing under a river of tar that stuck to everything it touched, ruining it. Deb's only consolation now was that their mother hadn't been alive to hear any of it. She'd always done her best to protect Deb, but it had probably only made Cordelia's hate worse.

An eye was looking through the door again, a gloating, pleased eye that promised more humiliation, more fear to come.

Adam heard Kate crying and looked at his clock. It was four in the morning. He knew he ought to get up to ask what was wrong. He lay there, listening to the sobs, half stifled in a pillow, trying to work out whether she'd meant to wake him. If she hadn't, going into her room would be an intrusion.

He hoped she wasn't going to wake the younger ones. He'd had an awful time with Marcus, who'd been struggling with his maths prep and hadn't been able to bear to ask for help. Adam had tried unobtrusively to offer advice, and been blitzed with a stream of contempt from his son. It shouldn't have hurt, that sort of thing, but it had. Marcus's last fling had been the worst bit: 'If you'd looked after Mummy properly, she'd be here now. It's your fault.'

At that point, Louis had looked up from his books, his big

blue eyes flooded with tears. Between the two of them, trying to soothe Louis's fears and Marcus's inexpressible anxieties, reassure them both in their different languages that one day Deb would be back with them, Adam had almost lost it. He'd been tempted to yell at them that he had needs, too, that he couldn't always be calm and kind and strong. Luckily he'd just managed to hold on, but he wouldn't if he had to deal with Kate as well. She might need him, but he hadn't got anything left to give her.

He strained to hear what was going on and was rewarded with silence. She must have got over it then, whatever it was. Perhaps it was a boyfriend or a spat at school. Adam turned over and tried to ignore the space on the other side of the bed. One day he might sleep well again. One day.

# Chapter 18

Trish's head was buzzing from a difficult conference. Her day in court had gone well, but the two clients who'd come to see her in chambers afterwards had been in such anguish that she couldn't now think of anything else. They wanted the court to force their local health authority to pay for experimental treatment for their daughter, whose leukaemia had just been pronounced incurable.

Tonight it seemed to Trish as though she would never get away from miserable families. If they were not tormenting each other, they were bludgeoned by fate or else by impersonal agencies, whose priorities could never match theirs. For the health authorities, there would always be at least fifty equally deserving cases to be balanced against each other.

She remembered the way Anna had involved her in Deb Gibbert's case in the beginning. 'Families being what always get you going,' Anna had said. Or something like that. But didn't they worry everyone? The hurt, the quite unnecessary hurt that washed about in the unhappy ones, seemed more important than anything else sometimes. Everything else came from it, after all; certainly most of the crime she'd ever come across.

This was the kind of evening when Trish needed George, but he was off on another frolic of his own, so she'd have to get herself back together again – and get her own supper. Do me good, she thought, if I've got the energy to eat anything anyway.

She'd probably end up washing off the sweaty grime under the shower and taking a huge glass of wine to bed, to fall asleep watching a light-hearted video. She knew she shouldn't have been quite so tired, but she'd been working on her papers most nights until well after midnight, and she was still angry with Anna.

Trish reached her iron staircase and put her hand on the banister. Suddenly the fifty steps up to her eyrie seemed like Everest. She hauled up one foot and put it on the bottom step. The metal reverberated under her heavy tread. She hadn't been this knackered for years. So much for the summer meaning less work.

'Hello?' said a young, vaguely familiar voice, which sounded very scared.

Trish looked upwards towards her front door. A figure was uncoiling itself in the dusk. Kate Gibbert.

'I say, are you all right?' Kate asked, staring down in the dark.

'A bit tired.' Trish gathered her forces and achieved a smile. 'I'm sorry I wasn't here when you came, Kate. How are you?'

'Fine. I'm really sorry to hang about, but I had to talk to you. And this is the only address I had. I tried to phone your mobile, but it wasn't taking calls. And I . . . I haven't any money to go anywhere else.'

'How long have you been here?' Trish had forgotten how tired she was and had almost reached the top of the steps.

'Since five thirty. I sort of thought you'd be out of work by then. I didn't realise.'

'You've been here for five hours? Kate, my dear child, I'm so sorry. Come on in.'

Trish flicked on the lights and rushed to find wine and biscuits to put into Kate before she even tried to think what real food there might be to cook. With a tin of Roka cheese biscuits under her arm and the bottle in one hand, two glasses and a corkscrew in the other, she came back to see that Kate was in tears.

Trish put down her load and offered a hug. Kate tried to relax into it, but they couldn't get it right. Trish withdrew, wishing George was with her. He'd be just the man to deal with this. Trying to think what he would have done, Trish persuaded Kate to sit down. She found a box of Kleenex and dumped it on the black sofa, poured the wine and thrust a brimming glass at her guest.

'Oh, thanks. I'm sorry.'

'Don't worry about it. You've been having an awful time, I know.' Trish sipped some of her own wine, letting it trickle slowly over the back of her tongue and down her dry throat. 'In any case, anyone would be in a state having had to sit out there on their own for so long, not knowing if I was ever coming. What did you want me for?'

'I needed to talk. I couldn't . . . I can't tell my father.'

'What?'

'It hurts him if I talk about my – my real father.' Kate looked shyly over the top of her wine-glass. 'I don't know if you knew, but my real father was the man who's just been shot.'

'Malcolm Chaze. Yes, in fact, I did know. I recognised the likeness.' Trish smiled. 'It's not hard to spot when you know what to look for. I'm so sorry he's dead. It must make an already difficult life hard to bear at times.'

Kate put down her glass and rubbed a screwed-up Kleenex over both eyes, sniffing.

'It seems so unfair. You see, I'd only just met him. And it was . . . He was amazing. Dad, my ordinary father, told me the truth when Mum went to prison, but I didn't think I'd need him . . . you know, Malcolm.' She smiled shyly. 'Then, one weekend, after I'd heard he was going to work with Anna Grayling to get Mum out, I somehow thought I'd better meet him. I just wanted to talk. That was all.'

'I know you went to his house.'

Kate looked astonished, her mouth opening and shutting like a hungry carp's as she tried to ask a question. All the shyness had gone and her eyes were angry.

'We've all been asking a lot of questions of a lot of people since he was shot,' Trish said gently. 'We've had to. I heard that you'd been round to Pimlico.'

'Sorry. I didn't think.'

'I never had a chance to talk to him about you. Did you like him? Was he kind to you?'

Kate nodded, her eyes leaking again. She gulped some wine to try to get control but only made herself choke. 'He was wonderful. He said he'd often wanted to find me, get to know me, but didn't think it would be fair to unsettle me. He didn't know if I knew about him, you see. He said he'd been watching me from a distance.' Kate's face was full of the kind of shaky pride Trish had felt when Paddy had first come round in front of her in the intensive care unit. 'He said he'd found it hard to wait, but he hadn't wanted to throw me off my stroke till after my exams next year.'

So he charmed you, too. 'And did you ever see him again?'

Kate shook her head. But her eyes warned Trish there was more to come.

'Or talk to him?'

'Once or twice.'

'When?'

'Once was the night it happened.' Kate raised her head. Her long straight hair flicked itself across her face as she moved, and she pushed it away impatiently. 'The A-level English group came up to London to the National Theatre that night. It was the last week of term.'

Her voice rose towards the end of the sentence, as though to make sure Trish knew what she was talking about. Trish nodded.

Kate was chewing her lip and looking as though someone was poking a hot wire into the soles of her feet. 'And I phoned him,' she said. 'In the interval. There was a phone near the loos, you see. I thought he might tell me how his campaign for Mum was going.'

'That seems fair,' Trish said encouragingly when Kate brushed a finger over her eyes. She shook her head again.

'It was only an excuse. I was being selfish. I wanted to talk to him for me. Not her.'

'Did you get through to him?'

'Yes.' Kate was staring straight ahead. The wires still seemed to be being driven up into her feet. Then she shook herself all over and produced a brave smile that didn't convince Trish for a moment. 'We talked for ages, nearly all through the interval, and he was . . . well, lovely, really. He promised he would get Mum out if it was the last thing he did. He said you were being brilliant.'

'Was that exactly what he said?' Trish asked, wondering who else he'd told. Kate nodded, apparently too full of her story to see the significance. 'I don't mean about me, but about your mother?'

'And he said that when that had happened, he and Mum and I would get together and work out how to make up for everything that had gone wrong in the past. Then his doorbell rang. I heard it even down the phone. He said there was a motorbike messenger there. He could see down to the front steps from his study window. He had to go.'

Kate stared at Trish, blank dread in her eyes. 'That must have been when he was shot.'

Trish felt wholly inadequate. She could advise on all sorts of legal and family problems, but she had never yet had to console a girl of this age for such a horror. 'Have you talked to the police about this?' she asked, carefully avoiding any hint of doubt or censure.

'No.' Kate sniffed and rubbed the back of her hand under her nostrils. She remembered the Kleenex and cleaned first her hand and then her face.

'I think maybe you should,' Trish said, as calmly as though she were advising a brisk walk in good weather. 'They need to know everything that happened that night. It's a bit late now, but we could talk to them tomorrow. Look, why don't I make you up a bed in the spare room? You can get some sleep and we'll call them first thing in the morning. Now, does your father – I mean Adam, does he know you're here?'

'No. I left a note saying I was going out.' Kate looked up. 'The little ones are OK, honestly. A friend of mine's sleeping over, so even if Dad was late they couldn't have been alone.'

'That's fine. But he's probably worried. I'll give him a ring now. You drink your wine. It'll help you sleep later. Are you hungry?'

'Not really. But, please?'

'Yes?'

'If he says he wants to talk to me, I– It's so hard. I don't want to have to explain. Not now.'

'Don't worry. I'll say everything that has to be said. You concentrate on getting some rest. I'll be back in a minute with some sheets.'

Trish phoned Adam from her bedroom. As she'd expected, he was jittery with anxiety, talking faster than usual and sounding aggressively demanding. Trish explained her plan for the morning, adding that she'd see Kate into the hands of the police herself, and make sure she got safely to the bus or train that would bring her home.

'I see.' Those two words had come out slowly, leaden. Trish

detected understanding and distress in them, but couldn't be sure whether she was imagining the menace. 'Thank you. D'you know what triggered this flight?'

'No. I haven't wanted to ask too many questions. She's in quite a bad way, but I think she'll be better after she's slept. If there's no improvement tomorrow, I'll take her to my doctor before we talk to the police. He's very good. Now I must go. I'll phone again as soon as there's any news.'

'I need to talk to her. Now.'

'I think, Adam, that it really would be better not. She's very tired, and very emotional. And she feels so guilty for upsetting you. Could you let her off, just for tonight?'

There was a brooding pause.

'So be it,' he said at last. 'Give her my love, if you think that wouldn't upset her too much.'

Trish briefly closed her eyes, but she didn't protest at the sarcasm.

'And tell her I'm not angry with her.'

That was better, she thought. That sounded almost sincere.

'Sure. I'll phone you tomorrow, Adam. Good night.'

With her arms full of bedclothes, Trish made her way down the spiral staircase into the great open living room. Kate was lying back against the sofa cushions. Her eyes were pink and swollen. There was still a lot of wine in her glass.

'I don't really like wine, much,' she said, noticing the direction of Trish's gaze. 'I'm sorry.'

'That's fine. Don't worry about it. It couldn't matter less, and I should have asked anyway. I've got Diet Coke, if that would be any better. Or mineral water. Let me make up the bed and then I'll fetch whichever you'd prefer.'

'I can do the bed. I'm used to it.'

'We'll do it together.' Trish led the way to the spare room. A few minutes later, as they were bending down at either side of the bed, tucking in the bottom sheet, she said, 'Did your real father talk at all about the time when he and your mother were together?'

It wasn't fair to press Kate when she was in such a turmoil, but there might never be another opportunity.

'Yes, a little. He said he'd come to understand that she was the real love of his life, but at the time when they were having their . . . when they were together, he was in so much of a muddle about himself that he hadn't realised that.' Kate looked up, hooking her long straight hair over her shoulder. 'And he said that she never told him about me. Not till much later. He didn't know why not.'

Trish wished she'd been able to talk to Deb herself about all this before she heard Malcolm Chaze's version filtered through whatever censorship he'd applied for Kate's benefit.

'So, I asked her.' Kate was looking older than usual and her voice had taken on a bitterness Trish hadn't heard from her before.

'When?'

'When she phoned me on Friday.' Kate's eyes flooded, and she was a child again. 'Last Friday. We were talking about his death. Dad sends her phonecards every week, you see, and she always phones me on Fridays before school.'

Kate dropped the sheet and stood up, staring at Trish. 'She told me my real father had lied to me. She said she'd told him about me as soon as she'd had the pregnancy test and he'd said she had to have an abortion.'

Trish finished the hospital corner she was tucking under the mattress to give herself time to think. She wasn't sure if she was angrier with Malcolm Chaze or Deb.

'And when she said she couldn't ever kill her baby, he said in that case it was her responsibility. He didn't want to have anything to do with it or her. That's what she told me he'd said. He called me "it".'

'Kate, he didn't know you.' Trish could see she wasn't

helping. She tried again. 'It wasn't you he was talking about, just a responsibility he hadn't expected and didn't know how to cope with. Try not to take it too personally. Your mother wouldn't want you to think like that.'

'But she does. She wants me to be angry with him. She said it was important I didn't go turning him into a hero. That Dad had looked after me and loved me, and that she and I owed him everything. That my real father had been selfish and mixed-up, and although she'd once loved him, she couldn't let me believe in his lies now.'

Trish had huge sympathy for Deb, but this was not the time for such cruel honesty. 'Listen, Kate, your mother is living under enormous stress at the moment, like you. I know she's been very unhappy at your real father's death. Maybe . . .'

'But he wanted me to be aborted. He didn't want me.'

'Your mother wanted you,' Trish said quietly. 'She loves you more than she loves anyone else. When I went to see her about making this programme, it was you she was thinking of. Not herself, not your legal father, or the other children. Just you. She cares so much.'

'But she doesn't understand.'

'I expect she does. Sometimes it's difficult to talk about that sort of thing, especially in her situation when she can't even see you. Now, I think you're too tired to talk about it any more tonight. Why not have a hot bath? It's only a trivial kind of soothing, but it usually helps.'

'All right.' Kate wasn't built for submission, but she looked like the humblest of dependants as she waited for the rest of Trish's orders. It diminished her.

'The bathroom's just there. And try to get some sleep. You've had more to put up with in the last couple of years than most people have in their whole lives. But you'll come through.'

'Will I?'

'Yes. You're strong and brave. Now, I'll start the bath running. Don't let it overflow, will you?'

As Trish let herself fall into her own bed, she wondered whether she ought to have offered Kate one of her own over-the-counter sleeping pills. She'd been in the kind of state that often made it impossible to sleep.

Still trying to decide whether any member of Kate's family would ever dare take a pill from someone else, Trish didn't notice when her own mind went blank. The next thing she knew was the radio turning itself on at six thirty in the morning.

She silenced it at once. As quietly as she could, she padded downstairs. The door to the spare bedroom was open. Trish put her head round it and was relieved to see that Kate was lying on her back, her hair spread all over the pillow and her mouth open.

Trish left her to it and checked her diary to make sure she didn't have to be in chambers early. Luckily she had no commitments until the following day. She put on the kettle, planning to deal with her paperwork until Kate woke.

It was too early to phone the police, or Sprindler's, or George. She made herself a mug of tea and sorted through everything she'd stuffed into her briefcase last night.

When the post came an hour later, she leafed through it and found a letter addressed in Deb's writing. Glancing over her shoulder, Trish was glad there was no sign of Kate. The letter was quite short.

Dear Trish,
I have to trust you. There's no one else. Kate told me how kind you've been to her and she's going to need a lot more help soon. I don't know whether you've guessed, but she's not Adam's child. She's Malcolm's. Adam's always known

and he told me he'd never blame her because he hated Malcolm so much. And he's been true to his word. He's been the best father Kate could ever have, and the most loyal, loving husband I could have asked for.

But Kate's going to need more than he can give her now. Could you see her, talk to her? We had a row over the phone when she asked me about Malcolm and I don't know where else to turn. You've done so much for us all, I feel awful asking you to do this too, but there's no one else.

It's not the sort of thing Anna could do.

Yours, Deb

Trish drank a mouthful of cooling tea, contemplating the letter. It suggested that Deb still trusted Adam completely and made Trish ache for her and her inevitable disillusion. Memories of his doubts about Deb's innocence mingled in Trish's mind with echoes of the loathing Cordelia had poured out. Did anyone ever really know the truth about the people they loved?

It seemed astonishing that the letter in front of her could have been written by the same woman as the vituperative outpourings Cordelia had passed on. The photocopies were still in the bottom drawer of Trish's desk. She leaned down to get them out again.

The handwriting was clearly the same, but everything else was different. Startling phrases leaped off the page, just as bitter as Trish remembered from her first reading.

You were always selfish, Cordelia. Too selfish to risk having children of your own. But now that it's too late for you, you've seen what mine are like and are trying to grab them, just like you've always tried to grab anything good I've ever had.

It's never been enough for you to know that I'm not as successful as you, has it? You've had to cut the ground from under my feet at every possible opportunity, whatever I've been trying to do.

You always hated Mum and me, didn't you? Did it ever occur to you that we might not be the villains you think? Did it ever so much as cross your mind that you were just jealous of me supplanting you as the baby? I know you've always wanted me dead. I suppose getting me convicted for murder was the next best thing.

You could have had anything, been anyone, done anything; but all you truly cared about was making sure neither Mum nor I could ever be happy. Now you tell me you want to steal Millie from me as well. Well, you won't be allowed to get your hands on her. I don't want her life ruined, too. And keep away from Kate. I know what you're trying to do and I'll stop you if it's the last thing I do.

You're a destroyer, Cordelia. You only have to see people being happy to want to ruin it. You and Dad were a fine pair: all you cared about was each other and making sure no one else got a chance to do or have anything you might want.

Trish put the photocopied letters down and ran her hands under the hot tap in the kitchen, pouring washing-up liquid over them and scrubbing as hard as she could bear.

It would have been useful to see the other half of the correspondence to find out what provocation there had been in Cordelia's letters.

The sight of the clock warned Trish that Kate might be waking soon. She dried her hands, put the letters out of sight and forced herself back to work.

She was peacefully sitting at her computer in one of the XXL T-shirts she wore in bed when Kate emerged from the spare room, rubbing her sore eyes. Trish swivelled round, making sure the T-shirt still covered most of her thighs. The slogan on it was more apposite than usual, trumpeting the fact that 'Eve was framed'.

'Good morning, Kate. Did you sleep?' she asked.

'Not much till it was nearly light. That's why I'm so late. I've only just woken. I'm really sorry. Am I in your way?'

'No. I thought we might have breakfast first. We can phone the incident room then. Now, what do you like to eat at this time of day? I can do toast or muesli or eggs.'

'Can I cook myself some scrambled egg? I'm a bit hungry. I didn't have anything yesterday. I couldn't really eat at all.'

'Of course.' Trish got to her feet in a hurry. 'But you don't have to cook them. Let me do it for you. D'you like toast with them?'

'It's all right, honestly. I'm used to cooking. I don't mind it. It sort of makes me feel safe, if you know what I mean.'

'Not really.' Trish wondered whether George found cooking made him feel safe and, if so, what she had done to make him so scared that he wanted to cook whenever he came to Southwark. 'But I'm delighted for you to do it if you want. Come on, I'll show you where everything is. Then I'd better put some clothes on.'

# Chapter 19

Caroline Lyalt was waiting for Trish to bring Kate Gibbert to the incident room. It had been a good morning so far. Almost as soon as she'd arrived at work, she'd taken a phone call from Dave Smart, her contact in Incident Room II, with news of Spike Hamper.

They had arrested him on suspicion of drug-dealing and were questioning him now about his possible involvement in the Chaze murder, Dave told her, but Spike was still denying having had anything to do with it. He might be telling the truth. On the other hand, he was also denying taking any drugs to Mandy in the prison and having been her pimp, and that didn't convince any of them. He had a record for living off immoral earnings as well as possession with intent to supply, so they were sweating him now. They had another five hours before they had to turn him loose, and if Caroline would like to come on over, or send someone else, she'd be welcome to sit in and hear the denials for herself. But it would have to be quick, because five hours was the limit, according to the Super, unless the officers searching Spike's flat found anything that would let them charge him with drug dealing. Oh, and by the way, they were dead grateful for the tip off.

Co-operation like that made Caroline believe she could have a future in the Job and one that was worth staying for. She'd phoned Femur on his mobile and been glad to hear that he wanted to sit in on the interview himself. In the meantime, she had gone back to the long list of Malcolm Chaze's girlfriends.

They'd got back to 1983 now, ignoring most, phoning some, and visiting a few. They'd turned up all sorts of fascinating stuff on the victim – his taste in women and his sexual habits, as well as confirmation of Deb Gibbert's suggestion that he was something of a social climber – but they hadn't yet found anything to explain his death. Luckily it sounded as though both the other incident rooms were floundering, too.

Caroline had spread the word of that already, and morale was higher among her team than it had been for some days. After all, it was they who'd turned up Spike Hamper and he was the likeliest suspect anyone had found so far. Things were definitely looking up.

'Sarge?'

Steve Owler was posing in her doorway. He looked even prettier than usual. His short, razor-cut hair was wet, as though he'd just had a shower, and his skin was glowing with health and exercise. The smooth black T-shirt was tucked into narrow black jeans, both beautifully ironed and showing off all his carefully honed muscles.

'Yes. What is it?'

'The girlfriends. I've just thought. There's one called Crackenfield, isn't there?'

'So? She wasn't on any of the drugs or suicide cross-lists, was she?' Caroline frowned. She didn't want Steve getting even cockier. What had he spotted? 'Am I missing something?'

'No. But don't you remember that story the other day in the papers about a junkie who died of an overdose while he was supposed to be looking after his baby? Wasn't he called Crackenfield?'

'Coincidence,' she said instinctively, even as she admitted to herself that he might have a point.

'Maybe, but it's not a very common name,' said Owler. 'At least, I've never heard it before. Have you?'

Caroline sighed. She mustn't be prejudiced just because she didn't care for his rat-like tendencies or the way he flaunted his good looks. 'OK, check it out. Get on to whoever dealt with the death and see if there is a connection.'

'Will do.'

She watched him go jauntily back to his own desk, showing off his taut, cheeky buttocks. She hoped he'd only just noticed the coincidence. She wished she'd seen it herself. The lists of Chaze's girlfriends had been in the incident room for several days now. In her peripheral vision she saw Femur shambling towards her.

He looked worse than ever. He'd had five shots of The Macallan to her one in the pub last night. She hoped he hadn't had more of something else when he got home. His eyes were slightly bloodshot. 'Morning, Guv.'

'What's new, Cally?'

'Not a lot. How did they get on with Spike Hamper?'

Femur shrugged and rubbed his hands through his rough hair. 'I'm sure they're right about his innocence of the Chaze killing. He never reads the papers, has no interest in politics, didn't react to Chaze's name, and seemed genuinely and completely ignorant of his identity, significance, and everything else.'

He looked a bit more together by the time he'd finished talking. Gallons of hot, sweet tea and a greasefix in the form of several bacon sarnies, and he'd probably do fine.

'Right,' Caroline said, aware too late that it was his favourite way of acknowledging a subordinate's report. She grinned at him, hoping he'd take that as an apology, but he looked back blankly.

'What have you been up to, while I've been flogging over to IR Two?' he asked, clumsily, as though his tongue was swollen or bitten.

'We've got one new line of inquiry going this morning, although I'm not sure it's worth much.'

He nodded, so she told him about the dead junkie and Chaze's old girlfriend. Femur's blank expression sharpened. 'It could be worth looking into,' he said. He even smiled. 'Well spotted.'

She wrestled with her conscience and lost. 'It was Steve Owler who picked it up, Guv. Not me.' She turned back to her heaps of paper.

'Well done for that, anyway,' he said, in his old voice. She looked back and saw that he knew how close she'd been to taking Owler's credit. Femur's smile broadened and looked much more affectionate. 'You'd better see Chaze's daughter on your own. I'd only get in the way. But let me know how it goes.'

'Will do, Guv.'

In the interview room, Kate was repeating everything she could remember of the night when she'd phoned her real father from the theatre. She looked as though she was carrying the world on her back, but for most of the time her eyes were dry, and her voice hardly shook. When Caroline asked for the background to her relationship with Malcolm Chaze, Kate recited the facts of her parentage and her discovery of it, with a coolness that didn't seem real but was brave.

Caroline, who hadn't found much in Malcolm Chaze to like or respect, began to think there must have been some good in him to have produced a daughter like this one. Considering that she was already having to deal with her mother's conviction for murder, an outrageously snotty, selfish aunt, far too much domestic responsibility, and the discovery that the needy man she'd always called Dad was nothing of the sort, she was handling herself well. Add to that the fact that she was now in the local nick, answering questions about the murder of her real – hardly known – father, and you had someone with the kind of courage that left you breathless.

Caroline had always been a sucker for courage, and she was having to hold on to her impulse to reassure and comfort this beleaguered child. There might be a chance to do that once they'd found Chaze's killer, but until then, she had to keep herself cool and detached.

Luckily, it was more than clear that Trish Maguire was acting *in loco parentis*, and doing all that anyone could to support Kate. For form's sake as much as anything else, Caroline asked Kate to repeat everything she could remember of her earlier conversations with the dead man. That didn't produce much beyond a whole slew of encouraging waffle about how he'd help her find a job as soon as she needed one, give her money for her gap year and so on.

'And what about his wife, Laura? Did you talk to her at all the day you came to his house?'

Kate's eyes brimmed, but again she held on. She waited a moment, coughed, then rubbed her eyes with a screwed-up piece of loo paper, nodding at the same time.

Caroline Lyalt exchanged glances with Trish.

'What was she like, Kate?' Caroline asked gently.

'Snooty. She came into the drawing room, where he was talking to me.' The tears were well under control now. Kate's voice was stronger too. 'Then she said, "So this is the famous daughter, is it?" "It" again, you see.'

Trish Maguire patted her shoulder but didn't interrupt.

'Then she looked me up and down, obviously not liking what she saw, and said, "Yes, I suppose there's no doubt. She's got your awful bulbous nose, Malcolm."'

Caroline felt her eyebrows twitch. From where she was sitting, Kate's nose looked anything but bulbous. There was a slight thickening around the nostrils, but it was hardly noticeable.

'"Well," she said to him, "make sure she doesn't embarrass either of us."' Kate's voice took on a clipped patrician intonation when she was impersonating Laura Chaze. Caroline had no idea whether it was an accurate impression, but it effectively created the idea of a busy, antagonistic, grand woman of several generations past, the kind of woman Caroline detested.

'"If she wants money, give it to her and get her out of here as soon as possible."'

Caroline wanted to say something helpful, but she couldn't think of a single thing. She saw Trish pat Kate's shoulder again and hoped it was helping. The girl gulped. 'Then she turned to me and sounded a little bit less snotty: "I know he's your father, but he's not in a position to have you living with him. I don't wish to sound unkind, but it's better that you stay with the people you've known all your life. Do you understand?" So I said of course I did. I just wanted to meet him, talk to him. I promised her I wouldn't get in the way, and that I didn't want anything from either of them, especially not money. All I wanted was to know him, just a bit.'

Trish Maguire looked as though she wanted to intervene, but Caroline gestured to her to let Kate finish uninterrupted.

'And then she said to me, sounding nearly nice, that in his work he needed to be above reproach and that to be known as the father of a child whose mother had committed murder would ruin his career, and I didn't want that, did I?'

'That must have made you angry,' Caroline suggested.

Kate looked surprised for a moment, but then she nodded. 'Well, yeah. I suppose it did. But it was all so difficult then, I didn't have time to be cross. I just said no, of course I didn't, even though my mother hadn't killed anyone and shouldn't have been in prison. Then she smiled properly and said she was glad I was so sensible and she hadn't really meant it about the nose, and that she'd do her best to help me when I was through university, so long as I went on being discreet about my father.'

'That's very clear,' Caroline said, when she'd got her breath back. Laura Chaze sounded like a right cow. If anyone was going to be shot, it should have been her.

'Then she went away and my father made a pot of tea and opened some biscuits.' Kate smiled suddenly, revealing a childishly open delight for a second. 'They were called Chocolate Olivers. I asked where I could buy some because I'd like to take some back for Millie and the boys, and he told me to take the rest of the packet home with me. He was kind, you see. He let me tell him about the children, and he said he could see they really needed me. Even more than he did.'

Trish leaned forwards. To Caroline's surprise, she said, 'Kate, did he ask anything about your legal father, about Adam?'

'Yes, a bit.' Kate looked as surprised as Caroline felt. All the delight had been extinguished. 'Why?'

'I just wondered. They'd known each other when your parents got engaged, hadn't they?'

'I didn't know that.'

'OK. Never mind that now,' said Caroline, glaring at Trish. This was not her interview and she should've known better than to interrupt. 'And what did he say about your mother?'

'Just that he hadn't realised how much he loved her till it was too late.' Kate rammed the hardened lump of tissue into her eyes again and sniffed. 'I told Trish all this yesterday, Sergeant Lyalt.'

'I know. But it helps me to hear it, too. And which day

exactly was it that your mother phoned you and told you how he'd wanted her to have an abortion?'

There was a stillness about Kate as she sat with her hands in her lap and her eyes slowly leaking. She said nothing. Trish looked surprised and as though she was about to intervene again. Luckily she held her tongue. They both waited. Kate was blushing and her long hair hung down, hiding her face as she stared at the floor.

'Kate?' said Caroline firmly. 'You must tell me the truth, you know.'

'It was Friday,' she said, looking up at last. Her eyes were huge and hurt and the tears were falling faster. Caroline went out to find some Kleenex.

'This last Friday,' she said, when she came back with a small, unopened packet, 'or the one before he was shot?'

Kate's blush betrayed her. Trish sat forward, but Caroline didn't want her to protest.

'Kate?'

'The one before he was shot.' She started howling then, like a child taking refuge from punishment in a sobbing fit.

'Sergeant,' Trish said firmly, back in her professional persona, 'I think it would be a good idea if I had a chance to talk to Kate privately.'

'It's all right.' Kate sniffed. 'It's all right, Trish. I didn't mean to lie. It just seemed easier not to go into details about it. I'm sorry, I really am. I rang him from the theatre because I was so upset by what my mother told me. That's why I wanted to see him again.'

Caroline saw that Trish was about to tell her not to say anything else, so she leaned forwards, smiling kindly at Kate, and said, 'It's much better to get the whole truth out in the open. You told him, did you, what your mother had said?'

Kate nodded.

'And what did he say?'

'That I had to try to understand. That it wasn't me he didn't want, just any kind of baby. Like you said last night, Trish. That he'd never had anything to do with children, and hadn't reached a stage in his life when he was fit to marry. He said he was incredibly immature and that he'd regretted it ever since. That's why he was so glad I'd found my way to his house and why he wanted a chance to know me and help me now, to make up for everything he'd done wrong before.'

'Did your father . . . I mean, did Adam know what your mother had told you?'

Kate sat very still. Her lips didn't move but her eyes looked as though she was working out a complex problem in her head.

'No,' she said.

Caroline didn't believe her.

'Are you sure?'

'Quite positive.'

Caroline looked at Trish, who wouldn't meet her eyes.

'All right. I'll get this typed up and then you can sign it.' Caroline knew she would have to send someone to interview Adam Gibbert again before Kate got to him. She already had his work address and phone number and had talked to him several times.

Kate was looking ill. Her eyes were dry again, for the moment, but her skin was the colour of uncooked potatoes and a few incipient spots showed up against the greyish pallor.

'Would you like some tea, while they're typing it?' Caroline asked. Kate nodded.

As soon as the sergeant had gone, Kate turned to Trish. 'She thinks I killed him, doesn't she?'

Trish shook her head, and touched Kate's shoulder again. It was a ludicrously inadequate attempt at comfort, but she couldn't think of anything else to do. 'No,' she said, wishing there were words that could deal with Kate's difficulties. 'No one in their right mind would think that.'

'Then it's Adam. I know she was suspicious of one of us. But he wouldn't kill anyone. I know he wouldn't. He couldn't.'

Trish smiled and hoped it hid her thoughts. Whatever Kate knew or didn't know about her stepfather, Trish was well aware how violent weak pleasers could become when driven beyond the limits of what they could bear. Kate's pale beige skin flushed again. She was shaking. Her eyes were still red, but now they were quite dry. 'I have to get home. How long is she going to be? I have to be back to look after Millie and the boys.'

'It's OK, Kate,' Trish said, dreading the outcome of Caroline's investigation. She couldn't think of any solution that wouldn't add to Kate's distress. 'When Adam gave permission for me to be the responsible adult with you when you gave your statement, he said he would arrange to have a friend look after the children. I can take you to the bus when you've signed the statement, if you like. Or you can stay up here another day with me. Get some proper rest without all that cooking and childcare.'

'I need to get home. I need to talk to Dad.'

'Kate . . .' Trish stopped, wishing this could have been one of the occasions when the words fountained out of her brain without conscious control. Unfortunately today she was all too conscious and every word that suggested itself seemed worse than the last.

'It's all right,' Kate said, 'I'm not going to ask him if he killed my real father.'

Trish watched her fighting for composure and had some idea of the maze Kate must be treading towards the ultimate discovery of who and what her two fathers had been all her life. 'I know he didn't. Just like I know Mum didn't kill *her* father. But I have to talk to him about this. If he overheard my phone calls, he'll know I was talking to my real father, and I don't want him hurt any more. He's been hurt enough already, Trish.' Her eyes were welling again. 'I have to get back.'

'God, you're brave!' Trish couldn't help the exclamation, but she was glad she'd made it as she saw Kate's colour returning to normal and a tiny movement parting her lips. She shook her head, but she was – just – smiling again.

Eventually Caroline brought the statement back. Kate grabbed a pen and pulled the paper towards her.

'No. You must read it before you sign it,' Trish said, horrified. 'Kate, you must never – ever – sign something without reading it first.'

'Particularly not a statement,' said Caroline, joking to warm up the atmosphere a little.

Even so, Kate looked scared and sat reading the typed sheets, stopping every so often to go back a line or two, as though she couldn't concentrate with the two older women looking at her. Trish led Caroline to the corner of the room and started a quiet conversation about Caroline's next planned holiday.

Between sentences, she could hear Kate breathing more easily. After about five minutes, she said, 'I've read it. It's all OK. I'm signing it now.'

Trish came back to sit beside her and insisted on reading the statement herself. Caroline stood on the far side of the table watching. Trish thought she could read pity and admiration in Caroline's expression, but that might have been just because she hoped they'd be there.

'Terrific, Kate,' Trish said, as she put down the Biro. 'I take it you've finished with us, Sergeant?'

'Yes. Thank you for coming in, Kate. You've helped a lot.

Try not to worry too much, and if anything else occurs to you that you think might help us, will you ring me?' She handed Kate a slip of paper with all her phone numbers on it, then added, 'Me, or Trish. She'll keep us in touch.'

'Thank you,' Kate said, gripping the piece of paper as though it was a safe conduct out of the police station.

When she was already half-way out of the interview room, Caroline said, 'Trish, could we have a word later?'

'Sure.' She trusted Caroline Lyalt. And in any case, she had no information to reveal and no client with something to hide. The more questions Caroline asked, the more Trish would learn and the easier it would be to protect Kate.

As soon as they were out in the street, Kate said, 'She *seemed* kind.'

'She is,' Trish said. 'Now, would you like to come back to the flat, or shall I take you to the bus?'

'I want to go home.'

'OK. The bus it is. The sergeant was right, you know, Kate, you shouldn't let yourself worry too much. You can't change any of the things that have happened by worrying and it's hard enough for you already.'

Kate stopped and turned. Her face was desperate. 'But there is only me, now that Granny's dead.'

'Granny?'

'My mother's mother. She was kind, too, and she sort of took care of us all when my mother . . . when the police took her away that first time. *She* didn't think my mother had done it either.'

'Did she talk to you about your grandfather's death?' asked Trish quickly.

'Not specifically, no. But I know she didn't think Mum was guilty. And after she had to go home that time, when they let Mum come out on bail, she wrote to me every day.'

Trish felt like a hound that has caught the scent of a fox.

'Was that usual? I mean, had she always written to you, or did it start then?'

'Oh, no, she'd always sent me letters, but only kind of like once every two weeks or so.'

'Have you kept the letters?'

'Of course.' The big dark eyes were welling again.

'Do you think I could see some of them? Some of the ones she wrote in the months before your grandfather's death?'

Kate stopped again. It was clear she didn't like the idea.

'It might give me ideas about how your grandparents lived, and that could help with the TV film,' Trish said, carefully not suggesting that the letters might contain clues to the truth.

'OK,' Kate said at last. 'But you will let me have them back, won't you? They're important.'

'Of course. Now, we'd better hurry. I looked up the times of the buses and there's one that goes in fifteen minutes.'

Trish bought her a ticket and saw her on to the bus. There was a taxi outside the bus station, so she hailed it and was back in her flat twenty minutes later.

Among the messages on the answerphone was one from Meg, tentatively asking for news of Paddy now that he'd been back in his flat for over a week. Conscience-stricken, Trish dialled her mother's home number. It was her half-day, so she ought to be back from the surgery by now.

'Trish, how lovely! Thank you for ringing back so soon. How is he? I don't feel I can go ringing the flat. Or dropping in. It's not like the hospital.'

'You were so good to him, Mum. He seems fine. I don't go in every day any more, or even every other. He's threatening to go back to work, he feels so well. He swears he's eating sensibly and getting enough sleep. I don't see that there's any more we can do.'

'No. Probably not. Is Bella around at the moment? Or is she back in the States?'

Trish couldn't speak. She had no idea her mother knew anything about the woman.

There was a laugh at the other end of the phone. 'Oh, Trish. You don't think I mind, do you? He doesn't mind about Bernard.'

'Oh, good.'

'It's a quarter of a century since he walked out. Of course I don't mind. I'm only glad she's around to look after him some of the time. I wish it were full-time.'

'Why did he leave, Mum?' Trish hadn't known she was going to ask the question until she heard the words. It wasn't one she'd ever put to her mother before.

'That's ancient history.'

'But you were hurt?'

'Of course I was. And humiliated. But that's enough of Paddy. How are you, Trish-love? Still working too hard?'

'Naturally.' Trish felt better. 'And getting ever more involved in this film project of Anna Grayling's, in spite of all my attempts to get out of it. Look, Mum, I wonder if you could help me with something on that?'

'If I can, I will. What d'you need?'

'Some medical information. Anna's being hopeless about getting it for me. D'you think one of your doctors might be prepared to look over some medical notes for me and see what he thinks about the condition of the people involved?'

'They don't like interfering in other doctors' work.'

'Even if it's only to give me some advice to help stop Anna humiliating a practising doctor on screen?'

'Maybe. I'd have to see. Mike Bridge would be the best. He's a lovely chap, very kind and unflappable.'

'Any good at geriatrics?'

'He doesn't do much. He's too young to make the older patients feel safe. They prefer greyer hair and a few wrinkles in their GP and don't see the benefits of recent training. But

Mike's the sort of doctor who asks or looks it up if he doesn't know the answer and that's worth a hell of a lot. Send me the notes, with a list of questions, and I'll get him to have a look at them for you.'

'Is your fax machine working?'

'Is it really that urgent?'

'Sort of. It would help enormously if he could produce some answers within the next few days.'

'OK. Fax the questions through. I'll give him a ring, see if he wants to drop in for a drink on his way home this evening. He occasionally does that.'

'You, Meg Maguire, are a jewel among mothers. I'll go and see Paddy and will ring with a report.'

'I didn't need a *quid pro quo*, but that would be kind. I like to know he's all right. Thanks, Trish. We'll talk later.'

Trish put down the phone and sorted out the medical notes, switching on her computer to type out a list of questions to go with them. She wished her mother was on e-mail, but Meg always said that faxing was bad enough and that if anyone wanted to write to her they could do it in a civilised fashion with an envelope through the post. As Trish sat at her own computer, working on the questions, she realised that they boiled down to two:

1. Could a woman in Mrs Whatlam's state of health have had the strength and enough balance without her stick to suffocate her husband?

2. Was there anything in Mr Whatlam's galaxy of illnesses that could possibly have made him stop breathing or produced a cardiac arrest, and yet have left no evidence?

Trish printed off the pathetic list, faxed it with all the sheets of medical notes from the case files, then set off to visit Paddy.

# Chapter 20

Paddy seemed surprised to see Trish in the middle of the day, but pleased enough to let her in and offer tea.

'That would be great,' she said, following him into the kitchen. 'I'm glad you're not back at work. Meg wanted me to find out how you are.'

Trish knew she'd made a mistake as soon as the words were out. The air temperature seemed to drop by several degrees. Paddy plugged in the kettle with an audible grunt, as though the force needed was immense. 'She'll be sending me another bloody diet sheet next.'

'Another?'

He gestured to a pile of glossy leaflets beside his fridge.

Trish shuffled through them, impressed all over again at her mother's good sense and generosity. In the absence of any follow-up from the hospital or a visit from the community nurse, the leaflets should at least give him the crucial information about his condition and its management. 'But these are great. She must have got them from the surgery. All this healthy diet stuff is just what you need and what that wretched hospital couldn't be bothered to provide. I—'

'Will you stop it, Trish? I had a heart-attack. But I'm better. I'm a grown man, for God's sake, not a baby. Now will the pair of you leave me alone?'

He banged down cups and saucers on a gold-bordered

black metal tray. Trish looked more closely at the picture in the middle of it, to see lettuce leaves and flower petals, and a small, realistic slug.

Paddy tipped the kettle over the open teapot, splashing boiling water over the slug. He shoved the kettle to the back of the worktop with a bang, cracked down the lid of the teapot and picked up the tray.

By then Trish knew better than to offer to carry it for him, so she merely opened the door to let him take it through into the sitting room. He poured the tea, adding a good slug of whiskey to his own cup. Trish didn't comment and was glad of the restraint when she saw him watching her. She stuck her tongue out.

'That's better. Now, Trish, it's always good to see you, but I don't want you here if you're going to behave like my old mother – or spy for your own.'

'Spy?' Trish was outraged. 'Meg wanted to make sure you were all right.'

'That's spying,' Paddy said, definitely. 'Now, tell me about your work or your fat lover. Anything but good advice on my health.'

'Why *did* you leave Mum and me?' She hadn't meant to ask, but the question was out, and she couldn't take it back. Listening to the silence, aware that she'd broken a taboo, she felt as though she'd been throwing stones on to a newly formed – and fragile – ice sheet.

'Oh, for the Lord's sake! Will you not leave me alone now?'

See what you've done! she said to herself. But it was done now; with the ice sheet cracking all round her, she could only go forward.

'I'm not trying to harass you, Paddy.' She looked down at the wet slug on the tray. 'But when you were in hospital, nearly dead, you made me face all sorts of things I've been feeling for years without understanding any of them. Then that day, when I thought you actually *were* dead, I – I need to get it all straight. Won't you tell me?'

He sighed. She looked up at him again. He didn't meet her eyes. Abandoning his tea, he poured an inch of straight whiskey into a glass and sat sipping that.

'Your mother's a saint, Trish,' he said at last.

'I know.' She was glad he'd recognised that, at least, but it didn't answer her question.

'And I didn't want to be married to a saint. In fact, I didn't want to be married at all. But I didn't know that at the time.'

Trish could feel her flesh tightening against the cheekbones and something like a steel rod holding her neck braced.

'Not because I didn't love her – or you. We had great games, you and I, when you were little and still liked noise and mess and stories.'

Trish nodded. 'I remember some of them.'

'But I didn't want to eke out my life ounce by ounce, or be reasonable or tidy or middle aged. There I was – me – commuting to and from Boring Beaconsfield every day, tripping off the train at seven, sitting with your mother over a wholesome supper and a glass of water, for God's sake, watching some awful soap on the telly with her and going to bed at half past ten.'

Trish couldn't help smiling at the picture. His voice warmed in response and he sounded younger: 'I tried, Trish. I tried hard, because I knew 'twas the life she wanted. But then I started stopping off for a quick one with the boys from work, and then I'd come home a bit the worse for wear and she'd get all hot and bothered if I woke you up to play – or disturbed your homework, once you were a bit older. And by the time we sat down to eat, the food would be burned or spoiled, but she'd never complain about that.'

'No. She doesn't complain. It's a point of honour with her.'

''Twould have been easier if she had. But no, she'd just sit there looking like a holy martyr, who'd never allow herself to raise her voice. Until one day I knew I had to make her angry.'

He stopped, looking right through Trish. She tried to remember if she had ever seen her mother lose her temper. Only once, she thought, and even then it had been a dysfunctional oven that had aroused her fury. Meg had stood in the kitchen yelling at the oven and kicking it. Even that had shocked Trish at the time. 'And did you?' she asked.

Paddy shook his head. 'I couldn't, however hard I tried. So one day, when I was drunk, I hit her.'

Trish felt her heart jolt, as though someone had thumped her in the chest. Paddy's face was reddening and he was glaring at her, as though it was she who'd done the unforgivable thing.

'And she still wasn't angry,' he said, still full of old resentment. 'Or maybe she just wouldn't let it show. Maybe that would have lowered her to my hog-like level. Wasn't she always a one for trying to make me face up to my responsibilities?'

'So, what did she do?'

'She picked up the chair that had smashed when she fell across it, and put it tidily back against the wall. Then she fetched a cloth to deal with the blood from her split lip and said she'd sleep in the spare room that night. That was all.'

Trish fought for detachment, using everything she had learned in her excursions into family warfare in the courts. She couldn't believe that Meg had never even hinted at this past violence, had even encouraged her to get to know the perpetrator. Her father.

'And I suppose that drove you even wilder?' She was quite proud of the cool steadiness of her voice. Her head seemed to be filled with cotton wool and there was a ringing in her ears. She realised she'd stopped breathing and made herself start again.

'To be sure. But I tried still to be the kind of man she wanted, and the father she wanted for you. I went on trying for another whole year. When I was drunk I didn't come home. I couldn't trust meself. But there were times in between when I did come back. And each time she forgave me and was such a perfect saint that I wanted to batter the patience out of her. So I left altogether. 'Twas the only safe thing to do.'

Anger was boiling just below the surface of Trish's mind. She held it down as firmly as she could. She'd been manipulated into liking – even loving – a man who could beat up his own wife. She was the daughter of a woman who could put up with that kind of abuse, yet still be prepared to forgive Paddy and visit him in hospital a quarter of a century later. Trish thought of Deb Gibbert's stories of the battered women she'd met in prison.

She wanted to be out of her father's flat, out of his life. And she never wanted to see him again.

But she sat where she was, telling herself to grow up and stop being so melodramatic. She wasn't an emotional teenager any longer. Her parents' battles could never be her concern. Whatever they had done to each other was their business. It was ancient history. If Kate Gibbert could cope, at the age of seventeen, with everything that had confronted her in the last few years, then Trish could smile and be polite about this.

'And do you hit Bella?' she asked calmly, but not at all politely.

Paddy poured some more whiskey and drank it down in one noisy swallow. Trish saw he was making a point and recognised exactly why her mother had refused to show anger even as he was hitting her. That should have made it easier, but it didn't.

'No, Trish, I don't. That was a part of a life – and a

relationship – that's gone. And 'twas only ever the once that I really hit her.'

He waited, maybe hoping for absolution. But it wasn't hers to give, and even if it had been, she wouldn't have given it. In any case, she didn't believe he'd lashed out only once. Men who hit their wives don't stop after one go, however much they may weep and beg to be forgiven and promise reform after each bout.

'I shouldn't have married your mother and she shouldn't have married me,' he said, perhaps still hoping Trish would understand. 'We loved each other once but that was never enough. We wanted different things from life. But that's all I'm telling you now. It's dead and gone and I don't want to talk about it. D'you understand me now, Trish?'

'Naturally. Thanks for the tea.' She stood up, swallowing the last of it and bent to put her cup back on the watery tray. 'I'll see myself out. Take care of yourself. If that's not too intrusive a comment.'

'Now, Trish, don't be childish. I'll see you again, I hope.'

'Call me if you need me,' she said, over her shoulder. ''Bye.'

She thought he looked a little forlorn, but that was too bad. He'd asked for it.

'I notice that you haven't moved in with that fat lover of yours,' he said casually. 'Or married him or had babies with him.'

Trish stopped, her hand on the door.

'You're a chip off the old block, so y'are.'

She let herself out, wishing she hadn't brought the car with her. She needed air and exercise. And she didn't want to get home too soon to face Meg's questions. It would be almost impossible to conceal what she was feeling. Meg had a kind of extrasensory perception when it came to her only child's moods.

There had been times in the past when she had phoned

from hundreds of miles away when Trish was in a particularly frenzied turmoil, asking quietly whether everything was all right. And Trish had never yet managed to conceal an anxiety – even a trivial one – if they were actually talking to each other over the phone.

It was years since she'd felt this rocky. Paddy's heart attack had started the process, and the whole Whatlam-Gibbert affair was upsetting in itself. Families! she thought again, shuddering. She didn't want to probe another single one. She'd had secrets and hurt and parent–child damage up to her throat. Perhaps she ought to switch to the commercial Bar. The rewards were much higher and the *Angst* must be less.

Whether she tried to switch her professional life or not, she had to clear her desk and fulfil her obligations to Anna and Deb, so she'd better get on with it.

She drove back to Southwark, avoiding the potholes, working out what more she could do to help Anna. Half-way home, she thought of a reason to go in to chambers, which would probably help get her back together and would fend off Meg's phone call for a little longer.

Dave greeted Trish with a sheaf of messages and the welcome news that the couple whose daughter had leukaemia had been phoned by their local hospital to say the health authority had suddenly decided to fund the treatment they needed after all.

'Thank God,' Trish said. She'd been worried that by the time the case came to court the damage would have been irreparable. 'That's great, Dave.'

She walked down the dingy corridor to her little room at the back of the building. One day, if she did take up Heather Bonwell's suggestion of applying for silk and got it, she might see about taking over one of the better rooms.

There were several voicemails on her phone, including one

from Anna: 'Trish, I'm really apologetic about having taken so long to get the medical information you wanted. But I've done it now.'

Trish sighed. Typical, she thought, Anna takes weeks to do something and once I've wound up someone else to produce the information, she disgorges. Still, she might as well listen to the full message.

'Here goes. In most cases of suffocation there wouldn't be anything to show whether a pillow or a plastic bag had been used.'

I know that, thought Trish in exasperation. Even Phil Redstone got as far as checking that out.

'There's nothing in Mrs Whatlam's medical notes to prove that she couldn't have held a pillow over her husband's face, but a practitioner who'd been treating her would be in a better position to assess it. There's nothing in the notes to suggest Dr Foscutt's evidence should be doubted, so you should assume she couldn't have done it. Then my source goes on to say: are we sure the angioneurotic oedema hadn't extended to the glottis? That can be fatal in itself. Does that help? I hope so. 'Bye for now.'

Ignoring the other messages and all the work she should have been doing, Trish switched on her laptop and opened the file with the trial transcript, which she had scanned into the computer when Anna had first sent it. She scrolled through until she reached the pathologist's evidence of his autopsy.

Sure enough, there were details of the angioneurotic oedema, but no mention of its affecting anything but the victim's face. Trish searched for 'glottis' but nothing came up, presumably because there had been nothing to report.

Her phone rang and she picked it up, absent-mindedly saying her name.

'Trish?'

'Meg, yes.' All her questions about Ian Whatlam flew out

244 | NATASHA COOPER

of her head, and the other, much more difficult ones sat there like sharp-beaked birds, waiting to peck away at the trust there had always been between the two of them. Trish breathed and smiled and hoped her voice would sound normal. 'How did you know I was here?'

Meg laughed down the phone. 'You said these medical details were urgent and you weren't at the flat. It doesn't take the world's finest detective to . . .'

'Of course. Sorry. Look, I was miles away. D'you mean your tame doctor has already read the notes?'

'Yes. And I thought I'd put you on to him so that he can tell you direct.'

'You've got him there? Great!'

'Ms Maguire?' said a robust young male voice, with a faint Scottish intonation. 'I'm not going to be able to help you much over the victim's wife's ability to suffocate her husband. There's nothing in the notes to prove anything either way. But if he was in a deep enough sleep not to wake and fight back, it wouldn't have taken much strength to hold a pillow over his head.'

'I can imagine,' Trish said.

'On the other hand, it's hard to see how he couldn't have woken if he was bagged. The antihistamines he'd taken weren't the sedating kind. And there are indications of possible defence injuries – the bruise on his hand and another near his neck – which suggest he might have been awake and fighting back. If so, I'd have said it's unlikely that it could have been someone in his wife's condition who did it.'

'OK. Now do you think it's possible that this rash-thing he had could have spread to his glottis – is that right? – and not been detected at either of the autopsies?'

'No. Any pathologist would have seen it straight away and would never have ignored it. But there is one interesting possibility. Have you any information about the food and drink the old man ingested that day and evening? I can't find it in the notes you sent.'

'No, I don't think I have,' Trish said, frowning. 'Although it must have been recorded in the autopsy, mustn't it? They always check the stomach contents.'

'Should do. That's why I'm curious.'

'Do you think the rash-thing could have been an allergy? Shellfish or something? His daughter told me once that his doctor had told her there was no cause.'

'That can be true. But not always. Angioneurotic oedema can be a reaction to penicillin, and various other things. But his doctor's right: there's often no allergen or apparent cause at all.'

Well, that's something, Trish thought. Good to know that the ghastly Dr Foscutt got one thing right at least. And penicillin wasn't among Ian Whatlam's many medicaments.

'But can you find out about the food and drink?' said Dr Bridge, sounding impatient. 'It could be important.'

'Why?' said Trish.

'I'd rather you told me what he'd ingested before I say. I don't want any suggestion of . . .'

'Leading the witness?' Trish said, and heard a breezy laugh.

'Yeah.'

'If you're right about whatever this mysterious clue is, would you be prepared to come on the TV programme to talk about it?'

'Could do. It's an interesting case.'

'Great. I'll be in touch.'

'Fine. Now your mother wants another word.'

'Trish? Will you phone me later, when you're through with this case?'

'Sure,' she said, ignoring the urgency in Meg's voice. She knew what it meant. 'And thanks for this. You've been ace, as always. 'Bye.'

For the first time in days Trish felt hopeful. She phoned Anna and left a message, asking for any information she might have missed or not been shown about the dead man's stomach contents. Then, too impatient to wait, she rang Cordelia Whatlam, who, luckily, had not yet gone abroad.

'Ah, Ms Maguire,' she said, in a voice that could have cut through a glacier, 'I owe it to you, do I?'

'I'm sorry?'

'So I should hope.'

'I wasn't apologising,' Trish said steadily. 'I meant that I didn't know what you were talking about.'

'Didn't you send the police here? The ones investigating Malcolm Chaze's death.'

'Certainly not,' said Trish, relieved to know that Femur – or perhaps Caroline Lyalt – was taking all aspects of the Deb Gibbert connection seriously. 'I didn't know you were in touch.'

'We'd met – when he tried to interest me in this ludicrous campaign to get my sister out of prison. I told you that.'

Trish blinked, wondering why she'd forgotten, and why Malcolm hadn't told her he'd seen Cordelia recently.

'The police appear to believe that I could have been so afraid of what your friend's farcical television programme might reveal that I was prepared to have Malcolm Chaze shot to have the project stopped.' Cordelia's breath hissed as she inhaled. 'And my taxes are used to pay the salaries of clowns like that!'

'I thought Malcolm Chaze's death had something to do with drugs,' Trish said, not sure how long she could play the innocent, but prepared to try.

'They appear to be running round in circles in a complete fog, accusing anyone who had even the most tangential connection with him. So, if their visit had nothing to do with this call, what is it you want?'

'Partly to thank you for sending me those copies of your sister's letters.'

'Revealing, aren't they?' Cordelia produced a hard little laugh, as though she was regrouping, changing gear almost. 'As you see, Debbie is considerably more complex than the good, quiet, domesticated, martyrly daughter you thought you knew. As Malcolm Chaze would have discovered, if he hadn't had the good sense to dump her all those years ago.'

Cordelia's bitterness was like the sound of nails shrieking across porcelain.

'Why are you so angry with her?' Trish asked, in genuine, if irrelevant, curiosity.

'Isn't my father's death enough?'

'I don't think so, but . . .'

'I don't have time for this. Why did you ring me?'

'I wanted to know whether you had any idea what your father ate and drank in his last few days.'

'What?' The gears were obviously changing again. 'Why?'

'To tell you the truth, I'm not exactly sure. But I have been advised to find out. And there's nothing in the files I've had access to.'

'I can't tell you, because I wasn't there.' The anger and contempt were still hardening Cordelia's voice. 'I know what he would have wanted, but whether Debbie would have had the decency to give it to him, I can't be sure. I rather suspect not. It would have been an easy way to punish him.'

It took Trish a moment to control herself.

'OK. Tell me what he liked, what you would have given him.'

'Fine. White toast, butter and honey with Twinings English Breakfast tea and semi-skimmed milk for breakfast. A glass of grapefruit juice at mid-morning. He'd read somewhere that it was better not to have citrus fruit or juice first thing.'

'I'm surprised he had it at all with his ulcer. I mean, aren't all citrus juices pretty acid? Wouldn't they make the ulcer worse?'

'It was pretty quiet when I was last with him. I don't know whether juice made it worse. It's true he never used to eat mustard or anything spicy. But he never said anything about the juice.'

'OK. Fine. What else?'

'Something reasonably soft and easy to eat for lunch: shepherd's pie, fish pie, stuffed pancakes, fricassée, something bland and soft like that. His teeth weren't very good. Then a cup of Darjeeling without milk at tea-time and a slice of cake. A glass of sherry at six. Supper of soup or eggs, something light, occasionally a blandish cheese, and then a final, long glass of grapefruit juice with his pills. He couldn't drink much alcohol and hated the gelatinous sensation of all those capsules he had to take, so he liked something as sharp and distinctive as grapefruit to get them down.'

'I see, thank you.'

'But, as I say, Deb probably didn't bother with what he liked. She was always trying to make him drink cranberry juice. He hated that, said it made his teeth feel all woolly, but that didn't stop her forcing it on him.'

But he never complained about your grapefruit juice tickling up his ulcer. And something as acid as that must have hurt. Did he keep quiet because that came from you and the cranberry from Deb?

'I see. Thank you. I'll write to her to find out. You've been very helpful.'

Cordelia did not produce any polite comment, merely a short sharp 'goodbye' before she put down the phone.

Trish typed a short note to Deborah, asking for the information about her father's last meals, printed it, put it in an envelope addressed to the prison and stuffed it into her handbag to drop into the nearest post box. It would be much quicker than getting a visiting order sent and going to ask her in person. Then, at last, Trish picked up the phone and dialled Meg's number.

She wasn't there. Trish mentally filed all the questions about her parents' past and left a cheery little message of thanks for all Meg's help with the medical questions. Then she abandoned Deb, Kate, Anna and the whole lot of them, to get down to her real work.

George phoned her mobile at half past nine to find out where she was and warn her that dinner was in danger of being seriously overcooked. She promised to be home in twenty minutes and walked back across the bridge, facing yet another way in which she was like her father. But, full of anger though she sometimes was, at least she had never hit George – or felt the slightest temptation to do it. And it was a while since she had got drunk. She was her own woman, not a clone of Paddy.

# Chapter 21

Deb was sitting on the bed in her cell with the door open, reading Trish Maguire's second letter, and wishing she knew why they needed to know about her father's meals. Presumably they were hoping for some kind of allergy story, but she hadn't given him anything he hadn't always had. She was sure of that. She'd always taken trouble to make sure he had everything he liked. Meals were just about the only thing she'd always been able to get right.

His taste in food and drink hadn't changed as often as some of his other requirements. She'd been well used to being yelled at one day for doing what he'd demanded only the day before. That habit had made caring for him almost impossible.

Deb got up to find a pad and felt-tip to write back to Trish Maguire, wincing as she moved. All her muscles seemed to ache these days, even in her tongue and jaw. She didn't know why.

A shadow passed her door. She looked up from the sheet of paper and saw Gill, whose cell was at the far end of the landing. She was the wing boss, more powerful in her own way than the screws. Deb smiled tentatively, despising herself for being a crawler.

'I've just heard they've got Mand's pimp,' Gill said casually.

'Oh?'

'Yeah. He said he never brought her no smack, but he'd

been here the day she OD'd.'

'She sent the pimp a VO?' Deb was appalled. 'A man who'd done that to her?'

Mandy had been so excited at the prospect of her visitor and so happy when she waltzed back into the cell after that last visit that it had never occurred to Deb he might have been the man who had abused her for so long. All Mandy had said was that Spike Hamper was an old friend who came to see her from time to time.

Since then Deb had assumed that Mandy's happiness had been anticipation of the hit to come. Now she thought sickly that it must have been the result of the same old game of trying to make your tormentor love you. She knew the rules of that game backwards.

It was a game from hell. You couldn't win except by walking away. And you couldn't do that because then you'd lose hope.

'Anyway,' Gill was saying, looking at Deb as though she'd grown green whiskers, 'I heard today that they turned his place over and found a bag of the same stuff Mandy took.'

Deb got up so fast she had to hold on to the wall to keep from falling over. Through the swinging in her head, she heard Gill's voice: 'Cut with paracetamol, like.' Gill shrugged. 'That must be why the screws've stopped harassing you now.'

Deb leaned back against the wall, her head tipped back, staring at the vaulted brick ceiling. It was painted the horrible colour of her father's false teeth. She couldn't think why she was crying again. Not now. Unless it was just relief. She tried to make her mind work, to thank Gill for the news, but all she could do was cry. Again. It was nearly as bad as the day she'd humiliated herself in front of those police officers. Even though her head was right back, she couldn't stop the tears flooding down her face.

She felt a rough towel against her cheeks and a gentle hand

on her head, straightening it. 'It's OK, love. Let it out. 'S not your fault Mand died. We knew that all along. And the screws know it now. They prob'ly won't tell you – or say sorry for what they did to you – but they know.'

Deb let herself fall forward against Gill's shoulder and felt more comfort in the tight, wholly sexless hug than she'd had since her mother picked her up the time she fell off her bike and skinned both knees and her chin, and Cordelia had laughed.

'It's OK, love. Let it out.'

After a bit, Gill stood her upright, gave her back the towel and said she was going to make some tea and why didn't Deb finish her letter then come and join the rest of them?

Deb nodded damply and wrote a quick list of everything she could remember giving her father to eat or drink during her stay and put it in an envelope addressed to Trish Maguire. Then she went out to be with other people again.

They were much kinder to her than usual and even talked about what they'd done to land them in prison, and why. For the first time Deb started to tell them about her father, then found she couldn't stop, even though she'd been banging on for what felt like hours.

'So I had to face the fact that not only would I never be good enough for him, but that I actually brought on this beastly skin condition,' she said at one moment, closing her eyes, as though that could quench the memory of his face, his pain, his loathing. 'And the ulcer.'

'What?' The question came from Gill, as so often articulating what the rest of them wanted to say but couldn't or wouldn't.

'He nearly always had an attack when I was there. Never with my sister and hardly ever with my mother. It was only me that brought it on. I just had to cross the threshold and straight away he'd have come up in these awful bumps.'

But did he hate you because of that or did it happen because he hated you? she asked herself, forgetting the other women. Their faces turned into a pinkish blur in front of her. She could hear their voices, but not as clearly as the ones in her head:

'What is it about you that makes the people you love despise and hate you?'

'You were never good enough for Dad or for Malcolm, were you? Why couldn't you face that, instead of trying to make them change when they couldn't bear to have you anywhere near them?'

And then came the accusations:

'You ruined their lives and Kate's and Adam's, too. You should never have married Adam. You only did it to give Kate a father when Malcolm threw you out. You cheated Adam. You never loved him. You gave him the twins and Millie to make up for that, and you've never loved them properly either. You spent your whole married life dreaming of Malcolm, and Dad. Neither of them ever did love you and now they never will. You'll never be good enough. And you'll never be loved. You're not lovable. That's really why you're here. That's why you're in prison and you'll never be let out. You don't deserve to have a proper life.'

Something moved in the pink fog in front of Deb and caught her attention. She saw that the other women were staring at her, but they could have been on the other side of a glass wall. She was cut off from them as well as everyone else. All the warmth she'd felt earlier had gone. The nightmares were back, jostling for space like maggots on a rotting body. More and more of them all the time.

Had she had a brainstorm that night and fed him pills she shouldn't have and put his head in a bag then forgotten all about it? Could she have been sleepwalking and done it then? Could her subconscious have imagined the whole elaborate story of the false teeth and made her believe it? Was she mad? And evil like Cordelia had said? And unlovable? Unlovable and in hell.

'Sarge?'

Caroline Lyalt looked up to see Steve Owler peering round the edge of her door. He looked indecently cheerful, still wearing his tight black jeans but this time with a dark purple T-shirt. The colour made her feel hotter than ever. Steve's face was glistening, but hers was positively dripping. She wondered if the Met would ever be able to afford air-conditioning in all their local stations.

'Steve. Well done spotting the Crackenfield connection. I should have had more faith in your intuitions. Have you traced the daughter yet?'

'Not yet, but the parents will tell us where she is, and we know how to get to them. That's not what I came for.'

'No?' Caroline rubbed her hands over her eyes, feeling them smart, and realised she was copying one of Femur's most familiar gestures. She hoped he wasn't in some bar somewhere, drinking himself stupid.

'Your mate in IR Two phoned and asked me to say they think they've got the gun that was used on Chaze. Ballistics are reasonably sure the bullets were fired from it.'

Her eyes already felt less bad. 'Great. Where did they find it?'

'A skip in Brixton. A woman saw it poking out of some rubbish and for a miracle called it in. Inspector Smart phoned while you were busy just now and asked me to let you know.'

'The first ray of light.'

'Apart from Spike Hamper.'

'Yeah, but he was a dead end. Still, we'd better see the Crackenfields before the end of the day. You found them, so you can come with me.'

He looked disappointed. Caroline suppressed a smile. The idea of talking to some law-abiding OAPs in Pimlico wasn't going to be half as exciting as chasing illegal guns in Brixton. But there was no way he'd be invited to join the IR II team, and it would do him good to see some tedious, dogged, necessary police work. Clip his wings a bit.

'Did you have any luck with Adam Gibbert's alibi?' she asked, making him look even gloomier.

'Yeah. The neighbours were round there having a meal with him. He'd been going to go to their house, but he couldn't get a babysitter, and the eldest daughter was away in London on a school trip to the theatre, so he asked the friends to come to him. They brought the food with them and reheated it in his kitchen.' He grinned suddenly.

'Something amusing you, Steve?'

'You should have heard the neighbour on the state of Gibbert's kitchen. Said she really pitied that oldest girl, Kate, having to do all the cooking there.'

'Kate, yes.' Caroline felt her headache tightening. 'Are there any fingerprints on the gun they've found in Brixton?'

'Some. None identified yet.'

'OK. I've got to finish this, but be ready to come with me to the Crackenfields' in half an hour. OK?'

She was still working when she heard Femur's voice outside the office. He sounded less pathetic than he had for days. Caroline pushed away her notes and went out to tell him about the gun. He already knew, clearly having his own snout in the IR II team.

'There's very little doubt it's the one used to kill Chaze, but it doesn't get them much further. They need a name, a face, or a useful set of prints, and it hasn't produced those. Is there anything new in the reports of the house-to-house or CCTV?'

'Nothing, Guv. But I'm about to go round to these people, the Crackenfields, to talk to them about Chaze and his relationship with their daughter and find out if he knew their son, who died the other day. I was going to take Steve Owler, but it'd be great if you could come with me. You'd spot a lot more than him – or me.'

'Flattery, Sergeant. Flattery.'

Her smile widened at the sight and sound of his obvious cheerfulness. She wondered if he'd had news of Sue or was just psyched up by the discovery of the gun.

'I'll come, but don't build too much on them. Didn't you tell me it's thirty years since Chaze went out with the daughter? The reasons for this killing aren't going to be found that far back. Come on, Cally.'

'More than thirty, Guv. You may be right, but it can't be coincidence. With a name like that? And with her brother dying too? We can't ignore it. They live only three streets away from his house. It won't take long. We have to follow it up, even if it does look like leading to another sodding dead end.'

'OK. Give me time for a leak first.'

'And a sandwich? I don't suppose you had any lunch.'

'You're as bad as Owler.'

'No one's as bad as Owler. Where he puts it all, I'll never know. I'll tell him he's been let off, and I'll meet you at the canteen in fifteen minutes,' she said, dismissing her boss.

He raised a finger to his forehead in a mixture of salute and insult and went off to obey.

They walked round to the Crackenfields' because there was no point getting out one of the cars, only to have to trail round finding somewhere to park. Their route took them past Chaze's house.

Femur thought again about Laura Chaze and her lack of misery. He knew colleagues who'd have had her in the interview room for that alone, interrogating her about hitmen and how to hire them.

He still thought she could have done it, even though no one had come up with any evidence. She was rich enough, and ruthless enough. But she could have thrown him out and divorced him, so what would have been the point of the hit? And she hadn't capitalised on the death, which she might well have done. Being in PR, she must have been tempted: the suffering heroine, tearfully appealing on TV for information about her beloved husband's killers. But no, she'd refused to do that, even when their press officers had wanted her to. Said it wasn't dignified and she didn't think it ever did any good anyway.

She was right there. Information tended to flood in, but it didn't often help. In fact, usually the police had a suspect all along, sometimes even the person making the appeal. It could be a handy way of keeping the suspect confident of his safety while the police collected the evidence that would convict him.

'Here we are, Guv.' Caroline had stopped outside a tall, thin house, which had seen better days. Unlike the clean paint of the Chazes' building, this one was chipped and grimy.

The elderly woman who opened the door was anything but grimy: a tall, elegant creature in a linen suit that was almost the colour of her blue-grey hair.

'Yes?' she said, as Caroline shook out her warrant card, introduced the two of them and said she was looking for Mrs Crackenfield.

The woman sagged a little. 'I am Margaret Crackenfield, but surely there isn't any more you want. We've had the inquest; the child isn't our son's, we've answered all your questions. Surely we can be left alone now.'

'Forgive me,' Caroline said quickly, 'but we haven't come about your son's death.'

Mrs Crackenfield looked as though she was about to faint.

After a second, she recovered herself and stood away from the door, saying, 'Oh? You'd better come in, then. My husband's not here just now. Did you want him? Or just me? Is it something about the car?'

'You would be fine.' Caroline was smiling in a way that would make anyone trust her, Femur thought.

Mrs Crackenfield led the way into a pleasant enough sitting room on the right of the front door. The decoration was shabby, but it had a sort of country-house kind of charm: all chintz and polished wood. The real thing, too. A house like this made you see the point of the style.

Mrs Crackenfield invited them both to sit down, but she didn't offer them anything to drink.

'We came,' said Caroline after checking that Femur didn't want to begin, 'to ask you about Malcolm Chaze.'

Mrs Crackenfield raised a trembling hand to her forehead. 'Poor man. It was dreadful, wasn't it?'

'You did know him then?'

She shrugged her slender shoulders, making the linen jacket bunch up around her ears. There were tiny pearls in the large lobes, looking incongruous and out of place.

'Not nowadays. He'd become so awfully important. But I remember him well enough as a schoolboy.'

'We understand that he had a relationship with your daughter.'

Mrs Crackenfield looked puzzled. 'Only a trivial boy-and-girl affair.' She shook her head, frowning. 'Don't misunderstand me, Sergeant Lyalt, not an affair in the current sense of the word. They were seventeen or eighteen. It was one Christmas holiday, they'd go to the cinema together or to dances held by some of our friends. Malcolm didn't know many people – our sort of people – so it was nice for him, and Georgie was glad enough of a guaranteed partner. She was at the age and stage when the idea of dances was rather daunting. She wasn't as pretty then as she became later. Even a little dumpy.'

'What made them break up?'

'I have no idea.' She sounded impatient. 'Heavens above, it's decades ago. You can't seriously believe that my daughter's friendship with Malcolm Chaze has anything to do with his death?'

The sight of Cally's face, beady and obstinate, made Femur decide it was time to take a hand. 'I'm afraid, Mrs Crackenfield, that with this kind of case we have to look into every possible aspect of the victim's life. It is a bore for people like you, but we need any information we can get about the man and, of course, any connections he may ever have had with the sort of people who might have wanted him shot.'

She flinched. He wasn't surprised. Violent death didn't fit anywhere in this old-fashioned, gentle, lavender-scented room. He saw that her face must once have been lovely, fine-boned and very elegant, before the whites of her eyes had faded and the wrinkles in her skin had made it look like crêpe paper.

'I can assure you, Chief Inspector Femur, that my daughter does not move in contract-killing circles at all.'

'No, I'm sure that's right. Where does she live now?'

'In Scotland. She's married.' Mrs Crackenfield seemed to find Femur's emollient voice easier to deal with than Caroline's uncharacteristic abrasiveness. 'She's been married for twenty-five years to a delightful farmer up there. They have five children, and she hardly ever comes south.' Her soft, wrinkled face twisted. 'Unfortunately for me and my husband.'

'I see. Could you give me her address?'

'I don't think . . .'

'It's all a question of eliminating people from our inquiries. As you can imagine, they have been extensive already and because we've got nowhere we have to look further and further back in his life for an explanation.'

'If you're looking to people who have not seen him for as long as Georgina, you must be desperate,' she said, with a little more energy warming her voice.

'The address?' said Caroline.

With obvious reluctance, Mrs Crackenfield dictated it.

'And you really never saw him yourself?' said Caroline, in the tones of prosecuting counsel asking the defendant whether he really expected the jury to believe a transparent tissue of lies. 'That seems odd, when you live so close.'

A faint flush seeped along Mrs Crackenfield's cheekbones. 'Naturally we saw him once he'd moved in round the corner: in the street, on television, occasionally even at neighbours' Christmas drinks parties. But we rarely spoke. It would have been rather undignified to try to make some kind of friendship with him now, simply because he used to come to our house as a schoolboy, don't you think?'

'Perhaps.' Caroline looked at Femur, eyebrows raised to find out if he wanted to ask anything more. He shook his head slightly. She stood up. 'Thank you for seeing us, Mrs Crackenfield. If anything occurs to you that might be helpful to our inquiries, will you let us know?' Caroline handed over a card. 'This gives you my mobile number, and I've written down the number of the incident room, here.'

'I see. Thank you.'

'And I would just like to say, once again, how sorry I am about your son's death. It must have been hard for you to deal with – in the circumstances.'

Suddenly Mrs Crackenfield looked as though she'd been stabbed and the life was leaching out of her. Femur, who'd had plenty of recent experience of feeling half dead with misery, saw that she wasn't going to be able to say anything. He thanked her again briefly and hustled Caroline out.

'That was a bit tactless, Cally,' he said, once they'd reached the street. 'Not like you.'

'I wanted to see how she'd react.' She sounded much harder than usual and he stared at her. 'There's something odd going on there.'

Femur had always respected her judgement, but this surprised him. 'She was perfectly frank, just didn't want us bothering her daughter. I'd have thought most mothers in her position would have been the same.'

'She was too tense for it to be just that, Guv. Couldn't you feel it? And didn't you look at her hands? They were clutching each other the whole time we were there. She's frightened of something.'

'Her son's just died in squalor. Wouldn't that make anyone tense?'

'Not as much as that. I think I might phone the daughter when we get back.'

'I'm surprised you're not planning to fly straight up there,' Femur said, with unusual sarcasm.

# Chapter 22

Playing phone tag had never done much for Trish's temper and she was beginning to wish she had never involved Dr Bridge in her work for Anna. When he hadn't been incarcerated with patients, Trish had been in court, and vice versa.

She was sluicing herself clean of irritation in the shower at the end of the day when she heard her phone ring. Grabbing a big red towel, she stepped out, sliding on the wet tiles, and picked up the phone just as her machine was about to click in.

George was peacefully cooking again, and delectable scents of fresh coriander and chopped red onion were wafting up the spiral staircase.

'Trish Maguire,' she said into the phone, cutting into the recorded voice.

'Oh, good. This is Mike Bridge. I thought I'd missed you again. So, you've the list of food and drinks. Terrific. What did the old man have before he died?'

Trish read out the list that had arrived from Deb that morning, which matched exactly what Cordelia had already suggested. It was going to give Trish considerable pleasure to tell Cordelia how closely Deb had followed their father's preferences.

'Grapefruit juice,' said Dr Bridge with satisfaction, the Scottish accent clearer than usual in the rolled R and the very precise U. 'In that case he had the whole package, didn't he?'

'I don't understand. What package? And what does grapefruit tell you?'

'Your list of his prescription drugs includes an anti-histamine called terfenadine.'

'I know,' Trish said, trying to curb her impatience. 'And it's never prescribed concurrently with astemizole, which was also found in his body. Together they can, in rare cases, cause arrhythmias that can be fatal. But no one suggested that there was enough astemizole to do that. It was only a minute quantity they found, just enough to throw extra suspicion on his daughter.'

'That's not what I'm talking about. Although that adds to it.'

'Oh?' Trish wished he'd get on with it, but he'd done her a favour by even looking at the medical evidence. She'd have to put up with whatever games he wanted to play. She just hoped he'd finish them before George was ready for her. The sharp, spicy scents from the kitchen were making her mouth water.

'Terfenadine is quite a lot cheaper than astemizole,' Mike Bridge told her. 'The kind of thing a practice might well prescribe for an older patient if they were trying to keep down their drugs bill.'

'And?'

'And it has a rare but occasionally fatal . . .' He paused, as though for dramatic effect.

'Fatal what?' demanded Trish impatiently. 'Come on.'

'Interaction with grapefruit juice.'

'You're joking.' Of all the possibilities Trish had been trying to believe, that had never crossed her mind.

'Nope. Grapefruit juice can inhibit the metabolism of terfenadine, which—'

'—would explain the apparent overdose the pathology labs found,' said Trish, who didn't want to play games.

'Precisely. And that's not all. That's what I meant about the whole package. Now, listen, Trish.'

'I am listening, and I'm taking notes.'

'Good. Your Mr Whatlam had gout, which used to be treated with NSAIDs. You know what they are?'

'Non-steroidal anti-inflammatory drugs,' she said crisply.

'Yup. Now, NSAIDs can, particularly in the elderly, cause peptic ulcers. OK so far?'

'I can just about manage to keep up.'

'Great,' he said, apparently unaware of her mood. 'When Mr Whatlam's ulcer flared up, his doctor correctly advised him to stop taking the NSAIDs and instead put him on a maintenance dose of allopurinol. And to deal with the ulcer, he was put on Cisapride.'

'I remember that, too,' Trish said, wondering whether this was leading anywhere or whether Dr Bridge was so recently out of medical school that he wanted to parade his knowledge.

'And Cisapride should never be prescribed with either astemizole or terfenadine.'

Trish felt as though her whole body had shut down for a second. 'Why?'

'Well,' said the doctor, as though he was enjoying himself, 'the combination increases the possibility of arrhythmias, and in some very rare cases, those arrhythmias have been fatal. The Cisapride would have been a lot more dangerous to him than the tiny trace of astemizole. Add the grapefruit juice and you've a cocktail of interacting drugs, all liable to produce arrhythmias.'

'Are you telling me, Dr Bridges, that you think his heart could have stopped without any suffocation of any kind? Either bag or pillow?'

'Just that.'

'But why didn't they think of that at the trial?'

'They? Which they would that be, Trish?'

'The GP, the pathologists, the labs that tested the bodily fluids. Anyone.'

'Or even the lawyers?'

'Even them,' Trish said, through her teeth. Phil Redstone should have checked every possibility. She couldn't think why he hadn't had a medical expert combing through every aspect of old Mr Whatlam's medical state and treatment to see if there was anything in the autopsy and lab reports to explain any of it. If it was all as obvious as this, why hadn't anyone noticed?

'When was the death, exactly?'

'Just over four years ago,' Trish told him. 'And the trial happened a year later.'

'There's your answer. I don't think anyone had picked up the grapefruit juice problem then, or the interaction of the drugs. It's only in the last two or three years that doctors have become aware of it. And there are still some doctors – and some pathologists – who haven't come across it to this day.'

Trish suppressed her outrage. No one could have knowledge that hadn't been discovered, but she still felt, viscerally, that doctors ought to know everything about the treatments they gave and the drugs they handed out. It sounded as though Foscutt's prescriptions had been as dangerous to old Ian Whatlam as the heroin-paracetamol mix that Mandy's pimp had provided.

'But we're still left with the astemizole,' she murmured

'You know that has a very long half-life, I suppose?'

'Yes. That point at least was made at the trial. It sounds as though it was one of the very few that was.' Trish was boiling with rage on Deb's behalf. 'Unfortunately, it had never been prescribed for anyone who was anywhere near him except for the daughter who's been convicted of his murder.'

'Yes, I know. And unfortunately I can't help you there. I can't see anything to account for it.'

'How long before he died might he have taken the astemizole for some of it to remain in his system?'

'It's hard to say, Trish. In the elderly, drugs are not always metabolised as well as in your younger patient, which is why one's supposed to prescribe a lower dose.'

'But it could have been weeks?'

'Oh, easily. Maybe months. I looked it up to check and the directory recommends that women of child-bearing age who are prescribed it should use contraception while they're taking it and for several weeks afterwards.'

So, if we could only find someone else who'd ever been prescribed it, Trish thought, we might be home and dry.

'Thank you very much, Dr Bridge.'

'Call me Mike. Your mother does when we're not in surgery.'

'Thanks. You've been very helpful.'

'It's a pleasure. Meg's always been one of my greatest supports here. I'd do anything for her. Maybe she'll introduce us the next time you're down here.'

'I'd like that. And if the programme goes ahead, I'll get the producer to get in touch with you.'

'Sure. Oh, before you go . . .'

'Yes?'

'You might like to know that both allopurinal and Cisapride can induce rashes – in other words, urticaria. And angioneurotic oedema is only a severe form of urticaria.'

Trish could hardly breathe as the rage boiled over. When she could produce any sound out of her throat, she said, 'You mean that the whole horrible, terrible situation he was in was caused by the mixture of prescription drugs he was taking?'

'Could have been. It's not that uncommon, particularly in

the elderly. Pharmacists are often very good at picking this kind of thing up, but unfortunately in your old man's case, the doctor's surgery dispensed the drugs, and the dispensing nurse probably never dreamed of doubting her boss's skill. If the doctor was under time and emotional pressure – as he seems to have been from your notes – he might not have checked too carefully when he was prescribing.'

'But it's an outrage,' Trish said, the last word erupting from her mouth. She wanted to see Dr Foscutt in a cell the size of Deb's for the rest of his life, surrounded by the noise that battered her eardrums for twenty-four hours a day.

'All drugs have side effects,' said Mike Bridge peaceably, far too peaceably for Trish's taste. 'It's nearly always a question of balancing a patient's need for relief or cure with possible side-effect damage.'

'Well, it shouldn't be.'

'You've probably had antibiotics yourself at some stage and then had to deal with the thrush they allowed to occur.'

That was true enough, but it did nothing to cool Trish's fury. She was never going anywhere near a doctor again if she could possibly help it.

'But I must go now. Goodbye.'

Trish put down the phone, wondering if she looked as weird as she felt. Light-headed and not at all sure of her balance, she thought she might faint from rage. For the first time she felt true sympathy for old Mr Whatlam.

'Trish?' George called up the stairs. 'We're ready.'

'Great. On my way.' She shook her head to clear it and reached for her leggings and T-shirt. Staggering, she reached the bottom of the spiral stairs two and a half minutes later.

George looked up. He was arranging an elaborate-looking salad on plates already holding grilled lamb chops and tiny squares of fried potatoes decorated with some herb or other. She sniffed and thought she could detect rosemary.

'You all right, Trish? You look as though you've had a shock.'

'Yes. But ultimately a good one. Progress in the Deborah Gibbert case.'

'Good.' There was enough heaviness in that word to make Trish raise her eyebrows and ask what the matter was. 'I only thought how nice it'll be when it's over, this film of Anna's. I might get you back then.'

'Oh, George,' Trish said, her conscience twisting inside her like a bit of barbed wire. Perhaps all the unusually elaborate food he'd been cooking had been intended to make her notice him and see how he felt. And perhaps, now she came to think of it, the unusual number of evenings when he'd had dinners out. 'Have I neglected you?'

'Not exactly,' he said, in the kind of voice that means 'yes'.

'I'm sorry.' She didn't immediately rush into questions about his own cases, which would have been a bit unsubtle, but gradually she worked round to them. His old cheerful smile told her he knew what she was doing, but that was all right. It was cheerful again. That was all that mattered.

Dr Foscutt turned his head on the scratchy pillow to check that Molly was still asleep. Her lips were a little parted and she was breathing quite noisily, for her, but regularly. He should be safe. He pushed back the single sheet that covered them both and slid out of bed, pausing to check on her. She slept on. He stared at her, as he automatically retied his pyjama cord and twisted the trousers round so that the unfastenable fly wouldn't gape.

In the moonlight, which looked so cool but wasn't, she seemed decades younger than in the daytime. He wished he could wake her. She might be able to make it all seem less awful. But she needed her sleep. He couldn't disturb her until he was certain, and even then he wasn't sure it would be fair to tell her.

Every time he thought of the Whatlams or their daughter, his guts felt as though he was dropping forty feet into a crevasse. He couldn't go on like this. The uncertainty was agony. And his patients were suffering. Oh, God! His patients.

He left the bedroom, clutching his grey-flannel trousers and a pair of tennis sneakers. He put them on in the hall and, almost silently, let himself out of the house to drive to the surgery.

At least in the middle of the night he'd have a free run with the records. There was no one around at that hour, and unless the on-call partner had to come in for something, there wouldn't be anyone until seven in the morning.

The waiting room looked odd with no one in it, and the locked door to the dispensary was like an accusation. He averted his eyes and went into the archive room, where all the dead patients' notes and old surgery diaries were kept. He ignored the notes; he knew there'd be nothing there. He'd checked, the police had checked, and the Crown Prosecution Service lawyers had checked. Even the defence lawyers hadn't questioned them.

The surgery diaries were exactly where they should have been, in a neat pile, each one bound in dark blue with their metal spiral bindings gleaming. He found the one for the year of old Ian Whatlam's death and leafed back through it, past the death, weeks past, months. He got all the way back before Christmas before he gave up.

He'd been right. There had been no surgery visits from either of the Whatlams. And yet he had seen her, poor Helen, he knew he had. She'd phoned in one day, months and months before the death, absolutely desperate. She'd been in such a state that his receptionist had asked permission to put her through, even though interruption of surgery patients' five-minute consultations was something he never allowed.

He could remember the morning. He'd been discussing young Mary Haskett's recurring urinary infections and had had to break off his instructions about taking a glass of cranberry juice every day to talk to Helen Whatlam.

She wouldn't be soothed, and she'd started to cry when he'd told her to bring Ian into the surgery the following week, as practice protocols demanded, so he'd been forced to say he'd call in on his way home to lunch.

He'd done it, too. His memory, which had blanked out the whole episode, was tormenting him now with pinpoint accuracy. He'd parked outside the Whatlams' front door and had been locking the car when she'd emerged, hobbling towards him. Her stick had made the gravel rattle as she'd pushed herself off with it at each step, hurrying as though poor bloody-minded Ian had been chasing her.

She'd asked if they could sit in the car because she didn't want Ian overhearing what she had to say. So, they'd sat there, and he'd listened to her and sympathised and done his best to help.

It had been the angioneurotic oedema causing the problem again. Ian had suffered from one form or another for years, and it hadn't been possible to isolate any particular trigger. Helen had begged him, with tears in her eyes again, to try some different treatment.

He could see the picture now: Helen weeping and himself embarrassed and sympathetic. Sweating, he knew he'd reached the crux of it. This was the memory that had been waking him night after night for the past week, and sending his guts into freefall whenever he thought of it during the day.

He had told Helen Whatlam that he had just seen a drug-company rep, who had given him samples of a particularly effective proprietary antihistamine. He had told Helen that she could have one packet, provided she promised not to exceed the stated dose.

Helen had agreed, so he had given her a packet of thirty tablets. And that had been it. He hadn't had time to add it to Ian's notes there and then. He had fully intended to write them up when he went back to surgery that afternoon, but he had forgotten to do it. He must have forgotten, because there was no record in the notes of anything prescribed at the time of that unscheduled visit.

Had the tablets been astemizole? He couldn't remember the names of the drugs companies that had sent reps that week. But the surgery diary would tell him. He looked up astemizole in the *British National Formulary* and saw that it was made by one of the manufacturers whose names were in the diary.

He put his head in his hands. His eyes were tight shut. He flogged his memory like the dead horse it had been. Why hadn't it produced the information before? He thought he knew the answer to that, too.

Deborah Gibbert had made him so angry with her outrageous behaviour in his morning surgery and the appalling things she'd said to him that he had believed her capable of murder. And his subconscious had buried everything and anything that might have cast doubt on her guilt.

Carefully he tidied up the archives to show no sign that he had been there. Nasty little tempting devils in his mind were trying to seduce him into erasing all mention of the drug company's rep from the surgery diary. But he managed to vanquish them.

He drove home, wondering what to do. It didn't prove anything, this recovered memory of his. Deborah Gibbert's fingerprints were still on the plastic bag and her father's saliva inside it. She had probably suffocated him, even if she hadn't given him some of her own prescribed astemizole.

If it hadn't been for that bloody lawyer and her television-producer friend, he could probably have ignored the whole thing. But if they dug it up for their wretched film, he'd be exposed to all kinds of unsavoury publicity and accusations of goodness knew what.

He wondered if Molly would be awake when he got back. He needed her. But it wouldn't be fair to wake her. She couldn't help with this dilemma. He'd always protected her against all the awful decisions he had to make, and he'd continue to do it. She had to move among his patients and their friends every day in the village. She had to be above it all, safely ignorant. If he couldn't even protect his wife any longer, then what was left?

When he reached the house, he opened the front door as quietly as possible and walked silently over the huge doormat.

'Archie?' she called, from the shadows near the hall fireplace. 'Is that you?'

'Yes. It's me,' he said, as he switched on the light.

She was sitting in the leather chair by the empty fireplace, wearing her summer dressing gown. Her grey hair was unbrushed, flying all over the place, and there was fear in her eyes. As he smiled and patted her shoulder, her eyes cleared. But something happened to his smile before he could speak, and his lips started to tremble. His eyes felt hot.

Molly got to her feet and held out her arms. 'What is it, my dear? What is it?'

He let her embrace him, and he tried to tell her.

'I can't hear,' she said, pulling back, but still smiling at him. 'Archie, I can't hear. Come along.'

She took him by the hand and led him into the kitchen. When she had made him sit down at the table, she poured him a glass of her home-made raspberry drink from the fridge.

'Now, what is it?' Her voice was the gentlest he'd ever known and it slid over him, soothing and analgesic, like cough linctus. 'I've known for days that there was something wrong. Tell me.'

He did. He could see from her face that she was listening, but it showed nothing else. When he glanced at her hands, noticing the new swellings around the knuckles, they were clenched around each other. They must be painful. He should have noticed that thickening of the joints; it was almost certainly arthritis. But she'd never complained. He wondered why not and looked away, trying to remember what he'd been saying. Oh, yes. He finished his grim little confession with difficulty and stared down at the table.

He felt her hand on his shoulder and looked up again. She was still smiling. It was going to be all right.

'It's a pity you didn't make a note of what the sample was when you gave it to Helen, but it sounds as though you did it far too long before his death for the pills to have had any bearing on it.'

'Yes, if Ian took all thirty tablets then. But what if they improved the rash and he stopped? Don't you see, Molly? If it got better, Helen would have stopped feeding Ian the tablets and put them away. Then she might have got them out again when he was next in need, which could have been much nearer the time I wrote the terfenadine prescription for Deborah.'

She still didn't understand. She was pouring more raspberry drink into his glass, and her face was blandly kind.

'Don't you see? It could have happened like that, Molly. Helen could have given him the last astemizole tablets at any time up till Deborah's arrival at the house for that last dreadful visit.'

'Yes, Archie, it could have happened like that. But you have no proof that it did. And no one ever suggested it was the mixture of terfenadine and astemizole that actually killed him.'

'Didn't they?'

'No. You've let this get on top of you, my dear. It's understandable, but it's not rational. The labs found hardly any astemizole in him. As far as I can remember, at the trial the prosecution lawyer said the trace they'd found went to show that Debbie had drugged her father to enable her to suffocate him, not that it had caused his death in itself. Don't you remember? You've run yourself ragged over this because you're so tired, and you've got it all out of proportion, my dear.'

He just stared at her. Could it be as easy as this? Could the last week's agony have been simply a manifestation of long-term stress?

'Come back to bed, Archie. You're worn out and not thinking straight. Come to bed and get some sleep.'

'Terfenadine,' he said suddenly, his eyes dilating. He could feel them, as he could feel the shock pumping up his adrenaline levels. 'Where's the *BNF*? There must be one here, too.'

'What are you talking about?'

'The *British National Formulary*,' he said impatiently. Suddenly Molly was no longer the source of all absolution and comfort; just a middle-aged woman whose mind didn't work quickly enough.

He got up, tripping over his unlaced sneaker, and grabbed his black bag. There should be a copy in there. Yes. Thank God for that. He leafed through, looking for the anti-histamines. He couldn't find them. What was the matter with him? He knew his way round this volume as he knew his way round his own surgery. The index would help. Yes. Thank God. There it was.

He looked at the last paragraph of the entry for terfenadine, searching for the note of the counselling that had to be offered to patients prescribed the generic form of the drug. 'Driving,' it said. And that was all.

His heart was banging in his chest. The rhythm was all wrong. It seemed to stop and start again, as though he'd been taking a dangerous mixture of antihistamines himself. He looked higher up the column for the side-effects. They were all right. The cautions were all right, too, just about pregnancy and breast feeding.

For a moment he breathed easily, and his heart slowed back to its proper tempo. His memory must be playing up. A sure sign of stress. He really ought to think about another locum so that he could take Molly away for a good long holiday, away from everyone.

He looked up from the thick red paperback to smile at Molly, to give her some reassurance. But even as his eyes moved up the page, he saw it: 'avoid grapefruit juice'. It was there, after all.

No one had known of the problem when he'd handed the prescription to Deborah Gibbert. That wasn't his fault. But he should have remembered when the news started filtering through that grapefruit juice might be dangerous with terfenadine. He'd been holding to his certainty of the woman's guilt, knowing she'd given her father an overdose. Now he had to face the fact that she might not have done it. He felt as though the very floor beneath him was unstable. Stemetil, he thought. If you've got vertigo, take Stemetil.

Then the terror retreated, like the sea sucking back over the sand on a shelving beach, and his heart steadied once more. The floor felt solid again. What was he worrying about? No patient with gout and ulcers was going to start drinking something as acid as grapefruit juice, for heaven's sake. He smiled at Molly.

He heard her voice buzzing in his ears and tried to listen.

'What's going on, Archie?' she said, very clearly. 'You keep changing colour and you're sweating. My dear, what is the matter? D'you want me to call one of your partners?'

'Heavens, no, Molly. I'm not ill. In fact I'm quite all right again now. It was just a dreadful moment.'

Seeing that she still looked worried, he told her, nearly laughing at himself for having been so irrational as to think that grapefruit juice could have been relevant to Ian Whatlam.

Trish was woken by the phone. Sleepily, she picked up the receiver and said her name.

'Trish? It's Anna. What's this fantastically good news you've got for me?'

Trish blinked and felt George turning over at her side. After what he'd said last night, she hadn't wanted to phone Anna in his hearing. But she'd had an opportunity, while he was reading the paper and she was doing the washing up. She'd rung from the kitchen, only to be answered by Anna's machine. Trish had left a brief message.

'Hang on a sec,' she said now. 'I'm just going to the other phone.'

She kissed George's rumpled hair and told him to sleep on. Downstairs at her desk, she got back to Anna and passed on the news about the interaction of grapefruit juice and terfenadine. There was an enormous gusty sigh from Anna before she said, 'Thank God. I've got a meeting with the channel this morning so that I can make my pitch. They like the preliminary stuff I've sent in, and if they're satisfied after the presentation, they've said they'll commit to all the money I need. I can even pay you now, Trish.'

'So this came just in time.' Trish knew she sounded sharp, but that was too bad. If Anna hadn't pretended to have researchers, or had got off her bottom to find the information sooner, they could have been here weeks ago. And if Phil

Redstone had done his job properly, Deb Gibbert would never have been convicted. If . . . if . . . if.

'Yes. I've made up a very slick presentation document, but I've just got time to add this to the end. It'll be the perfect final cherry on the cake.'

'Anna, it's still not certain that it'll be enough to get Deb out. It's only given us another possible cause of his death.'

'I know. But it's all we really needed. You've done brilliantly.'

'Don't get too excited. There's a long way to go.' Trish rubbed her eyes to get the sticky grits out of the corners. She tried to push her brain up to speed.

'Oh, bollocks to that, Trish. In any case it'll make for a fantastic confrontation.' She sounded excited. 'I've been racking my brains for the climax of the programme. This will be it.'

'Confrontation?' Trish had taken the phone into the kitchen and was trying to fill the kettle while they talked. The phone was clamped between her chin and shoulder and she was holding tight to stop it falling into the open kettle.

'Yes. With Dr Foscutt. Can't you just imagine it?' Anna's voice was lighter and quicker than it had been for a long time. 'And so, Dr Foscutt, when you were prescribing . . .'

'Anna, you're not to spring this on him on screen.'

'Oh, Trish, grow up. It's a rough old world out there. If he made a mistake, and it's looking to me as though he did, don't you think he deserves to be exposed?'

'Not like this. Evidence has to be tested in court. Not on the screen.'

'You're too squeamish. I have to fight for my living. I can't afford your sort of gentlemanliness. I'm going for the jugular: both jugulars.'

'Both?'

'The doctor *and* the lawyer. You've got just what I wanted.

I knew you would. We'll have Phil Redstone on camera, too, and ask him – all sweetness and light – what steps he took to check the effect of the grapefruit juice on a man taking old Mr Whatlam's medicines.'

'No one knew the danger then, Anna.'

The sound of George getting out of bed echoed down the cast-iron spiral staircase.

'Anna, I'm going to have to go. But think carefully about this. The doctor is a pain, he treated Deb badly, he was clearly arrogant. But he's a professional man, and he didn't warn her about grapefruit juice because no one knew of the problem at that date. You can't pillory him on TV for that.'

'I don't see why not. I'll let you know how it goes with the channel commissioners this morning.'

'Anna, I've . . .'

'Don't go yet.' Anna's voice was dangerous enough to make Trish hold on.

'Be quick.'

'I want your word, Trish – your solemn promise – that you won't tip off either Phil Redstone or Dr Foscutt.'

Trish was silent.

'Trish, I have to make you do this. Say you promise.'

'Anna, I can't deal with this now.'

'Then tell me you promise not to talk to them today. And we can sort it out this evening. Will you at least promise me that much, Trish?'

Trish felt as though she were being pulled apart.

'Just till this evening. Haven't we been friends long enough for you to give me that much?'

'Yes,' she said at once. Put like that, there wasn't much else she could say. 'Till this evening.'

' 'Bye, Trish.'

Trish made breakfast and went to dress. It seemed too hot to put on her tights and shoes until she absolutely had to, so she pattered down the spiral staircase in her bare feet. She could feel each bump and roughness in the cold iron treads.

Downstairs, George was tucking into toast and coffee. 'Come and sit down and have something to eat for once, Trish. I really don't know how you get through the day without either breakfast or lunch.' He set about adding a lavish layer of butter to his next slice of toast. 'I'd be dead.'

Trish sat sipping black coffee, watching him tucking in. 'There's not as much of me to keep going,' she said cheerfully.

'You are a monster. Who was your call from?'

She looked at him from under her lashes as she drank her coffee.

'It's OK, Trish. Last night I was feeling a bit weak, I admit it. But this morning I'm as tough as you like. You can tell me. Something about your Gibbert case, I presume?'

She nodded and reached for one of his slices of toast. 'Tell me about what you've got on today,' she commanded, 'while I eat this.'

He laughed, but he did sketch in a light-hearted account of the clients he was supposed to see later, and a couple of his more difficult partners, and a new outdoor clerk.

'I wish we could persuade him to take up the law as a career,' he added. 'He's a bright lad, but he's on his way to drama school in September. Clearly thinks we're all barking mad. He can hardly keep from laughing at the lot of us all day.'

'He's got something, George. No solicitor is entirely right in the head.'

'At least we're not a bunch of leaky mountebanks like you lot at the Bar.'

'Mountebanks!' Trish was laughing as she tried to swallow the last corner of naked toast. 'What a ludicrous word! Anyone would think you were a hundred and ten.'

George was about to retaliate when they heard the post thump on the mat. He wiped his mouth on his napkin and went off to fetch it for her. Trish accepted the pile, which included a fattish Jiffy-bag, with a smile and put it at the far end of the table.

'Oh, go on, open it,' he said, hauling open *The Times*, which he had picked up from the mat at the same time. 'I don't mind.'

Trish raised her eyebrows at the unresponsive newspaper and ripped open the envelopes, piling bills in one heap, letters to be answered in another, and dropping the empty envelopes and the exasperating circulars and advertisements on the floor. At the bottom she came to the Jiffy-bag.

Inside it was a bundle of letters in the kind of shaky but elegant writing an elderly person might produce, along with a note in much more modern scrawl.

Dear Trish,
Thank you very much for being so kind to me. I don't know how I would have managed if it hadn't been for you. I've talked to my dad about it all, even a bit about my real father, and things are easier now. It'll be all right when Mum comes home, I know.

I went through Granny's recent letters to give you a selection that show what she was like. You said you'd send them back to me when you'd finished with them, and I would like that.

Thank you again for everything.
Yours sincerely, Kate Gibbert

Trish hardly noticed that George had poured more coffee into her cup. She picked it up and drank as she read what Helen Whatlam had written to her granddaughter.

The letters were, as Kate had originally said, evidence of a kind, sensitive woman. They didn't say much about her own life, except to describe what was out in the garden and which friends she had recently seen, but they offered Kate a lot of helpful, sound advice for dealing with bullying schoolmates and unhappy siblings. To Trish they were redolent of the kind of common sense and gentleness that Meg had always given her. But there was nothing revelatory in any of them, until the last.

You are sweet, Kate, to be so sympathetic about your grandfather's ailments. It's true, he hasn't been very well these last few days. His rash is very much worse, and this time it's spread beyond his face and hands.

To tell you the truth, I was at my wits' end to know what to do, but luckily the doctor came after all. He's given me some extra-strong pills with a name I can never remember. It sounds rather like semolina, so that's what I call them. Unfortunately your grandfather didn't think it was at all funny. Still, the pills are doing him some good and he's much more comfortable now.

He sends his love, and so, dear Kate, do I. Don't work too hard. Exams are very important, especially nowadays, but your health and happiness are even more important than doing well at school.

'And that,' Trish said aloud, 'is presumably how the astemizole got into Ian Whatlam.'

George put down the paper and smiled to show how receptive he was. But Trish thought he'd listened enough for one breakfast and told him they ought to be getting to work.

While she was going through her post in chambers, the phone rang. It was Meg. 'So,' she said straight away, 'what's the problem?'

'Nothing,' Trish said, making herself concentrate on work

and Deb. 'I've got a big workload at the moment, but I'm ploughing through it.'

'Don't waste my time, Trish,' Meg said. 'Or your own. You were all of a doo-dah the other day when Mike Bridge was here. And it's nothing to do with work. You'd been to see Paddy, hadn't you? Did he upset you?'

'We should have got past all this ESP by now.'

'I think I'll always know when something's hurt you, Trish,' Meg said, in her usual matter-of-fact voice. There was nothing sentimental about her. 'What did he say?'

'He told me he used to beat you up.'

There was a pause, but it was very short. 'Not very often, Trish. In fact, only once, really badly.'

'Why didn't you tell me?'

'Come on. He's your father, you're half his. I hate those women who slag off their husbands to their children. It's not the children's fault if the marriage has gone bad. And it's not fair to make your child feel responsible for her other parent's misdeeds.'

It was breathtaking. Literally. Trish had to make herself suck in air.

'Sometimes I think you ought to write a guide to good mothering,' she said lightly. 'But why, how, and how did you bear it?'

'It's ancient history. He made me angry, Trish, and I didn't know how to deal with it, and so I let myself gee him up. He—'

'Don't blame yourself.' The words came out with an urgency that shocked even Trish. 'Victimised women always do that. It's how the whole syndrome works. You—'

'Stop it, Trish, and listen.' Meg was sharp enough to be obeyed. 'We played stupid destructive games, Paddy and I. I didn't understand them then, but I do now. He likes drama, as you know. That's why he's always falling in love. He likes the passion and the excitement, and he enjoys raising people's demons. Do you know what I'm talking about?'

'Not entirely,' Trish said. But she had a fair idea. She'd done a bit of it herself in the past, until she'd understood.

'We all have them living in the primeval swamp, somewhere in our subconscious. D'you know what I'm talking about now?'

'I suppose.'

'Well, Paddy likes digging them up and watching them frolic. What he's not interested in is seeing them for what they are, hosing them down, and making them walk calmly side by side with someone else's.'

'And that's what you and Bernard . . .?'

'That's what anyone in a successful relationship has to do, Trish.' There was enough quiet emphasis in the words to make her understand that Meg had wanted to say this for a long time. Trish made an encouraging noise, which was all she could manage.

'If the pair of you can't make your demons walk in a well-behaved crocodile, then there's no hope. Not in the long-term, anyway.'

Trish was struggling. She knew what Meg meant, but the implications were more than she wanted to deal with just then.

'I'm not sure there are all that many well-behaved crocodiles, Mum,' she said. 'And if there's ever been any animal more like a demon in the primeval swamp than a crocodile, well-behaved or otherwise, I've never heard of it.'

'You'll work it out, Trish,' said Meg, adding casually, 'Bring George for Sunday lunch one weekend. Bernard likes him, too.'

# Chapter 23

Caroline and Jess were eating cold chicken and dill mayonnaise on the roof terrace of the flat, watching the sun turn the sky the colour of smoked salmon behind the high-rise flats across the road. Jess had only one more day's filming to go, then she would be back signing on and going after every possible audition. But she seemed much more sanguine than usual at this stage. And she was pleased with the work she had done, which always made her happy.

'That was great, Jess,' Caroline said, licking the last of the mayonnaise off her fork. 'Thanks.'

'I . . . Oh, bloody hell, sodding, fucking hell,' said Jess, as Caroline's mobile cheeped on the teak bench beside her.

'Sorry. Got to answer.'

'I know. It's a murder. I'll get the fruit. Don't move.'

'Sergeant Lyalt,' Caroline said into the phone, watching Jess's slim back view disappear into the flat.

'This is Georgina Painswick. You left a message for me to call a couple of days ago. I'm afraid we've only just got back from Spain. Is it about my brother, Henry Crackenfield?'

'Thank you for phoning back, Mrs Painswick. No, it's not in fact about your brother. I wanted to ask for some background information about Malcolm Chaze, the MP who was shot last week. I take it you do know he's dead?'

'Naturally. But I doubt if there's much I can tell you. I

haven't seen him since I was in my teens. What made you think I could help?'

'We've been collecting the names of all his girlfriends and talking to each one.'

Georgina Painswick snorted. 'I was hardly a girlfriend. It was a Christmas holiday fling when I was too young to know any better.'

'Why did it end?'

'Because term started,' she said crisply. 'I went back to school, and so did he.'

'Did he ever talk to you about drugs?'

There was silence, broken eventually by a sigh. 'You must know that he did, if you've got on to me. This is what it's all about, isn't it?'

'I don't understand.'

'Oh, come on.' She sounded angry. 'It's not *my* relationship with Malcolm you're interested in, but Henry's.'

'Why do you say that? Did your brother try to introduce Malcolm Chaze to drugs?'

Caroline hardly noticed Jess coming back with two large flat bowls filled with raspberries.

Georgina Painswick laughed unpleasantly. 'Can it really be possible that you don't know?'

'No. I don't understand what's amusing you so much, either.'

'There's nothing remotely amusing about this. Malcolm Chaze never had any money.'

'So?'

'And Hen and I were spending quite a lot that Christmas holidays. We'd inherited a bit from a kind of trust our grandfather had set up. Not a real income, but more than just an allowance. There were a lot of parties that year, and we all needed to pay for clothes and drinks and taxis. I think we even went to Annabel's once. Malc hated being left out, or looking wrong, or not being able to pay his share, so he needed some cash.' Mrs Painswick paused.

Caroline thought she knew at last where this was going, but she didn't want to lead her witness. 'OK,' she said. 'What happened?'

'Malc got hold of some heroin from somewhere and started trying to flog it. He had a go at me, but luckily I was scared enough to refuse.'

'I thought he'd always been fanatically antidrugs,' Caroline protested.

'Filthy hypocrite. I can tell you, Sergeant Lyalt, that when I read in the paper that he'd been shot by a drug-dealer I thought it was poetic justice, I really did.'

'We did hear that he had once experimented himself and had a bad time. Was that while you knew him?'

'Malc take heroin? You have to be joking. He wasn't going to shoot up his profits. He was only ever in it for the money.'

'So when did he start being so vociferously anti-drugs?'

'When he decided to go in for politics and was afraid that his past might catch up with him, the slimy bastard. D'you know what he did then? Have you any idea?'

Jess was beginning to get restive on the bench opposite Caroline's, but this was far too important to risk interrupting. Caroline got up with the phone held against her ear and went indoors in search of pen and paper. She heard Jess's voice behind her but ignored it.

'No, Mrs Painswick. What did he do?'

'Went round to my parents' house to call on them and tell them that he was trying to get into Parliament in order to put something back, make up for what he'd done, and said that he wanted them to forgive him for wrecking Hen's life.' Each word came out as though it had been spat.

'How had he done that?'

'You must know. For God's sake, he made my brother buy

heroin, watched him get addicted and introduced him to a real-life big-time dealer to carry on where he, Malc, had left off.'

'What?'

'Now d'you understand?'

'Yes, I think so. Tell me, did your parents know what Malcolm Chaze had done?'

'Of course they did. Hen could never keep anything to himself; and he was rather proud of being a friend of Malc's. Old Malc was always a charismatic bugger, even at school. That's why Hen did what he wanted in the first place, and bought the bloody stuff off him. Listen, Sergeant, that man deserved shooting – in fact, he deserved a whole lot worse. Don't waste your sympathy.'

'Mrs Painswick, why didn't your parents ever expose him?'

'Because they're too damned decent, and probably because they didn't want to betray Hen's weakness to the world. But when Malc came on his creepy quest for forgiveness, my father gave him an ultimatum: stay away from drugs; keep your nose clean; stick to the party line if you ever do get accepted by a constituency; accept the whip; and do not ever come anywhere near any member of our family again. My father said he told Malc that if he ever stepped out of line the whole story would go straight to Central Office.'

'Thank you, Mrs Painswick. Thank you very much indeed. You've been very helpful. I hope you enjoyed your holiday.'

'It was terrific, thank you, especially once I'd heard that Malcolm Chaze was dead.'

'Right. I must go now. Thank you for your help. Goodbye.' Caroline was already dialling the number of Femur's mobile as she ran back to the roof terrace. 'Jess, darling, I've got to go.'

A metallic voice told her that it wasn't possible to connect the call.

'I'm really sorry about the raspberries. I hope tomorrow goes fantastically well for you. I'll be back as soon as I can. I love you.'

Caroline ran out of the flat. The lift didn't move when she whacked the button, so she ran down all six flights of stairs. Even so, she was hardly panting as she unlocked the car. All that weight training and running had paid off.

She drove to Femur's house, praying that he hadn't hit the whisky or gone out to the pub. There were lights on downstairs. She couldn't understand why he'd switched off his phone. The car had never been so badly parked before, but she didn't want to waste time straightening it. She didn't even lock it, just ran up to the front door to ring the bell and bang the knocker.

'Hold on,' Femur shouted. He didn't sound plastered. Thank God for that. She waited. She waited a full five minutes, punctuated by the occasional reassurance that he would be coming in a moment. At last she heard footsteps and then the door opened. He looked stone cold sober and a lot happier.

'Cally?' He sounded surprised. 'What's up?'

'You all right, Guv?'

'Yes. Why?'

'Five minutes to answer the door?'

'Was it that long? Sorry.' His smile was almost blinding and his eyes were gleaming like diamonds again. 'That was Sue on the phone. She's coming back.'

'Great. But now we've got to go back to the Crackenfields'. I'll explain on the way. I'll drive.' She suddenly realised how momentous his news must have seemed and took the time to smile properly at him. 'It's really great about Sue, Guv. But let me tell you what I've just learned.'

She could hardly bear the time he needed to put his shoes back on and lock all the windows he'd opened to cool the house off after a day's stultifying heat. At last he was ready. Even then he wouldn't let her start her explanation until they were sitting in her car and she was heading towards Pimlico.

'And so,' he said, at the end of her breathless outpouring, 'you think it's possible that Crackenfield had Chaze shot after his own son died of the drugs that Chaze had introduced him to?'

'Yes. Steve Owler's notes show that Crackenfield spent all his working life in the army and still has close links with his regiment. He could easily have heard the names of squaddies who'd come out and gone underground.'

'That does happen,' Femur admitted. 'Yes, it is a possible answer. We'll have to look into it.'

It was nearly ten by the time they were parked outside the Crackenfields' house. Femur let Caroline go up the steps first. The door was opened by Mrs Crackenfield, looking just as elegant but even more washed-out than the first time they'd been there. She was wearing a discreet black dress with three-quarter-length sleeves and pearls. As she recognised them, she produced a tiny smile.

'Sergeant Lyalt, what a pleasure. But could this wait until the morning? My husband and I have relatives with us tonight. We're in the middle of dinner – I mean, we've just got to the pudding stage.'

'I'm really sorry, Mrs Crackenfield,' Caroline said, 'but we need to have a word with your husband. It won't take long, but we do need to speak to him tonight. Now, in fact. I wonder if you could maybe give your guests their pudding while we talk to him somewhere else?'

'What is it, Margaret?' demanded a loud male voice.

'Darling,' she said clearly, half turning her head away from them, 'could you come here for just a second?'

A man as tall as she was, but a great deal broader, emerged

into the hall behind her. He was still wiping his lips with a large white damask napkin. Mrs Crackenfield smiled faintly at the two police officers and left them with her husband. They saw her move silently down the hall, brush his arm with her hand and move into the room where he had come from.

'Well? What is all this?' he barked, clearly angry.

Caroline went through the usual performance with her warrant card.

'Haven't we been bothered enough? My son is dead and buried. The whole terrible story is surely over now. Must you come worrying us again?'

'This has nothing to do with your son's death,' Caroline said, not quite accurately. 'Could we come inside? We need to ask you a few questions. Perhaps your study would be suitable?'

Femur moved up to join her on the top step. He could carry quite a presence when he chose and she was glad to see that tonight he had chosen. He seemed as powerful as she'd ever known him. Brigadier Crackenfield yielded, turning away to precede them to the stairs.

His study was the small room over the front door, which had been turned into a bathroom in most of the similar houses Caroline had known. There was room for a big Carlton House desk in the window and both sides of the room were lined with books. There was a strong smell of pipe smoke, unlike the rest of the house, which smelt only of flowers and polish.

There was a tilting swivel chair in front of the desk and a velvet-coloured wing chair in one corner. That was all.

Brigadier Crackenfield sat at his desk, swivelling around to face them. Femur gestured to Caroline to take the wing chair and he himself leaned against the bookcase nearest the door. Caroline opened her mouth to start, but caught Femur's eye and let him speak.

He did it well, she had to admit, sounding clear and unemotional as he ran through the few facts surrounding Malcolm Chaze's death, then followed them with everything they had learned about the dead man's connection with the family.

Crackenfield sat with a very straight back, listening. At the end, he took his pipe from the pocket of his suit jacket and held the bowl comfortably in his hand. He made no effort to fill or light the pipe.

'Admirably put, Chief Inspector. But I do not understand why you have forced your way into my house, interrupting my guests' dinner, to tell me all this.'

'Because we have to talk to everyone who could have been involved in Mr Chaze's death,' said Femur, committing himself at a much earlier stage than Caroline thought either right or sensible.

She saw from Crackenfield's slack jaw and staring eyes that he was dumbfounded.

'Don't be a fool, man. Do you really think that if I had stooped to take revenge on that man for what he did to my family I would have chosen something like this?'

'No?'

'Good God, no. Think about it, Femur. I had only to lift the telephone and talk to Central Office to have him blacklisted by the Party. I had only to talk to a journalist, and, God knows, we've had enough of them sniffing around since my son's death, to have Malcolm Chaze blazoned all over the front pages as the hypocritical blackguard he was. Why should I of all people want to have him shot?'

'I'd have said you had plenty of reason. Either of your two other scenarios would have involved publicity for your family and the further blackening of your son's name.'

'My son had no reputation left.' The quietness of his voice did nothing to sweeten its bitterness. 'He had not had any kind of public role, not even a job, for over twenty years. I am retired. My daughter lives hundreds of miles away under her married name. None of us would have been damaged by the publicity.'

He looked at his pipe, polishing its side on his handkerchief. When he let his eyes lift again, Caroline saw that they were bleaker than ever.

'It is possibly the worst, certainly I hope the last, humiliation my son has wreaked upon me that the police should come to my house to accuse me of murder.'

A slight cough made them all look towards the door. Margaret Crackenfield stood there, with a light mackintosh over the black dress. A small suitcase stood on the floor beside her.

'Margaret, have you gone mad? Our guests!'

'I asked them to go. As soon as I realised what these officers had come for, it seemed best. We don't want a horrible scene.' She smiled first at Caroline, then at Femur. 'Shall we go?'

'Margaret!'

'Don't, my dear. Let's have some dignity.'

'They have no reason to question me, Margaret. And so there is not the slightest need for this magnificent, but absurd, gesture. Take off your coat.'

'It's no gesture, John.' She sounded very tired. 'I did it. Or rather, I had it done.'

The three of them stared at her.

'It seemed suddenly impossible that that man should live while my son was dead.'

'Margaret.'

'Mrs Crackenfield,' Femur said. She turned her head to smile sweetly at him again. 'Mrs Crackenfield, I must caution you that you do not have to say . . .'

'Yes. I know all that,' she said, long before he had finished. 'That's quite all right, Chief Inspector. But shall we go? I am not sure quite how much more John can take.'

'But why? How?' Her husband's big hand squeezed around the polished bowl of the pipe and he was breathing fast and hard. But there were no other signs of emotion.

'Oh,' Mrs Crackenfield said almost casually, 'I thought Hen's dealer would probably know someone who could shoot Malcolm for me. And it wasn't that expensive. I was surprised. I had thought I might have to sell my pearls.' Her hand stroked them. 'But in fact it didn't cost much more than a month of poor Hen's smack.'

'Margaret. You're not telling me that you—'

'Bought his drugs? Oh, yes, my darling. He couldn't afford them on benefit, and he had to have them. Methadone never worked for him. He couldn't get it right or something. And it was better that he was happy and addicted and safe, instead of burgling and going to prison again. You know what happened to him there.'

'Margaret . . .'

'His dealer was trustworthy. Quite a nice boy. And I knew the smack would be clean this way, not cut with something lethal. It was better, my darling. It really was.'

She left the suitcase where it was and crossed the short distance to his chair. There she took his head between her hands and kissed his domed, sweating forehead.

'I think if the baby had turned out to be ours, it might have been different. There would have been something to live for, to stay out of prison for. But he wasn't, and so we have nothing left of Hen. Georgina is safe and happy. And you'll be all right. You don't need me. And I could not go on living in the knowledge that Malcolm was swaggering around these streets and writing articles in *The Times* about the evils of drugs and drug dealers. And "everyone who cares about real justice". I could not bear it. He had no right to live, you see.'

She turned to smile at Caroline again. There were tears in

her eyes, but her voice was remarkably steady. 'I think we ought to go now, Sergeant Lyalt,' she said, 'before things are said that shouldn't be said. Will you help me?'

'Yes. I'll help you. Come along, Mrs Crackenfield.'

Caroline took her arm and felt her shake. Together they walked out of the room, Caroline picking up the suitcase as they passed.

# Chapter 24

'And so, Trish,' said Femur's voice in her ear, 'I thought it only fair to let you know that we have a confession for the Chaze killing. It had nothing to do with your inquiries into the Deborah Gibbert case. So you're safe.'

Trish hadn't realised he'd known how frightened she had been.

'Confessions aren't always real,' she said lightly, trying not to give any more away. 'Don't forget Deb's mother's.'

'This one holds water all right, and it's taking us a lot further than I'd even hoped.'

'Mixed metaphors, Chief Inspector.'

'Not necessarily. If a boat doesn't hold water, it can't take you anywhere. If it does, it can. Right?'

For a moment she thought he was insulted, then she heard the laughter and joined in. 'Right,' she said. 'So, what have you got?'

'The name of the person who put out the contract, the one who accepted it, and the go-between, who also provided a channel for the money. We've recovered most of that – cash, of course – and there are enough prints on the notes to make the case against all three of them as near cast-iron as your lot will ever allow.'

My lot, thought Trish. Now I am insulted. I owe you one for that, Femur.

'And was it a dealer, as you always thought?' she asked sweetly.

'There was a dealer involved, yes.'

Trish wasn't sure what he was holding back, but she knew enough about him by now to know that she wouldn't get any more unless he chose to give it to her, so there was no point asking.

'He's being sweated now. With luck he'll cough and we'll get whole chains of supply as well as all the conspirators to murder, but the dealing details will just be bunce as far as I'm concerned.'

Trish tried to suppress her curiosity in the interests of dignity – and to pay him back for his crack about the Bar – but it was eating at her. She needed to know who had hated – or feared – Malcolm Chaze so much and why. She gritted her teeth.

'It was good of you to let me know. I don't suppose you're going to tell me who it is or what the motive was?'

'No.' There was a pause before he added, 'But you won't have long to wait. It'll be in the papers as soon as we go to committal. You know I can't tell you any more just now, don't you, Trish?'

'It wasn't either Kate Gibbert or her father, I take it?'

'No. Not them.' Trish could hear that Femur was enjoying himself, so that was the last question she'd ask.

'Good. Well, thank you very much for letting me know. It was a kind thought.' That was better, she decided. That really sounds as though I don't even want to know the rest. He may not believe it, but it's enough to save my face.

'I'm curious, too, you know,' he said suddenly. She smiled to herself, but said nothing. Let him ask. 'Did you ever turn up anything definitive in the Deborah Gibbert case?'

'You'll see all the details on Anna Grayling's programme. It shouldn't be long now, because they're starting to shoot next week.'

'Fair's fair, I suppose.'

'Absolutely, Chief Inspector Femur. You have to observe your professional discretion, so do I.'

'Who'll be appearing on your friend's programme – apart from you, of course?'

'You may be a trained interrogator, but I think I'm probably proof against your probing,' Trish said, with a laugh that was supposed to conceal her continuing anxiety for Deb and Kate.

They were no longer Trish's responsibility, but she couldn't stop thinking about them. She'd already taken far too much time away from her own work, and as soon as Anna's bank had stopped threatening her and Deb's solicitors had briefed one of the best silks to handle her appeal, Trish had handed over all her information and intuitions and picked up her own practice again. Dave would probably never forgive her for the risks she'd taken with that.

Phil Redstone's hostility worried her less than Dave's. Even though she'd made it clear that she wasn't acting for Deb in any capacity and had refused to take any public part in Anna's film, Phil was badmouthing her all over the Temple. That was a pain, but she didn't think he carried enough weight to do her any real damage.

'Probably,' Femur said, sounding much more friendly than Trish would have expected. But then Ian Whatlam's death hadn't been one of his cases, so he had no particular axe to grind. 'Well, good luck with the programme.'

'Thank you. I expect we'll meet again one of these days.'

'I hope so – at least so long as it's a social meeting. I don't want you on any more of my murder cases, Ms Maguire.'

'I'll do my best to keep out of your way next time, Chief Inspector.'

'You do that. Goodbye. And congratulations – if they're in order. I rather suspect they will be. I've sometimes wished I had you on my team.'

He didn't wait for a comment, and Trish was left to wonder just how much he had picked up of the supposedly secret information Anna was going to use in her film.

Trish put down the phone and turned back to her cooking. George was due any minute and there were still things to be done. She checked through what she'd achieved so far. The flowers were already arranged on the table and the candles waited to be lit. The champagne was chilling, and the oysters were ready opened on their beds of cracked ice, with tasteful trails of seaweed decorating the edges. Buying the seaweed had been more laborious and expensive than almost anything else, but the more difficult it had become, the more determined she had been to get it.

The whole dinner was a cliché, a kind of seducer's Valentine's Day dinner, but George shared enough of her sense of humour to appreciate it. It was important to have a joke going if she were to show him, as she wanted, that she was back – properly back and undistracted by Anna, Deb, or even Kate. George's mask of interest and support had cracked only once more, but Trish now knew just how distracted she had been. And she wanted to make it right. Making him laugh was probably the best way of doing that.

His key grated in the lock and she turned away from the elegant table to see a huge bunch of dark-red roses advancing into the room over a pair of long, sturdy grey-flannel legs. So, their minds were still moving in the same direction. As Trish laughed, George looked round the flowers.

'I just wanted to say sorry for being so childish,' he said. Trish moved aside to show him *her* gesture. He put down the flowers and reached for her.

Later, when they'd eaten the oysters and drunk most of the champagne, he raised the subject of Anna's film himself.

'In fact,' Trish said, reaching for the bottle, 'I'm not going to have anything to do with it.'

The sudden anxiety in his eyes made her feel maternal.

'Not because I don't think you could cope,' she said, grinning at him, 'but because I've got too much work, and I don't want to muddy my professional reputation with this kind of thing. I've given Anna everything I've found out, so it's her job now. And it's one she's very good at.'

'Do you know who she's got to appear?'

'She's done fantastically well. The appalling Dr Foscutt has agreed to speak on camera, admitting that he had no idea of the interaction of grapefruit juice and terfenadine at the time, which . . .'

'Which is fair, isn't it? I mean, not many people knew then.'

'Right. But what wasn't fair was ignoring the information when it did come to light.'

'That isn't a crime, though.'

Trish wrinkled her nose. 'Maybe not. But I think he was grossly negligent, both in his treatment of the old man and the way he behaved to Deb. If we could only have proved that he did at some stage give Ian Whatlam astemizole we might be able to get him charged with perjury, but I can't see it happening now.'

'So he'll get away scot-free?'

Satisfaction made Trish's finger ends tingle as she thought of her most recent conversation with Adam. He might once have believed his wife guilty, but he was making up for it now.

'Not completely. Deb's husband has made an official complaint to the General Medical Council. It may not stick and the frightful Foscutt probably won't come before the disciplinary committee until after Deb's appeal's been heard, but it does mean that he'll experience some titchy part of the misery he visited on her and her family.'

'Revenge?' George said lightly.

'Oh, yes. I may have learned to control my vehemence,' Trish said, raising her glass in a toast, 'but I haven't lost one scruple of my rage. I want him punished, and if making him live in anxiety about his professional future is the only way, that'll do. His mistakes caused appalling misery and I don't think he'd have made them if he hadn't let himself hate Deb. If there hadn't been any malice in what he did, I wouldn't be so angry. But I think there was, and so I think he ought to pay.'

George was looking at her with an expression she couldn't read. She hoped he wasn't preparing a little lecture about the illegitimacy of vengeance.

'What?'

A slow smile revealed the man she'd always known he was, even when he retreated behind one of his disapproving masks.

'Don't go soft on me, Trish,' he said seriously. 'I know your rage scares me sometimes, but it's part of you. I can cope with it. And I couldn't cope with knowing I'd made you pretend to be less than you are. OK?'

She let the reassurance spread its warmth up and down her spine, freeing muscles and feelings that she hadn't even known were constricted.

'OK, George.'

# Epilogue

For the moment there was peace. Millie and her friend Steph had been persuaded to play up in her room, well away from Marcus's sarcastic tongue. Deb had given him the new ointment for his hands and it seemed to be helping. The awful rash had first appeared in the week after her release, and it had got worse over the two years since then. Everyone had told her that her return was the miracle her whole family had been praying for. Marcus's hands told the true story.

He was sitting at the dining table, opposite Louis, quietly doing his homework. Deb and Adam were sharing the sofa and the newspaper, which neither of them had had time to read that morning. Adam reached out a hand.

Deb put down the foreign news and took it, trying to feel what she knew he wanted to give her.

The old gas fire in front of her was sputtering. It only just gave out enough heat, and it made the small untidy room stuffy. She glanced at her watch.

Adam must have seen the movement, because he let go of her hand, carefully smiling at her before he went back to the sports pages. He was a good man. She knew he'd not found it easy to have her back. Life was better now than it had been just after her release, but there were still times when they didn't know what to say to each other, or how to be easy together. Sometimes when she saw him bracing himself against the irritable outburst he knew she was about to produce, she hated herself for making his life so hard. At other times she hated him for not understanding how difficult it was to come back from where she'd been.

Occasionally, when the children were all out or sleeping over with friends, they tried to make love, but it was hard. Maybe they expected too much, or maybe they just didn't trust each other enough yet. Still, they were beginning to be able to achieve these odd casual caresses, a light brushing against each other in the kitchen, even a kiss sometimes.

Deb smiled, almost loving him, just as the phone began to ring. Marcus flung down his pen, shouting, 'How am I supposed to get anything done in this place? It's like Piccadilly Circus. If you two had the slightest interest in my future you'd arrange a quiet room where I could work in peace. Or let me go and live with Aunt Cordelia as she wants me to.'

He's only eleven, thought Deb. What will he be like in five years' time? And why can't Cordelia leave us alone and stop making my life so bloody hard? Hasn't she seen me punished enough yet?

Deb caught sight of Louis's scared face and tried to smile. The phone was still ringing. She hoped it wasn't Cordelia at the other end, pretending to try to make peace so that she could have another opportunity to grind Deb's face in the mud. On the other hand, it might be Kate. Deb reached for the phone, hearing Adam say firmly, 'You're down here with the rest of us, Marcus, because you made Millie cry by sneering at her game with Steph. If you'd treated them properly, they'd be down here, and you would be upstairs in your room out of earshot. Until you can learn to be kinder, Marcus, you'll find yourself having this kind of trouble all the time.'

'That's stupid.'

Deb tried to concentrate on the love and patience in Adam's voice instead of the contempt in Marcus's. She knew the raw skin on his hands was hurting him. She knew he couldn't help it. She glanced over her shoulder as she left the room with the phone clamped to her ear. Marcus's face was withered and withering with contempt.

'Mum?' called a bright voice down the phone. 'It's me, Kate.'

'How lovely, darling! How are you?'

'Fantastic. Great. And you?'

'Things are going well.' Deb longed to pour out all her difficulties and miseries, but that wasn't fair. There was nothing Kate could do about any of them, and she shouldn't have her university years spoiled with worrying over her mother's problems. 'What's the news?'

'They are letting me switch to law next year.'

'Oh.' Deb tried to forget how much she hated lawyers. She summoned up all her memories of pleasure to colour her voice: 'That's really exciting, Kate. I'm so pleased.'

'Me too. It should make it easier for me to read for the Bar. Did I tell you how great Trish Maguire was last week?'

'Yes, you told me.'

'She showed me all round the Temple and took me to court with her and then out to supper. She thinks I'd make a really good barrister, and when I've got all my exams, if I'm still keen, she'll talk to the head of chambers about me. She can't guarantee that they'll give me pupillage, of course, but she—'

'Whoa, whoa, Kate. Hold on a moment. I thought you were thinking about being a solicitor. It's dreadfully expensive being—'

'At the Bar. I know. Trish went into it all with me. You can't get a grant and it's two years before you're even ready for pupillage. You hardly earn anything as a pupil and are unlikely to get up to a proper living wage for several years after that, and you have all sorts of expenses. I know. But it's what I want, more than anything in the world. Trish says she's sure I can do it.'

Damn Trish Maguire, thought Deb ungratefully. Damn her.

Without Trish, she knew she'd still be behind her door in the prison. But she could have done without this.

'We'll do our very best, Kate, but we may not be able to afford it. There are the other three to think of, too.'

'I know that, Mum.' Kate's voice was fat with confident happiness.

Deb could hardly bear to think of all the things that might drain it out of her. Life's emotional liposuction, she thought.

'And I'm not expecting you to pay.'

'It's not likely that you—'

'Mum, wait a moment and listen.'

'You deserve to have whatever you want, Kate, and I long to give it to you. But we may not be able to afford it.'

'But that's why I'm ringing.'

Deb stared at the photograph of Kate hanging on the wall ahead of her. She hadn't heard Kate sound as excited as that since she was a child young enough to be thrilled by birthday-cake candles. She didn't think she could bear to be responsible for quenching that thrill.

'I've had a letter from Laura Chaze's solicitors. You know, my . . . my father's wife.'

'Yes. I know who she is. What did the lawyers want?'

'To tell me that my father's will has finally been proved. It was all terribly complicated, apparently, partly for tax reasons but also because he wrote a codicil just after he met me that first time, and because of the way he'd worded it, it meant he'd set up a trust. They've been trying to work out how to deal with it ever since.'

'A trust?' Deb didn't realise she was frowning until the pain of her tight skin reached her brain. 'Did he leave you something?'

'Sort of, but in the codicil he left instructions that if anything happened to him his widow was to pay for whatever professional training I needed to follow the career of my choice.'

'How very kind of him.' Deb felt as though she was speaking round a tennis ball stuck in her throat. 'But it may not be—'

'No. Listen, Mum. This is important. Legally she's got to fund me through whatever post-graduate qualification I want to get. The lawyers even say that my father specified . . . Hang on, here it is. "Medicine or law or accountancy – whatever she chooses. I want her to have a proper profession and enough money to fund a decent life while she qualifies."'

'How generous.' Deb wished she could feel pleased. Through the open door she could see the chaotic living room, and the back of Adam's head. His dandruff had got very bad while she was in prison and it had dusted his shoulders with gritty white particles. Marcus was still ranting from the homework table and now Louis was sniffing. From where she stood, at the foot of the stairs, she could hear every word of Millie's game of going to prison. Deb knew she should be glad that Kate was getting out of all this. She *was* glad.

'And Trish has said that she'll introduce me to everyone in her chambers between now and then and show me how to make myself acceptable to them all. Isn't that great?'

Deb felt warmth rushing through her whole mind and body, washing out the resentment that it should be Malcolm's money that gave Kate what she wanted, that once again she was going to be left behind.

'Yes, my darling,' she said. 'It's great. But you don't need anything like that to prove that you're acceptable. Anyone would accept you as you are.'

'That's sweet, Mum, but there's a hell of a lot I've got to learn. I must go now. Love to the others. 'Bye.'

'Goodbye, Kate,' she said and, still holding the phone, went back.

'Can't you shut the door?' said Marcus bitterly. 'There's a frightful draught.'

'Hush,' said Adam, pointing to the television in the corner. The six o'clock news was on and a familiar figure was posturing on the steps of some grand building. The newscaster's voice said, 'Dr Archibald Foscutt appeared today in front of the disciplinary committee of the General Medical Council. He was cleared of all charges of gross professional negligence in connection with the death of Ian Whatlam.'

There was a short pause, a rustle of papers in Archie Foscutt's hands, a dry cough and then an obviously prepared statement: 'While I have every sympathy for the sufferings of Deborah Gibbert during her dreadful ordeal, I could not have prevented it. At the time I prescribed the antihistamine terfenadine for her father, there was no generally accepted knowledge of its interaction with grapefruit juice. My failure to warn him of this was therefore not negligent. I have always served my patients to the best of my ability. I am glad that has now been recognised. These last few years have been extremely difficult for my wife and myself. Thank you.'

Ignoring the questions of the journalists and rubber-neckers, Dr Foscutt took his wife's arm and led her to a waiting car. It looked a great deal more luxurious than any car he'd driven in Norfolk. Deb wondered who was financing him. She also wondered whether only she and Anna Grayling still believed that he had to have been the source of the astemizole that was found in her father's body at autopsy. There was no one else who could have provided it. But Deb couldn't do anything about that. It was the kind of argument that had been used to convict her and she wasn't going to do the same to anyone else, even Foscutt.

'Will you shut that bloody door?' shouted Marcus, picking at the shredding, painful skin of his fingers. 'And turn off the TV. I can't concentrate.'

Adam hit the remote control to silence the television and looked at Deb. Her eyes were like stones in the white, dead face. Then Marcus said something else and her eyes changed. She looked dangerous. Without thinking, Adam took three quick strides to stand between her and his son.

He moved back almost at once. But she had seen and understood. The damage was done. All his careful, patient, painful work on his own fears and on hers counted for nothing. He had thrown away the only chance they had. She knew now and for ever that he thought she was guilty. He wished he was dead.